THE PETE ZENDEL SERIES- BOXED SET

JOY OHAGWU

LifeFountainMedia

Kouts Public Library
101 E. Daumer Road
Kouts, IN 46347

BOXED SET OF 3 BOOKS

WHISPER
THE SECRET HERITAGE
HUNTER

VOLUME ONE

WHISPER

WHISPER- The PETE ZENDEL Christian Romantic Suspense Series-

A NOVEL

*To **JESUS**- The One Who laughs. Your Holy Name is my Crown of Glory.*

A CONTEMPORARY CHRISTIAN ROMANTIC SUSPENSE SERIES

Get Joy Ohagwu's starter Library for **FREE**. Details are at the end of this book.

Foundational Scripture

"I am the Way, and the Truth, and the Life: no one comes to the Father but through Me."-**JESUS** (John 14:6)

1

"Then you shall know that I am in the midst of Israel: I am the Lord your God and there is no other. My people shall never be put to shame."- Joel 2:27

"911. What's your emergency?"

Rita Gonzalez gripped the phone tighter, covered her mouth with the other hand, and squatted low in a corner of the small, smoke-shrouded room. If she had still been in the outer office fixing appointments where the fire began, she feared she would've been history. But she'd gone to the file room to replace the client files they'd used earlier today, fix the notes taped to each file, and lock the cabinet drawers.

She came out only to see a fire raging from the reception area. The gasoline smell stung her nostrils as the fire spread, and the heat tingled her skin. So she yanked the fire alarm. Then the explosion thudded in her ears. She dove into this file storage room and shut the door just before a second explosion rocketed through the building. She'd clasped her hands over her ears then felt her cellphone bulging out of her pants' pocket. She pulled it out and dialed 911.

Hungry flames licked the edges of the doorjamb, and the fire threatened to burst into the room, teasing her with yellow flashes underneath the door.

Any moment now, the fire will breach the last barrier—the door. "There's a fire. Please help me." A cough interrupted her and she doubled over. "It's almost inside here. The office is burning." Another bout of coughing halted her speech, and she flattened her palm on the brown carpet and bent over, inhaling a deep breath.

"You're going to be fine, honey. Find a place in the room away from the fire and get as close as you can to the ground. Use any clothing to cover your nose and mouth. If there is water around you, wet the cloth when you place it on your nose. Are you hurt? Are you alone?"

"Yes, I am alone."

"What's your address?"

She managed to call out the address before more smoke seeped in and white, smoky clouds blurred her view of the door. Fire crackled underneath the door, making her squirm. She was clearly trapped. "Please hurry."

"Help is on the way. I'll stay on the phone."

The operator kept speaking with her, but Rita scarcely

heard her over the one question vibrating through her head: would the firefighters make it in time?

A spark shot farther from beneath the door. That drove her deeper and closer to the second-story window. She huddled near the glass, but when she glanced outside, she couldn't imagine going down so far. She could fracture a bone, so she refused to take the risk to jump.

The door burst open, and burning heat slammed her skin. She screamed, and the phone dropped from her hand, sliding closer to the flames.

A figure appeared out of the fire. But as he held out a hand to her, something about him made her pause. Clad in all black, he didn't have a county firefighter badge on his chest.

He wasn't a firefighter. She withdrew her hand, even though she was now finding it tough to breathe.

At her hesitation, he came closer. He bent over and caused her to shrink farther away as her heart pounded. "There wasn't supposed to be anyone in here." He crouched low and tipped her chin, forcing her to look up. "Now I have to take care of you too. Come here."

She pushed his hand back. "No!" Smoke stinging her eyes, she teared up. Yet she fought back.

He pulled her by her hair and forced her up to a standing position. He showed her a printed photo, but she didn't look. "Where can I find this? I need the information."

"What?" She didn't look. "I don't know what you are talking about. Please leave me alone."

He yanked her arm and drew nearer to the fire burning the entrance. "Where are the files?"

"What files?" Had she heard a loud bang before going in the back to organize the file room? She was getting confused about what she heard and didn't hear. "Please let me go. I don't know anything."

The clog in her throat blocked even the smoky air, and gasping for breath, Rita started crying.

Another figure appeared beside him. "Let's go. It's not her we want. It's her boss. She's just the secretary. Hurry up. People are coming."

Voices calling out for any survivors reached her ears from afar, and Rita screamed with all the air left in her lungs. A slap hit her cheek and left it tingling and slammed her face to the ground. Then the man cursed. He shoved her to the corner, punched her face, and just before she blacked out, and the firefighters—the real firefighters entered—he left through the window. The accomplice followed. She was gasping for breath, and cough spasms wracked her body when a man rushed for her.

Caring arms lifted her and carried her out. "You are going to be fine. Hang on." Sure that she was now safe, she let her eyes slide shut.

"Hey, come and listen to this," Tatiana Stone, 911 operator, called to her supervisor. "Our last caller dropped her phone at some point, but I heard someone else there when she'd said she was alone. I think I also heard her scream. Maybe the fire wasn't an accident?"

She waited for her supervisor to listen to the recording. Then he nodded. "You might be right. I heard something. Send that to the police and let them handle it from there." He patted her shoulder. "Good job."

She picked up the phone and called the SSPD.

MIRANDA SOW LISTENED TO SOFT MUSIC AS SHE FLICKED ON HER blinker and made the same set of turns down the valley as she'd made every Friday evening for two years, heading toward her office building. She turned off her AC and rolled her window down.

Then the burning smell hit her nostrils. As she drew closer and peered in the distance, her eyeballs rounded. She blinked, then gasped. From afar off, she saw fire department trucks had surrounded her building.

Huge flames flicked upward, and her hands tightened on the steering wheel. Wasn't that her office—on *fire*? Her chest constricted. She stepped up on the gas pedal, and just then, a car struck hers from behind. She gripped the wheel and righted the vehicle. Then she rounded the second to the last set of hills and slowed down, catching a glimpse of the dark Tundra behind her. Why did he hit her? If this wasn't an unsafe place to stop to prevent an accident, she would stop now. But she moved forward toward a wider section of the road.

"Maybe he's new around here." The car neared at a higher-than-average speed, and instead of passing like she expected, it slammed her rear bumper again, harder this time.

Her heart pounded in her chest, and she scrambled with her other hand for her phone. This wasn't an accident. This person meant her harm. If she could find her phone with one hand, hidden inside her purse, under her last patient's files, she might just...

Her fingers fumbled fast. A third ram sent her car into a

double spin across the road. Losing control, she pumped her brakes to prevent it from skidding off the valley, but the wheels wouldn't grip the asphalt. Off it plunged into the grove of trees and tumbled down the valley. Her head hit the steering wheel twice, and her own voice screaming provided the last sounds she heard before the car burst into flames.

2

"Then the remnant of Jacob shall be in the midst of many peoples, like dew from the Lord, like showers on the grass, that tarry for no man nor wait for the sons of men." Micah 5:7

"What do you mean you can't come? We planned this vacation together. Now, we're in Mexico, but you brought work along? That's not fair." Lips compressing, Violet Zendel listened to her brother give what sounded like a rehearsed formal answer, quite suited to his controlled personality.

"Fine. We'll meet you back at the hotel in an hour. Meanwhile, we're stopping by this place near Highway Plaza in the old city. Tim wants to show me a nice view from there." Her voice came out tight, but she managed to contain her frustration. This was not the time to exchange words with Pete.

"See you later." She hung up, slid the phone into her back

pocket, and tugged at her friend's arm. God knew she was grateful Tim Santiago came along on this vacation—their first one together in four years—or this would have turned into a work-away-from-home situation.

She lifted her gaze to his. "Pete's not coming. Let's go." With the tightness constricting her throat, even her voice couldn't hide her disappointment.

"Sorry to hear that." Tim, an eyewitness to her troubled relationship with her brother, touched her hand, lending a sense of comfort to ease the ache in her heart. Why couldn't Pete ever think of her, demonstrate, through just a little thing, like a touch of the hand, that he cared? "This way."

She followed him and lifted her chin, resolved to enjoy their last day before returning to Maryland and her college Chemistry students.

THERE WERE THREE THINGS VIOLET HATED—THE DARK, SPIDERS, and uncertainty. Yet all three were happening. Right this minute.

Crack.

She froze on the steps and spun to Tim. "Did you hear that?"

No response.

Violet gasped, then blinked against the faint lighting and inhaled the dank air in the old mansion as she lifted her leg to climb higher. She swiped at a cobweb, swiveled, but could barely make out his slim form close behind.

"Embrace your fears, Violet, and they'll turn tails and run. Don't be scared."

This was not how she heard other people's trips to ancient ruins turned out. They usually returned with memorabilia and nice photos. This didn't feel nearly relatable to those tales. Yet here she was fighting off cobwebs from her hair with almost no light to make out where next to plant her feet.

She turned to find her best friend, Tim, who now breathed close to her ear, and was standing one step below her. He smiled as she flashed her cellphone's light on him, and he blinked hard against the light. She punched his arm. "Don't laugh, Tim. It's not funny! You know I hate dark places. Why did you bring me here? And why didn't you tell me you were right behind me?"

His dark Italian curls bounced as he shook his head. "Seriously, Vi? And miss the rounded eyes that looked at me when you heard something?" Still shaking his head, he ushered her forward. "Ha. No way. Let's keep moving. We're almost there. You'll thank me for this later."

She shifted the light off his face and back on her path. "Cindy visited old Greek coliseums last year and returned with amazing photos. Now, I'll be lucky to take one picture that won't make it look like I'm lost in some underground mine and waiting to be rescued." Violet grunted but resumed climbing. As soon as she saw the top, she slowed down for Tim, who came up and stood tall next to her.

"You were excited right before we turned to climb these stairs so I'd suggest you quit complaining. Moreover," he shrugged, "maybe it was time you lost your fear of the dark."

She didn't respond, preferring to bask in the light rays and escape from the darkness. Now awash in broad daylight, she shaded her eyes from the sudden brilliance, not complaining when Tim led her toward a walkway, through which they climbed some steps to what looked like an old gallery. She dusted off cobwebs from her hair while he studied a map in his hand and switched off his cellphone's flashlight as she did hers. "You know, we could've taken the easier route the site escort offered."

"And miss out on the fun of taking the ancient way the mansion guards used in climbing up here?" Tim inched up a brow. "Nope. Not for an archeologist. We're always pursuing the secrets hidden in the dark."

"And I hate the dark." Violet sighed. "Which makes me wonder why I chose to follow an archeologist here. I could've been relaxing in the hotel with a cool drink, not crawling up holes and ruining my clothes."

Tim's laughter echoed through the old walls of the empty space as they emerged at an opening with descriptive wall plaques in the local language. "I know why you did it. Because you're my best friend. And that's what best friends do." He offered a charming smile, then dusted something off his cheek. "Come on. I'm so excited to show you a secret compartment I heard of but didn't see the first time."

"Another secret place?" She felt her eyes roll even before she spoke. "If it's dark…um…no, I don't think so."

He tugged at her arm. "Come on, Violet. There won't be dusty tunnels this time. Just stairs. Old, but well-lit stairs." He paused to allow her to choose.

She nodded. "Fine then." But she glimpsed a vivid view of the ruins of the old city walls and was drawn in by them. Crumbling bricks were hugged by beautiful green and purple-flowered shrubbery dotted with surrounding large trees. Flowers grew through the crevices of the cracked wall and lent it some strange beauty.

Violet let go of Tim's arm and approached the rectangular window. Glancing through the rough-edged window and careful not to touch it, she observed the rustic beauty. "Wow. I love this." His soft steps whispered closer on the worn carpet behind her, and for a moment, she felt a calm wave soar through her spirit. Smiling, she leaned on his shoulder and drew in a deep breath.

He curved a hand around her shoulder. "There's a reason why people leave the old to move to the new. But exploring their beginnings, and the places they abandoned, teaches me a lot about human nature. We need each other and will leave places to stay close to people we love. But you know what?"

She spun. "What?"

He let go of her shoulder. "Where a people started tells you a lot about their journey-to-become. And you can learn a lot from that."

Violet smiled. Tim had been the best thing to happen to her in recent years. He'd first asked her out, but she'd refused, knowing it wasn't God's will for them, at least, for her. She'd learned to know that every man God led into her life wasn't meant to be in a relationship with her. She asked the Lord for godly direction after meeting Tim, especially knowing she felt nothing more than friendship for him. Soon, he'd shared a choice he'd been torn about making—accepting a job offer from two different colleges across state lines.

So, they'd prayed. And after that prayer, it became clearer who God wanted Tim to be toward her—a friend and a prayer partner.

As time went by, they grew to become close friends, and then prayer partners, then travel buddies. Last year, they were both too busy to travel and had opted for Mexico this year.

Violet still wasn't sure whose idea it had been to include Pete—and she'd been shocked when he'd accepted to come.

And, since Tim was soon leaving for a year as part of a South America research archeologist exchange program, she savored today's outing even more. This was the last day of their vacation, and it wasn't lost on her that, as they returned, he would begin earnest preparations for a possible return to either Mexico or South America. Truth be told, she was already missing him.

She drew in a deep breath and chose to be present in the moment. Faded paint on the old structure met with overgrown weeds and brushes to contrast beautifully with the eroded marble. She glanced up at a rusted chandelier, long past its heyday. What must have been a red-color rug beneath their feet had been worn down by time, dust, and human traffic to bare, shredded white threads at the center while spots of stubborn red color clung to the fringes.

The tall galleried room they stood in flowed into the far outside wall connected by flagstones like a well-planned palace. The owners must've been rich. Gorgeous nature wound with primitive technology provided the impetus for an appreciation of God's divine nature and how much power He gave to man on earth to build whatever he wished.

At that moment, Violet realized Tim waited for her to drink her fill of the area before leaving. So, having seen enough, she turned and followed him. He asked another person who idled by to take a photograph of them, which they graciously did before leaving the area to explore a bit more. Contrary to her expectation, with the dark stairs behind them, she was finally enjoying this. Other tourists took the longer walk from outside to come around to enter the galleria while she and Tim climbed the stairs.

At her prompt, they exited the large hall, walked down a few stone steps, and crossed a clear space toward a smaller, older ancient ruin. When they reached it, it appeared to be like a servant's quarters with narrower steps and smaller rooms than the mansion.

"It was rumored that this small place was the birthplace of the father of one of Mexico's richest families—the Nunez family—about one century ago. Although it has never been proven true."

"Interesting." She fell in step. "How old is this place then?"

He shrugged. "I'd say maybe a few hundred years old."

Luckily, some sunlight streamed in through cracks in the walls and lit up the space. The stairs, cracked in several places, seemed narrower, and the blue paint on the inner wall was faded. Holes above in the rusted zinc roofing, provided little shade from the overwhelming heat as she drank the last of her water from her bottle and tossed the container into a labeled garbage bin.

Observing the one-story structure ahead, Violet was surprised that the doors still stood and that the internal walls remained intact. It portrayed the excellence of the builders. As she approached, she noticed that the few other tourists had remained at the galleria, and some uneasiness coiled in her belly. "I don't see other tourists entering this one, Tim."

One white sign with red arrows indicated where the stairs were. He led her up the flight of steps and paused midway. "I don't see any signs saying it's out of bounds either. Come on, we won't stay here too long."

When they reached the top step, a torn, dirty curtain—the

size of a sedan car window—fluttered to her left. "Tim, there's a curtain here." She stepped past him. "For such an old place, is that normal?" Surprised to see something that modern in a building so old, she approached and flipped the curtain aside with a finger.

"No, it's not normal and shouldn't be there. Any curtains should've been long gone," Tim confirmed, a worried line creasing his brow.

She peered out the window and felt her eyes widen. "What in the world...?" A dark-blue van idled afar off. Considering the crushed lawn and low wooden barricade it had crashed and driven over, it was in the wrong place.

Near it, a group of men stood in a huddle like they were trading in something secret. A heavy, black-nylon bag was exchanged for wads of cash, and just then, she saw a man standing on the other side of the window, much closer to her than the two men afar off. The curtain flapped again, his gaze met hers, and he frowned. She knew what his frown meant—she shouldn't be here.

His gray eyes bore into hers beyond the sweaty, dirt-brown scarf tied to his forehead, and something told Violet she wasn't supposed to have seen the exchange she had. A weapon clicked, and she gasped as Tim approached her and stopped. Then she felt him trailing her gaze to the weapon in the man's hands because Tim echoed her next words, "Gun!"

They ducked beneath the curtain and raced down the stairs. Being one floor up, they had an added height advantage. But bullets aiming for them bore holes into the ancient structure with thudding sounds. Either the man was using a silencer, or the walls were stronger than she thought because they weren't hit—yet. Her heart pounded in her chest, and she ran down like she was being chased by a helicopter.

"Jesus, please shield us!" Tim shouted as they exited the structure, taking the last few steps, two at a time, and landed at the outer door. Some sparsely armed security men, shouting orders to themselves, flanked the structure, and two swept past her and Tim.

She wanted to warn them that they were outgunned, but she froze when she heard a whimper. A boy, no more than six, crouched low playing with some pebbles at the edge of the structure. With his trembling lips, he seemed really scared and frozen in shock. No one else appeared to notice him.

Tim grabbed her hand to lead her out as more gunshots rang out and shouting vibrated from inside the structure, but she wouldn't leave. Her heart wrapped the boy in a hug. So, she sprinted toward the side of the structure.

"Violet!" Tim shouted behind her, but she raced forward until she reached the boy.

Panting and squatting low, she sighted the fear caught in his big brown eyes, but she didn't let it deter her. Shoving down her own fear, she extended a hand to him. "Come. Come with me. It's okay. You'll be all right."

Once his little arms wrapped around himself, he shook like the earlier fluttered curtain.

"Violet! Come over. It's getting bad," Tim shouted again above the chaos.

But she wouldn't leave without the boy. No. She won't.

She guessed his weight with a sweeping glance. Quite slender, he didn't appear heavy. So, she offered the only thing she could— her body as a shield for him. "I'm going to carry you out of here, okay? Don't be scared." Without waiting for an answer, she slung her purse like a sling bag across her shoulder. Then she bent lower and swept her arms beneath his thighs and, with a grunt, scooped him up and hefted him onto her shoulder. Loud voices coming from inside the building warred with sporadic gunshots, but she ran as fast as she could across the distance toward safety.

Jogging under his weight, she moved quickly, praying not to get hit as she managed to reach Tim, dash behind a wall in the galleria, and set the boy on his feet before an explosion rocked the smaller structure, leading them to dive for cover.

"Violet, you could have gotten killed!" Tim barked as they ducked behind the place she had stayed to admire the view not long ago.

She covered her ears. "I wouldn't leave the kid!"

He shielded the boy, who was now hugging Tim's leg. "Neither would I, had I seen him. But that was no excuse to put yourself in danger."

They bent over for cover as another round of explosions shook the ground. They waited for a few moments until calm settled. Then Tim carried the boy, grabbed her arm, and rushed her out of the mansion, taking the stairs two at a time again. With all the noise, surely someone must've called the authorities, but Violet wasn't waiting to double-check.

They managed to exit the space completely, tumble into the street and into normalcy before catching their breaths. Soon, the wail of a police vehicle approaching disrupted the seeming normalcy. Then another, and yet another. And not long afterward, a black truck pulled up close, and police officers rushed into the mansion.

She, Tim, and the boy stepped aside to let them through. She wasn't sure about the significance of what she'd seen, but it could have been some sort of drug deal gone bust. *Thank You, Lord Jesus, for getting us out of there safely.*

Tim's shuffle caught her attention, and she jerked her neck sideways, still fraught. Then she smiled as she saw it was him. "Violet, what you did back there was incredibly brave. You saved this boy's life." He squeezed her shoulder and his Adam's apple bobbed. "While my concern was saving yours. I feel responsible for you since I brought you here." Tim set the boy down on his feet. She dusted sand off the arm of Tim's sleeve.

"It's okay, Tim." Violet swiped sandy sweat off her brow. "I know you were worried. Thank you for looking out for me. I appreciate it. Let's go to the hotel. For starters, I could use a cool bath in this burning heat. Moreover, this was definitely not the museum or archeological visit I envisioned. This is more Indiana Jones's style, which I can definitely do without."

His wide grin worked to bring her worry down a few notches and eased her heart rate. An average-height lady in a red dress, with spiral waves of sandy-brown hair bouncing over her shoulders, rushed to them and gushed in Spanish to Tim, who replied with acceptance of her gratitude. Tim informed her in Spanish that Violet had saved the boy's life.

Despite the lady bending and holding out both hands to the boy, Violet held on tightly to him, not wishing to hand him to a stranger until she confirmed the woman's identity. She paused until she heard the boy call her mama, reach out, and smile at her before she released him. Relief swept through her as the moment had become tense, but she wasn't regretting making sure the woman was his parent first. It would've been worse rescuing him only to hand him to a complete stranger. A police officer approached and paused, speaking to the lady first.

He must've demanded an ID because she dug one out of

her purse and showed it to him, plus a photo of the boy standing with her now. While she spoke with the cop and he examined the documents as well as asked her more questions, the little boy faced Violet.

He blinked sparkling brown eyes full of innocence beneath dark lashes that melted her heart into a puddle and served as his thank you to her. She dipped into her pocket and gave him a granola bar, and he stepped closer and enclosed it with eager hands, smiling wider before turning back to his mother whom the police now cleared to leave. Reunited with her son, she scooped him up into her arms and kissed his cheeks, and Violet was sure she would scarcely put him down anytime soon as they both disappeared into the street's foot traffic.

The officer interviewed them next, and after they each gave their statements, providing their names, addresses, and contact information, they were cleared to go. Soon, the area was cordoned off with yellow Do-Not-Cross tape.

Leaving them all behind, Violet and Tim returned to where he had parked a rental car. Luckily, the garage was easily accessible and not cordoned off. They paid at the meter and climbed inside the sedan. She made a mental note to add getting shot at to her list of things she hated.

She slid her seat belt across. "Well, can you make sure next time we go to a museum of any kind, we're going to be safe before we pop into a possible drug deal?" When Tim's eyes widened, she laughed as she sat up straight. "I'm joking. Well, not about the safety. But I know there's nothing you could've done about today's occurrence."

"Thanks. You had me gaping for a second. I can't get enough of your professorial attitude ever, can I?" He grinned when she opened her mouth to reply, then realized he teased and shut it again.

"One of these days, Vi." Tim eased off the curb and entered traffic, and soon they were heading toward their hotel.

Pete would hardly believe what she had just experienced when they reached the hotel and she told him.

Relieved and sure they were safe for now, she heard her phone ringing. Still catching her breath, she dug it out of her purse, pressed Answer, and raised the phone to her ear. "Hello?"

"Violet? It's Pete."

A frown pinched a curve to her eyes. "Pete?" But he rarely called, if ever. She usually did the calling.

"Yes." Her brother came through rather coolly, a contrast to the situation she had just encountered.

"Is everything okay, Pete?" She pressed a hand to block her ear against a loudly-tooting horn from a car nearby. But the next words weren't what she expected.

"There's been an emergency. I need you to return right away." A slight pause followed, and Pete wasn't the pausing type.

That got her heart pounding again. And scared.

3

"In that day, the Lord of hosts will be for a crown of glory and a diadem of beauty to the remnant of His people." -Isaiah 28:5

ANGEL MARTINEZ USED THE BACK OF HER HAND TO WIPE condensation from her windshield as she veered off the highway exit at two in the morning. Thankful to be heading home—finally—she resisted the urge to massage the stiffness gripping her neck. Well, considering the cases she was handling, her unease was like small change. It had been enough that a local psychiatrist ended up dead in a suspicious accident on the same day her assistant narrowly survived dying in a fire. As she read the cases, hard as she tried, she couldn't fashion a reason for the arson or for the murder. The names of the possible suspects they had so far hadn't shaken anything loose, nor had the victim's birthplaces nor anything else given a clue as to the identities of the architects of these crimes. With time, something would give, but when?

She navigated past the slow car, wondering if the driver was falling asleep at the wheel considering his tires wobbled between lanes. While she passed him and flashed her police cruiser lights briefly as a warning, he straightened up in his lane and sat up, giving her a generous smile. A nod sufficed for a polite response before she returned her sight to the road. The ringing of a phone drew her attention back to her vehicle, and she pressed the hands-free Bluetooth earpiece to answer. "Hello?"

"Send backup! Shots fired…Hurry." A scramble followed in the airwaves. Then the call disconnected.

"Pierce?" Angel blinked at the phone atop her purse even though she recognized her partner's voice. He'd hitched a ride with her because his car had a flat tire. Having just dropped him off at his house, she was still close enough to return.

She grabbed her radio and alerted the SSPD, and then swerved her vehicle to the shoulder until all four tires scrunched on gravel and she was free to turn.

She flipped on her sirens to full blast as she drove against the traffic until she found a safe place to join the southbound lane. Driving fast, she was soon back to the road leading to Pierce's home. She prayed he would be safe until her arrival. Within minutes, she pulled up at his driveway as the spark of gunfire lit up the dark interior.

Angel grabbed her gun, jumped out of the cruiser, and ran, head down, toward the house. The front door was unlatched, and it hung open. She pushed it wider, entered, and groped through the hallway using her hand. No other identifiable sound reached her ears, so she had to do something.

She took out her cell phone, which she'd grabbed from the car, and flicked on the light function. Then she slid it as far as she could to the other end. As though in response to her action, gunfire exploded from both the living room and the bedroom door at the end of the hallway. Angel ducked.

"Pierce! It's me. Where are you?" She had to know so she wouldn't hit the wrong target. Once during their training years ago, she had mistakenly hit a camouflaged target and had learned her lesson then. Now was not the time to risk her partner's life.

"Over here!" echoed.

Good. He was still alive. "To the living room then," Angel muttered. She would risk getting hit by the shooter from the open bedroom doorway if she attempted to cross while standing. So, she trotted to the edge, dove across, and landed with a hard hit on the living room floor. Gunfire shot past her, but she had been quicker. Her partner's rapid breathing whizzed as police sirens whirred close by. She peered at him in the darkness, then whispered, "What happened? Are you okay?"

"I came in and saw this guy robbing my house. He was unplugging the TV about to cart it away. Clearly, I had surprised him, and he didn't know I was a cop. He panicked and shot first, and I ducked. Then I flipped the lights off from the control. But we clashed. As I turned to call you, he lunged at me, and I lost the phone. He ran to the bedroom and hid there. We've been exchanging fire since then."

"God be praised, you're still alive." Angel felt for his feet and heard him wince. "Are you injured?"

"I might have taken a hit to my leg because I'm having a hard time moving it."

"Stay here." She rose to her feet but kept her head low. "I'll try to draw him out."

"Please be careful."

"Okay." She moved one step closer to the hallway listening for any sounds. Before she could take another step, an object hit her back, and she fell.

It was the shooter now leaving the bedroom.

She lunged at him in the shadows and kicked the gun from his hands, which she could see from the reflecting light from her cellphone afar off. Then she flipped onto her back, pointed the gun, and froze. She couldn't tell why, but all of a sudden, it was her and her first foster parent again. The images flashed in her mind.

Him towering above.

Her struggling underneath.

Then the gun in her hands went off.

Angel shuddered but managed to shake the trauma from her mind long enough to see the attacker dive toward her. She swung her leg, and it made contact with his jaw. He groaned, then began struggling for her gun. The door burst open, and other police officers had arrived. Lights flashed around them, but the struggle continued.

"Police!"

"Over here!" Pierce shouted as the place flooded with lights. The officers closed in. Soon, seeing her uniform, an officer shot the attacker in the back, and he slumped on her. She pushed his weight off her and rose.

"Thanks. He entered the property and was robbing my partner."

Another officer cuffed the unconscious man, while another called for an ambulance.

"Pierce is injured so we need two ambulances."

She slid over and sat up against a window, breathing hard. "I need someone to unmask him so we'll see his face."

An officer standing close by did so. Then he flipped the man onto his back, and she took a look—short brown hair, narrow nose, and scanty brows. Satisfied, she leaned back and waited for the officers to process the scene.

It was going to be a long night.

4

"For there is nothing hidden which will not be revealed, nor has anything been kept secret but that it should come to light." –Mark 4:22

∼

Two days later, Angel sat in her office at the SSPD and lifted her eyes when she heard someone approaching. She blinked, sure she was seeing double. Her brother stood in the front of her office, and, a moment after her shock wore over, she beckoned with a wave for him to enter. She pushed back her chair and almost sprang to her feet, eager to go over and hug him. But considering the last time they saw each other—the day he called her a hateful, religious freak—was the same day he left town, she wasn't sure how well that hug would go over. So, she simply settled for a question. "John? What are you doing here?"

Hit by a throbbing headache, she rubbed her forehead as he took the seat opposite her desk. His rugged blue jeans were washed out, his orange T-shirt could use a round in the washing machine, and his disheveled hair needed an introduction to a comb. Was he homeless? Refusing to make assumptions, she waited for him to state his mission. She set down the file she was working on and locked her PC's screen and faced him fully.

He clasped his hands. "I hope you don't mind me coming here."

She eyed his short hair and rough beard but said nothing. It was barely three years since the last time they saw each other. Ten years her junior, John had grown so tall it was impossible to spot any age differences between them unless you were close to their family. But at only twenty-two, he had aged more than he should. "Sure."

"That's fine. How can I help you?" She wove her hands together and settled them on the desk, fighting back an exhausted yawn stemming from the attack two days ago. Going to the hospital and rotating between stopping at the floor where her partner was being treated and the floor where the attacker was in custody had worn her out.

So had giving her statement and writing up and submitting her report, which had pretty much consumed the better part of yesterday morning. She'd gone home, showered, changed her clothes, and then returned to the hospital after buying Pierce food. Since he was a widower, no one was taking any meals to him. He had appreciated it. Then she headed to the station to dig further into her current murder case.

Luckily, the girl who'd survived the fire had woken up and

given her statement. Without her seeing the arsonists' faces, Angel was almost thrust back to the start.

"I'm here because I need your help." John appeared to hold his breath while waiting for her answer. Then his gaze dipped.

"John, what's the matter?"

Finally, the yawn escaped. Obviously, her last cup of coffee had washed down her belly without doing its job—working to keep her awake. Next, her eyelids would likely be drooping. But she wasn't leaving until she made some headway on this case—and heard her brother out.

"I..." He pinned his gaze to a point past her head. "I need a place to stay. For now."

She felt the frown deepen her brows. "Why?"

His Adam's apple bobbed. "I got into a situation and...I lost all my money and my house."

Angel crossed her arms. "What kind of situation?"

He studied his open palms. "Gambling. I moved to Vegas. Me and the guys were out one night, and we went to the casino. One thing led to another, and before we knew it, it became a habit." He ran a hand through his hair. "Listen, if you can't help me, that's fine. But can I crash on your couch for a few days until I figure things out?"

She stayed silent as she thought through his revelation and reeled at the level of indiscipline.

"Please?" In the past, John didn't apologize or beg. He simply took and walked away when things got tough. For him to beg her now, he had to be desperate.

"Fine. But you need to apply for and get a job soon."

His shoulders slacked and he nodded. "I will."

Based on his recent revelation, she didn't have to ask about his credit score. It might be hard for him to find a decent job.

"You might want to look at construction companies that could be hiring. They could hire you more quickly."

"Okay, I will." He stood and wiped his likely sweaty palms on his jeans. "And thank you."

She reached for her purse, stood as well, and dialed her supervisor. "I need to go to my house for an hour. I have a family emergency." After giving him a brief explanation, she walked out with John in tow.

Their parents had died when they were young. Of all her siblings, John was the most troublesome. He had been hard to tame when they were younger, living with their foster parent who beat them up when he got high—until the day he'd called her names, then tried to strangle her with his belt and she shot him with his own gun. She'd been afraid to report him to authorities, fearing her siblings might get split up. That was when her life changed irreversibly. Luckily, they found someone who wanted all of them in their home. Since then, she was basically the parent to her four siblings and had managed to get them settled in various jobs. The youngest had graduated college last year and was working as a computer analyst in some tech company. One was a banker. The other, a truck driver.

By God's grace, every one of them was settled in life career-wise, except John. Did he suffer because he found her sobbing after shooting their foster father who'd tried to strangle her while high, thinking she was his ex? Angel wasn't sure. She just knew that, from that time onward, John had changed. He was more aggressive, didn't listen to instructions, joined some street gangs, and it had taken sustaining a gunshot wound to make him accept to go back and finish school. She'd thought the nightmare was over.

Yet here he was today with a new tale.

How long would she have to carry him? He was not a Christian. And praying for him and his conversion to Christ had been at the top of her agenda. But she was feeling like God wasn't ready to answer her yet, and she was tired of praying for it and seeing things get worse and not better.

Even when they were moved to a foster home with absentee parents and a middle-class paycheck, she had delayed her own dreams of going to college and worked night jobs to help her siblings out. By the time she finished supporting the last sibling to start college, she had turned thirty and had no time to pursue a relationship. But four years earlier, she'd admitted to herself that she couldn't handle the waitress jobs and the inconsistent hours any longer, so she applied to join the police force.

Surprised by her acceptance, she filled out the form and had smiled sadly as she circled Single yet again. Now, years later, many could not understand how she was single at almost thirty-one. But she couldn't explain that she had been too busy raising her siblings to think of having a relationship. Since her youngest sibling just finished school and started her own life, Angel was excitedly looking forward to settling down. But would she have to put her life on hold again to help out John?

She started her car, and as John buckled up, she turned to him. "Listen, I know you might not understand this, but each time you get into criminal behavior, you set the timer of your life backward. Aren't you tired of playing catch-up? Won't you ever change?"

She gripped the wheel with desperate hands, willing them to change someone they couldn't. "Look around you. No one is here to help you. So next time someone tempts you into doing something wrong, ask yourself whether they will stand with you when everything hits the fan? Only Jesus stands with you through thick and thin, whether you like to hear it or not."

She tapped a finger on her chest. "Do you think I'm here because I'm better than you? I've been single all these years, and I've not yet faced a problem that God allowed to overwhelm me even with my imperfections. Do you think it's by my own power that I was able to support you, Stephanie, Grace, and Hughes?" She shook her head. "Of course not. Without the grace of God, we wouldn't have made it, John. So, I'm asking you to take a minute and think about where your life goes from here. If you continue in this path and end up in jail, I can't help you."

He simply sat there and said nothing. So she started the car, revved the engine, and drove from the lot, hoping and praying she could scale this new challenge with John, without losing her patience with God.

Between the murder case, her partner's robbery, and John's fresh issues, could she handle anything else? Why did she fear things had just begun?

5

"But I would strengthen you with my mouth, and the comfort of my lips would relieve your grief." –Job 16:5

∽

FOR A DAY OF VISITING AN OLD MANSION AND GETTING SHOT AT, Violet was sure she could handle one bad event for one day. But another? Certainly no.

She'd waited on the phone, and her brother, Pete, had stayed silent until she could take it no more. "Pete?"

Whatever he had to say wouldn't he just say it? Or better yet, did she truly have to hear it?

Silence, heavy with apprehension, hovered like a dark cloud full of ominous rain.

"What is it?" She swallowed hard and waited for what felt like another full minute, though it might've been only a couple of seconds. "Tell me. I can handle it." Maybe she could handle it, but she couldn't shake the dread filling her.

Tim nudged her arm. "Is everything okay with Pete?"

She squeezed his hand near her arm before he returned it to the steering wheel and smiled but said nothing, waiting for her brother to speak when he felt able to get his words out. This was highly unusual for him. He was pretty much a say-your-mind-and-get-it-over-with kind of guy.

"Dad is dead."

Violet blinked, her vision a blur as her world spun off its edge. "Pete?" She clasped her forehead.

Did she hear him right? "No."

"I'm sorry, Vi. He's gone." An echo of his words chilled over her sunburned skin like a block of ice.

Her dad was fine. He had to be. "He wasn't sick when we left the States, Pete."

"I know. But something happened, and they couldn't catch it in time the doctors said." The last time his voice got this grainy was when their mom had passed. He had been close to their mom, even though he would have nothing to do with her faith in Christ.

"What are you saying, Pete? What happened to Dad?" Her ears rang with the words, and she wished some horn would toot and blast the words away with them. She felt her fingers clench the dashboard as she hunched over and settled her head there. Something had to feel real here beyond the pain rising in her heart and threatening to drown her.

"It was a brain aneurysm. They said he collapsed while walking in the community garden. Someone found him and called an ambulance. They took him to the hospital and suspect no foul play, but they couldn't do anything to help him. It was...just too late. He's gone, Vi."

But she was no longer listening.

"No." She pounded her fist on the dash and wished she had gotten the call. She would've insisted they do more. "They can't say it's too late. They can try something, anything," she pleaded, weariness burying the tail of her words while pain swelled in her heart. "Dad can't be dead. I refuse to believe it."

"I'm sorry, Violet. So sorry," Tim whispered to her ear as he flicked the blinker and parked by the roadside curb beside a shoe store.

"I pushed them for more details, and they said it's been twenty-four hours already. They tried to verify his identity when he was first brought in. Then they reached out to those who'd taken him to the hospital. It took some time, hours later, before someone knew who he was, but he had been pronounced dead by then. He's been gone for twenty-four hours already."

She almost challenged Pete further, but she would be blaming the wrong person. It was indeed too late. Pete knew how much their dad meant to her, and he wouldn't have called her if it wasn't true.

"Noooo. No. No." Her voice grew weaker with realization. Her world had just shattered. The phone fell from her trembling hand, tumbled to the floorboards while sobs wracked her body. She didn't know when Tim came around the car and opened her door. She simply felt his strong arms wrapping around her shoulder and drawing her in as she wept.

Her hero was gone.

∽

Angel stepped out of her patrol car and slammed the door. Eyeing the law offices of Sanderson and Curtman, she approached the redbrick building. With it tucked away at the other end of town, it had taken almost an hour to drive down here. But Reggie Sanderson had been the last man to see Miranda Sow alive, and Angel was going to find out why the late psychiatrist had visited him that afternoon. And if that had anything to do with her death.

She reached the doors at the second floor, pressed the bell, and waited. Soon, a receptionist with blonde hair opened the door, flashed a smile, and swung the door wider to allow her entry.

"Welcome to Sanderson and Curtman. Please have a seat, and someone will be with you shortly."

"I'm here to see Mr. Sanderson on an official police matter." Angel took a seat between two offices facing each other with one receptionist desk at the center. Soon, someone emerged, and based on the DMV records she'd checked, it had to be Mr. Sanderson. But she waited until he drew close and identified himself.

The short man with double-rimmed glasses and a bald center on his head extended her a hand. After introducing himself, he led her into a spacious office where bookcases full of tomes lined both sides of the wall. Long bookcases covered all areas of the office, scarcely leaving space for a walkway or desk or chair. "Please, have a seat."

Angel sat down, focusing on the framed photo on his desk of him and a young boy playing soccer. He didn't appear to be much older than she was. And suddenly, she yearned for a husband and child of her own. Seeing her peers married and living with their own spouses and kids raised a desire in her.

But she was also aware of the uniqueness of her situation. She knew God was in control and would sort her out at His time.

She tore her eyes away from the image to the man himself. "Yes, I'm Officer Martinez. And I'm here about Miranda Sow. My understanding is that she came to see you a couple of days ago. Can you tell me what that visit was about?"

He clenched his mouse and stopped moving it. Then his gaze darted toward the door, and his Adam's apple bobbed. "I'm sorry, but is Miranda in any trouble? Does she require legal representation?"

"Miranda is dead. She was killed in a hit and run—run off the road in what appears to be a deliberate attack. We're trying to determine why she was killed and by whom."

Color drained from his face, and she edged forward in her leather chair. "You can help us by telling me why she came to see you."

"Dead? Truly? She was just here... hale and hearty." He shook his head, scratched a short beard, and then met her gaze with resolve. "Miranda came to me and asked if she would be able to retain my services in case someone was targeting her."

"Did she say who?"

He nodded. "She said she thought she might be in danger. At first, she wouldn't say who she suspected. But I convinced her our conversation was confidential."

Angel cleared her throat, wanting him to conclude faster. "Interesting story. Do you have the name of the individual in question?"

He hesitated. "You did not hear this from me."

A frown twisted her face. "Why? Who is he?"

"Richard Danielson III. She said he might be the one, though I doubt it."

Angel blinked. Then her eyeballs rounded. "The congressional candidate? Son of Congressman Danielson II?"

He nodded. "One and the same."

"Wow. What was Miranda's connection to him?"

He stared at her. "I was too shocked to ask. I just told her to come back when she had more evidence."

"What evidence did she share, if any?"

"A postcard. Mailed from a high school up north. Very tidy lettering said, 'Remember us?' She shoved it back into her purse and didn't share anything more. Frankly, I figured she was just too scared. I could see it in her eyes, like she was reliving a nightmare. I thought a few days away from her job would do her good. But I told her to go to the cops if she felt unsafe or took the threat seriously."

"Unfortunately, she ran out of time." Angel equally nodded and rose. "Thank you very much for your assistance." She settled a card on his desk but doubted he would use it. Lawyers rarely called back, in her experience. "If you remember anything else, give me a call."

He stood and shook her hand. "Of course."

With those words, she left Sanderson, sure that she now had some direction for her investigation. But once she drove off the lot, she knew. If she was going to get the criminals involved in Miranda's murder and the arsonists behind bars, she had to hurry. Or she might run out of time—especially if they were powerful politicians with things they'd rather keep hidden.

If they had killed Miranda to hide evidence, they'd be willing to do it again, and she'd likely be their next target if she got too close to the right answers.

After working hard on her cases that afternoon, Angel pushed back her chair and drew in a deep breath, breathing in the scents of stale coffee and paper—the banana peel from her makeshift lunch rotting in the trash can definitely didn't help settle the frustration swirling her stomach. Nothing had given way to corroborate the lawyer's story. She couldn't go to a congressional candidate's office with an accusation or suspicion of murder—or anything else—without facts and corroboration. She had to find a connection between Miranda and the congressman, who was several years her junior.

Was there something she overlooked? She scooted closer to the desk and studied the files before her again, determined to figure things out, even if it was a loose thread.

An hour later, she paused everything and made herself a cup of coffee to keep her awake after another long night the previous day. She soon needed another and allowed the next cup of coffee to sluice down her throat before attempting to read anything else.

She settled back in her chair, both hands wrapped around the mug. She could use some reorganization. Files were growing at a fast pace, now stacked one atop the other on the right side of her desk. Matter of fact, she smirked, the seats were the only empty spaces.

With her partner out of commission, her work had doubled. A reminder popped up on her screen, alerting her to proceed to interview the building manager of the burned building tomorrow. Her partner's notes mentioned the manager had been away both times Pierce had checked on the man. Luckily, the scribbled address on the notepad showed a place not too far from the station.

Angel headed to the office fridge for the sandwich she'd

brought for lunch, then called her brother to see how his job applications were coming.

"I applied to ten places today," John said, some lightness lacing his voice. "I already got a call from one asking about references. May I use you as my reference?"

She returned to her office, sat down with her meal, and thought about it. "No, I don't think family members can refer you, or at least, I doubt personal references are taken very seriously. I can, however, call the supervisor of the burger place you'd worked at over the summer a few years ago. He lives in the area, and we attend the same church. I'll explain your situation, and we'll go from there."

"Okay. I'll wait to hear from you before calling them back. Thanks."

"You're welcome. See you later." Angel hung up and hoped her friend, Tim, would be willing to help. Granted, John hadn't been the model employee, but Tim was the only option he had now. For her sake, he'd probably help John. Maybe, after this, John would make empowering choices and stay out of trouble. Her ability to support him in these situations was wearing thin. She could only do so much before her hands failed her.

Angel hadn't spoken to Tim for a couple of weeks. She finished eating her lunch and dialed.

"Hello?" his familiar voice answered.

"Tim, it's Angel Martinez. Do you have a minute to talk?"

Rustling sounded over the speaker. "Please hold for one moment."

She waited until he returned to the call. "Sorry if I'm interrupting something. I can call back."

"No, that won't be necessary. It's good to hear from you. I'm in church, attending a funeral, so I had to step outside. Please continue."

"You remember my brother, John? He left town about two years ago but had worked with you."

A chuckle sailed through, slightly easing Angel's tense heart. "Of course, how could I forget him? Is he okay?"

Hmmm... How should she frame things, without lying and without disclosing the whole story? "Physically, he's fine. But otherwise, not really."

"How so?"

"John showed up at the station yesterday, having lost all his money due to some gambling. I'm housing him temporarily, but he needs a job. And he's applied to a couple of places, but now, they need a recommendation. Usually, they ask for two, but it seems they would like him to start soon so they can accept one referral. Would you be willing to provide it? He'd be grateful." She paused then, as she unwrapped her sandwich and eyed wilted lettuce, added, "I know he wasn't a model employee. But right now, he's flat on his back and could use a good word in his favor."

"You don't need to worry, Angel. I will provide him with a recommendation. It won't be glowing, but he will have a good enough chance to get the job. Tell him I'm inviting him to fellowship, and maybe, he might pick up a few things to help him reshape his choices. I should clarify that this isn't a condition for helping him, more like an addition so he can get his life permanently on the right path."

A thrill shot through Angel's tired mind and chased away her exhaustion. She gripped the phone tighter and wished she could hug Tim. "Thank you so much. Tim, you're a great friend."

"And you're an awesome sister. Everyone here knows you literally raised those kids like they were your own."

"I appreciate your kind words." She flicked a dollop of mustard from the edge of the bread and reached for a napkin. "Thanks a lot."

"You're welcome. Please pass along my contact information to John for requesting the recommendation, and I'll talk to you later."

"Sure, I'll do that. And sorry for interrupting the funeral."

"No problem. A close friend's father passed away unexpectedly, though he was an old man."

"I'm sorry for your loss. Goodbye, Tim."

"Thank you. Bye, Angel."

As soon as she hung up, Angel lifted her eyes upward. *Thank You, Jesus.*

She dialed John next and gave him the update. She could hear the excitement in his voice.

"Oh, man. Thank you. I will call him and email him the recommendation request form. Thanks, sis."

"You're welcome. Don't mess this up. I have no one else to call on your behalf," she warned, sandwich still in hand, but not a bite in her stomach.

"I won't. Thank you."

"He also said to invite you for fellowship. An invitation you might want to respond to when you speak with him. I'll leave that choice between you two."

Silence followed. "I will go. I will accept his invitation to attend the fellowship."

"Oh, okay." Wow, had he really accepted to go for the fellowship? What a pleasant surprise. She wasn't even sure which fellowship it was for—men's fellowship, weekly Bible study, or another—but that didn't dampen her joy. Considering she'd invited John several times and he'd turned her down, this was one serious miracle. "I'll see you later."

"Okay, thanks again."

She wrapped up the call, checked the time, and exhaled, pushing back her chair—her small break was over. So, leaving the sandwich uneaten, she pulled her purse and her coat off the wooden coat rack then headed out to interview the girl who'd survived the fire. Maybe, with a chat, she could jog her memory a bit and unveil some new information, which might give her a sense of who Miranda had been afraid of the day she died.

6

"A friend loves at all times, and a brother is born for adversity." – Proverbs 17:17

∽

ONE WEEK AFTER HER DAD HAD PASSED ON, VIOLET REMAINED IN shock. In her heart, she could still hear her dad's authoritative but trusting voice echo through the waves that splashed from the river and ended where her feet wiggled into the sandy bank. *What I love about Jesus is that His death is as powerful as His words. His resurrection as renewing as His creation of the world. His power is loving and gentle, but also fierce.*

Coolness, as determined as the memory weaving through her, covered her toes. *You can trust Him, especially in those times when you're in pain or hurting. Always lean on Jesus, my daughter. He's big enough to carry you, dear. His arms are sure larger than mine.* Her dad's words filtered through the waves of memory into her hurting soul as she stood on the same shores where they had spent so many sweet family moments.

"Lord Jesus, I miss Dad and Mom, even though she's been gone for a while. I love them so so much," she swallowed past a choked throat, "and this hurts badly. I feel totally...alone without them here. I know they're with You, but is it selfish that I want them here with me?"

Violet shivered against a cool breeze wafting over her skin. Then she stared beyond the shimmer of the rising sun cast over the face of the calming water. Overcome, she sighed, wishing away what had to be done—what had to happen today.

She wove her hands together. "I'm crawling through pain, Lord, and I'm just breathing in and out and hoping this numbing pain would go away." She bowed her head as another bond of sorrow roped around her heart and she pressed a hand there to ease the knot. "I came here to draw strength to get through this event. Please help me, Lord, because I can barely stand, let alone speak a word without choking up. Grace me. Please." She drew in a long breath, then exhaled.

Moments later, and feeling slightly less burdened, she bowed her head and prayed again. "Dear Lord Jesus, every fiber of feeling, every thread of thought, and every challenge that today represents, I surrender fully to You." She raised her hands above her head. "Like Dad said to do, I give it all. Even though I don't understand why he had to go, I choose to trust You."

Her father—Paul Zendel—the now-late CEO of the Cortexe Corp., was a Christian, saved and baptized with the Holy Spirit, a God-fearing man. At this time, nothing else mattered. Knowing he was now at rest at the bosom of the Father lent her peace of mind. And she knew it with certainty.

It is well with my soul. She drew in a deep breath again and felt the burden of sorrow ease a little more. She picked up a white rock washed by the waters lapping against it near her feet. She ran a thumb over its smooth edges and managed a small smile. Her dad used to pay her in quarters with each smooth stone she picked when she was little, stones like David had in Scripture. He said it was good that she worked for her money, and that had ingrained good values into her at an early age. She learned not to take anything for granted. Holding the stone now tightly in her palm, balled into a fist, soothed her heart—which felt heavier than the object.

Catching some movement from the left, she spun toward the brushes leading back to the family cottage. Footsteps followed behind the trees, and soon, her driver emerged on the footpath, approaching her. She shifted away from him, not yet ready to go. He seemed to get the message and stopped a few yards away.

She still had one memorabilia in her pocket to digest before she faced today. She reached into her pocket and brought it out. Violet cradled the fifteen-year-old picture in her hand and swallowed hard at the faces staring back at her.

All so happy and so united. All she had left of the four persons in that picture—Dad, Mom, Pete, and herself—was Pete, and he was far from being counted as her person right now. He'd grown even more distant in the past week, even though she needed him more now.

He was her twin.

We were supposed to be best friends forever. But that was now in the past too.

A drop of rain splashed on her hand and drew her attention back to the picture. She studied the joy on her parents' faces.

Her mom's long, dark hair had swept over part of her own face but nothing could hide the joy in Violet's lively eyes. It was the best family vacation she could remember. This was their family's trip to see the Northern Lights in Alaska. She had been so enraptured by such display from nature that a love for science was born in her. There she decided to study science, to seek to understand the beauty of God's universe. And Pete had enjoyed it too. He was truly her brother then, ever so protective. She had treasured this photo so much that it stayed by her bedside even now.

Violet circled a finger around her dad's smiling face near her mom's. She sniffed back a tear and lowered her hands. "Dad, I'm going to miss you." Her heart felt heavier with each word she uttered. "I look forward to seeing you again in heaven. Adieu, Papa." With those words streaming through trembling lips, she tucked the photo into her pocket, then glanced at the smooth stone she still held.

Well, learning from her Bible, she knew something could still be done with a smooth stone. She walked over to the old tree that stood weathered against time by the riverbank and found what she'd hoped was still in a Ziploc bag nailed to a meet of two large branches. She tugged at the head of the nail, and soon, it eased loose, rusted but strong.

She opened the package, pulled out the old wooden slingshot, and smiled. Testing the rubber tied to both ends, she knew it would still work. So, she pinned the bag to the tree with the nail, and walked back to the beach, watching the current.

She tucked the smooth rock in her hand into the ten-year-old slingshot she and Pete had made and left on a tree hump many years ago and shot it over the crystal-blue waters. It landed with a thudding splash and sounded as decisive as the choice she was faced with. Today was the day she dreaded. And she would face it with faith and courage, not fear or dread.

A familiar voice broke through her thoughts. "Ma'am, we have to leave for the funeral. We're cutting it close with the time." Her driver drew closer. Usually, he stayed in the car. But not today. Everything and everyone was out of sync. She could hardly think through the coming event without tears clouding her eyes. How was she supposed to know that the last time she saw Dad would be the last time, *ever*, on this side of eternity?

Violet swiped a stray tear and nodded even as she felt a hand on her back. She spun and, through a misty gaze, saw her driver had drawn even closer.

The gray-haired man's face crinkled with a warm smile, and understanding shone in his eyes. With one hand gently on her back, he nodded. "I'm so sorry for your loss, ma'am. Your father was a good man. I'll miss him, and so will everyone at the company. But, so we don't get people worried…we really have to go now." Always a kind man, he had picked her up from school a couple of times when she was younger, so he was no stranger to her.

Appreciating his caring attitude, she swallowed hard, shoved aside the memories of the sweet times her family had enjoyed, including the ones on this private beach, choosing to treasure it in her soul, and turned fully. "Thank you, Mr. Raison."

He lifted her purse off the ground where she had set it on the stone walkway a couple of steps away while she slid her toes into her shoe, and shoehorned the back with a finger. The stone cottage hugged the grassy plain surrounding it, well maintained year-round by the groundskeeper. A tip of its brown curved roof peeked in the distance, and the warmth inside beckoned to her.

Clutching her sweater to ward off a slight chill, she strode with equally heavy steps back to the cottage, to get ready for her ride to the church, while hoping she could still wake up and find out she had been dreaming.

Ready or not, it was time to bury her dad.

7

"...But with the temptation, [God] will also make a way of escape...."
-1 Corinthians 10:13

∼

Her visit the previous day to see Miranda's office assistant who'd survived the fire had yielded no new leads, so Angel hoped this trip across town to the building manager would lessen her frustration. She wasn't ready yet to actively pursue the angle of the congressman. Especially without any proof.

She had to find a connection, but despite searching through DMV records all day yesterday, phone numbers, and addresses listed, she could find no connection between both individuals. But if there was a possible link, then someone knew something, and she wasn't going to rest until she found out who and what.

When Angel arrived, a lady stood locking the lone office door.

"Excuse me." Angel hustled forward. "Is this the office for Spencer Leasing?" And why was she locking the door? Angel checked her watch. It was barely two p.m.

The brown-skinned lady jerked at her words, and the keys fell from her hand. Angel waited for her to pick them up and straighten before she asked again. "Can I see Mr. Spencer?"

"He...we're closed," she stuttered and swallowed.

"Closed? Are these your normal hours of operation? You always close at two every day of the week? Or did something happen?" Angel pressed a hand on her hip.

The lady darted her gaze. "No. I mean, it's complicated."

Angel staggered her stance to show she wasn't leaving. "I'm listening."

The lady swallowed again. "Officer, I promise I don't know anything. I only do what my boss tells me. I think it's better you speak to Mr. Spencer himself. He should be at his house."

Angel observed her narrowly. "His address?"

"Homestead Court—3210 Homestead Court."

Angel walked back to her cruiser and set the address into the GPS. She arrived there within twenty minutes and parked some distance away then sat there, cautious as she observed the home for movement. Seeing none, she drew closer on foot. When she reached the front door, she radioed her location and status to the station before knocking. Soon, someone shuffled to the door and peeped through the peephole. With the pause that followed, she was sure the only reason he cracked the door open was due to her uniform.

"Yes?" A short man with razor-fine hair darted his gaze to the street beyond her.

"Mr. Spencer?" she prompted.

"Yes. How may I help you?"

"I'm Officer Angel Martinez. I have a few questions about the fire on 210 West Forest Valley Road and the accident that occurred not far from it."

His Adam's apple bobbed before he opened the door wider.

She stepped into an affluent home, and her boots clicked on the hardwood. Pieces of original vintage art decorated the dining room wall while white leather chairs and a cozy-looking gray leather couch occupied the living room.

He strode toward the center of the living room and curled his arms. "You shouldn't have come. Now, they will come after you too."

She walked toward where he stood, then paused as he drew to a stop. "Who are *they*?"

His lips curved upward. "It's complicated."

"Same thing your secretary said." Angel tipped her chin. "How so?"

"I was warned not to leave my house and to tell no one about it." He beckoned her to follow. "I don't know about the accident or the fire, what caused it." He led her to a home office near the living room, the plush white carpet softening his steps. "But…" He pulled out a file and handed it to her. "Not long ago, we were notified about pests and mold being present in that building, and we scheduled a visit with State authorities. At the time, the correspondences for this request all looked legitimate."

He sank into a black swivel chair, and judging from the circles around his eyes, he had clearly not been sleeping well.

"So, what happened?" Angel pressed a hand to the glistening desk.

He sighed and moved his mouse. "I grew suspicious when they asked for keys to the building and for unescorted inspections. But afraid to lose my business, I gave in."

"That isn't standard protocol, I assume?"

"No, far from it." He shook his head. "We usually send a staff member or two to follow them and monitor the process and record any findings so we can fix anything they uncover."

He shook his head, and a frown dented the side of his mouth. "Little did I know, they weren't from the State, that instead they had duplicated the keys and returned to the building the next day."

"The day of the fire."

"Yes." He wiped a hand over his face, the rasping sound of his stubbled jaw grating her nerves. "Then I was warned to make sure I told no one about it, which I didn't because they said they will burn down my house too. And not to leave my house, which I haven't. But I had my secretary call the State to verify, and they said there was no scheduled inspection according to their records. It was all fake, even though the notification letter arrived with original stamping. I have no idea how they got it. I almost called the cops, but..." He shrugged. "I love my family. They warned me the next day not to contact the State office again, so someone in there could be collaborating."

He closed his eyes, puffing a slow breath across thick lips. "I'm so confused. But one thing I'm sure of—the people behind this are powerful and seem well-connected. A vehicle makes rounds of my house a couple of times a day... perhaps just so I know they're watching me closely. What I don't know is how or who."

Well, she was starting to have a good idea. She pushed away from the desk and paced a few steps before facing him again.

Yep, she had a lot of random info being thrown at her from more sources, and yet she just had no proof. How was she to figure all this out? She started with the question uppermost in her mind. "Do you know why the psychiatrist was targeted? Did anything stand out about her? Was there anything saved from the fire that we can take a look at?"

Angel didn't wish to scare him with her rapid-fire questions, but she also needed as much information as possible.

Spencer powered down his PC. "No, I'm not sure what ax they had to grind with her. She seemed like a really nice lady. Been in that building for more than seven years." He rounded the desk and paused. "The fire department saved a major portion of the last room in her office, the one housing client files. I guess you can look at the file cabinet with the list of her clients. They were in the back and untouched by the fire, save some smoke damage."

"Yes, please, I'd like that."

Stunned at the unraveling events, Angel began to wonder whether the answer to the woman's murder lay somewhere within those files. Her client list would be a great place to start. Thoughtfully, she straightened and approached the window.

Just before she reached it, a boom ruptured the quiet outside, and she peered through a crack between the curtains. Her cruiser was on fire. A second explosion rocked her cruiser —the only vehicle left in the front street-level curbside parking —and then the lights inside the house went out. She dove beneath Mr. Spencer's desk, pulling him down with her. His phone rang, and he picked up the call, then hung up.

"They said I shouldn't have called the cops." His voice shook. "They know you're here. They said they will…"

She pressed a hand to her lips. "Shhh. I never swallow an

enemy's threats. Come with me. What's the farthest room from the entrance?"

"The kitchen. It leads out to the backyard."

Angel dialed the station as he led her, guided by natural lighting. Thankfully, they reached there safely, and she got her captain on the line. "Please send for backup. Someone blew up my cruiser and threatened to burn the property manager's house down. Also, send a team to retrieve the file cabinet with the deceased victim's files. Our answers could be in there." She dictated her current address again, just to be sure they had it, and was told to sit tight until help arrived.

But she wouldn't stay idle.

She led the man to duck near the edge, away from the kitchen door, then realized she'd forgotten to tell the captain where in the house she and the man were hiding. On second thought, she figured they might leave their current location if forced to, and so she didn't bother.

"Were you close to her? I mean, Miranda? What kind of person was she?"

"We weren't personally close, no. We maintained professional contact." He managed to say, though still wide-eyed. "But she was nice. She invited me and some of our staff to a Christmas party years ago, and we met some of her clients. Some were college students. One was the owner of a hospital, and there were also some professors. It was many years ago, so the details are sketchy. Sorry, I can't recall more."

"That's okay. You're doing great. Could any of them have targeted her?"

"Honestly, I don't know. At the time, they all had high praises for her, so I hope not. I guess people can change."

She dialed the captain to update him on their location as

soon as the wail of sirens echoed down the street. Then the front door burst open with a loud gunshot, and she pulled the man away to hide behind the kitchen table.

She cut the call, silenced her radio, and they both went silent. Clicking sounds trailed the shot as footsteps moved around the house. She raised her hand and grabbed a plastic bowl from the counter. Then she laid low and slid the bowl across to the kitchen door. It rested against the border between the kitchen and dining area, just where she wanted.

She hid again as voices called out threats.

Another voice took over, a female voice. "We promise to make your end quick and painless." Harsh laughter vibrated through the hall.

The crash of glassware, likely the ones on the dining table across from them, resounded nearby, and Angel squinted but didn't move. Another set of glassware crashed to the ground.

"The tougher you make this, the rougher it will be for you," the male intruder warned.

But the sirens were upon them now.

It was only a matter of seconds before the other police officers arrived to help. *Sixty seconds to go....*

Until then, they just had to stay alive. *Lord, please shield us.* Her host gripped her arm, causing her to turn her head. She pressed a finger on her lips, and he nodded. Then she waved for him to keep his head down, which he did, although she doubted he was planning to get up unless forced to. She pulled out her gun, disabled the safety, clutched it with both hands, and waited.

Angel crept around the left side of the table as the click of a boot approaching from the right reached her ears. She clamped the sturdy leg of a chair close to her with one hand and peered, weapon pointed first. Someone kicked the bowl she'd tossed forward—so they'd entered the kitchen. Gunfire being exchanged outside ratcheted things up, but she stayed focused.

Less than ten seconds to wait for police....

Any moment now, she would face the intruders.

The eyes of the Lord are upon the righteous and His ears are open to their cry, the Scripture worked into her conscious mind, leading her to utter another prayer in her heart. *Lord, please guide me with Your eye.* She flattened on the ground to gain an angular advantage. As she crawled on her belly to the end, all sounds ceased. Had the intruders spotted them?

She flipped on her back, and her gaze collided with that of a masked man in black-and-black towering above her, his drawn brows indicating he was still unsure if he was seeing correctly. But that bought her enough time. She shot first, then scrambled to her feet. The bullet hit his mid-thigh, and he grunted and planted a hand there.

"Run!" She pushed Mr. Spencer out the kitchen door as she spotted an officer racing toward them from behind the shooter. But the lady accomplice had the police officer within her sights.

Angel pointed ahead to warn him. "Shooter!"

The officer flipped around and shot before making a full turn, and that move saved his life and took down the female intruder. Her attacker, the man, had reversed and was reaching for his fallen gun.

She spun and raced out the door, following Mr. Spencer. Then the man must've reclaimed his gun since he returned fire, and she ducked behind the door, on the other side. *Bam! Bam. Bam.* Rapid fire echoed as the officers fired at him inside.

So, defying all odds at the risk of getting hit, she jumped up to her feet, ran across the backyard, and fled with spraying fire behind her, just as his shots grew closer like he was chasing her.

But she kept running, determined. She would escape terror or die trying.

8

"...Weeping may endure for a night, but joy comes in the morning." – Psalm 30:5

By the time Violet was dressed up and had reached the church, a limousine bearing Pete drew up and parked next to hers. They had planned to meet up this morning, if necessary, at the cottage where she'd been staying should last-minute changes or anything else crop up.

With them living on opposite sides of town and across state lines, this arrangement eased the logistics for the past week since the cottage was closest to Pete's house, only minutes away, across the river, by road. It had also given her the opportunity to relive treasured memories of their family there.

To her surprise, well-wishers had gathered in the parking lot close to the church entrance. They drew closer to offer support. Soon, she smiled at the first person, Shelby, her dad's former secretary who'd retired last year and moved out of state to live with her kids.

The silver-haired woman with a frail frame wrapped her in a hug. "Vi, dear, I'm so sorry for your loss!" Violet returned her hug and accepted the flowers as Shelby wiped tears from her cheeks with a trembling hand. Osteoporosis had turned Shelby into an indoor person, but her agility remained visible in her clear gaze.

"Thank you, Ms. Shelby. And thank you for coming." Grateful to have her driver standing close by, Violet passed him the flowers. Soon, someone else came close and hugged her, gifted her a bouquet, and then shook hands with Pete, who was idling quite some distance away. They were offered more condolences. Violet gave the flowers to her driver one more time.

Most of the small crowd were her dad's friends, former and current employees of Cortexe Corp., plus some older gentlemen who'd been among the first to join the company but no longer worked with them. She greeted everyone warmly and accepted the flowers and food they gave. The aroma of casserole sailed into her nostrils but couldn't stir hunger in her grieving belly.

More people handed her warmhearted gifts like packaged food, drinks, and so many flowers that her driver and Pete's took turns getting them all into both cars.

Her driver drew close and whispered into her ear. "We have to join the service now."

She acknowledged him with a nod, then waved to those remaining around them. "Thank you so much. We are touched by your sympathy. May God bless you. We have to go now." The crowd dispersed, and almost everyone filed ahead of her into the church.

But she couldn't get her feet to move. She stood in place, overwhelmed by the love of her community, feeling like they'd collectively hugged her. The past several days, her church family had surrounded them with their prayers and sent heartfelt emails and text messages and phone calls. That alone gave her strength to face the task ahead. Of course, she alone responded to their messages, since Pete considered those ones to be strangers. But Violet didn't mind. She worked to remain the link between her family and the church.

She made her way to Pete as her driver parallel-parked, and both siblings managed a brief nod. He squeezed her hand and swallowed hard before letting go, but his face was wound as tight as twined ropes, lines etching deeply into both sides with heavy eyelids sitting over them. The hour they had both dreaded had arrived—and if not for God's grace, she didn't feel even a tiny bit ready for it—and matter of fact, at this point, Violet figured she never would.

No one was ever ready to say goodbye to their parent, no matter how bad or good those parents were in their lifetime. Thankfully, she had only great memories of the man whom they had called Dad and of their mom. Pete waved her toward the church doors, and when she didn't move, he walked ahead of her up the steps. The sharp sound of a red-breasted sapsucker pecking at a maple tree near the church doors helped unglue her feet.

Violet held her breath and strode with heavy steps into the Christ Believers' Church. She brushed off dry fall leaves from the left shoulder of Pete's black pantsuit, which might have fallen from the maple tree. Knotting her lime-green scarf—her mom's favorite color—over her black dress more tightly, again, she wished she was dreaming. But she wasn't. Her heart ached with the loss of a man who was more than dad to her—he was her hero.

Pete's dark hair, much like their dad's, reminded her of him afresh and blurred in her vision as tears threatened to overtake her will not to cry. Though his face had seemed calm earlier, his shoulders hunched over with his obvious fresh realization of their loss. At least, his head had blocked her view from the faces watching their entrance or she would lose it completely. Today, no matter who she saw, a smile was out of the question. Sliding past the full church in attendance, she caught a few surprised brethren and friends staring at Pete. Of course, they would stare.

He hadn't entered this church in a long time, much too long. And only their dad's funeral could've squeezed him through those oak doors. She caught his side-glance as he turned to check on whether she followed. Then satisfied, he advanced. The hardness of his countenance was only surpassed by the rugged quarter-sawn oak pew on the left aisle, which they were moving toward at the front row.

Violet managed to swallow past a tight throat, wishing for a private moment to gather her emotions but knowing that was not an option now. Having spent the better part of the night in tears, and the morning getting emotionally and physically ready, she already felt spent. And the service had barely begun.

Her voice was likely gone too, but she couldn't be sure as she had barely spoken to anyone but God since she woke. Putting her clothes on and thinking of going to bury her dad had been a struggle. But she'd forced herself up and out the door. Even the cottage had felt empty without their parents.

Before leaving today, she'd glanced at a framed image inscribed with choice words from her dad's favorite poem. The art decorated the space between the entrance to the cottage and the fireplace.

She'd smiled sadly as she walked past and made a note to move it to her apartment instead of donating it like they'd decided they would do with the other items in the cottage that weren't personal effects or company property.

They'd also decided not to sell the cottage. Too many sweet memories remained there, and a stranger wouldn't appreciate its worth. What a relief to agree on that with Pete since they hardly agreed on anything the past several years, leading to the distance yawning between them—distance she alone made concerted efforts to bridge.

She also saw no need to sell furniture since she had more than enough and so did Pete, and thanks to the great foundation laid for them by their parents, they had a good life and lacked nothing. However, some of the non-furniture items in the house had sentimental value, and those they would definitely not give away. This morning she just wasn't in the right frame of mind to start putting things away, even though the moving boxes she'd ordered had arrived.

She would need some weeks off to go through everything since they'd accumulated a lot of stuff over the years. And, even without asking, she knew Pete would leave all those choices to her.

Now guided by the ushers toward their seats, Violet stopped where her name was taped to the back of a pew, entered the aisle, and sat beside Pete. She set her purse down and glanced at him. His stoic face—and square jaw still hard as granite, as it has been the past decade and a half since he came home from school a very different person—was unreadable.

Yes, biologically Pete was her twin brother. However, since he changed from being the warm, protective brother she knew, denied his faith in Christ, and grew this hardened shell, the difference was as night and day. She could easily confront Pete each time he behaved badly, but that would've put even more distance between her and her only sibling—distance she hadn't wanted.

Torn between getting him to the good side, and loving him, she'd cut him a lot of slack, which probably didn't help. Right now, she'd wished for a glimpse into what had changed her brother. But each time she dared to ask, he shut her down, *fast*.

As she faced forward and listened to the Word while tension reverberated from Pete, she shoved the rising pain downward. His stiff frame and clenched fists did more to increase her nervousness than to quell it.

In her heart, Violet was tired of being the one who worked to hide that their resemblance was simply facial. Her heart hurt each time he huffed when the Word of God was being shared, like now as his grip fastened with whitened knuckles on the ring of car keys looped on his middle finger. Or like the way he'd shifted away from her whenever they ate together, as soon as she blessed her meal before eating.

Nevertheless, she held on to hope for him, even though the more she hoped, the more it appeared like he was getting farther away from God. But no matter what, she'd keep loving him. He was her brother, and she hoped to glimpse the kind of brother he once was—a Christian, loving and caring. She hoped that day wouldn't be too much longer.

9

"Nevertheless, God who comforts the downcast, comforted us...." -2 Corinthians 7:6

∽

"Amazing Grace" filtered into Violet's ears. The age-old music playing from the organ soothed her grief. Thinking about her dad, she scarcely managed to keep the tears at bay. Knowing their mom had passed some years ago made this even harder.

At the time, Pete, who was on a flight returning to the US from Spain, spoke to their mom by phone about an hour before she passed away at the nursing home where she was being cared for, due to Alzheimer's. That experience and her sudden loss were in no way comforting. They had hoped that their dad would live longer—much longer than four years afterward.

Tears disobeyed her instruction not to flow and dropped

down her left cheek. Another followed as she recalled the shadow of their mom praying for Pete every night on her knees, with her head bent, after tucking Violet into bed, and often sharing a Bible story with her. Violet would pretend to be asleep.

But her mom's audible groans toward heaven remained indelible in her memory—and had seared the commission to continue praying for Pete's conversion into Violet's heart. Little did she know that until today, now with both their parents gone, Pete would still be the way he was—locked behind a glass seal where nothing spilled through—nothing.

Violet dipped her lashes and used the tip of her finger to swipe the tear dangling along the edge. At a tap on her shoulder, she lifted her gaze and met Pete's.

Her eyes dropped to his hand where he held out a fresh set of tissues. But she had spotted some softening in his glance. His brown eyes still appeared swollen, and the edges were wrinkled more than before. He was in pain too. She could see it. He just fought hard not to show it. But why? She sighed inwardly.

"You can have mine, Vi." His first words today. He swallowed hard, and his Adam's apple bobbed as she accepted them. "We'll be fine, *mi querida hermana*."

His Spanish endearment, meaning my dear sister, was his first attempt at softness in a long time. Like an answer to prayer, it sluiced through her heart and soul, bringing a drenching of hope to the parched places within her. She replied with a nod as her long black hair tumbled over her shoulder. "Gracias."

Since she was born, Violet learned Spanish from her dad, even though the Spanish language was rarely, if ever, spoken in their house despite their Hispanic family origin.

Simply because they usually had non-Spanish speaking

friends and church family members around, English became their primary language of communication. Spanish was also like their little-known secret that allowed her to hear what people said when they thought she or Pete didn't understand. On rare occasions, or during hard times like now, when communication was tough, they switched from English to Spanish.

Pete faced the altar again as the funeral service continued with songs and hymns she'd chosen from her parents' favorites, played by the choir. She managed to follow the service as eulogies of her dad were given by family friends and colleagues and an elderly aunt. As she listened, her nerves calmed until her eyes met an object placed by a minister gingerly at the center of the altar, and her gaze froze on it as he walked back to his seat.

Their dad's cremated remains in an urn stared back at her in an unreal manner. She darted her gaze away and noticed she and Pete both avoided looking in that direction as their gazes shifted rightward. She would burst out in tears if she chanced more than a glance at it. No. This wasn't how she wished to remember him. Her dad was more than what was in that container.

Violet instead allowed herself to flourish with memories of the sweet man—lively, vibrant, and jovial. Always had a smile for everyone, and never intentionally hurt anyone. Gregarious and fun to be around.

It warmed her heart how he would play soap bubbles with her as a little girl in between phone meetings with his staff whenever he worked from home. During the winter, on snow days, Dad would pull her around in a sled on snow and glue on a white beard like Santa riding on a sleigh.

Then the day after Christmas, he'd drive the entire family,

in their real car, to a Christmas dinner in the city from the cottage, their Christmas home away from home. Maybe that was why the cottage was, by far, her favorite place. Homey and hidden behind a grove of tall trees, just outside the city limits, it hugged the hillside with the cityscape on one side, farms on the other, and the river flowing along its southern border.

Its gray stone walls always welcomed her from afar, and the view warmed her heart with expectation even before the fireplace inside was lit. A narrow, stony trail led toward the river where she and Pete—when they were younger—would play with rocks and build sand dunes on the beach.

In the evenings, their parents would build fires and roast some meat or fish on it, if they caught one. Then they would set a blanket and enjoy the meal while their mom read them a book or their dad read a poem—usually his favorite poem —"O King".

Violet swiped another tear, but more great memories followed. She swallowed recalling her cottage bedroom's reading nook with its pirate lantern dangling from the edge. The nook had a wooden sword for a coat hanger and cozy red, white, and blue throw pillows coupled with a pink blanket.

Many summers were spent there devouring book after book and leaving a large pile at the foot of the bed. The best part of her day was when she'd later learn that her mom had ordered fresh book supplies at the local library and had swapped them for the finished pile.

Surprising herself with an unexpected chuckle, as a procession of the choir for a special presentation began, she recalled covering herself with a blanket to hide that she was reading a gripping tale, only to have her mom reach in and slip the book from beneath the covers and slap it closed with a thud—forcing Violet to sleep.

Christmas and New Year celebrations, usually spent at the cottage, were always memorable—until now. Considering that this was still early November, Thanksgiving and Christmas this year would be hard, *very hard*, to get through.

Last Christmas, even though her dad had been sick with what they had thought was pneumonia but turned out to be an issue with his lungs due to heavy smoking as a young man, he had insisted the three of them to go to the cottage to spend the holidays. Pete had accepted the invitation when she pressed on him how much their dad said he'd wanted to see his children together. But Pete warned that any praying would be without him. She'd agreed, excited to see their family under the same roof.

She'd spent time reading selected Scriptures from the book of Psalms and Proverbs, his favorite passages from the Bible, to their dad, who sat on a rocking chair in front of the fireplace. She smiled when she reached verses he liked. He would usually reward her with a smile, as well as mumble a repetition of the Scripture from memory or give other commentary while she continued reading out loud. Pete left them to it at some point and went fishing, though he returned hours later, having caught nothing.

At the end of Christmas Day after the reading was done, Dad had laid a gentle hand on her arm, then asked her to read his favorite poem, "O King". Even though she'd known he had been fond of that poem her whole life, at that moment in time, she realized the poem meant a lot to him.

And for that reason, she would ensure the poem's art still hanging prominently on the cottage wall was moved to her house. If nothing else, it would keep the memory alive. She remembered feeling somber that day as night fell, and they'd shared mugs of hot chocolate and marshmallows as she missed their mom. Clearly, they all missed her.

Then they'd watched some TV and prayed together when it got late, without Pete. That was the evening her dad officially gave over the reins of the company to Pete, signing all the paperwork, and handing them to his secretary who'd stopped by. He'd also named Violet to be in charge of the lab, as well as the ex-officio deputy to her brother. Though surprised at the move, she'd been fine with it since she still enjoyed her full-time job. She always suspected her dad may want her to move to work fully in his company someday, and she realized that the day was nearer than she'd wished for it to be.

Overall, that had been a better Christmas than she'd expected, better than they'd had for a long time. Not because they were completely taken with each other. No. But because they learned to love one another and accommodate each other's differences, without alienating anyone. They were a family once again, without prejudice. They knew each other's buttons and avoided pushing them. They gave without an expectation to receive.

Before going to bed then, they'd exchanged gifts. Pete had surprisingly bought Christmas gifts for them too—a blue sweater for their dad and a pair of pajamas for her, with a box of chocolate. More surprisingly, he'd recalled how much she loved her reindeer pajamas many Christmases ago and had bought her a pair. Which left her wondering...how much of the past did he remember? Did he recall his faith in Christ? She'd thanked him for the gift, but that spurred something else in her—a burden to pray. So, instead of wearing the pajamas, she took them and presented them to God in prayer on her knees.

Clearly, there was still some kindness left in Pete, a kindness she knew God could expand. She cried to Him to grow that patch of softness in Pete's heart until he repented and received Jesus afresh. She'd prayed for Pete long into that night, like her mom would typically do, then exhausted, she fell asleep.

An usher beckoned at her, and the wave drew Violet back to the service. But the elderly lady wasn't calling for her, but for her brother. So, she scooted to let him through. As Pete rose, he climbed to the altar. Soon, it would be her turn to speak.

As Pete stood there, he shared about who their dad meant to him, making it impossible not to see how much he resembled the senior Zendel. He spoke like him, paused in between sentences, and tilted his head when he was ruminating on his next words. "Dad was a very good man, a great father, and an admirable example to us."

Pete glanced toward Violet and swallowed hard. "He taught Vi and me how to hold our own and never back down in front of a challenge. He taught us that with hard work, and…God's help, we could achieve anything."

His gaze traveled to the urn, but she refused to follow it there. Then when he looked up again, his eyes were misty. "He always said today is more important than yesterday, so make sure to seize the day and don't waste it regretting what happened yesterday. Meaning, we should forget the past, optimize today, and plan for the future."

His Adam's apple bobbed. "Dad said to always do your best today because you are not guaranteed tomorrow. And if you get to see tomorrow, count yourself blessed and do it all over again."

He placed a hand on his chest. "I've held those words close to my heart as I learned to lead an organization he pioneered from the ground up. I've seen respect and admiration for him in the eyes of everyone whom I've met since taking up the duties of the CEO at Cortexe Corp."

She hardly heard his following words as her heart twisted with grief. Pete's voice, so much like their dad's, reminded her afresh that he was no longer here.

Violet jerked her head leftward moments later when someone called her name and beckoned her out to the aisle. Pete had finished speaking and returned toward their seat.

She drew in a deep breath, stood, walked past Pete, and then took the stage at the altar. As she stood there, she was grateful for the sheer number of people who had come to honor her dad. The church was full. She gripped both edges of the podium as her feet turned to jelly and her heart was melting with coming tears. She blinked and lost her struggle not to look at the urn. No. It couldn't be her dad in there. The gray oval sat unmoving, in contrast to the man he'd been.

Her eyes fastened to it, and she wanted to ask the urn to give back her dad but knew it couldn't. Her eyes swam with tears, and someone stepped close and rubbed her back, though she didn't look to see who it was as she returned her gaze to the packed church watching her.

Violet glanced at Tim wearing a black suit seated behind the first row. When their eyes met, he nodded, giving her strength to continue. It had to be a sign, a gift from God, to give her strength on a tough day, while caught in a moment she wished she didn't have to go through. She inhaled another deep breath and cleared her throat.

Violet fixed her eyes to a point past their heads—and

settled it on a cross affixed above the church entrance—as she spoke. She didn't allow herself to look at the urn again and undo the composure she was struggling to maintain. "Thank you all for coming to celebrate the life of our father. I appreciate your presence, your prayers, and your support.

"Losing him has been a hard blow." She sniffed past a tight throat. "Dad, our dad," she began, "was my hero. And I can't believe he's gone." Her voice broke. "He wasn't just Pete's and my dad." She waved to where she saw faces she'd recognized. "He was a dad to the youth church he pastored, whose members I see in the audience today." One of them nodded as her eyes met his. Through the corner of her eyes, she saw Tim rise, with a phone pressed to his ear, and step out the side door. She returned her focus to the service as someone started recording on video across from where she stood. She didn't mind as she'd seen how much effort the church had put in to support the funeral today. They must've hired the videographer.

"He was a father to his employees, his community, and as many of you have said to me, a mentor in this church." She bowed her head and prayed for grace to get through this. This was her eulogy of a man she honored and respected. She *would* get her words out. She *would* get through this.

"My best memories of him were at our family cottage where we often spent summers, Christmases, and New Years. He would roast marshmallows over an open fire at the private beach, and then read us a poem." She smiled painfully as the memories flooded her.

Her heart breaking, she lifted her head higher. "I could go on extolling him, but instead, I'll settle for sharing his favorite poem with you, a poem he said had been passed down from his dad. I'm not sure about its origin. Maybe it was something his dad wrote. I just know he'd read this to me from childhood, and I like it."

Her next words came effortlessly having heard and recited "O King" over and again throughout her lifetime. "The poem says:

Long may you live, O King!

Escape the Hunter when he comes

His heart is dark, his dagger is cloaked, and his finger is cut

He comes for Kings

And none see him coming

Escape the hunter every way you can

For the King is favored by God to live

Live among the orchards, vineyards, and garden of roses and blossom

Fresh as the air, sweet as the berries, and refreshing as the rain

Long may you live, O King!"

AS SHE UTTERED THE LAST WORDS BY HEART, SHE ALLOWED THE following applause and the standing ovation to strengthen her for her walk back to her seat. "Adieu, Papa," she whispered.

Pete patted her arm as she reclaimed her seat. The rest of the funeral passed in a blur. But she felt comforted by all the friends and well-wishers who hugged her and followed them to the burial cemetery, and her heart broke even further as they buried him.

As far as she was concerned, her last safe place was gone, and only Jesus was truly her place of rest from now on.

She wrapped a hand around herself to ward off a chill as

she entered the vehicle and headed to the lawyer's office for the will reading. There were no surprises. Her dad would want her to go to work for him at Cortexe Corp. alongside Pete, and his will indicated that. She chose to do so and to leave her teaching job at the college. She loved both equally, but preserving her dad's legacy through his company came out on top. By the time the lawyer was done, she felt drained.

This day—surely the longest day of her life—left her exhausted when she returned to the cottage with Pete. They ate some pizza in silence, grieving together, after which she said goodnight to Pete, who fielded business calls and responded to condolence callers.

With shoulders as heavy as ever, she went to her room, showered, changed her clothes, and slid beneath the covers. Battling sleep, she closed her eyes, thanked the Lord for gracing her through the funeral, and soon, she fell asleep.

10

"Do not marvel that I say to you, 'You must be born again.'" –John 3:7

∽

Angel woke up with a sharp pain shooting across her midsection. She groaned, sucked in her breath, and blinked behind heavy eyelids. As the smell of disinfectants hit her nostrils, she was sure of one thing—she was in a hospital. She tried to move but couldn't. Unable to recall how she got here, she pressed a hand to her forehead.

How long had she been out? If the signatures and get-well-soon wishes written all around her cast were anything to go by, she must've been out for more than one day. Some were dated Monday, one Tuesday, and another Wednesday. She eased away the oxygen mask blocking her view of her body. As she struggled to lift herself to rise, more pain shot up her legs, and she groaned and settled back down.

Then she saw she wasn't alone.

"Stephanie? John?" Her siblings sat flanking the bed, each holding onto the bedside railing. Were they...*praying*? Maybe Stephanie, but certainly not John.

Just then, the door opened. Her partner shuffled in with a slower stride, probably due to his injuries during the attack at his home.

Her little sister, Stephanie, covered her face, sobbing quietly.

Angel turned her glance to John, who was muttering... something. A prayer? Quite unlikely.

At her words, his head lifted. Then he drew closer, eyes rounded. "Oh, you're awake. I was worried." Concern lined his thick brow. "I got home from the fellowship I attended with Tim. Then I went to the store to buy some milk when the call came. They said you'd been shot and were in surgery."

He rubbed his brow. "So I called Stephanie and the others. We waited until you were out of surgery. Hughes and Grace will be back in an hour."

John then bowed his head and raised it. "You scared me. And I prayed for the first time. I prayed so you won't die. And," he gulped, "I wasn't sure God would hear someone like me. But I'm glad He answered. I didn't expect that." The room grew quiet, and, unable to speak past a tight throat, she squeezed his hand when it settled in hers. "I may reconsider my rejection of Christ after all."

Was she hearing correctly? After all these years of praying and hoping for him to accept Christ and giving up hope were they truly one step closer? "So, you'll go to fellowship again?"

"Yes." A lone tear rolled down his cheek. John was never the type to shed tears. Whatever happened must've shaken him. "They said you coded twice, Angel. I'll go to church again. If only to go and thank God for saving my big sister's life. I appreciated your worth when I woke up and you weren't there. I've... taken you for granted." His voice broke. "I knew I had to have a chance to apologize. I'm going to clean up my act, arrange to settle my debt, then get my life together. For good this time."

"I'd applaud you for that choice, young man." Her partner, Pierce, stepped forward. "It's better doing it with Jesus, John. I know these are the things you want to do, but I also know from experience, that the road to getting those things accomplished successfully, and without any more regrets, passes through Jesus."

"I appreciate your words." John nodded. "Like I said, I'm willing to give Jesus a try."

"Fair enough." Her partner turned to her, and his smile seemed to lift the pain pinching his eyes. "And it's good to see the sleeping beauty is now awake. You scared us all. What were you thinking landing into a dangerous place alone like that?"

"Justice..." Angel managed before her throat tightened again, still reeling over the news—She'd coded? And John was getting serious with Jesus? She adjusted her pillow to lean up slightly. Could she dare to be hopeful for him after virtually giving up?

"Lady Justice, you need to stay alive to execute justice, too, so no more taking excessive risks." He wagged a reproving finger. "Next time, you wait for me or someone else before going to interview a suspect. We never know when things might turn ugly. Are we agreed?"

Angel grunted her disagreement, and they all laughed, except her. She wanted the criminals caught, not waiting to pet them into talking. Granted, she'd taken a risk, but it had paid off with the information.

The weakness making her drowsy again, she slid down the pillow. "Thank you all." She would need a couple of weeks to heal. But she would get back on those criminals' trail. Then, as sleep shuttered her eyes, she muttered, "Soon."

∼

Violet took three weeks sorting through their parents' belongings before finally getting comfortable enough to resume her full-time duties at Cortexe Corp.

She found a few surprises. Like a golden heart locket bequeathed to her by her parents and which she now wore everywhere. Plus, they'd left the cottage to her, while Pete inherited their family home. Then they left her a key. She wasn't sure where it fitted into or what it was for, and so had a jeweler unseal the locket, insert the little key, then seal it again since she wore the locket everywhere. Hopefully, one day, she'd figure out what the key was for.

Still missing her dad, she grieved his loss, but she'd admonished herself that sitting indoors and crying wouldn't bring him back. So she tried to resume her life, starting with Cortexe Corp., which was running smoothly under her brother's leadership. For the past year, she'd been working at the Cortexe Corp. lab with the technicians while unofficially functioning as the Deputy CEO, who had retired the previous year. She had a management office on the top floor next to Pete's, but enjoyed her hands-on lab work. A day-to-day chief scientist managed the staff there, but she oversaw their work when needed. She also supplied whatever the technicians and staff requested.

Pete had an undeniable knack for leadership. But working with him for the past year, while teaching at the college showed he also had an aggressive ambition that had to be monitored. She hoped to help him balance both sides of his personality without clashing as often as they recently had in private. Since the funeral, things had been calm, but she couldn't assume they would remain so.

Upon arriving at the complex, she stepped out of her white sedan and, while walking toward the towering complex, uttered a quick prayer for her first full day to go smoothly, especially with Pete. She strode past the familiar Cortexe Corp. inscription on white marble and entered the expansive lobby.

A life-sized banner image of Pete smiling greeted her. Standing at the entrance and with her eyes shielded by large dark sunglasses, she halted her stride, inhaled the pine-scented air-freshening fragrance, and released her breath with a single word, "Interesting." He was sure putting his stamp on the company. But was this new addition his idea or did someone suggest it?

Sometimes, it struck her, like right now, how much they looked alike. Of course, she chose to wear large sunglasses today to avoid the stares she'd get without them. Her nerves were wound up enough already.

"Miss Zendel?" She spun to a security guard approaching with cautious steps, one hand idling on his weapon.

She raised her hand and took off the glasses. "Yes."

He closed the distance and shook her hand, and his shoulders dropped upon recognition. "This way, please. Your security escorts will be waiting at the elevator. Both of them." He ushered her forward. Then they took a turn, and two broad-chested men fixed their gazes on her.

She swallowed. She had bodyguards? A driver had been enough. And even then, she'd asked to drive herself in for a few days to have privacy to pray during her commute.

When she reached them, she paused, and they greeted her with a wave and a small smile. Then one held the elevator for her while the security guard returned to his duty post. She managed to stop herself from smiling when she saw the numbers on the elevator buttons were now math symbols not digits. Another change Pete had made, but this one she liked. When they were kids and had visited their dad's office, Pete said he'd do it. She hadn't realized it had meant so much to him then.

The elevator doors closed and, after a soft bounce, carried them up to a secure floor. As soon as they exited, Pete was standing there.

"Welcome, Vi. Glad to see you here." A quick hug followed.

"Thanks." She returned his hug.

His gaze dropped to her neck. "You got the locket." He said it as a statement of fact.

"Yes. I didn't know about it, but Dad and Mom apparently left it to me. I found it with a note addressed to me in their bedroom drawer. You knew about it?"

Pete nodded. "I saw it years back and had asked Dad for it. He said it was for those in the family who followed The Way. I guess I didn't qualify."

"Oh." The Way meaning Jesus. Was this that important? "I didn't realize. I'm sorry?"

Pete shrugged. "Hey, it's their choice and I respect it. I'm glad you got it at least."

He stepped aside and pointed forward. "This way, please."

Her bodyguards-cum-security escorts trailed his bodyguards as he led her down a long stretch of offices, introducing her to the COO, among others. She smiled and managed to hold onto as many names as she could. But she'd need more interaction to know them at a glance. As they passed office after office, almost all the staff members, who had worked closely under their dad's leadership, were gone. Did Pete fire them or did they leave on their own? Some worry crept up her spine. She would find a chance to ask Pete why he made all the physical and managerial changes—and perhaps, what other changes were coming in order to better support him.

Their leadership styles were different and could prompt a mass exodus of people who preferred their dad's family-style work atmosphere to Pete's formality. But she hoped Pete would retain some sense of community so the oldcomers wouldn't feel estranged.

Her phone rang inside her purse, and she paused and picked up the call. "Hello?"

Heavy breathing followed.

When a clicking met her ear, Violet curved her brows and moved the phone away to look at the screen. She blinked at the white words against a black background. "TELL ME ABOUT THE POEM." Then the call disconnected.

Pete walked back to her. "Vi? Are you all right?"

Raising her glance to him, she wasn't sure how to explain what had happened as the words, like grainy sand, cleared off her phone. "Someone called me, and instead of talking, typed out a question asking about a poem."

"Dad's poem?" His brows inched up. When she nodded, he frowned. "Why would anyone care about an old poem?" He reached out and took her phone, handing it to one of her bodyguards. "Take this to the lab and investigate who the message was from." While the man left with her phone, Pete ushered her forward, appearing to be more intent on getting started with their day than in dealing with her caller. But she'd been rattled.

"The bigger question is how does he know about dad's poem?" How much could the team find out? There'd been no voice to analyze. The call barely lasted ten seconds and came from an unregistered number. But she relented, not interested in arguing with Pete. "Could it be as a result of my presence here? Did someone object to my working here as Deputy CEO? Or was there a disgruntled employee since the call came in now while I'm here?" But why would someone be against her role in her dad's company?

Pete gave her a bland look. "Really, Vi?"

"Sorry, but I have to ask." She pushed back. "I take my safety seriously."

"As do I," he replied. Some silence followed. Then he led them forward again. This wasn't how she wanted things to start.

"Fine. Let me know what they find out."

His nod ended the conversation, and she trailed him to his office for their first official meeting. But something told her things would only go downhill from there.

11

"Nor is there salvation in any other, for there is no other name under heaven given among men by which we must be saved." –Acts 4:12

∼

"I got the job," John's announcement helped Angel through the final round of her physical therapy for the day. She climbed down from the machine and hugged her brother, sure that he wouldn't mind a sweaty hug. Angel was so thankful that every day she felt stronger and stronger. Beyond the occasional pain and scarring, she scarcely suffered lasting injuries.

"That is the best news yet I've heard today. Congratulations!" She held him at an arm's length and wished words could describe how much he'd changed—and how happy that made her. In the weeks since he'd returned, she'd seen him mature, both physically and spiritually.

He'd become more patient, attended fellowship with Tim

every week this month, and was going again next week. She found him spending time early in the morning studying his Bible and praying. That was new—and pleasant to see. She prayed harder in her heart for him to come to salvation in Christ, and with the way things were going, it seemed that would only be a matter of time.

It was not a secret that John had ruined his life. But it was also not a secret that God was turning things around for the better for him. Getting this new job being the latest in that trend. The restoration of his relationship with their younger sister, Stephanie, being the first. Stephanie had found it hard to forgive him for cutting off from them, and they'd had issues for a decade. She had been angry over the way John had been living his life. But, in recent weeks, they'd grown close, arriving at the hospital together, going out for lunch, and him saying amen when Stephanie prayed before they left Angel at the hospital. This new family that God gifted her was so good that it left Angel speechless most times. She just watched the miracles unfolding and thanked God.

"Thank you." John supported her with a hand as she knelt to get her pearl earring that had fallen during her exercise.

When she straightened, the hospital therapist gave her a thumbs-up. "Now, you're in such good shape, and you're about ready to go home. But after you're discharged tomorrow, I suggest you rest for an extra two weeks before returning to strenuous work. I will recommend that to your doctors."

Knowing she was getting discharged had also been a blessing. "Thank you. But can I work from home?"

Her therapist nodded. "As long as you follow the exercise and therapy and rest regimen, you should be fine." She moved toward the exit. "I'll see you for a checkup in three weeks."

Eager to leave the hospital setting and not step foot in one again as a patient for a long time, she was definitely grateful for the freedom to go home. She spun to John, who was collecting her items—sneakers and her purse for her for transport back to her room—while she grabbed the sweaty face towels and switched from sneakers to flat boots. "When do you start the job?"

"I let them know I'm available now, and that works for them. So, I'll be starting tomorrow. But I'll be home to check on you around one p.m. I'm a site supervisor, so I won't do the hands-on work but rather ensure things are running smoothly." John led the way toward the exit.

∼

IT TOOK TWO WEEKS AND THREE REMINDERS FOR THE SECURITY team to get back to Violet about the strange call. By then, she had settled into her duties and mastered the art of avoiding conflict with Pete. They'd clashed on company issues twice, once in the presence of others, and she wouldn't allow a repeat.

But Pete was changing fast, thanks to his growing friendship with the newly hired COO. Apparently, the guy had been hired just before their dad handed things over to Pete a year ago, but he had played a minor role in primary decision making until now. And he considered her an enemy.

She wasn't about to allow some criminally-minded fellow ruin her parents' company. So she stood up to them both—like right now with both men in her office convincing her of a need to purchase additional security and hire more manpower. "Guys," she folded her hands on the smooth-polished mahogany desk before her—her dad's desk—and drew a deep breath, taking comfort from the connection to him, "if what we're trying to achieve is to restructure the company, I'm all for it. But starting an internship, building a campus here, and paying for more software is currently outside our budget and our scope of operations. Why do we need to do all that?"

"Expansion." Pete slid into the chair in her office while his bodyguards hovered beyond the glass doors. "We have to expand. The world is moving forward, and we need to move ahead of the curve. We need to take on progressive projects, and I have just the idea for that. One scientist at the lab has been working on it for some time now."

He spread out his arms wide. "But I want it bigger. We can only attract heftier investment when we go big. I know a contact who works with foreign investors, and I gave him a call. He has interested parties standing by. He's simply waiting for our go-ahead."

When she shook her head, Pete leaned forward. "Vi, this is our chance. We seize it or we miss it. I have to build on what Dad did here. The security industry needs more eyes in the sky. I will provide them with the equipment by leveraging what already exists and connecting them all. That is why I commissioned The Rulebook, which the tech team is working on. But we need more money for the project to continue, and there are investors willing to finance us."

Violet also leaned forward, palms down now on Dad's desk, the strength of the man who had sat there for decades seemingly holding her up. "Do you know about the possibility of possession of any criminal records by your potential investors? Granted, I spend all my time at the lab, but I also care what decisions you make up here. If you need me to step in and be the voice of caution, I will."

Crossing his legs, Pete narrowed his gaze at the COO. "He'd said you wouldn't listen. And I wished he was wrong. I wanted us to do this together, but it appears I need to go it alone." Some desperation cooled his tone and sent caution racing up her spine.

"Pete, do you know the identities of these investors?" But he was silent, as though his mind was made up. He was going with the COO on this, against her wishes.

That caution shivered deeper into her heart. Feeling double-crossed, she still spoke her mind without fear. "The company is not in trouble. We're not strapped for cash and looking for investors. We're fine. If we keep doing what we're doing, we can expand slowly. This Rulebook project sounds dicey to me, and there are no guarantees of success. If I were you, I'd tread carefully."

Even as a kid, Pete disliked anyone standing up to him, so she took a risk. She had quit her professorial job, so her full-time income now came from Cortexe Corp. But she fought for her parents' legacy. They had sown all they had into this company, truly grown it from the ground up, and she wouldn't allow Pete to mortgage all that on a scientific experiment with possible criminals.

"Either you come along or you don't." Pete rose and approached the door. At her voice, he paused.

"I think I'll prefer to spend more time down at the lab. I'd rather not be in your way since your mind was made up before you came asking." She pressed palms deep against the desk, sadness achingly echoing in the finality of her words. "Oh, and please keep your bodyguards. I'm sure I can navigate this building by myself."

He squeezed the door open without looking back. "Suits me

fine." The COO led the way. Pete followed, and as soon as the door closed, Violet didn't have to ask. Battle lines reverberated through their exchanged words and left little room for dialogue. Was this truly the beginning of the end for their peaceful collaboration? "I'm sorry, Dad," she whispered.

Her phone rang, and she picked up the call. "Hello?"

A clicky sound followed, and she jerked the phone back from her ear.

"I WANT TO KNOW ABOUT THE POEM." The call ended like it had the first time, and she slid the phone into her purse, rose, and headed down to the lab, determined. She was a computer analyst and wouldn't wait for someone else to find out who was bothering her. Then she called the police to report the incident, also informing them about the first one. She was done waiting for Pete. And done trusting him with her safety. He was uncontrollable.

12

"...Make known what are the riches of the glory of this mystery among the Gentiles: which is Christ in you, the hope of glory." – *Colossians 1:27*

∼

Angel arrived at work two weeks after leaving the hospital, to a rousing round of applause, a cluster of balloons dancing over her desk, and a warm welcome. Hugs, followed by appreciation for the risk she had taken, were given by her colleagues, and she couldn't feel any more loved and appreciated. Or more ready to dive into her case afresh.

As soon as she settled into her seat, her cellphone rang. She frowned at it. It was a bit early to be getting a call. "Hello?"

"Hi, Angel?" a vaguely familiar voice asked.

"Yes. Who is this?"

"Tim Santiago. Do you have a moment to chat? I promise it won't take long. But you'll want to know about this."

She swallowed hard. "Sure. What's up?" Tim had become like second family since he and John became friends. He'd progressed from a spiritual coach for her brother, to a life coach, and now a trusted friend. His positive impact had altered their family for good, and she had expressed her gratitude to him several times.

"Actually, I think you may want to be a part of this."

Her curiosity piqued, she batted a yellow balloon aside and used a paperweight to pin its curly ribbon further away. "Um, part of what?"

"John's water baptism. He received Jesus in the early hours of this morning after we'd talked for almost two hours. He called me around three a.m. And I suspect the only reason you haven't heard is that he might be asleep."

Angel sunk into her chair, a gray balloon floated skyward, and tears pooled in her eyes. "Are you kidding me?" A happy sob escaped her lips.

"No, I'm serious. Congratulations. He had a lot of questions, and I walked him through the answers I knew from Scripture. I was thrilled when, as we wrapped up, he said he wished to receive Jesus. So I led him in confessing the Sinner's Prayer. Mission accomplished. John is now a part of the family of Jesus."

Tears warmed tracks down her cheeks as she waved off Pierce's concern over her crying. "I'm so happy. You just made my year. Thank you for sharing this news. And yes, I will come for his baptism. Seven p.m. is the usual time, right?"

"Yes, it is. The pastor is taking care of this one."

"Thank you for everything, Tim. Really, thank you. Heaven

knows how grateful I am and will repay you for this labor of love."

"My pleasure, Angel. But remember, it is the Lord who uses us to accomplish His divine purpose, not us. I am only a vessel."

"A willing vessel. That made a huge difference."

Static joined Tim's chuckle. "Well, you're right about the big difference we've seen in John. I'm also glad to hear you're feeling better. Stay safe out there."

"See you later, Tim. And...thanks again."

As she hung up, Angel was sure her day and life had just gotten brighter. She smiled at the bright yellow balloon, dancing between her monitor and her stacked desktop file tray, feeling herself to be just as cheery and light weight. If anyone asked her, this was as close to the best day of her life as she could imagine. John was saved. She hummed "Amazing Grace" as she powered on her PC. *Thank You, Lord Jesus. You did it for me.*

∽

Violet alighted from her car at the Cortexe Corp. complex with heavy steps. She and Pete had just had their worst argument over the phone last night. How could she even come into work today? But they had a scheduled meeting she couldn't afford to miss. Weeks upon weeks of her hard work dangled in-between Pete's ambition and the company's wellbeing.

Massaging her forehead to ease the dull ache with one hand, she felt for her purse in the front passenger seat. If she chose to go through this day with her brother, taking a pain reliever would be a must. She rummaged through her purse, found some Aleve, and drank two. Then she returned the remainder of her bottled water to the cup-holder, stepped out, and slung the purse over her shoulder. At the door, she spun around. She hadn't locked the car. She sighed and shook her head, choosing not to return to lock it. It should be fine within the complex with the heavy security.

She clutched her purse, pushed through the doors with weary feet, thanks to a sleepless night, and paused to check the time. She smiled—7:44 a.m. She had fifteen minutes to settle into her office, put her purse down, and then head to the meeting.

As soon as she stepped past the rotating lobby doors, she froze. Pete stood there looking directly at her, with one hand shoved into the pocket of his black pants. He'd dyed his hair a strange color somewhere between golden brown and milky white.

He was a different person from who she'd left here the previous day. Ignoring the hair color, for now, she closed the distance between them and stopped within a handshake's distance. Anger swirled around him, and with his lips pinched white, he must be working hard to contain his fury.

But she wouldn't give in to whatever his demands might be—if that was why he stood here. She hitched her purse higher on her shoulder and arched her chin, trying not to think about how perfectly matched their heights were when so little else now seemed the same. "Why are you waiting for me here? Our meeting is at eight."

The COO emerged from behind him, so there had to be trouble. Without acknowledging him, she didn't let her gaze waver, holding Pete's eye to eye unflinching.

The COO cleared his throat, and peripheral vision revealed

an evil grin as it twitched his dark mustache. "That would be my fault. I should've called you to give you a heads-up." He slid a hand into his pocket and winked. "Oops."

Her frown deepened, pinching her own lips to match Pete's. "A heads-up to me about what?"

"We're restricting your building access." Pete moved closer. "You will be granted full access to the general entrances and exits, as well as the lab. But no more than that."

She crossed her arms. "Since when? Remember, I also have authority in this company. You cannot make unilateral decisions as you choose."

He turned, and the bodyguards advanced before he took a step. "If you violate these conditions, disciplinary actions will follow, up to and including termination. Are we clear?" Of course, he turned his back to her. He couldn't say that to her face. But his bodyguards? Fear laced their eyes for her brother. And her heart constricted with a similar yet stronger fear, for him, not about him. Did he become so obsessed with power and control that he forgot to be good-natured?

She strode around the guards to stand face to face with him, eye to eye once again. "Dare you say that to my face, Pete? You might have the executive authority, but I can petition to take over the company if you're going in the wrong direction."

Something blazed in his eyes, making her wish for his previous coolness. Lurching forward, he stood inches from her face. "Only if I'm incapacitated, and I'm not. You lack the legal grounds for such. And I will fight you. Are you ready to get into a stinking fight because this will be ugly?"

Pete knew she loved him and would hesitate to engage in a public spar.

He guessed as much with her frustrated silence. "Sorry, sis. I remain in charge. And you don't dare flout my rules around here or you face the consequences." He stormed off, leaving everyone in the lobby quiet at the altercation.

So, she squared her shoulders and marched to the lab. There, she asked about the lead scientist who worked on The Rulebook. Something was going on.

"The roster was edited to say he was on leave this week," an assistant informed her.

"Thank you." She massaged her neck as she entered her office and sat. Her office at the lab was much smaller, but more peaceful, though, in this moment, she would have loved to touch her father's desk, envision him sitting there, guiding the company. If only Pete had cared to take that desk. Would memories of the man behind it have tempered him?

Shaking her head, she got to work on the tasks she had set up for the day and refused to think about Pete. Anything she did now would be out of anger, and she wasn't going to react like that.

Around lunchtime, her phone rang. She smiled at Tim's contact. "Hey."

"Hi, Violet. How's your day going?"

She wondered whether to answer in a formal respectful manner or to share her problems. But this was Tim. "To be honest, Tim, I could use a friend right about now."

Tim huffed a sigh. "It's Pete again, isn't it?"

"Yes."

"If you want to talk, I'm a friendly ear. Hey, can we do lunch? Right now? There's this restaurant, La Mesa De Comedore, not far from you there. Can we meet up in say, one hour?"

"Sure. I haven't eaten, and my belly is growling. I know where it is, and I'll see you then." As she hung up the call, she prayed for grace to get through her day without further bad occurrences.

~

Inhaling an appeasing breath, Violet allowed the savory dishes before her to soothe away some of her worry.

"What happened?" Seated at the La Mesa De Comedore, Tim forked some roasted corn and some mayo as well as chicken to his plate from the large dish they'd ordered.

Violet followed suit to serve herself. And as soon as she'd taken a bite, she sat back to figure out how to shape her response politely. "I don't know what Pete is doing. And I think he wants to force me out."

"Out of the company? That's impossible." His eyes narrowed. "Right? I mean, the will stated that you both have ownership stakes in it as the only surviving children."

She offered a brief nod and sipped some water to douse the hotness of the soup. "Yes, but Pete has the executive authority. I'm more involved in the lab, and I only take over if he is deemed incapacitated."

"Well, he's not sick so..." Tim swallowed, and a dark line tightened his brow. "But with Pete being the way he is, that's not good either. I don't think your parents foresaw this. What are you going to do?"

She let her spoon sink deep into the chicken tortilla soup but didn't immediately lift it, swirling vegetables and black beans into a whirl. "If it was someone else, it would've been easier." She swallowed her food and shook her head. "What can I do, huh? He's my brother, and as much as I don't want to see him ruin everything, there is nothing apparently wrong. If I took this to court, nothing could prove the company is being jeopardized, beyond my gut feeling."

"And Pete's animosity. Don't forget that." Tim set his fork down. "And stripping of some of your authority."

"Right, those too." Violet ate some more as Tim picked up his fork and ate in silence. "Again, I'm trying to avoid a public spar. It will jeopardize future investment prospects. I'm stuck between tough choices. I want to hold out hope for my brother, and I choose to relinquish any power he wants. After all, I have more than enough to meet my needs."

"This is plain wrong. Vi, let me know if there is anything I can do. You can always go back to teaching." He toyed with the edge of his napkin. "It's an alternative."

"Yes. But...well, something about seeing the only family member you have left heading toward ruin and taking everything else down with him makes you not want to let that happen, even if you can't stop it." The words, a whisper, seemed to strain through her closed throat. Why was she even trying to eat?

"Maybe you should both talk to a professional. A mediator might bridge the gap."

Violet choked a laugh. "Does Pete seem agreeable to a mediator to you? He is in charge, remember?" She edged the bowl away. She couldn't stomach another spoonful. "I think I lost my appetite."

"If you're going to face Pete, you need to eat. I have an idea of something you can do."

A spark of curiosity, and faint hope, shot through her. She scooted forward, studying him for a clue. "Okay. Tell me."

He winked. "Only after you finish eating, so eat up."

Sighing, she picked up her spoon and ate some more.

"So, you say you were getting strange messages. Have the cops identified a culprit? Did they find anything? Or did you?" Tim asked as he too rounded off the meal with a belch a little louder than he probably would've liked. "Sorry about that."

That led her to chuckle. "No apologies, it's a natural phenomenon."

They both laughed. "Just like Professor Ben used to say."

The memory calmed her a bit. "Actually, I didn't find anything. The number was a dead end, and the cops haven't seen anything to flag. So, there's nothing. They blamed it on a possible sick prankster taking advantage of my dad's passing."

"Sick prankster indeed." Tim sipped some water, wiped his mouth with the napkin, then sat back too. "But don't you find it weird that a prankster, however sick, would resort to hiding his identity, risking police trouble, and doing it twice just for a prank? I'm not sure I accept that version."

He sat up as she finished eating and pushed her plate aside, sure that she couldn't consume another morsel. "That's where my suggestion can come in handy in identifying this culprit too. You hear me out, then choose what to do."

"I'm listening, Tim." She prayed that whatever he suggested she could legitimately do. Sure, Tim was a Christian, but she had to keep her own conscience clear in whatever she put her hands into. "It's just…with my and Pete's emotions being so raw after our dad's death, grief could partly account for his recent behavior. It might not be, but I want us to keep that in mind. He could also be trying to establish himself, although I deem it unnecessary. I'm not excusing him, but I wanted us to keep all the relevant pieces in perspective."

"And that's why I'm suggesting you play along until you find out what this is all about."

"Ooookay." Violet tapped a finger on her water glass, unsure how to react. "Go on."

Tim leaned over the table. "Look at it this way. If Pete is involved in something wrong, or if this Rulebook thing is worth pursuing, how would you know from the outside? You can only know if you're still inside the company, working with him. Moreover, you might also utilize the lab facilities to discover who your mystery caller is." He rolled up his sleeve and paused. "I'm sure you love your brother, but the same cannot be said of him, unfortunately. You don't have to take my word, but based on what you've shared, I don't see any other viable options for what you want to have happen. So, I've got a second piece of advice for you."

"Sure. What is it?"

"Get a journal. Write everything down. Everything you do from here on forward." He shrugged. "Including how this whole situation makes you feel. You know, write it down, especially if you can't tell anyone about it. So that tomorrow, you can find the strength to face what comes next. You won't be able to do that if you bottle it all up inside. And thirdly, pray. Pray like you've never prayed before, Vi. This is a storm of life. And no storm comes without a mission. But prayer turns those waves around to work for you, instead of against you. I'll be praying for you too. You can be sure of that."

Violet appreciated her friend's advice, knowing it came from a perfect heart, full of only concern for her. She settled a hand on his arm. "Thank you. I love everything you've said and will keep it in mind."

She closed her eyes, trying to envision how to handle this better than he'd suggested. Unable to find other suitable alternatives, she popped her eyelids open as BREAKING NEWS came on the air. Tim seemed ready to say something, but he turned to the wall-mounted TV as well.

"We interrupt your scheduled programming to inform you that a body found at a construction site downtown has been identified as this man." An image flashed on the screen, and she blinked at the TV, then swallowed hard. It was the Cortexe Corp. scientist supposedly on leave.

13

"For there is nothing hidden which will not be revealed, nor has anything been kept secret but that it should come to light." –Mark 4:22

∽

"Tim," Violet's ears tingled, and she rasped. "He was said to be on leave. He's...*dead*?" She clutched her chest, gasping.

"You know him?"

She pressed her fist harder against her chest. "He's the lead analyst for The Rulebook, and I was told he was on leave for one week. He had argued with Pete on Friday. I didn't get involved, and I wasn't listening. I had my earbuds on. I figured they'd work whatever it was out."

She and Tim stared at each other, pondering, knowing, wishing they weren't thinking it. But one of them had to say the words.

Violet braved it. "You think," she gulped, "do you think Pete had something to do with it? I'm scared, Tim. If he did this…" She ran a hand through her hair. "This isn't who he was. This isn't my brother." Words failed her. "I don't know who Pete Zendel is anymore."

He touched her hand and held his there until she met his gaze. "Don't make any assumptions yet. Ask him, hear him out, then make choices. I hate how this looks, but please," his eyes bore into hers with seriousness, "I know Pete has contacts with the police, but find a cop you can trust and tell him everything. My police friend would've been perfect, but she just survived a shooting and is dealing with some family issues. I would hesitate to expose her to anything potentially dangerous so soon. Considering this new development, it is even more important to write everything down now. Make sure you document as much as you can."

He paused like he was thinking and sucked in his lower lip. "I'm not sure it's wise for you to quit now even if you were thinking about doing so. Since you were at the same lab as the deceased guy, if you leave now, it will seem suspicious. Moreover, with this guy out of the picture, Pete will likely rely on you for the completion of this project."

"If he asks for me to take over, what do I do then?" Everything was happening so fast the room spun and developments left her with no space to think. Since Tim wasn't directly involved, surely, he had a clearer perspective which she could count on.

"There are two options. You walk away—he succeeds in securing someone willing to create something that threatens the world instead of protecting it. Or you stay and destroy it. If he offers you the chance, I'd say, you should accept it. But if it turns evil, you make sure you take the program down—unfailingly. Don't be responsible for a catastrophe, Vi. Everything is now on your shoulders. And I'm sorry you've found yourself in this unenviable situation."

He cast a glance at the TV again. "And if Pete did this, then he's covered his tracks pretty well. The problem we're facing now is this—if he killed once, he'll do it again. Don't be a victim. Be careful and get out if you feel unsafe."

She nodded and squeezed his hand. "I will."

"Promise me," he pressed.

"I promise."

He leaned back, then drew a long breath. "Good. Because while I'm away for a year, I need to be sure you'll be okay."

"Wait." Violet blinked. "Where are you going to?"

"I wish I knew all of this was going on before I took the position of adjunct faculty at the Department of Archeology in the University of Mexico." He sighed. "I can't cancel it now."

"Oh no, don't cancel it. We both knew you wanted this. But what a great surprise. Congratulations. I'm glad we came for lunch this afternoon then." She smiled. "I'm going to miss you." She tapped on his chest with a finger. "Don't go wandering into museums and getting shot at. You be careful too."

His laughter rang out so normal—and sounded like sweet music to her ears. It had been long since she heard those sounds. At least, she had something to smile about, even if only for a moment. And she was sure going to miss Tim. "Text me your email address, your phone number there, and your mailing address. Every form of communication possible. Skyping, whatever works."

"Of course, I will." He folded the napkin and set it beside his plate. "There is someone I led to Christ last night, or shall we say, early this morning. I'm heading to church tonight for his baptism."

"Oh, that sure makes me glad to hear. Congrats on that too. Unfortunately, Pete is far from the possibility of such an occasion happening for him."

"Don't give up, Vi. God can work a miracle tomorrow. In fact, He will, at His time. Keep praying and thanking Him in advance."

Nodding, she gave what she was sure was a sad smile. "When do you leave for your assignment?"

"In two weeks. Just enough time to know you're okay around Pete before I get on the plane."

"Thank you." Tim was looking out for her like her brother should, like Pete should. Tim paid for their meal, and they rose to leave.

As soon as they exited the restaurant, her phone rang. It was Pete. Since the day he called her to tell her about the loss of their dad, she dreaded picking up his calls, suspecting he called when something was wrong.

With recent developments, she needed time to think before talking to him, so she let the call go to voicemail. At the valet parking, while she waited for her car to be brought to the front, she listened to the message. "Vi, it's Pete. Please come back to the office. We need to talk."

That was it?

She sighed and hugged Tim. "Thank you for lunch. And... for your advice. I appreciate it."

"Remember everything I said." He held her gaze, waiting.

A slight nod dipped her chin. "I will. You keep me posted about your plans."

"Will do. Bye for now, Vi." He shrugged his coat tighter to ward off the slight chill.

"Bye, Tim." As she watched him drive away, she felt like she lost her only friend and remaining family in the same day. Tim was more than a friend—he was a brother, a brother in Christ. She prayed she wouldn't have any emergency that would make him cancel his trip. It meant too much to him. Then she entered her car and drove off, en route to Cortexe Corp.

~

When Violet arrived, Pete was pacing at the lobby. Their eyes met, and he moved toward the elevators. She followed his bodyguards.

He marched forward, pushed the button, and while they waited, confusion and caution warred in her heart. So, she prayed. *Lord Jesus, I'm not sure how to handle whatever Pete is about to throw at me. But give me grace, wisdom, and direction in Jesus' name.*

The elevator pinged, and one by one, they all filed in. Then the doors sealed them in oppressive silence. But she was tired of avoiding confrontations while his choices degenerated from bad to worse. It was time they had at it, and whatever came out of this situation, God would take control.

She added a few more words to the prayer. *Lord, I know how much he hates to see or even hear about Jesus. It's almost like a taboo. He's my only family left, and while I can tiptoe around him to keep a semblance of a relationship, this time calls for being explicit with Your permission. Please, help me.*

The elevator chimed again at the executive floors. Pete led them toward his office, and her eyeballs rounded at the sheer size of the team working upstairs now on this project. So, Pete had hired the new employees and scaled up The Rulebook projected timeline—judging from the wall timer—all without telling her? What more was happening that she didn't know?

They walked into his office, and by then, she felt like her heart would burst. Staying calm was a struggle.

"Please, have a seat." He pointed to a swivel chair.

She shook her head. "I won't need a seat for this." She turned to his bodyguards. "Please excuse us. I need to speak with my brother alone. Now."

They stayed rooted, glancing at Pete, but he said nothing.

A fire rose from the pit of her belly and burst out of her lips. She reached out and flung the door open. "Get out! Now!" she roared. Without waiting for Pete, they marched out, and she kicked the door shut with a resounding thud. She spun, curled her arms, and faced Pete again, after adjusting her pinstriped suit.

Pete shrank back with a step. "Wow. That, I have never seen from you. Well, I guess we have all changed, haven't we?"

"Actions and reactions are equal and opposite, scientists say." She pressed her lips tightly and looked Pete in the eye, a mirror of hers. "And no, we haven't all changed for the worse." She pointed at him. "But you have."

She leaned forward and pinned both hands on the glistening glass desk. "I want you to tell me what you did to that dead young man. Something tells me you had a hand in his demise. I know you are capable of a lot of things, but killing an innocent man wasn't one of them. Yet. Tell me that hasn't changed."

Pete spun and walked off to a cabinet, uncorked a bottle of wine and poured it over ice. He took the glass, returned to his desk, and took a sip. Then he gulped half the glass, set it down, and laughed. "You know, Vi, you might be my sister, but there are things you never ask a man. Who he sleeps with and how he makes his money."

She held his gaze with her steady one. "I didn't ask you any of those questions. The truth never hides from discovery forever, no matter how long you conceal it. Now, you tell me what role you might have played in that young man's demise or I'm going to the cops. And if you did anything complicit, I will go to the cops anyway."

That jerked his eyes into a frown. "You want to call the cops on me?" He came around his desk and loomed a breath away. "How dare you!" he drawled. "Try that, and I'll rend you before nightfall."

"You don't scare me, *mi querido hermano*. I'll call them *only* if you're guilty, Pete." She remained unflinching as his alcoholic breath poured on her face. "So, now is the time to say whether Pete Alejandro Zendel has become a murderer or if he's just the mean bad boy he's been for the past decade." She edged closer until their faces were inches apart. "Did you kill the man?"

His hand lifted for a slap, but she bridged it with hers without looking away, then wagged a warning finger. "Don't you dare hit me, or I will surprise you by how well those self-defense classes have paid off. I don't think your pride can handle that in full view of your men, can it?"

He sneered at her. "I thought you were a Christian. You shouldn't hit back." A wicked smile she'd never seen turned up a corner of his lips and sent a chill over her spine.

"Yes, I am a Christian. But I won't be bullied by my own brother. You can be sure about that."

His hand swung to his side, and he stepped back as though

he was also stepping away emotionally. "I'm done entertaining your tricks. I have no response to your allegations. But I do have an update about your status here."

Silence followed. When she said nothing, he continued. "I have directed the staff to know you will take over the project, henceforth known as The New Rulebook. Since our dear friend's unfortunate demise left a gap, that gap will be filled by you, and you will meet up with the deadline I provided to our clients. Since you say this is our company, its time you act like it and actively support our main project. If these terms are not agreeable to you, please feel free to quit now."

He glared at her, almost sure she would quit. Disbelief shivered through her. Tim's words were coming true. She had a choice here, and besides her, no one else would dare to oppose Pete. None.

So she leaned forward, smiled, and planted both palms on the cool table again. "Of course, I'll work on The New Rulebook. After all, I like a good challenge." She straightened, then spun toward the door, determination brimming in her. If what the scientist had shared about The New Rulebook was true, then she had double duty on her hands—build what Pete asked for, and then build in a factor to ensure its destruction—at the same time.

And she could not fail in either task. "I'll see you around." She walked out, slammed the door, and strode to the elevator, out to the parking lot and entered into her car. She prayed for God to send her a police officer she could trust without jeopardizing her safety. Then she revved her engine, slid the gear into drive, and exited the main gate.

It was time to buy that journal.

14

"So, I prophesied as I was commanded; and as I prophesied, there was a noise, and suddenly, a rattling; and the bones came together, bone to bone." –Ezekiel 37:7

~

Angel looked up from her PC when her office door creaked open. The captain leaned against the doorjamb.

"Sir?"

He scratched his short, gray beard, entered, and sunk into a chair. "Listen, I've got this man here who said he came to report Miranda Sow missing."

Her eyes widened. "Missing?"

"Yes." He nodded. "Apparently, he doesn't yet know she's dead. But, before we suspect him of complicity, I think you should listen to him. His is quite an interesting tale—it might just crack this case wide open."

She grinned widely. "Sir, I have researched everything I can, and yet, this case has frustrated me for weeks now. Where is the man now?"

He pointed behind him. "Waiting in my office."

"Do you want me to interview him there?"

The captain shook his head. "I'll escort him over. But take his statement. Matter of fact, record it and ask for his permission before doing so, please. If any of what he says is true, you're about to get swamped with leads. If so, I'll definitely be assigning more officers to support you. Good luck."

"Thank you." Angel sat up like she'd just gotten a jolt from an energy drink and searched for the recording app on her PC while she waited. She found it, then called the lab to have them back it up on their server while it recorded. When they assured her it was done, she hung up the call and waited. She preferred to secure the information in case something damaged it on her system. She tested her recorder and verified it was working. Then she announced the date and time on it after its confirmation just as both gentlemen walked in.

A tall, broad-shouldered man wearing a black UM polo shirt and rugged jeans, with a golf cap entered. His eyes were sharp, sharper than she would expect for a civilian. She stood, approached them, and smiled. "Hello, I'm Officer Angel Martinez. Please have a seat."

She pointed to a spare seat. He extended her a hand. "David Lynn. It's a pleasure to meet you." He took the seat she offered, and the captain walked out and shut the door.

She returned to her seat, glided back in, then rested her gaze on him while he tapped his foot in impatience. Finally, she cleared her throat. "My captain says you're here about a disappearance?"

He gave her a photo, and she accepted it. Yes, it was a younger image of Miranda Sow. High cheekbones, same set of blue eyes, and dark hair.

"Miranda Sow is a friend. She has not shown up at her place for the five days I've been in town, and I've checked there every day. Her office was sealed off with a Do-Not-Enter sign when I went there after checking at her house all these days. If something happened, I haven't heard anything in the news. Therefore, I came here to report her missing."

Angel eyed him. "And you say your relationship with her is...?"

He glanced away. "It's complicated."

It's complicated? Seriously? Angel was getting tired of hearing that phrase with regard to this case.

She sat back. "Listen, I'm going to ask for your permission to record this interaction. Is that all right?"

His tapping fingers went still. Then he shrugged. "Well, sure. If it will help us find her. No problem." He fidgeted and tapped his foot again. "Listen, can you please put out a statement in the media or something so someone can start looking?"

"You didn't say what your relationship with her was, Mr. Lynn. I'm going to need that to make sure you're not someone we should be looking at for a missing person."

"Call me David." His brows drew together. "Of course not. Not with the stuff she mailed me. Which was the reason I came here in the first instance."

Angel crossed her fingers. "And what did she mail you? Do you have it with you here?"

He fished in his pocket and handed her an envelope. "Here."

She accepted the letter, opened it, and extracted a single

note out. Then she flipped it open and read. "I THINK THEY FOUND ME. HELP ME, DAVID." Followed by Miranda's house address scribbled at the base, along with her cellphone number.

"Interesting." She glanced up. "Who are they? And why was she scared of them? And why were they searching for her, Mr. David?"

He shifted in his seat. "It's a long story. One I can't get into except we commence looking for her. Time is of the essence."

His impatient puff reached her ears. She had to reveal the truth to him. If Miranda trusted this man enough to inform him she was in danger, then maybe, just maybe, he might have something to say to help unravel this case.

"I'm sorry, Mr. David. But Miranda is dead."

He stared at her like she had spoken a different language, and his face turned pale.

"She was returning from a visit with a lawyer when arsonists burned down her office building, and then ran her vehicle off a valley road. She died that day. I am the officer investigating her murder, and we are trying to identify the culprits but haven't had much success. Any information you can share will help us bring Miranda some measure of justice. I'm very sorry."

He stood, wobbled a bit, then paced her office. From the manner with which he clutched his chest, it seemed like he was hyperventilating. He sat back down and stared at her with a crestfallen face. "So they did find Randy," he said slightly above a whisper.

"She's Miranda," Angel clarified for the recording to be sure they were speaking of the same person.

He nodded, then lowered his head, and a lone tear slid

down his right cheek. "I know. She was Randy to me, to *us*, back then."

Angel leaned forward. "I know this has come as a shock to you and you're grieving. I also know it's a lot for you to take in, but the more we wait, the more these criminals cover their tracks. They were trying to hide something, and I want to uncover what that is. Can you help me?"

He lifted his head, wiped his cheeks, and nodded sharply. "I will. For Miranda's sake. We'll get them all."

"How many are the 'all'?" Angel held her breath.

His gaze became resolute, and again, Angel wondered if this man seated before her was a civilian, but this wasn't the time for a getting-to-know-you chat. It was time to get information, and she would not be distracted from that sworn duty.

David ran a hand through his hair, then fisted his hands, arms flexing as though about ready to exact revenge as ever. Then his gaze settled on her. "There are ten people involved. And it all began ten years ago…"

15

"Therefore the law is holy, and the commandment holy and just and good." –Romans 7:12

∼

TEN YEARS EARLIER...

Miranda glanced at the science teacher sitting at the end of the bench, and her heart warmed. Their date had ended perfectly. A meal at Buena Casa de Costillas, an evening spent walking along Crescent Drive with decorative lighting, then an unexpected return to the school, where they both taught, so she could get the anxiety pills she'd forgotten to take home. Now back on school grounds, they'd left his bag and her purse in the car, locked it, and took the car keys along on the walk to the sports complex. After a ten-minute trek, she unlocked the doors with her keys, entered, and he followed her to the staff changing room where the lockers—and her pills were.

She kicked off the high heels she'd worn and set them in place next to her sweater. Then she slid her feet into the leather flats that were a constant in her staff locker.

Hardly anyone was in the sports center of Andres High School, where she was a swimming instructor. She was finishing her degree in nursing, and with one semester left, she could hardly wait to leave the part-time swimming job and start her dream career of helping people get better.

"I've had a lovely time tonight, Randy." David leaned, arms folded across his chest, against the doorjamb.

She couldn't help a chuckle. "Me too. Except when the waitress mistook us for newlyweds and served us free slices of special red-velvet cake."

He laughed and swung to face her as she searched for a bag to package her high-heeled shoes into. They were going to walk a long way back to where they parked close to the boarding school gate, and she wasn't doing it twice in one night in heels. Especially not after their nice walk in town. "Yes, it was awkward telling them they had the wrong table and that we were on our first date."

Comfortable silence stood between them.

He reached out and took her hand loosely, making her pause her action to peer in his face. "I do hope we get there, someday. If today is an indication of what me-with-you will look like, I'll give it a chance."

"I—" Miranda began saying, but a shove of the changing room doors, followed by loud rancor, and thudding feet interrupted her. She counted off the boys as they entered, and each settled their gaze on her. Ten boys, all high school students with affluent parents—donors crucial to the school's funding—seemed drunk and high on substances and perused her with unworthy intentions. The way each ran their eyes over her made it clear what they would do to her, if given the opportunity.

"Hello, Miss Randy." One boy with dark hair and blue eyes stepped out from the pack and linked a hand over her neck. "How are we doing?" When she didn't respond, he sank onto the bench and sat between where she stood and where David sat.

"How did you get in here? This space is for staff only," David queried. Her eyes met his. David, being a slender, nonathletic person, was no physical match for these boys, with muscular athletic build and who played various sports well. Moreover, he couldn't tackle all ten. She'd heard a rumor about a clique formed by these, and that they occasionally broke the rules without penalty. So, any attempt David made to defend her could earn him some violent attacks, especially since the boys were under the influence of substances.

Nevertheless, David took a step toward her. But another boy, with light-brown hair and gray eyes, stepped between them. Then another followed him. And yet another. Until four boys were between them. They were spoiling for a fight, one she wished to prevent.

One of them, the first one who'd sat down, stood and sauntered to David. "I believe we asked the lady a question, and you were not invited to answer."

A chorus of laughter followed.

She faced them all but didn't address the boys. "Dave, I'm going to the maintenance area to find something to pack my shoes in. I'll be right back."

She stepped out the door, and one of the boys blocked the entry to prevent David from following her, which he couldn't easily do with the four bulky frames in front of him. She bit her lip. Her plan hadn't worked. They knew what she was doing—planning an escape—and the boys made sure they held onto something, *someone* she wanted, in order to ensure her return.

～

MIRANDA STRODE DOWN THE HALL AND TURNED RIGHT TO ENTER the maintenance area. She contemplated her options and didn't like any of them. First, she could call the police, if she had a phone on hand. But they would speak with the school security guards, who would inform the police that the boys had done nothing wrong.

The boys might get in minor trouble for being under the influence. However, with their parents in powerful positions, they would be freed in a little while, if they even saw a jail cell at all—and they would return for payback. Also, she wasn't going to leave David and flee.

She had one option left with the least path of conflict—wait them out and hide here until they tired and left David. She entered a large room and spotted a coat closet. Opposite it was an open toilet. It didn't look like it was flushed so she tore out a piece of tissue paper, pushed the toilet cover over, and pressed it shut. This was the maintenance room used by the janitors who maintained the gym. Near the wall, a pile of gym laundry towels lurked in tied bags. Staff uniforms, washed and ironed, hung above the dirty laundry bags.

Good place to hide.

Miranda approached it. Never in her life did she think she would hide from some young men for potential assault. But this situation called for wisdom. Calling authorities when nothing had happened would increase the chances of something worse happening later, and she wasn't willing to risk it. She only had a semester left here. Then she was done.

She swept the uniforms aside, planted one foot behind the dirty laundry bags, and stepped beyond them to hide. Releasing the uniforms, she exhaled with a sense of relief as they swept over her upper body and hid her completely. Too bad, she'd left her purse in the car. At least, she would have had a phone to call for help. She just hadn't thought she would be in danger in a school where she worked. She thought of heading back to the parking lot, but someone who was likely a part of the boys' clique had lingered outside and might tackle her alone in the dark. So, left with no other options, she leaned against the wall, crossed her arms, and waited.

She must've fallen asleep. Because the next thing she heard was a loud bang as someone burst into the room and she jerked awake. She straightened as another set of footsteps tromped in, then another.

The stamping of feet drew closer. "Did you see her?" a young voice squeaked as more feet entered.

"Not yet, but I will. I've got plans, real plans for that chick. Did you see her legs?" the voice drawled sensually, and a low whistle followed, driving her heart into a panic.

The boys were here. They hadn't left, and their intentions were evil.

Another voice sounded closer. "When you're done, I'll take over."

Miranda clutched her chest. She'd never experienced anything like this, nor heard of it anywhere in this state. The boys moved like they were possessed by something simply intent to do evil that night.

"Then me after you. Man, it's going to be fun tonight," another boy added.

A frustrated sigh followed their fruitless search for her as buckets landed against the wall. "All that can only happen if we find her. Are you sure you saw her enter here? I won't be patient for much longer." Another object got tossed, and it knocked out the lone light bulb, throwing them into darkness. She could remember the path she had taken to reach her hiding place if she needed to run out in the dark.

More obscenities were tossed at her, and more evil plots shared. She covered her ears, disgusted by what they planned —for her. These boys were plotting a gang rape as though it was a normal occurrence.

But where was David? What had they done to him? Was someone guarding him to ensure he didn't come searching for her? He wouldn't leave her here. So, *what* happened?

That they hadn't left in what might've been thirty minutes since she left, meant they were serious. But if she had stayed there, and if they had tried anything with her and David shielded her, what would they have done to him to reach their aim?

The night was getting progressively worse. Since she had now heard their collective intentions, she would be right to call the cops, except she couldn't. And they would deny the allegation, and she would be back to square one. She might even get framed for something horrible and get locked up instead. For someone like her, struggling financially already, any legal expense was beyond her options.

Swallowing hard, she chose to stay hidden, hoping they would be unable to find her in the dark.

A very small interior room she had checked earlier, which

had nothing more than a toilet and washing sink in it, creaked open. Then someone slammed it shut. She listened as each boy dug deep into items, opened places, tossed objects, searching for her. She'd once heard about avoiding dark places because something bad could happen. Tonight, that couldn't be truer. She wrapped her arms around herself with desperate fingers and held her breath any time someone drew close.

Their search grew more frantic, impatience raising their voices. She wished she could flee but felt safest staying put as her heart pounded in her chest.

Then a hand pressed against her face, and she was sure her heart almost stopped beating. "How do you find something warm-blooded and alive on a cold, dark night, boys?" a boy mocked. "You wet your hands with cold water and trail the heat signal. I found her."

Her heart sank further. His hand clamped like a cold vice plastered against her face, and even though a uniform separated them, his clench on her face was strong, pressing deep into her eyes.

It was time to run. Or die.

Miranda slammed a hand against the wall, jumped over where she knew the dirty laundry was near her feet, then pushed his hand away. She ran toward the door and reached it only to come into the view of flooding light from the outer hallway. Two boys, who lay on the floor near the door—drunk and almost passed out—glanced up, and their eyes met hers.

"Hey!" one of them shouted.

But she didn't wait. She jumped high into the air and narrowly missed their hands lifted to clamp her feet to make her tumble. Her feet landed in the hallway. She ran toward the changing room where she'd left David as a trail of shouts followed. Curses rained behind her, and the other boys gave chase.

"David! They want to gang rape me!" She saw David appear at the doorway, punch the boy who stood in his way, dive out, and run toward her.

Caught between the boys chasing her, and the one racing toward David as he neared her, Miranda knew one thing—with her revelation, the chances of them leaving this night alive were slim—and if they did, she would be on the run for the rest of her life.

It was going to be a night that would change her life forever.

16

"Do not be overcome by evil, but overcome evil with good." –Romans 12:21

～

It wasn't until David stopped speaking that Angel realized she had stopped breathing. She drew in breath sharply and planted a hand on her chest as she slowly exhaled. "Wow." She settled against her chair. "So, this was what Miranda said to you, I'm guessing?"

He nodded. "Yes, almost word for word."

"So," Angel leaned up, "how did you both escape?"

He paused for a moment, then glanced at her with that intent look. "We didn't. Two security guards, who were making their rounds, got there just then and radioed the situation in. They asked us what the problem was. While Randy cried, I informed them, that they had planned to gang rape her. The guards called the police, and when they arrived, the boys said they were simply talking to each other and not about Randy. So, her case was dismissed."

"I'm assuming the story didn't end there as Miranda is now dead."

"Not nearly. They fired Randy two weeks later. Then I helped her land a job at another school. But she started receiving death threats, and someone broke into her house. So I asked some guys, and they helped us get her a new ID, with a new driver's license, and she fled. We chose to separate to save her life and to stop the boys whose parents had come to query Randy before she was let go at the other job. Clearly, she was a loose end they wanted to take care of to protect the boys' futures."

"At the expense of Miranda's." Angel brushed her hair back.

"Exactly. Randy chose to stay in the state to take care of her elderly grandma but changed everything else. And moved to an area where she least expected anyone to come looking. We did everything possible to make it hard enough for anyone to find her, and we hoped the last place they'd expect her to be would be within the same state. We also had little time to help her disappear so it was rushed and mistakes were possible."

"Well, if it helped to conceal her for ten years, then you both did a pretty good job. What prompted them to come looking for her?"

"I'm not sure. That's what I hoped to find out."

Angel opened a drawer to get a notepad and grabbed a pen. "Can you write down the names of the ten boys if you know them, please?"

"Sure." He nodded and accepted the items. "I could never

forget their names. They endangered a lady I loved and denied me a chance to spend my life with her."

Her heart hurt for the love those two sacrificed to protect Miranda. And as he wrote, Angel prayed that, if any of the boys were involved in the death of Miranda Sow, she would nab them in time.

∼

ANGEL DROVE HOME LOOKING FORWARD TO ONE THING—HITTING the pillow. It was late. Following her interview with David, she was happy to make some headway on the murder and arson investigation. She had two possible directions to focus on—Miranda's client files and David's list of ten boys, who were now men.

Because the first attempt against Miranda had been to burn down the office before killing her, Angel suspected the culprit was hidden somewhere within Miranda's clientele.

After going through the files with the clients' names and hoping for a miracle, she came to the same conclusion as Mr. Spencer. There were some powerful people in her client list, including past governors, state legislators, and famous actors. After obtaining the right clearances, she was allowed access to some sealed files tonight.

That took things to a whole other level. She unlocked a list of eight people who might possibly want Miranda dead. Those eight sealed-file client names listed two drug dealers; a gang kingpin who was already in prison but, after his recent release, had paid her a visit; a doctor who was sued for medical malpractice; two teachers, one who manipulated scores for students in exchange for favors, another who threatened a student with a deadly weapon; and three officers on administrative leave for excessive use of force in conducting various arrests.

Then the last one shocked her.

Tommy Moore—a promising candidate for the US House of Representatives, who was new to politics. The elections were happening soon, and he could be a prime suspect if he had something to hide. She'd dig into his files in detail tomorrow since the lawyer had said Miranda mentioned a congressional candidate. First, she would check her notes for the exact name tomorrow.

Stifling a yawn, she pulled into her driveway and parked outside her garage, meaning to drive inside after she'd gathered her purse, files, and other items. She leaned over to retrieve her purse from the front seat, when an object smashed into her right passenger window and rained shattered glass onto the seat.

Angel ducked beneath the steering wheel. She inched her head up slowly and found shards of glass all around her—and someone running toward the back of her house. So, she grabbed her phone, jumped out, then gave chase.

She reached her backyard, leading to her neighbor's backyard, too, where a rustle of leaves jostled in the distance. She chased along, but after jumping the low fencing and watching the figure disappear into a small path, she found it tough to breathe and had to stop to catch her breath. Obviously, her body hadn't healed enough to sustain a prolonged foot chase. She was also alone and chasing a criminal on foot, and in the dark, which wasn't too safe.

So, she relented much against her wish, but choosing to avoid an earful from Pierce, she doubled back to her car, then called the station. While waiting for a squad car, she gathered her things and walked around her car to see what she'd been attacked with. A piece of rock had been thrown at her window. She sighed but avoided the urge to touch it without gloves.

Soon, other officers arrived and cordoned off the area, studying the damage to her vehicle. An hour later, they had searched the surrounding areas but didn't find the suspect. Knowing he or she was likely long gone, she thanked them for coming and for stationing an officer to watch her place in case the suspect showed up again.

Her front door opened, and John emerged with puffy eyes. Had he been asleep this whole time? The way he rubbed his eyes suggested so. Considering he typically left for work quite early most times, she wouldn't be surprised that he'd been sleeping and hadn't heard a thing. He walked toward her, now wide-eyed. "What's going on?"

She sighed as the last officer waved goodbye before getting into the squad car. "Someone threw a piece of rock at my window, crushing the glass."

His brow furrowed. "What? You should've called me."

She shrugged. "You're not a cop. That would've put you in danger. Anyway, I chased him but he got away. So I called the station to report the attack."

"I'm glad you're okay." He waved her forward. "Let's get out of this cold."

As they entered the house and locked the door, Angel rubbed shivers from her arms, relieved to be safe. She crossed to the dining table, settled her weapon's belt, car keys, and purse on it.

An inviting aroma wafted into her nostrils from the kitchen

area. "Well, don't we have a surprise chef in the house? What did you cook or order?"

"Not ordered, I cooked." He grinned, and some pride curved his smile deeper into his cheeks since she'd smelled and appreciated the aroma. "Since you did all the cooking while we were growing up, I thought I would make you a meal for a change. It's your birthday, sis."

Angel face-palmed herself. "I forgot my own birthday. Great."

"We remembered for you." John loosely clutched her arm and led her toward the kitchen where five tall cards stood at the kitchen table, with a cake at the center of it. "Everyone wants you to know how much we appreciate all of your sacrifice. So, these are handwritten cards from each of us, saying thank you for your sacrifices over these years. We love and appreciate you. You are the best big sister in the whole world."

Angel teared up and wrapped her arms around him. His words and action hugged her heart even tighter. "Awww, John. You're going to make me cry. This means a lot to me. I can't believe you guys pulled this off. Thank you for at least remembering, because I definitely forgot."

"Poor Angel. Always saving everyone else." He teased and she laughed. "Well, now we all join to save you." A serious look smoothed his face. "Seriously, I love you, sis. You mean a lot to me, and I know the extent of your sacrifice."

He swallowed, and his head dipped a bit. "I know that, had you not been busy taking care of us, you would've been married by now. I'm sorry for the delay you encountered, and I pray God will lead the right man into your life at His right time. We're praying for you."

She hugged him again, this time, unable to keep the happy

tears from wetting her cheeks. "Thank you, Johnny. And I love you too. I will call the others tomorrow." Her other siblings must've gone to sleep, and she didn't wish to wake them up.

He propelled her forward. "Okay, come and cut your cake. I've been resisting diving into this delicious temptation while waiting up all day. Well, all night, too, since I got home from work a few hours ago. I must've fallen asleep on the couch."

That's what she thought.

John settled a knife next to the cake and set two flat plates on the counter. Angel rounded the table, picked up the knife, and sliced down the middle. "Thank You, Lord Jesus, for the grace to see another year. I give all the glory to You. May the coming years glorify You in my life. I'm very grateful for all You have done, and also for those You have not done. They all work together for my good. Thank You, Lord, in Jesus' mighty name, amen."

A slight hesitation trailed her prayer, which surprised her because these days John said amen to her prayers. Then, as she glanced up, John smiled. "Amen, sis."

She cut a slice for her and for him as he brought out the ravioli pasta from the fridge, along with spaghetti meatballs, and heated those in the microwave. The aroma alone had her mouth watering. John took his plate with cake, grabbed plastic forks for them, then sat down across from her.

The sweetness of the chocolate cake melted in her mouth, and her shoulders loosened. When had been the last time she'd relaxed like this? Her last birthday? Maybe not that long, but it sure felt like a long time.

John tapped the fork on his plate. "I have a question about the prayer you just prayed."

"Sure. Ask me." John had been ravenously studying Scripture since his conversion to Christ. If she couldn't answer a question, she directed it to her pastor. "What about it?"

"You'd thanked God for the things He had done."

She nodded. "Yes."

"But you also thanked Him for the things He didn't do. Why? Are you supposed to thank God when bad things happen too?"

She chuckled, wiped her mouth, and took a sip of water from a glass he set next to her plate just as the microwave chimed and he stood to retrieve the food. She waited for him to return with it. "You know what, John? Yes, we should. Scripture tells us to give Him thanks in *every* situation, not just the ones we like. Why? Because all things—the good, the bad, the ugly, including the unforgivable—work together, not alone, but *together* for our good. If we believe this, then we can and should thank God in every situation."

"Interesting," John replied between chews.

"Yes. It is." She poised her fork in the air while resisting the temptation to indulge in more cake. "I'll tell you three major things I've learned in my life. One, no matter how a circumstance looks, Jesus has the final Word. Two, Jesus is Lord above every situation, no matter how bad it seems. Third, God is good, and no depth of evil occurrences can change that. I grasp these as my weapons of overcoming the evil I see every day in my job, and I know that, no matter how things look here, these three things hold true."

She counted off on her fingers for emphasis. "One, Jesus has the final Word. Two, Jesus is Lord above every situation. Three, God is good."

John's fork had frozen midair while she talked, like he was

absorbing her words. "Jesus has the final Word. Jesus is Lord above every situation. God is good."

"Exactly."

"Thank you." He pointed at her dish of pasta. "Now, please eat your food before this turns from dinner into breakfast."

Angel laughed and tossed a fallen piece of cake at his face.

He eyed her narrowly. "Oh, no, you didn't." He finger-scooped some icing and flung it at her, and it got her ear after she ducked.

She set her fork down and staggered her stance. This was shaping up to be a food-fight kind of birthday. And after the long, bitter weeks she'd had, a food fight would be sweet. Angel eagerly dipped her fingers into the cake, scooped up more icing, and returned the favor.

17

"He delivers the poor in their affliction, and opens their ears in oppression." –Job 36:15

∽

THE FOLLOWING DAY, ANGEL STRODE TOWARD HER NEW POLICE cruiser, struggling to contain her anger. She had just left the congressional candidate's campaign office and almost had a cease-and-desist letter slammed in her face for querying the man over the phone. He was out of state for campaign matters, but his staffers were able defenders of him. Their candidate was perfect, they said, and had done no wrong nor harmed Miranda Sow.

She'd called her captain to intervene, and after he called the higher powers, two hours later, the candidate returned and she was able to sit down with him. He'd basically denied ever having had a shrink or needing one his words, not hers.

Which meant, she needed to find out why he'd gone to a psychiatrist. Then she'd practically gotten shoved out the door.

She entered her car, slammed the door, and returned to the SSPD. She got right into the files they had retrieved, pulled out his case file, and read through it. Then she flipped to the back of the file and froze before drawing the folder closer and tipping it to the setting sunlight streaming through the passenger window. Was that...? Yes, a scratched-out note with a date of...wait...a few days before Miranda's death?

She took the lone sheet to the captain. "Look, I think we found something. I'm going to need some help figuring out what was written and then scratched out."

"Get the folks in the lab on it right away." He nodded. "This man keeps resisting us at every turn. We'll get to the bottom of this. Great job."

With a nod, she proceeded to the lab, handed over the sheet, then went to grab some lunch with Tim. She'd been surprised when he had asked her out to lunch. But having no other engagements, she accepted.

When she arrived at Olive Garden, she easily spotted his dark hair peeking above the seat close to the door. She walked past the hanging plant suspended above the hostess desk, passed a couple being served their meals, and turned a slight corner toward Tim. Then she caught the whiff of spicy Calabrian chicken breadsticks sandwich, and her mouth watered.

Once he saw her, he smiled and pulled out a seat. "Hi, Angel. Please have a seat."

"Thanks for choosing a place so close to the station." She sank into the chair he had pulled out, rubbing her neck as a waiter approached. Hopefully, their food would be served soon, and they'd have enough time for a quick chat. "It's good to see you, Tim."

"You seem like you've worked hard enough for one day already. Those bags under your pretty eyes say a lot."

Chuckling, she blinked in surprise that he had noticed her eyes and called them pretty. "You can say that again. A murder investigation is never easy. People close up when police officers show up, and all you're after is the truth. I want this case sorted, and I'm determined to see it to the end."

"And there's our Angel. Always chasing the truth. John told me someone had attacked your car last night, so it's good to see you're fine. I've been praying for you."

"Thank you. I can use all the prayers I can get."

"Say, how is John doing? He's been busy, I presume, and honestly, so have I. As a result, we haven't spoken for a bit."

She smiled as the waiter took their orders, then left. "John is doing good, great actually. It's such a remarkable difference between who he was and who he now is in Christ. He's so responsible now it's hard to compare him to his past. I'm grateful, too, for the role you played in his conversion. Who knew all of that can come out of a job recommendation, huh?"

"Life is full of godly surprises." Tim played loosely with the edge of his napkin. "How about we add one more surprise to that?"

A waiter served their trademark free bread and set a bowl of salad at the center of their table. She wondered what Tim had in mind but refused to guess. She sucked in her lower lip. "How do you mean, Tim?"

He cleared his throat. "This morning, after speaking with John, I realized that time waits for nobody. The risk you faced with the attack weeks ago and the one last night showed me I couldn't wait any longer before saying this."

"Saying what?" She picked up the serving fork and served herself some salad. She took her fork and played with the food for want of something to center her. The longer Tim waited to speak, the more she wondered what could be so hard.

Finally, he cleared his throat and set a gentle hand on hers, and it stilled. "I want to ask you out on a date, Angel." Her gaze trailed his words to his eyes and held. "If you're not in a relationship." Hope glistened in his gaze.

Her eyes widened as he withdrew his hand and settled it on his lap, then gave her a disarming smile. "Tim, are you serious? I mean, I want to be sure this isn't a spur-of-the-moment thing."

He nodded, and the bounce of those Italian curls added certainty to his words. "Yes, I'm sure. It took me a while to pray through to know this is what God wanted. I want to go on a date with you, Angel. Would you give me the honor?"

She thought for a moment and chuckled. "If you're sure Jesus led you to ask, then, I'd say yes."

A vigorous nod followed. "I am certain."

"All right then." Surprised this had become more than a lunch between friends but had turned into something better, Angel wished she didn't have to go back to the station because all she wanted to do now was jump and squeal for joy. But she simply shrugged and maintained her composure.

Soon, their food arrived. But the coming date lingered pleasantly at the back of her mind as she ate.

She silently thanked God for it and prayed that, whenever it happened, it would be according to His will and for both their good. Caught by this surprise, she gladly enjoyed a happy surprise for a change.

Violet arrived home from work and knew she'd had it. Pete had cut off her access to the Executive Floor, made her have to sign in each time she entered and exited the lab, and basically reduced her status to a regular employee.

Confronting him yet again had yielded no positive outcome, leaving her with a broken spirit and a determined mind. Yet she had cooperated and worked very hard on The New Rulebook project. He had a goal, and she had hers—and both were polar opposites. It was almost finished. But he'd asked her twice if she was hiding anything, and she equally asked *him* if *he* was hiding anything. Of course, he hadn't admitted to having a hand in the death of their deceased employee, but he was never going to tell her the truth, so that became her sole leverage.

Today was the final straw for her. And while she had earlier contemplated allowing the program to run on a limited basis, the required separate adjustments would flag her actions to Pete.

That was why, today, she completed her construction of what would ensure its destruction. And she didn't regret it. She just hadn't safely extracted it out of Cortexe Corp. yet. Running against her brother's project pained her, but he'd left her to choose between his ambitions and the public good. It was clear that involving authorities would set alarms off and the deeply interested parties wouldn't quit until the program was re-created. Her only option now, knowing she was the one person who currently understood the program fully—was to ensure its destruction. But accomplishing it in a way that didn't alert Pete was as tough as climbing Mount Everest unguided. He had eyes

—and guards—everywhere and tracked her movements within the complex.

Violet set her purse near her couch, kicked off her black pumps, and relaxed into the cushions. She then bowed her head and poured her heart out to God. She'd used her lunchtime to visit their family lawyer yesterday, asking about the possibility of challenging Pete legally.

But their lawyer had indicated that any move she made to challenge Pete would be public and could attract severe backlash against them both. He'd advised that they sort out their differences privately, which wouldn't happen in the near future.

She sighed, stayed near the couch, and literally prayed all evening. She was tired. Of Pete. Of his harassment. Of being in the right, but overshadowed by her brother. Of having to choose between getting him to do what was right or having their family made into a public spectacle.

She needed divine guidance. So, she turned to the Word. For another hour, she just read the word of God and sought His leading for her decisions. Exhausted, she sipped some water, set it down, then continued praying. At some point, she slid down to the floor and rested her back against the couch.

She pulled her hair into a bond with a rubber band, and when her fingers caught at the tip of it, she tugged at it until it came through. Then she huffed and massaged her neck. Why was she struggling to maintain long hair? She'd better head to the salon and get a haircut tomorrow. Decided, she rose, made some dinner, ate, and then went to bed.

In the next week or so, with God's grace and guidance, she would finalize her work on the project and be free of it. For good. Then she could move on with her life.

Angel dipped her chin and studied the list of names in her hand. She'd met with David two more times to inquire about Miranda, and based on her own investigations, all the facts he presented played true. The ten boys had stuck together after leaving high school. They had even bought homes close to each other and led secretive lives. No online social media accounts, or such, which, for a bunch of thirty-or-so-year-olds, was odd.

Visiting all ten this week had revealed a mellowed-down nature for all but one of them, who got prickly when she mentioned Randy. She noted his reaction and jotted it down. They all denied having done anything to hurt Randy. Two claimed not to remember who she was, but their body language betrayed the lies.

She sat at her desk and toyed with her pen—*was* there a missing link? The only persons on both the client lists and the boys' list that she hadn't contacted personally were the two famous actors. It would be challenging, but before throwing up her hands in the air, she was going to shake those giant trees and see if any leaves fell down.

18

"Do not fear therefore; you are of more value than many sparrows." – Matthew 10:31

∼

THE PAST WEEK HAD BEEN THE MOST HECTIC VIOLET EVER worked, but that wasn't her present challenge.

It was this man.

Violet sat across from the tall man in plain clothes, sipping tea on the Silver Stone Metropolitan Transit train across from her as it chugged down the tracks and wondered what to make of him. The scenic view of green grasslands she typically enjoyed whenever she commuted by train to clear her mind from the pressures of her job was far from her vision as she tried to assess the fellow while he behaved as though all was well and he'd done nothing wrong. In addition, she'd asked a driver to send her car home for her while she commuted to protect this fellow, but she still wasn't sure what to make of him.

He set his cup down and, as though sensing her perusal, raised his head and locked his eyes in with hers. They had a certain kindness, but she was bent on finding out his plans for her company.

He smiled as if to ease her worries, and the dimple on his smooth cheek raised her heart rate, though she didn't return the smile. First, they just met hours earlier, and she literally saved his life from Pete. Secondly, he had to explain what he was doing sneaking into Cortexe Corp. and pretending to be an intern. Yes, she had prayed for God to send her a good cop, someone she could trust, but this wasn't the way she'd expected Him to do it.

She curled her arms and sat back, watching his every move and trying not to be distracted. His muscles bulged every time he moved his arms, definitely distracting her from her goal. What was happening to her? This was definitely not what she wanted, especially not today. She cleared her throat loudly. "You said you're a cop. What were you doing snooping around on my company grounds without a search warrant and pretending to be an intern?"

He settled a hairy arm on the small table between them and smiled warmly again. The warmth in his eyes was doing things to her belly that she didn't want to admit. Now was not the time for romantic admiration. She was at war with her brother who theoretically was working to destroy the world—with a click— as she strove to save it. "I want to thank you for saving my life back there. I'm grateful."

His voice moved like silk over her heart, and she found herself nodding in acceptance with little hesitation—and with a small smile. "Sure. You're welcome. My brother wouldn't be that magnanimous had you been taken to him instead. So, I'm asking you yet again, what you were seeking to find? I bought this ride home just for this time with you, so I hope you won't waste my time." She had to make it home on time to mail Tim an old letter. He *was* frankly the only person she trusted now, but she hadn't heard from him in almost one week. Moreover, the letter in question was from her dad's drawer. Seemingly old, it was written in Spanish, and some of the terms used in it sounded contradictory. Confused, she wanted Tim to take a look at it now—rather than wait until his return. Her gaze returned to the man across from her.

"I–I was searching for any information about something called, The Rulebook," he flatly said.

Oh, he meant what's now called The New Rulebook. But how did he know about it? Her ears perked.

He lifted both hands in the air. "Listen, I know how weird this sounds, but I've got a dead body in the morgue with those words written on him. A former employee of Cortexe Corp.—by the way. I think those two things are connected to why he died. My captain wants to see what you or anyone here knows about it. Your website is pretty bare, and there was no other way to gain access. So I entered as an intern. My apologies. And if you know nothing, then I'm sorry to have wasted your time." His gaze lingered on her face as though both studying it and admiring it. Then he sat back, and an announcement rasped overhead, saying her stop was coming up.

But if this man was a cop, and she needed a cop to talk to, maybe he was the right person.... She could at least tease the edges of trust with a few facts, see how things shape up, and then know whether she could trust him fully. Or not. "My stop is next. There is a Mexican restaurant I usually grab dinner at." She thought of the men she was sure Pete could have hired to trail her every move and knew she had to be careful. Then she added, "If you follow me there, we can talk."

"Yes, I'll go with you. The station will send someone to drop off an unmarked police cruiser, with the keys inside for me there. I can use that to drop you off later." His shoulders dropped in relief. "And thank you."

She bit her lip at her next brazen suggestion. "But we need to be careful in case my brother is watching." She saw a cross and John 3:16 tattooed along his elbow. Then her gaze returned to his face. "You'll act like we're on a date, and I'm sure we'll be fine."

She watched his reaction as a smile broke out wider than before. "A date? With a beautiful lady like you? That shouldn't be a problem at all."

Surely, her cheeks were burning with the way he swept her another admiring glance. Then a serious look overcast his gaze. "Then we can talk about why you need to hide from your brother. No one should be made to feel unsafe, especially not from one of their own. No one."

This time, the smile reached her heart. "Of course, you'll say that. You're a cop."

They exited as soon as the train stopped, looped their hands as they walked, arrived at the restaurant within minutes, and entered through the curved archway. Violet liked the floor here, painted to look like beautiful cascading stacked decks, while the hanging colorful red, green, and white lights over each table added to its ambiance. The atmosphere was usually calm and with no loud music, perfect for her to sit and clear her head whenever she had to.

She waved to Amanda, one of her favorite waitresses, and the woman waved back from behind the counter as she claimed her seat opposite the cop. While they ordered, she contemplated how much information to reveal while still protecting Pete. Maybe just enough to test him....

"Ma'am, can I take your order please?" a waiter holding a pen and a notepad asked, interrupting her thoughts.

"Yes. I would like a—" A hand tapped her shoulder, and she turned to see a scraggy-looking figure. Then recognition hit, and her eyes rounded as she lurched to her feet. "Tim?"

She hugged his thin frame, a far cry from the healthy man who'd left the US months earlier. "Good to see you. I've missed you, bro." She had missed him. But she was struggling not to reveal her shock at his change. He hadn't said a word yet so she beckoned him to sit. "Please join us."

He seemed to think about it, glance behind him toward the entrance. Then he swallowed hard. "I can't stay, Vi. I need to warn you first. I didn't want to lead them to your house so I came here, hoping to find you. How I prayed you would come!"

Struggling not to cover her mouth over how emaciated he was, she placed a hand on her chest. "Tim, what are you talking about? Who are they?"

He cast his eyes back like he expected someone to show up. "It's a long story, but the short version is this—there is a link between the contract I'm researching under in Mexico and your dad."

"My dad?" She pressed a hand to her chest. "He never lived in Mexico."

"Sorry, not really him, but his poem. I remember you saying he'd never lived in Mexico. But something definitely ticked someone off when I followed my results from your tests. I mentioned his poem in my class and asked them to translate it into Spanish. One month later, things began to happen."

"Things? Like what *things*?" She fought the urge to turn away from his stale breath as a waiter passed and gave Tim a questioning look. Tim was her friend and she would stand by him no matter what.

He planted a hand on his hip. "Random items began missing from my office. At first, I thought it was a thief. Then threatening calls followed, asking about the source of the poem, but...in Spanish."

"Wow." Violet touched his elbow near her.

"I'm not sure what this is about, but it seems I might've ruffled some powerful feathers because someone who's well connected is now after me." He paused and let his arm drop, as did hers from his elbow. "I never told anyone it was your poem or your dad's. So, they think it's mine, and they're pursuing me."

"Because of a poem?" the cop spoke for the first time.

Violet cast him an impatient glance—she hadn't introduced them yet! "Sorry, my mistake. Tim, meet Detective Mike Argan of the Silver Stone Police Department. He's investigating The New Rulebook. Mike, meet Tim Santiago. He's a seasoned archeologist with a specialization on South America. He's also my prayer partner and friend."

With the introductions done, she turned to Tim and patted on the chair. "Tim, I know you might be scared, and you're not making much sense right now. Plus, I think you could use a meal and a shower. But why don't you sit down first, and we can..."

He shook his head vigorously, and his dark curls bounced. He settled a hand on Violet's shoulder. "Vi, are you listening to me? Someone is trying to kill me because they think I'm you. If they knew you are the real owner of that poem, guess what will happen?"

"Did you talk to the police?" Mike folded his arms across his chest.

"In Mexico, yes. By the time I arrived at home, DEA was waiting, saying someone called in that a drug deal was going down in my house, which wasn't true. I didn't suspect foul play until I entered the house that night, and all the communication wires had been cut, phones disconnected, and a warning spray painted on my kitchen wall. 'WHAT IS THE POEM? WHO ARE YOU? DON'T CALL THE COPS OR WE WILL ANSWER.'"

Tim sighed and his shoulders hunched. "So, I fled. Not knowing who to trust, I didn't call the cops. I also didn't want to call you and get you into trouble. Instead of flying, I hitchhiked for a whole week to reach here."

Violet blinked. "From Mexico?"

"Yes, virtually, after I spent the cash I had. All the way from Mexico. I left everything behind—phones, luggage, *everything*. I couldn't risk withdrawing money from the ATM. When I arrived at Silver Stone today, I slept at a metro station not far from here for a few hours instead of going home in case someone knew my US address. Then I remembered you usually come by this restaurant, and I chose to risk showing up and warn you."

Violet felt her brow draw together. "But my dad never told me the origin of the poem."

"Ask him," Mike said.

"He's dead."

"Oops. Sorry about that. How do we handle this then?"

Mike turned to Tim. "I can take you down to the station and place you in protective custody. Will you prefer that?"

Tim appeared to think for a second as his brows arched upward. Then he nodded. "Yes. That is fine. But if we can pass by my place first, I'll appreciate it. At least, I can get some money from the house and a change of clothes."

"No problem." They rose, and Mike tipped the waiter for their free drinks since they had eaten nothing, and they rode in his police cruiser and, about a half hour later, drove into Realms Street where Tim lived.

She spun to speak. But he had dozed off, and his head leaned slightly against her shoulder. Her heart ached for her friend suffering through no fault of his own. It crushed her heart that, because of a family relic—*her* family relic—his life was turned upside down. But as they rounded a few turns and approached his house, she tapped his arm lightly. "Tim, wake up. We're here."

He lifted his head, popped his eyelids open, and wiped his face with a hand, then sat up straight.

Mike was easing in to park across the house, maybe to survey the area first, when she thought she heard a hissing sound. Across the way, a black Chevrolet approached slowly, then zoomed past them, driving much faster than it should in an inner street. Mike flicked on his police siren. They revved up their speed in response, and he called it in through the radio.

Then, behind them, an explosion rocked the road.

19

"Then the Lord said to him, 'Peace be with you; do not fear, you shall not die.'" –Judges 6:23

∼

Violet clutched her seat belt as Mike hit the brakes, the tires screeched, and she turned to see what it was. She closed a hand over her mouth. Tim's car—parked in the street-side curb—erupted in flames. Tim had taken out the car's battery, so it wasn't an electrical fault. Someone set his car ablaze on purpose, and that had her heart pounding.

Her eyes rounding, she gripped the front seat's headrest.

"Okay, this is definitely not a coincidence. Something is going on here." Mike grabbed the radio, updated the SSPD, and asked for a firefighters' truck to be sent. Then he turned. "I want to know everything about The New Rulebook, Violet."

She wasn't waiting. "I'll tell you everything." If danger was around the corner—against her or Tim or both—she'd do everything to stave it off.

"And about the poem," Mike added. "And about your late dad, who appears to be at the center of this."

"Yes, everything actually began in Mexico, two years ago, while I was on vacation with Tim and Pete."

"Okay, thank you. I'd like to hear more." He spun to Tim. "I don't know what you unearthed in Mexico. But tell me everything that happened since you arrived there and began digging into Violet's family's poem. And maybe we can get ahead of these manipulators."

He glanced at both of them. "Seems we've got a poem they think is worth killing for—why? Meanwhile, I'm taking you both to the station for Tim's account of his targeting and," he turned to Violet, "for us to wrap up our first date."

"Uh...." She opened her mouth to respond, but only managed a soft "oooh."

"I'm teasing." He tapped a finger on the armrest. "But not about getting to the bottom of these issues."

"Oh good." Her shoulders dropped as she exhaled. "And Tim and I will cooperate with you fully."

"After all, our lives depend on it," Tim whispered, clearly shaken. He curled an arm around his midsection and shivered, then gulped. His slim frame curved slightly, possibly under the pressure of the entire ordeal he had already been through.

She reached out an arm and touched his hand, smiling a little. "It's going to be all right, by God's grace, Tim. I believe it."

He gave a bare nod as her hand dropped. "I had locked up a few things in the car in case anyone broke into the house while

I was away. There were carved Ethiopian wooden art pieces in the trunk. I guess they will be burned too. To me, those are—irreplaceable. Including the gift you brought me from London."

"The miniature female diver sculpture? I know you like it and carry it everywhere. We can always get another one next time we pass through London." But that was poor comfort as his form curved even further and lines deepened on his face. She squeezed his shoulder. "I'm so sorry for your losses. I would take care of this if I could. I can't believe I got you into all this. It's my fault."

He shook his head. "Don't you dare say that. You didn't burn my car—they did. And whoever 'they' are, we will find them and make them pay."

Mike veered into traffic, just as the same black Chevy showed back up again.

And a bullet pierced her window and lodged in the front seat's armrest, missing her by a hair's breath.

"Shots fired!" Violet shouted and ducked her head.

But she was barely done speaking before more shots followed. Mike raced forward, but the shots pelting the cruiser shattered the side mirror and back window. The glass rained onto the street like popcorn. But that slowed the Chevy further as it veered sideways to avoid it, gaining Mike some distance.

Soon, Mike expertly maneuvered them several feet ahead of the black Chevy. Then he swerved to a side street, and melted into traffic, then navigated into yet another, even while he radioed for backup.

She exhaled in relief, although her heart still thudded. Then something damp wet her thigh. She trailed the source upward, and it rested on the blood flowing from Tim's shoulder onto her thigh. "Tim!" She lifted his shoulder with a hand, her breath clogging her throat. He'd gotten hit. Blood stained his blue shirt and arm. Pressing her palm to the epicenter, Violet stifled a gasp as blood seeped through her fingers. "Tim is bleeding. Please call for an ambulance."

Mike rushed a hand to his radio and did so.

Violet clutched Tim's shirt and prayed harder than she ever had, that her friend would not die. She prayed furiously, then pressed her lime-green scarf on it to stem the bleeding, but when Tim's blood soaked the scarf in a few minutes she cried out for help. "We can't lose Tim! Let them hurry please." She propped up Tim's chin as his head started drooping and he mumbled confusing words in slurred speech. "Stay with me, Tim. Please don't die."

"An ambulance is on the way." Mike veered off that street into an open commercial parking garage. Then flashing his badge and identifying himself, he ordered the security personnel to close the entrance. They scrambled to obey.

He turned off the vehicle and stepped down. Mike rounded the cruiser and helped her set Tim—who was now unconscious—on the ground gently. Then he lifted his gaze to hers, worry lines creasing his forehead as he darted his gaze between hers and the entrance. "As it stands right now, I'm outgunned until backup arrives, and I don't wish for anything else to go wrong here. I want Tim to live, but we can't make a sound until more police officers arrive with the ambulance. I can't risk losing you, too, without knowing what I'm up against. So, please, start talking."

Violet nodded and knelt on the opposite side, still pressing a hand on Tim's wound, while Mike stemmed the bleeding on

Tim's chest, both working as a team. "I understand, and I'll tell you all I remember."

So she began. "Pete, Tim, and I were on vacation a while ago in Mexico…"

20

"Death and life are in the power of the tongue. And those who love it will eat its fruit." –Proverbs 18:21

∼

ONE WEEK AFTER INTERVIEWING BOTH POPULAR ACTORS DAVID had mentioned, and visiting the high school in question, then leaving with more questions than answers, Angel decided all trails led to these grounds—the Fortitude Homes Estate. Observing the affluence surrounding her in the sprawling Odenton, Maryland estate, home of actress Liberty Stone, Angel managed not to allow her mouth to drop open. Angel had expected a small house since this wasn't the actress's permanent home. But if there was anything people knew about Liberty, only her love of guns and shooting, apparently, surpassed her name and affluence.

A Lamborghini sat parked under a zinc-roofed detachment,

beneath a tree, in the expansive gun range, which doubled as her home here. Standing about a hundred feet from the parking area beyond the gate where Angel left her partner sitting in the police cruiser—ready to proceed inside should anything go wrong—she spotted four buildings within the estate. An immaculate, white, four-story mansion, the shooting range, front and center, and a real garage—not the small canopy under the tree—three times the size of a middle-class home.

Arriving early in the morning meant the roads had been clear and the drive less than fifty minutes rather than two hours. She hoped Liberty would cooperate, since Angel had avoided a public display of force, as requested. They had come in plain clothes and drove an unmarked cruiser to avoid rousing media interest from those folks camped outside the estate.

Angel pulled out her radio, tuned the right dial, and spoke to her partner. "Pierce, I'm outside her shooting range. She suggested we meet in front of it, though I'm not sure why."

Static came over the radio. "Copy that. I'm here, armed and ready should you require backup. I'm keeping the SSPD looped, just in case." The line fell silent before his voice came over, softer this time. "Be careful, Angel."

Of course, he was caring and would say so. "I will. If you need to enter, here's the gate entry code." She dictated it to him. "And the shooting range is out front by your right. You can't miss it. Just walk toward where you see targets set up close to the distant boundary bushes."

"Okay. If you can't radio, keep me posted via text messaging."

"Will do. Over and Out." Angel visually tracked indented

steps in the sandy path ahead to a structure on the far left. With its flat roof and large windows facing the target props, it had to be the shooting range. In contrast to the rolling lawns of the estate grounds—manicured to perfection—gravel and sand lined the shooting range and the path leading up to it.

But where was Liberty? Facing the shooting range, Angel contemplated approaching the main building.

She spun a moment later when the low whir of a vehicle purred closer. Behind her, a golf cart pulled to a stop, and Liberty alighted. Instantly recognizable from her celebrity photos, the lady came close, offered a dazzling smile, and extended a sleek hand. Angel now understood why she got all the attention she did. "Hi, Officer Martinez, welcome to my humble home."

Tall and hourglass shaped, with bronze skin and long dark hair curling to her waist, she was part Jewish, but few people knew that. Instead, her Italian heritage was publicized since her family had fled Eastern Europe in the 1930s, migrated to Italy, and lived there until they moved to the US.

Angel almost spat at the description of the estate as a "humble home". Her own house could fit that description better, not this. Nevertheless, she accepted the handshake and smiled too. "I appreciate your time in speaking with me. Hopefully, this won't take very long." Depending on what they discovered.

While Liberty led the way to the range's double doors, the suited man who had dropped her off, drove to the side, and parked the golf cart, then trailed them at a distance. Likely, he was one of her security guards.

Liberty showed her into the cool interior. Dark brown walls and gleaming floors shone with a high-polished wood finish.

Low glass windows covered half the length from the floor to the ceiling, and a skylight roofing at the middle allowed ample light into the space. It was long, longer than it seemed from outside. Angel slowed her pace and allowed Liberty to walk past her deeper inside. Gun cleaning tables hugged the far walls, and opposite them were stalls marked as Beginner, others Intermediate, and Mastery. Hay was strewn across the floor within each stall, about thirty in all from a quick count. She wondered whether the hay was there as foot padding or as a simulation of natural ground, but didn't ask. Focused, she kept her eyes open. Safety warnings were taped on the wall. The Intermediate and Mastery shooting stalls, marked with yellow and red paint at the edges, were gated with safety warnings taped at the entrances and warnings not to operate a weapon without necessary approval.

Then Angel passed close to a room where a clear glass door revealed enough weaponry for a small army. A quick glance showed antiques and marksman rifles, obviously expensive guns she'd never seen in person before, guns you'd only find in specialty gun stores. She held her tongue until they reached an office at the far end and stepped into an expansive room with a desk, PC, and chairs surrounding it. A lady, sitting at what might be a receptionist desk, rose when the three entered.

"Good morning, Ms. Liberty. Are you ready for your morning practice? I have everything set up in your private practice room." The lady, who seemed to be around fifty years of age, started sitting but straightened again. "Oh, and I had them bring your morning coffee over since you said you had a meeting." The lady threw Angel a quick glance, so Angel dipped her head to acknowledge her.

"Yes. Thank you, Nellie," Liberty responded with authority.

"I will let you know if I need anything else. And please hold my calls until we're finished."

Beyond them outside, Angel had spotted a horse stable, hidden away in the back corner of the estate, now visible from the side window. A horse grazed outside it, and Angel wondered how Liberty could maintain all this. There had to be enough people working here to support her.

Liberty spun to Angel and paused. "Would you mind chatting with me while I practice? I have a flight to catch in about forty minutes, and I both need to chat with you and practice a bit before I leave."

After thinking for a moment, Angel nodded. "Sure." She took out her cell phone, texted Pierce an update, and then followed Liberty. They turned a small corner and entered a separate, larger stall with a door. Several guns rested in a locked case, which Liberty unlocked and removed two, handing one to Angel. "Since you're here, instead of watching, why don't you practice with me while we talk? I'd like to get to know you folks at the SSPD. One of the things I've been told is that you guys are good at everything you do, including shooting. Best me."

Angel accepted the gun, the safety glasses and ear protection, and her challenge. "Well, I'm not here to compete, but a little practice never hurt anyone." With only one stall here, she'd go one round and be done.

She took the time while they got served their rounds by the man who'd followed them, to observe the space. Here, the glass window ran from roof to ceiling, revealing a grand view. The targets were set farther away than the ones she'd seen outside. So she knew. This had to be Liberty's private practice area, further confirmed by the cup of coffee steaming on a table in the right corner.

"I'm here to ask you about Randy like I'd mentioned when we spoke." Angel kicked things off with the primary goal, not letting herself be distracted by the grandiose.

"Yes, I do remember you saying so. What questions do you have?" Liberty stepped aside and allowed Angel to take the first couple of shots. She hit the center and set the weapon and goggles down, keeping the earmuffs secure over her ears, then stepped aside.

Liberty whistled. "Good shot." As she applauded, her slim golden bracelet jingled. "I guess you're as good as they say you people are. I'll make sure not to land on the wrong side of the law, then." Liberty took her former spot and began firing.

So, Angel fired off a set of her own questions, undeterred by the applause. She was here for information to solve a murder case, and solve it she would. "Were you there that night at the high school?"

"I was on a late-night run as I couldn't sleep, so a run felt perfect to clear my head."

"Were you close enough? Did you see something?"

"Not at first. I started my jog at the cafeteria and rounded the bend to the sports complex before the loud voices alerted me that something was up." Liberty fired off a couple more rounds. They all hit their target's center.

"And from the records I was granted access to, both by local police and school archives, you were the only witness who hadn't submitted a report, although you were mentioned a couple of times."

"Odd." She shot a few more rounds, then frowned, straightened, and set her weapon down. Then she removed her safety goggles. "Is that what they told you?"

"Indirectly, yes." Angel nodded, leaning on the waist-high

bulletproof glass partition. "They mentioned not having a report on file, despite indicating you had been there."

"I was there. But I had told them what happened. How Randy's voice drew me to the altercation."

"Apparently, your report was skipped. It has been said that Randy was shouting to David. Did you hear what she said?"

Silent for a moment, Liberty lifted her cup of coffee, added sugar and cream, then stirred it and sipped. The steam had worn off, and Angel wondered whether there was still any warmth left in it. When her host looked up, sadness dimmed her eyes. Then, almost immediately, it was gone. "You know, something about being a victim of assault thrice makes you want to fight the signs anywhere you see it."

Liberty had been assaulted…thrice? "I'm sorry to hear that." Angel cringed. Would her questions raise things the lady would rather not chat about?

"Thank you." A quick nod followed before Liberty set her cup down, folded her arms, and braced against the partition. As her lips pressed tightly, a distance in her eyes appeared as though she was reliving…something unpleasant. "I recall the scream I heard that night. I ran from where I was jogging toward the sound. By the time I arrived, Randy had jumped out of the maintenance space. Yes, I heard what she said."

She faced Angel fully. "She said she was about to be gang-raped. I heard those words and the panic behind them. As a woman, I reacted instantly, and blood pounded in my ears, for her."

A sigh escaped her lips. "I saw the body language of the boys chasing her, and I knew—without a doubt—she was saying the truth. And as soon as those guards flashed their lights, called for backup, and involved the police, you had never seen better-behaved boys before." She shrugged. "Their gang-up against Randy's accusation the following day led me to speak up. I provided my statement to the school authorities who should've given it to the police. I guess my report didn't line up with the official school statement that there had been a misunderstanding. So, they must've tossed it out."

Angel scribbled on her note. "I'm guessing that must be why you got mentioned in the archive notes but not in the police report." She glanced up at Liberty. "Who signed the school report?"

"I'm not sure." Liberty shrugged. "Likely one of the counselors who are typically called in for behavioral matters. One was always available around the clock."

Angel notated that too. "Can I ask why you're so obsessed with guns?" She'd mentally searched for a more politically-correct query, but, finding none, she stuck with her first thought. No celebrity she knew of embraced their love of self-defense and weaponry like Liberty. But Angel wished to hear how much she embraced the love of preserving lives that weren't hers too.

"I'm sure it seems as though I'm addicted to guns and shooting. But the contrary is true. I've supported gun-control legislation for years. I've voted against allowing mentally ill folks, minors, and people in unstable domestic situations access to guns. I support ID, background checks, and criminal record and mental health verification prior to gun sales. And I support the retraction of permits when an individual's safety compliance status changes. After all, there are more than enough guns in the world if we chose to use them strictly for hunting. We don't need to kill. We don't exact justice. That's what the police, you guys, are for." She settled her weapon and Angel's on the counter, and the man took both to secure them.

"So, why amass weapons sufficient to arm an army?" Angel asked straightforwardly.

"Well, first and foremost..." Liberty looked up and smiled, one of the few times she did. "I'm not addicted to guns. Not in the way you think."

She led the way out of the private practice stall. "The main reason I do this is it serves as a place to clear my head while I engage my hands. A place where I can shoot and think without hurting people." They cleared the first room where the assistant had been, though she wasn't on her seat any longer. Angel waited while Liberty left her a note, then rejoined her walking toward the exit. "Another reason, which I don't publicize, is after the last assault I wished to empower myself. God defends me, but I have to take steps, too, to provide minimal defense the next time someone thinks I'm a piece of something." She paused as they reached the door. "The collection of rare guns began when my acting career took off."

When they stepped outside, Angel paused at the entrance. "Is there anything else you remember about that night? Have you been in touch with any of those boys since or have a relationship with them?"

Liberty shook her head. "I've got no reason to. Two of them are in Hollywood, but I have no interactions with them." She gave a slight pause and inched up an eyebrow. "Matter of fact, one lives twenty miles from here, and I don't think I heard you mention him when we spoke on the phone. Richard Fletcher, a son of old money. I'm not sure what he does for a living, but he was there that night and part of what went on. He stopped by once, but I warned him against coming here again. At the school, I remember that he'd smacked me once. I reported it, and the school authorities did nothing. But he was one of 'the pack' as we called them then, though usually lingering at the fringes of their activities most times, so he went scot-free. I wouldn't let him anywhere near my home. I'm not sure what he was after, but he sure didn't get an audience."

Angel perused her list with a finger and frowned. "You are right. I don't see his name on my list. I'll check once I get back to the office." Did David forget to include him or did he not know about the guy? She extended a card to Liberty. "Thank you very much for your time. If you remember anything else, feel free to give me a call."

A nod followed as Liberty walked back to the golf cart, her security man in tow. "I will. Enjoy the rest of your day. And I hope you nail whoever killed Randy. She'd suffered once before, and she didn't deserve to die."

"I concur." Angel left the estate, feeling even more determined to find and arrest whoever killed Miranda Sow.

21

"Woe to you who plunder, though you have not been plundered; And you who deal treacherously, though they have not dealt treacherously with you! When you cease plundering, you will be plundered; when you make an end of dealing treacherously, they will deal treacherously with you."- Isaiah 33:1

∽

ANGEL ARRIVED AT THE ADDRESS ON FILE FOR RICHARD FLETCHER with Pierce. Could this be correct? She cross-checked her notepad. Yes, it was. A frown curved her eyebrows. "This looks like destitution, not old money."

"Same thought here," Pierce said and stroked his beard.

They approached the isolated old house, a crooked roof framing ivy trailing over corroding redbrick walls. Buckling under nature's intrusion and time's cruelty, how did it even still stand? Although set in an area most people had moved away from, abandoning worn-down houses possessing little to no commercial value, it seemed only this house had smoke rising out of its chimney. Cautious, she motioned to Pierce, who took out his gun, and removed the safety, as did she. When they reached the house, she rapped on the door, held her gun facing down, and waited.

Soon, the door squeaked open, and an elderly lady peered out. "Yes?"

Her brown eyes matched her brown overall coat, a coat seemingly thick enough to serve as a winter coat.

Angel met her gaze and held it. "May we enter?"

The woman eyed Angel. "Not really. Give me a second."

When the woman shut the door, Pierce motioned to Angel. "Going to check the back."

Angel nodded while she waited.

Moments later, the door reopened, and the lady swung it wider. "You can come in now."

Angel stepped in and slowed her steps after entering the cluttered home. Bags of stuff leaned against the corners of the walls, and she trailed a narrow path to the living room. "Does Richard Fletcher live here?"

Almost as soon as the question was out of her lips, Pierce shouted from out back. "We have a runner!"

She jumped over the clutter toward his voice and exited via the kitchen door. Outside, two men tousled in the grass, struggling for a gun. One of them was Pierce. The other must've been Richard.

Angel ran toward them. Then a gun went off behind her.

"Hold it right there, missy," the older woman said to Angel, who aimed her gun right back at her.

"Why would I do so, ma'am?"

The woman held the gun pretty steady for a lady of her age. "I said, hold it right there." She took a few steps forward. "My grandson will not be used again as a scapegoat after what that tramp accused him of, robbing him of a decent life." She shook her head. "And you won't barge in here asking about him for no reason. So, I suggest you and your friend leave." Above her steady aim, her gray eyes peered back at Angel, just as steady, firm, and calm. "Richard won't leave this house. Ever."

"I'll say we're not leaving until we talk to Richard first." Angel waved her gun. "And I suggest you put the gun down before you hurt yourself."

The woman remained where she was.

Stalemate.

Grunts grated her ears from both men fighting for the gun behind her. Angel shifted toward them slightly, but the soft explosion of a shot, and the puff of dust following the gunfire between her legs, stayed her feet. She scowled at the elderly lady. "Ma'am, I am a police officer, and if you try that again, I will be forced to return the favor."

Silence.

"Put your weapon down, ma'am, for the last time."

"I won't. And I suggest you leave my property."

"We have to question your grandson."

"He's done nothing wrong."

"We'll determine that."

"Thank you, but I already did. No one is taking him anywhere."

"Who said anything about taking him somewhere, if he did nothing worth taking somewhere?"

Silence.

"I said, leave." Her hand trembled.

"No," Angel countered.

She winced at the thuds of blows exchanged by both men still locked in a fistfight behind her.

"The last person who came looking for him here, that Randy lady, ask her how it went for her, huh? Then you know how it will be for you. Again, leave before you regret it."

"Grandma? Where are you—" someone said from inside the house, then emerged fully, and gasped as he began reaching for something from behind his jeans.

Angel didn't wait. She shot his thigh before he brandished a weapon. Before his grandma could shoot at her again, she shot the woman's thigh too, and she fell to the ground. Angel rushed toward the lady to kick away the gun when the younger man who'd emerged earlier aimed at her.

She had no choice. She shot him point blank. His face seemed familiar, but she had little time to process it as she seized the woman's gun from the ground, spun, and rushed to support Pierce who was holding down Richard. She threw him some cuffs.

After cuffing Richard, Pierce swiped beads of sweat off his forehead. "Are we clear?"

She nodded. "I think we are unless someone else shows up armed and shooting. Let's call this in."

"What was going on there?" Pierce asked her as they lifted Richard and his grandma to their feet, after being assured SSPD officers were on their way.

Angel shook her head. "I'm not sure. But I guess this lady

knows something about how Randy died." She spun to the woman. "And I suggest she starts talking by the time backup arrives."

∼

Angel sat across from the older woman in an interview room at the SSPD and could hardly believe what Pierce and she had uncovered.

The lady's cuffs contrasted the character she had played on TV. "Mary Chambers, you played a cop for years. And now you shoot at real cops? And you're a killer?"

The lady was silent, and wiry gray hair fell over her face. Then she leaned forward. "Have you ever seen your only promising grandson's future go to waste because some girl accused him of threatening to harass her in high school? My baby was innocent. They were trying to smear him. He couldn't get into a law enforcement career because of her accusation. Frustrated, he went into drugs. Then the creditors came knocking, and we lost everything." She shook her head. "No, he had to find her. Had to make her pay, but he didn't have the spine for it." Hoarse laughter, unbecoming of the lady she'd portrayed for so many years in front of millions of people, came through her throat. "No way. I was tired of watching him wallow and wither away. So, I sent Collins. He had the heart to do what should have been done many years ago."

Collins was Richard's brother, whom Angel had unfortunately killed. "He killed Randy. You sent him to kill Randy." Her heart wrenched at the conspiratorial nature of this lady.

She spoke through gritted teeth and a burning gaze. "Yes, I did, and I don't regret it. She deserved it for what she did. She ruined our lives." What altered this lady from a beloved character to a criminal?

This wasn't the time to figure that out. Angel had no other option. Heartbroken at what needed to be done, she proceeded. "Ma'am, I'm placing you under arrest for the murder of Miranda Sow. You have the right to remain silent. Anything you say can and will be used against you in a court of law. You have a right to an attorney...."

As Angel read her her rights, the lady laughed hard, with pain written over her eyes. Angel wished she could help the lady heal, but it wasn't part of her job so she relented and whispered a prayer instead. Then an officer cuffed her and led her away, but it seemed she yet had one more thing to say as she paused briefly at the door. She pinned Angel with a gaze. "If you charge me, you have unleashed a storm. You won't live through it, I promise you. You might not even make it home. I suggest you release me without charges."

Angel leaned across from the table, unwilling to bow to any threats, even from people she pitied. "We shall see."

～

"PIERCE, TELL ME WHAT YOU GOT." ANGEL RETURNED TO HER office and hovered behind her chair, gripping it with a hand.

He flicked on her screen, took her chair, and revealed what he'd been working on. "Okay, while you were interviewing the suspect, I was digging, and I found something interesting."

"Spill it." Angel sat and rolled her chair closer to the PC.

"Their family was on the straight and narrow until something happened twenty years ago, inducing the woman to leave her acting career. Then, not long afterward, her husband divorced her. A few years after the divorce, her grandchildren moved home. And their wealth began dwindling. They got involved with some people who were suspected of dealing drugs largescale. And in the process, the grandkids became addicts. Little by little, they withered away their family fortune and were left with debt. Then, I suspect, the blackmail started. They made large payments to groups founded by local gang leaders and got roped into their circle. Richard's wife is a daughter of the leading local gang icon. It's a web. Another surprise? Richard and Danielson, the congressional candidate, are cousins. And he has a business partnership with some members of the gang. We have a whole situation that simply unraveled here."

"Wow." Angel curled her arms. "I guess Miranda was caught between powerful, rich, and determined enemies." The woman's threats began to make sense.

"And, get this, the deceased brother of Richard, a truck driver, owns a black Tundra."

Both her eyes rounded.

"And he frequents the roads serving the valley road area for water delivery, they say."

"He must've been delivering more than water."

"I concur." Pierce nodded. "But, since he knew the route well, it makes sense he'd be the perfect person they'd send to take out Randy."

"Well, let's check his truck for any damages and go from there," Angel said as the captain walked in.

But she still had one more question bugging her. "Why do you think the grandma confessed so easily? I'd expected some resistance."

Pierce shifted and faced her. "Because the minute we

knocked on her door, we had them. It would've only been a matter of matching traffic cameras from the accident, running the Tundra's registration to her grandson, Collins. And the rest would've fallen into place. It was game over."

Angel rubbed the goose bumps on her skin. "It's just so sad. I liked her TV character."

Pierce turned up a lip. "Me too. Does it matter that her ex-husband was a cop, they'd had an ugly divorce, and he'd left her and married a fellow cop?" Angel shrugged, not sure what to say, and let Pierce finish his thoughts. "But people change, you know."

"That they do," she concurred. "I can understand how those set of facts could make someone bitter, but she shouldn't kill because of it. Like you said, people change."

"Great job, you two." The captain shook their hands.

"Thank you, sir." Angel shifted. "And I need to ask a favor."

"Anything."

"Pierce and I will need police protection for the near future."

"Oh, I watched your interview. Good job there too." Then his smile flattened into a hard line. "And your request is granted. No one threatens one of my people without facing consequences. We'll put the necessary equipment and staff in place." He patted her back and left.

Pierce spun. "Why do we need protection?"

She moved closer. "I'll fill you in."

22

"O Lord, be gracious to us; we have waited for You." –Isaiah 33:2

∽

Violet sat in the hospital waiting room, clasped her hands, and settled both between her knees. She lowered her head and tried to make sense of the past twenty-four hours while doctors fought to save Tim's life. Tim, basically trekking from Mexico to avoid getting killed. Her, caught in her brother's crosshairs, and this cop, who showed up out of nowhere and dove headfirst into her life, company, and situation. She clasped her head between her hands. "Oh, dear Lord, this is not happening." She pressed urgent hands on her eyes, hoping to stave off the sleep forcing its way in. It had been a few hours since Tim came out of surgery. Although it had gone well, the doctors weren't sure when he would wake up. That had been the issue.

Yawning, she saw someone approach, and she turned fully, then stood. It was the cop, Mike. "Hey. How's Tim?"

Mike wore an unreadable expression. "He's stable for now, but he's in a coma. Doctors say it could be a while…"

Her heart tightened, but she managed a nod. "I understand, but I don't like it. Not one bit. Tim shouldn't get shot for me."

Mike took her arm, and gently guided her to a pair of seats. He squatted in front of her and looked her in the eye. "I don't want you to blame yourself. This isn't your fault. Yes, it may have started because of what you own, but you are not to take responsibility. Someone tried to kill your friend and possibly chased him all the way from Mexico. The license plate of the vehicle in question was grabbed by a security camera, and we traced it to a car rental facility in Arizona. We found the individual who was named as the car renter, but they'd fled to Mexico. We have a team headed there now. With assistance from the Mexican Police force with jurisdiction, we will find them, and we will protect you." He touched her arm. "You are not to blame."

The sound of a baby crying drew her eyes away for a moment. Then she focused back on him.

"Do you believe me?" As his gaze roamed her face, she saw how clear his eyes were, brimming with determination for protection and for justice, and she nodded.

"Yes, and thank you."

He squeezed her hand, and it rolled some of her worry away. "My men will escort you home and stay watch around your home overnight, but since they thought Tim was the owner of the poem, I believe you might be safe, for now." He released her hand.

"What happens when Tim wakes up? If they know he's still

alive, they could still come after him." She looked away, wondering how the nearness of a man she hardly knew could affect her when she wasn't even thinking about it. "I want to make sure Tim stays safe—for good."

"We can explore options when he wakes up, depending on whether he is still being targeted." Mike straightened.

Did he see her reaction earlier? Was that why he'd straightened? She couldn't tell.

"Options like?" she pressed.

He trailed his mustache with a finger, lost in thought, and blinked—oblivious to her swallowing hard at the gesture. This was not the time to think about Mike's handsomeness, but she couldn't deny being drawn to the man. However, she disciplined her mind to focus on Tim. "Depending on the threat level, if the worst comes to worst, we could issue a death certificate and, with his consent, change Tim's name and identity."

"Um, okay. That sounds extreme."

Mike scratched his head. "I know. Sometimes, extreme measures are necessary to save lives. He can continue his life, but he won't officially be in the witness protection program. It can be done."

"Is there an option that won't involve something so drastic?"

"Since we're so close to nabbing the suspect, I believe we won't go that far. But if it came to it, yes, we would consider granting Tim a new identity." Mike rubbed his chin for a moment. "How safe would you like him to be?"

She got his point, but she would have a hard time accepting a name change if she were in Tim's shoes. "Will I be notified of his new identity, if things get to that?" She prayed that it didn't and the team would be successful in catching the suspect or suspects.

"I'm sure he will tell you, but it will solely be Tim's decision about who to share such information with."

"I understand." She nodded. "Will he move to another city or state, if that should happen?"

"Possibly. When we encounter such aggression and an international threat, we take very good precautions to protect our people. Also, remember we don't yet know the culprits behind this. It's even more imperative we protect Tim's identity until we're sure he's totally safe." Mike glanced down the hall. "If he doesn't wake up soon, and we need to reach a decision about his future, we will get in touch with his family."

"He only has a living grandma, and she lives in a nursing home. I can provide you her information if you need it. Tim gave it to me, just in case."

"He trusts you." Mike watched her beneath a measured gaze. "You both are quite close."

Was that some spark of interest in his eye? She tilted her chin. "Yes, we are. He's my prayer partner and my friend." When he said nothing, she added, "And no, we're not in a romantic relationship, if you were wondering."

"Oh." His shoulders slackened.

Was he interested in her? She wasn't sure and didn't want to ask as her mind was occupied with ensuring Tim's safety. She blamed herself for suggesting she and Mike fake-date just to protect her from Pete. Maybe that was why she was seeing him in a different light than simply a cop. But it was all she could come up with on the short term considering she was trying to protect him and herself too.

Her heart longed to see Tim smile again. To see him laugh and to see him live. "Is there a time frame for when we get another update about Tim?"

Mike turned to glance at the clock on the wall. A dark stain smeared the back of his shirt.

Violet gasped. "You're bleeding. A doctor should check you out."

He twisted, then flexed his shoulders. "It's got to be some grazing. I had thought I bumped something there. Sure, I'll go down to the ER to get it treated." He took out a notepad. "I'm going to ask for you to give me your phone number, email address, home address, and other identifying information. If we need to reach you in an emergency, I want to have multiple options, especially due to The New Rulebook case. My captain will send someone to watch Tim while I report to the station to update our team."

Mike scratched his chin covered by a neatly-trimmed beard. "Although it would've been best to have you come with me to see the captain, since he might have questions, and to provide a report on your suspicions with the case on Pete, I decided against it for safety reasons to ensure your brother suspects nothing. Until we hear back from the team en route to Mexico, working with the Mexican law enforcement authorities for this case, everyone stays put. Meanwhile, I suggest you go home and get some sleep."

She shook her head. "I'm not going anywhere. Not until Tim has woken up."

Mike frowned. "I understand your concerns, but you do need to sleep. You've virtually been in this hospital, waiting, for almost a day now. You need some rest if you can be useful to Tim when he wakes up. And don't you have to go to work tomorrow! If you're gone for too long, Pete may suspect something, and we don't want that to happen. You can always call to check on him. And you can spend your evening here, after work, to sit with him. Maybe talk to him so he can hear a familiar voice. I was told people in a coma can hear you, and I tend to believe there could be some truth to it."

"Thanks, Mike, but I'm staying. At least for another day. I'll call Pete and let him know Tim is sick and in the hospital and I'm staying here. Nothing more. That should buy me twenty-four more nonsuspicious hours to monitor Tim's progress and to pray for his recovery." Unsure whether the man was a Christian or understood the power of prayer, she openly shared her intentions.

That seemed to catch his attention as he drew closer. "Oh." He blinked. "You'll pray? Are you a Christian?"

She nodded. "Yes, am."

"Me too. I'll pray for your friend." He observed her with that...look...again. "And for you too. See you in a few hours then. If anything happens," he pulled out a card from his wallet and handed it to her, "call me on any of these numbers."

She took the card, then gave him hers, thankful that the hospital had given her scrubs to change into after she washed Tim's blood off her hands and body. She'd gone to the gift shop, bought a brown T-shirt and black slacks, and changed. As she waited, she'd prayed and dozed off. Tim's surgery had lasted for hours, but the time passed quickly as she remained deep in prayers for him. "I'll see you later."

As Mike's shadow disappeared from the outer doors, she lowered her head to pray for Tim and, for herself, and for Mike —who was making small inroads into her heart.

∽

Two days later, as soon as Violet left work, she headed to

the hospital. She parked, walked past a departing ambulance that seemed like it had dropped off an emergency patient, took a left turn, and she spun toward the healing garden at the center. The greenery of the healing garden made the hospital seem less stiff and unwelcoming.

Striding past long-stay patients sitting on the benches while taking in some fresh evening air beneath early-budding cherry trees, she used the walkway to climb to the first floor, then caught the elevator to Tim's room.

After arriving in his room and having watched Tim until it was dark, she decided she needed to go to church and pray. A heavy burden weighed on her heart. So much was hanging in the balance, and she felt a need for a place of complete openness with God.

She turned to Mike, who stood briefing an officer who had arrived to watch Tim's room. Mike had faithfully been here every day, and they'd talked for hours before he would leave. They shared their interests, favorite sport teams, favorite Scriptures, and life experiences. They laughed together, shared meals to save themselves trips to the hospital cafeteria, and grew much closer. She felt like she knew the man well enough, even though it had only been a few days since their first chance meeting. "Mike?"

He glanced at her, raised a finger to request her patience, wrapped up with the officer, and came over. "Yes?"

"I need to go to the church and pray. I can't figure all this out on my own. I need some time with God. So please let me know if Tim wakes up while I'm there."

He was silent. Then he peered in her face with kind eyes. "Mind if I join you? I mean, with all that has happened, I could use some prayer time myself. It's been so busy at the station, tracking the team in Mexico... I haven't had time to pray either. And I was going to let you know that with help from the Mexican authorities, they've nabbed the driver."

Her eyes widened. "Really? Great." Some relief swept through her, and her shoulders slacked. "Did he say why he targeted Tim?"

"He didn't talk, but his collaborator did. She spilled everything, including who paid them. A group which specializes in relics paid them to do away with Tim."

Violet pressed a hand on her heart. "Why?"

Mike scratched his head. "Well, they had thought he had some gold stored somewhere since he was singing about kings, so it was apparently a robbery."

"A robbery?"

"Yes, but that's not the interesting part."

"What else?" Violet leaned on the wall as he faced her fully.

"She says she heard one of the group's members sing your dad's poem as a song in Spanish. When she asked, he said it was a folklore song within his local community. Apparently, digging deeper, it originated from travelers said to have had a former king from a Spanish island kingdom called Lanzarote, passing through the area some hundreds of years ago. Although, as the story went, there was no difference among the travelers, and no one could identify the king among them. He said that was what old folks in their place had told them growing up. As years went by, people feigned to be descendants of that king, but it was never proven true. The song was more in tribute to them because the traveling group had been armed but didn't attack them, so they sang their praises long after the travelers moved on."

Violet was gaping by then. "Huh. How come I've never heard this before? That's interesting."

Mike nodded. "It sure is. But that wasn't the direction of our investigation so we focused on our reason for being there—we nabbed the guys, and they sent a confirmation that Tim was dead. A photo of some random person who looked a little like him. We're hoping that satisfies their contractor's bloodthirst. I thought you might want to know the story, though."

"Goodness." She let out a whoosh. "An attempted robbery caused an international chase? I'm so glad he's safe now. At least, for as long as they believe the tale."

"You could find out more about the story and the said king if you like...." He studied her again.

Violet shook her head and waved the suggestion off. "Not while Tim is here fighting for his life, no. I think I've learned enough. I'm going to leave the past right where it is, and I'm sure Tim would say the same. But thanks for your readiness to support me."

"You're welcome." A brief smile warmed his face. "Sadly, we had to let the woman go free for cooperating. She said their job was finished, and the other fellow had been arrested. That was what she communicated to them. And she promised never to come after Tim or to enter the US again. We, and the Mexican law enforcement folks, already have a watch placed on her ID in case she changes her mind. So, for now, Tim is safe and can continue his life."

"Thanks, Mike." She hugged him. "This is the best news I could've heard right now."

"Thank God. We hope you can have some rest now, save for Pete." He glanced at a second officer who joined Tim's security watch. Mike waved at him, and he waved back, then went to speak to the officer already posted. While Violet thanked God in her heart, Mike returned his attention to her. "I'm off for a couple of hours, and I know I won't sleep so I'd rather pray. Then I'll head to the station to see what I can find out. My partner is already investigating the information you provided about The New Rulebook."

Not seeing any reason to refuse, Violet smiled. "Sure. You can come. But I should warn you, I don't pretend when I pray. With the way I'm feeling right now, my prayers can get intense."

He chuckled. "Suits my present mood too. I have both a heavy heart and weighted shoulders I need to lean on God for as this case with Pete keeps unraveling. New layers are uncovered every day, and I need godly direction and prayer. I'd rather do it with someone who wouldn't mind my intensity either."

Violet shrugged. "Fine. Let's go." She led the way out of the hospital, joined him in his police cruiser at his offer, and off they went to Christ Believers Church.

23

"In this the love of God was manifested toward us, that God has sent His only begotten Son into the world, that we might live through Him." -1 John 4:9

∽

UPON REACHING THE CHURCH, VIOLET LED THE WAY INSIDE, AND Mike followed to the front and settled into a pew. She spun to him and spoke in low tones as they were alone. In the wee hours, everywhere was quiet. "Please feel free to take any seat you like. And to pray however you like. I'm not sure when I'll be done praying, but I'll take a taxi home so don't feel like you need to wait for me."

He nodded. "Sure." He made his way over to the altar and wiped his palms on the sides of his pants. Then kicking off his shoes, he sat on a lower step and unbuckled his weapon belt, setting it down beside him. He leaned on a step and curled his arms around his knees. Then his lips moved in prayer.

Violet knelt down, disciplined her mind, and focused on her own prayer. Bowing her head, she thought about the chase, the shooting, Tim's injury, his surgery, and Pete. Violet tried to speak, but her heart felt fuller than her mouth. How could she verbalize how she was feeling? So much had happened, even in the last couple of hours, that it sapped her of words. So, she took her favorite form of prayer when words failed—whispering to Him where it hurts—and praying in tongues. *Thank You, Lord, for stopping the people who were after Tim. I'm grateful to You.*

She swallowed hard as the image of Tim lying in the hospital bed for days now in a coma, appearing vulnerable, yet surrounded by a strange sense of peace, overwhelmed her. She choked on a tear when she thought of how close he came to dying. *Thank You, my Father, for not allowing the enemy steal Tim from us. I'm grateful. Oh that he would wake now....*

Her mind moved over to Pete, and she could seldom breathe for the burden in her heart weighed so heavy. There was so much to communicate. No words seemed good enough, so her heart did the talking in groanings.

How much time had passed before she peeled her tear-filled eyes open when she heard a crinkling sound, she had no idea. Mike had his head bowed to the ground at the base of the podium of the altar, and the image stamped itself into her soul. But her heart was still heavy for Pete so it returned to praying for her only brother. Right now, she recognized that, in order not to be crushed under the pressure she felt regarding Pete's sharp behavior changes, she needed to pour some of these thoughts and feelings into words. She gripped the chilly curve of the chair in front of her.

"Dear Lord, I'm not sure how to begin, but I'm here before You, laying out my heart openly without fear. You have never failed me. You won't start now."

She lifted her gaze skyward and shook her head. *Do I have the courage to spill these painful words wrapped around my soul for so long they feel as though they were a part of it?*

Violet wasn't sure she knew how, but for her own sake, she had to try. She couldn't just give up. She had to pray and seek the face of the Lord. "Lord, I'm trying to understand why my life is changing at a rapid-fire pace while my brother's life is going the opposite direction." Feeling tears coming, she let them escape. As they trickled down her cheeks, she prayed more. "Lord, it's been many years since Pete served You. Every time I broach the subject, he turns against me. He doesn't go to church. He doesn't seek You. He doesn't revere You. He doesn't have the fear of God in his heart."

She crouched lower on her knees. "And that is the main reason his recent changes bother me. If I can only understand what's going on with Pete, then maybe I can help him." Violet prayed on until she felt Scripture impressed on her heart—"the battle is not yours. It is the Lord's."

Frustration crept up her heart because all she wanted to hear from God was that, yes, she could do something to change Pete. Or to turn him from the direction he was going, so she pushed back in prayer. "Lord Jesus, I love my brother, and I want him to be saved. I want him to do the right thing. I want Pete to make the right decisions. I don't want to lose my brother. Please change him through me." Yes, it sounded selfish, but she said what she wanted regardless. There were no pretenses between her and God.

Again, the Words overrode hers in her heart—"the battle is the Lord's, not yours."

Frustrated, Violet stood, moved to the altar, and sat in the center of the dais. When she'd walked past Mike, she heard him groaning in prayer. With his head lifted and tears flowing down his cheeks, she wondered about his anguish. But she had her own praying to complete so she faced the other way. Nevertheless, something struck her about his vulnerability, displayed without care for who heard or saw him, even when he knew she was there. So absorbed in prayer, Mike was completely focused on the Lord and not on anyone else.

She turned her back to him, folded her arms between her thighs, and lifted her gaze to heaven once more. This time, sure she was more exhausted by the response she was getting, than by being physically tired, Violet persevered in prayer. Something had to change. Something had to give. She was tired of making the same petition over and again for a stubborn brother who refused Christ and hoarded enough secrets to create a confidential cabinet.

Yes, she could make God change His mind about this. He could save her brother now. No, He wouldn't let Pete be lost forever.

The thought of Pete going to hell sent a shudder through her, and she pressed her eyes closed. "Lord, You are good. I don't want to see my brother grow worse. He has become distant and more cold-hearted. I want to see Pete saved, please," she cried her deepest prayer. "I don't want my brother to go to hell. I want Pete to make heaven," she groaned the prayer in her spirit, and sobs swallowed her speech. "I don't want to lose him.

I don't want him to commit a crime and go to jail. I don't want him to kill again, if he did before. Please, Lord, help me. Save him now."

And for the third time, she heard those words again—"the battle is the Lord's and not yours."

Violet buried her head into her hands and wept until her eyes throbbed. When she finished laying her burdens at the Lord's feet, relief worked through her. If this was God's will for her not to press further about Pete, she would relinquish him to God. Little by little, in her heart, she gave everything Pete had done to her, over to God. Violet allowed the Word she had received to comfort her instead of frustrate her.

She accepted that, as much as she wanted what she wanted, God knew what He was doing. "Lord, please take over. I accept to release this battle to Your able hands. I've fought it long enough and have realized how incapable I am for it. So, take this. Take over Pete, and let Your Righteous will be done." Peace flooded her soul. She sang one song of worship in a low tone. Then, as soon as she felt a release in her spirit, she simply sat there, soaking in the Lord's surrounding presence.

"Hey." Mike tapped her shoulder, and she turned. "May I join you?"

She nodded with eyes as puffy as his. "Sure. Please sit." She scooted over, even though the podium of the altar was large enough for them and more. "Are you done praying?"

He sniffed. "Yes, for now. Do we ever finish?"

Violet found herself chuckling. "No, we don't." She glanced at him as he crossed his arms around his knees.

The light at the altar shone on him and revealed his chiseled jaw and the curve of his trimmed hair above his neck. She couldn't deny that this man was handsome. "Were you praying for your family?"

He stared at her for a moment. "I have no family," his Adam's apple bobbed, "at least, none that will consider me their family—thanks to something I did in my past. I've learned the hard way that, sometimes, those who are closest to you are the hardest to offer you forgiveness."

She settled a hand on his arm. "I'm sorry to hear that."

He covered her hand with his own, and a smile softened his features. "It's okay. Let's just say I have an older brother who treats me sort of like yours treats you. We have that in common, so I understand how you are feeling."

She gulped. "It's harder when they are not saved. I love my brother, but..." She let her voice trail off.

He settled his arms on the floor behind him to support his weight. "Yes, it definitely is. You pray, and you want them saved, like right this minute. But it doesn't happen immediately because their will is involved. God wants everyone saved, but He won't force anyone to accept the gift of salvation. It's a free, fully-paid-for gift. But you have to want it. The process of creating that want is what causes the delay, bringing your will in alignment with God's will." He twisted toward her and offered a sad smile. "The more stubborn your sibling is, the longer the conviction journey. But every prayer of salvation is a seed on the altar, and they will accumulate and bear fruit one day."

Amazed at his wisdom and patience—patience which she didn't readily feel—Violet placed a hand under her jaw and kneeled her elbow on her thigh. "I know. I just...want it to happen now." Her eyes pleaded with his. "Before he gets worse and does something that can land him in jail." She shook her head. "He's too smart to be wasted. I want to see Pete saved." She sighed. "But, then again, who am I to dictate to God? His time is the best."

"Stop putting so much pressure on yourself, Violet. You can't make it happen by your own power." Mike reached out and placed a tentative arm around her shoulder loosely. She knew he was maintaining a respectful distance and appreciated the gesture. "I wished the same for my own brother for a long time. Then I realized that, in addition to being a valid witness for Jesus, sometimes, you just need to keep praying. Trouble is best avoided, but certain people will only see their need for Christ when *in* trouble, not out of it. I'll pray along with you, but I'll still do my job as a police officer where Pete is concerned. Will that be an issue?"

She shook her head again. "Of course not." His hand slid off her shoulder and returned to his thigh. "You have to do your job. I get it. I just wished it didn't have to be my brother at the center of it."

Mike rose and checked his watch. "Wow. It's almost two a.m." He helped her with a hand to get to her feet, and she dusted off the back of her pants as they made their way to where she'd left her purse after he clicked on his weapon belt. "Do you care for some food? I saw an IHOP on our way here, and if it's not too early to have breakfast, I'd like to buy you some food. I'm hungry too, and I'll be heading to the station after dropping you off at the hospital to get your car."

"Sure, breakfast sounds good. Though I've never had it this early, I feel hungry, so let's go." She seized the strap of her purse and slung it over her shoulder.

Mike winked at her, and her belly responded with butterflies. "Moreover, let's not forget you owe me a promised date."

Violet felt her brows curve upward. "I do?"

"Yup." He nodded and grinned. "From the train."

Then she remembered and laughed. "Oh, you know that was fake, for security reasons."

He swept her an admiring glance, sweeping color to her cheeks. "Not to me. Please, lead the way."

As she climbed into the vehicle and Mike drove them, she recalled something her pastor had shared during a special singles' meeting. She could almost quote it word for word.

Anyone, who can kneel with you before God, will stand with you before men. The place of prayer was a place of intimacy with God. And anyone who entered there with her and showed her their true face—vulnerable, unraveled, and with no self-pride —was worth taking a chance at love with. Mike was worth taking a chance with. "This is about the riskiest thing I've ever done, but let's make it a date then. A two-a.m. date."

Mike paused at the stop sign and lifted his eyes upward. "Thank You, Jesus, for answered prayers. Number one down, three more to go."

His eyes met hers, and they both laughed for a change. His eyes sparkled, and she wondered if her acceptance put the glint there. "I will give almost anything to know what the other three prayer points are."

"I'll spill it all on our date."

That sealed the deal.

24

"Great peace have those who love Your law, and nothing causes them to stumble." –Psalm 119:165

∾

Violet returned to work two days later and found herself struggling to focus. Her mind kept shifting toward Tim at the hospital until she finally called and checked on him twice before lunch. According to the nurses, he was still in a coma, and at this point, it was expected to last possibly for weeks.

Weighed down, she remembered how he seemed so peaceful the previous day as his chest rose and fell with steady breaths. His dark hair slid to the side of his face like a shield, his pallid skin giving the only indication of his suffering. As she'd stayed by his bedside after her early-morning breakfast-turned-date with Mike, she was amazed by how close the bullet had come to Tim's heart. Doctors said it was a miracle that he'd been alive. She thanked God for saving Tim's life because she wasn't sure what she would do had he lost his life on her account.

Thankfully, those who were pursuing him had disappeared. She longed for him to wake so she could tell him he was safe now.

She glanced at her PC and told herself the truth—she wasn't going to get any work done. The best option was for her to go back to the hospital. She informed Pete of her whereabouts and took off.

∼

Angel was at the station when the phone call came. John called her, and the moment she heard the tone of his voice, she knew something was wrong. "John?"

"Angel, I just heard from the pastor that Tim's in the hospital. He was shot, and had surgery at Silver Stone General."

Angel gasped. "I spoke to Tim last week. He can't be shot. He's in Mexico." She and Tim had grown closer after their first date weeks ago and were maintaining a long-distance relationship. They got to chat whenever she could spare the time, and they would be on the phone for hours.

"He was. But, from the information the police provided, things became dangerous with something he was working on in Mexico last week, and he returned unexpectedly," John said.

Was that why he hadn't replied to her calls? She'd gotten his voicemail and thought he was simply busy, though he'd usually called back within a day.

John continued, "He had barely arrived when he was shot in police custody near his home. I don't understand all the details, but since you're one of them, you can ask more questions internally. I wanted to let you know before I head over there. I'm so sorry."

So was she, for whoever attacked the man she loved. Tim had declared his love to her barely three weeks ago, and now someone was trying to snatch him from life? No way. Not if she could do something about it.

"Thanks for calling, John. I'll find out what I can, then head to the hospital soon."

"Sure. I'll meet you there." Then John hung up.

⁓

VIOLET SAT AT THE EDGE OF TIM'S BED AND LIFTED HER GAZE AS the door opened. "Hi," she greeted the man and woman who entered. The lady was in police uniform, while the man had crusted cement around the ankles of his rugged jeans. His hair was short, and his eyes were sharp.

"Hello," the lady replied, but her gaze settled on Tim as she moved toward him. Only when she drew close enough did Violet see her nametag—Officer Martinez? Where did she know...? "You're Angel." Violet smiled wider. Angel was in a relationship with Tim. "Tim told me about you. We're close friends."

"I am." Angel studied Violet's face. "You must be Violet, then." She reached out a hand, and a faint smile creased her lips.

She bobbed her head. "Yes. And it's a pleasure to finally meet you."

"The pleasure is mine as well. This is my brother, John."

Violet shook hands with John. "Nice to meet you, John."

"Same here." He gave a nod.

"What happened to Tim? I barely had enough time to get the details before I left the station." Angel grasped one of his bedrails and leaned over. "I just needed to see him."

"I understand." Violet gave her a summary of the events and the shooting.

"My goodness." Angel's gaze narrowed. "Do you know who might be after Tim? Any enemies of your family?"

"Besides my brother, Pete? No, I don't. Moreover, Pete wasn't close with our dad and has never cared about the poem or any family history. He has only one obsession now, and I'm the only person standing between him and it. I'm glad, though, that the culprits were caught and dealt with and that Tim is safe."

Angel exhaled, and her shoulders slacked. "Me too, Violet. Sounds like you're going through a rough time." Angel's voice softened. "If you need a sister, I'm here for you."

Warmth spread through Violet's chest. How special to have the instant connection of a sister in Christ—especially when her one sibling was... "Thank you. I appreciate that." She pointed at Tim. "In the meantime, I'm praying our friend will wake up soon."

"Amen to that." John stepped forward, his heavy boots thudding on the slick linoleum.

"Amen," Angel echoed and grabbed a seat. But John leaned against the wall. And the wait continued.

◊

ONE MONTH LATER, VIOLET LEFT HER OFFICE AND DROVE TO THE church. Tim still hadn't woken up. She entered the Christ Believers Church again with a heavy heart and sat on the first seat, pulled down more by weariness than by gravity. She sunk her purse into the next chair and lowered her head onto the backrest before her. Glancing at the cross at the altar, she blinked and closed her eyes. "My life is a mess, Jesus. And I'm going to tell you all about it." So she let go of trying to have it together and poured it all on Him.

"It's been one month, five days, and fifteen hours, Lord." She exhaled long and massaged her stiff neck. Working hard for twelve hours a day, six days a week had taken down her health. But that wasn't why she was here today. She continued her prayer, stifling a yawn. "Tim has been in a coma, under police protection, and we don't know if or when he will wake. It's taking too long." She slid to her knees and leaned her shoulder against a church pew.

"I have completed The New Rulebook design." She paused. "And tested to be sure its destruction worked as it should. Everything is set," she added, feeling a pang of guilt, pain, peace, and confusion all at once. "I'm not sure what to do. Pete knows I'm hiding something. I'm in love with Mike, and I'm not even sure how it happened." Laughter escaped her throat. "Pete could kill him if he sees him and knows what Mike and I are up to regarding his pet project." Another sigh followed. "Everything is so complicated now."

She rose to her feet, made her way to the altar, and fell on her knees once more. Sobs racked her body as the words poured out of her. "I'm alone, and I'm fighting Pete on my own. Many times, I want to end the duel, but I can't when I think about how much harm that will cause."

Tears streamed down her cheeks and matted stray hair to her face. "Today, I nearly got caught sneaking the journal out to the car had that young lady not shown up. Had I not been worried about Tim, I likely would have remembered to add the die holding my last ten-percent secret before now, and not have had to bring the journal from home. I'm not sure where to go from here. Pete knows the project is completed and will seek to activate it soon. How can I stop him?"

She peeled open passages in her Bible, and even though she was as tired as ever, she prayed. Prayed for Tim's recovery, prayed for Pete's change of heart. Prayed for The New Rulebook's scheme to be successfully overturned. Prayed about her feelings for Mike. Prayed for Cortexe Corp. Then, again for Pete. She sobbed so hard that, after what felt like an eternity, she grew limp, laid down there, and soon, fell asleep.

Soft sky-blue light glowed in her vision, and Violet saw herself standing where she'd been lying down. She felt swept off her feet and light as air, even though she still stood in a place she didn't readily recognize. Shining light surrounded her but didn't hurt her eyes.

Then across, feet glowed like the sun. "Violet," a Voice said. "Do not be afraid. I have heard your prayer and the gentle whispers of your heart—whispers that traveled straight from your heart to Mine. Well done, daughter. Your crown is waiting, and Pete shall be saved. Give the journal to whom I will show you. Then have My peace." The light faded away.

A sharp chill swept over her skin, and shivering, she jerked awake.

Again, she was lying down at the church altar, and silence surrounded her. She blinked, her heart thudding. Crawling away from there to her feet, she shuddered and wrapped her arms around herself. What just happened? God actually spoke —to *her*? She rehearsed the message, dwelling on every word.

Then realization dawned, and she bowed herself and wept.

Violet inched her face upward and let out the words she already knew the answers to. "Lord Jesus, are You saying what I think You're saying?" She choked out her next words in a gentle, painful whisper. "Is my time on earth done? Am I coming home?"

A quiet certainty settled on her heart. Yes. It was time.

She tried to accept God's will, but her heart wouldn't let her. "Lord, I want to see Pete saved. I've prayed for so long. So did Mom. It cannot happen in my absence. No, Lord! Please. Let me see it happen." She pounded her fist on a step of the altar's podium repeatedly until it throbbed while she sobbed louder.

Pete shall be saved, Violet, a Voice whispered in her heart.

She bowed lower, her shoulders shook harder, and her hair poured over her face and mingled with tears and every kind of fluid. She gripped the altar's edge and shook it hard. It took a while, but little by little, she considered a choice to accept God's will and her possible exit.

She pressed a finger to her throbbing lips. "I love Mike, Lord. I'd hoped to marry him if he asked me to." She rocked her feet dangling loosely off the first step, her faith and trust in God being stretched to snapping. Could she really accept this if it was His will?

That was what trust came down to. She shut her eyes, inhaled deeply. Then she exhaled until she had calmed sufficiently. "Thank You, Lord, for the heads-up." She swallowed and chose to forgive everyone who had offended her whom she might not have already forgiven. "Lord Jesus, I accept whatever is coming, if it is in Your perfect will."

Do not fear those who can hurt the body, but not your soul.

The Lord was so close to her, so close His Words were now physically audible. She'd just had the most vivid vision since she became a born-again Christian. Her spiritual senses were sharper than they'd ever been. She wobbled on her feet, still feeling like she floated.

What was happening? Violet bent her head between her thighs and wept bitterly as the thought of what may be coming swept over her afresh. "Please take care of my honey, Lord. If I must go, find Mike a woman who will love him better than I ever could. Make him happy, and please get him to heaven." With teary eyes, she looked skyward. "Because I'm not saying goodbye to him. I must see Mike in heaven."

Just then, her phone rang, and she walked away from the altar to go get it. She wiped her tears and managed to reach it before it cut off. "Hello?"

"Hi, this is to inform you that your prescription order is ready for pick up," a pleasant automated voice informed.

"Yes..." She opened her mouth to respond. But the church doors swung wide open, and familiar faces stared at her.

"Miss Zendel?"

She said nothing as the phone dropped from her hand and hit the floor. "Come with us, please. It's urgent." Pete's security guards, fully armed, stopped where she stood. Then they led her by the hand.

She shook off their hands and squared her shoulders. "Why?"

"You withheld company resources, unauthorized, and inconsistencies in your sign-ins in the lab's signature log today showed you left at unapproved times and likely in possession of restricted company property. Therefore, you are required to return to our site immediately to be questioned."

She froze, knowing she couldn't lie and say she didn't do any of those. But she also couldn't say that she did them for a good cause. Not to these guys. Of course, their response had been carefully worded for them by Pete. He was seeking to get his hands on the piece she withheld from The New Rulebook software. The 10 percent she'd withheld. And she would never give it to him.

It was no use calling the police. If she did, Pete's guards would rough-handle her before they arrived. And there was no guarantee they wouldn't kill her before then—and possibly endanger Mike—a chance she wasn't willing to take. Someone had to be alive to take down The New Rulebook. And if it wasn't her, she would find someone who would. But for now, she had to see Pete, face to face. Enough of these go-betweens.

So, armed with quiet determination, she lifted her purse, slung it over her shoulder, and faced the altar again. *Lord Jesus, You said You hear the whispers of my heart. So, here's one more. Thank You again for not letting me get blindsided. I'm not looking forward to whatever will happen, but thank You for promising to save Pete. I'm grateful.*

Casting one backward glance to the altar from the door, and recalling the vision she'd had minutes earlier, she strode with heavy steps out of the church.

25

"I know your works, love, service, faith, and your patience; and as for your works, the last are more than the first." –Revelation 2:19

∽

Violet sat cross-legged as she waited for Pete inside the Cortexe Corp. complex without access to her phone. The bodyguards had led her into a secure room on the ground floor and waited for her brother to join them to determine her fate. She admitted to no accusation they threw at her and simply insisted that she speak with Pete directly.

She'd spotted increased activity at the complex as they drove her in. Limousines were parked out front as soon as she stepped out. Curious about what was going on, she'd been too tired to ask. Moreover, they quickly ushered her into the room where she now waited, giving her no chance to socialize, leaving her tired, hungry, and thirsty. "Can I have some water, please? Also, if you have a sandwich or something, I'll appreciate it."

One of the bodyguards took steps to an adjacent room, then returned with a granola bar and a can of soda. "That's all I found. Sorry."

The poor man didn't appear too comfortable with the way she was being treated. She smiled and accepted the food. "Thank you very much. God bless you."

The guard opened his mouth to speak, but just then, the door opened. Violet took a bite of the granola bar and popped the can of soda open. She savored the fizzy liquid as it worked its way down, cooling her parched throat. Considering how the atmosphere in the room had changed, she knew who had entered without glancing up. She ate up more of the granola bar and drank half the soda before she met his gaze.

Arms crossed over his chest, he leaned against a table, watching her. And fumed. She could see it in his eyes. He dipped his chin. "Eat. We'll chat when you're done. Perhaps, then, you might be inclined to give us what we need."

She would say, no, she wouldn't. But she needed the food. So she finished the snack, drank the remaining soda, and set the empty can on the table. "What *do* you want, Pete?"

Moving away from the table, he drew a chair, flipped it around, and sat facing her, with the back of the chair to her. "I want what you're holding back. The ten percent. Now. No games."

"I don't have it."

"Who does?"

Silence followed.

"You've pushed me to my limit, Vi, and I'm sorry for what has to happen if you don't cooperate. You should have just done what you were paid to do and given it all over. Holding things back gets you in trouble."

Violet steeled her spine. "Handing things over places, possibly, millions of people—their privacy and probably their lives—in jeopardy. Is that a chance you're willing to take? Because I'm not."

Pete huffed. "Listen to me. There's no need to play a hero here. Simply do what you're asked."

"No. I won't." She pointed at Pete. "You should take a stand for what you know is right."

"It's not so simple."

"Yes, it is. Cancel everything. If you took anyone's money, refund it. Destroy this software before it destroys you."

"Destroy it?" Pete's brows furrowed the way they did when he'd faced a mathematical problem he hadn't yet found the answer for. "Never."

Violet sat back. "Then you're the one who made the wrong choice, not me."

Just then, one of his men entered, handed him an envelope, and whispered into his ear. Pete frowned, opened the envelope, took out something—Was it a photograph?

Before she could sneak a glimpse, he'd shoved it right into the envelope and swallowed hard. His face pale, he cleared his throat and glanced around the room.

Then his gaze settled on her. A hard edge curved his mouth, and determination glistened in his eyes. "Don't make this harder than it needs to be. I won't argue on this anymore. What you have done... Let's just say options as to what needs to be done to remove any obstructions in the way are not good. As a matter of fact, the only thing standing between you and...

certain death is me. And if you continue to reject cooperation..."

They stared at each other.

But Violet was no longer scared. She wasn't moved one bit.

Her focus shifted then. She wasn't sure whether his threat did it or plain exhaustion from fighting someone who was supposed to be protecting her. Her spirit grew burdened and full of pity for her brother once more, but the worry and despondency dissipated. Trusting the Lord to fulfill His promise about Pete, at His time, she leaned forward. "I'd like to remind you of someone I once knew." She crossed her legs. "Someone I looked up to at one time. They were my guiding light, and I trusted their example."

"Violet..."

She held up a hand. "If you're going to kick me out of this place built by our parents, Pete, give me the honor of saying my last words on these grounds."

He stared at her. And shut up.

"This person, like I'd started to say, had eyes like fire. But they burned to protect me. But not anymore. I held onto some sweet memories of our growing up over the years." She chuckled, reminiscing. "Like when you fought the boy who stole my snack money at Walmart. Or the day we walked home in a snowstorm, and Mom and Dad were stuck in Denver. You took off your winter jacket and gave it to me and walked home freezing. I never forgot that."

His Adam's apple bobbed.

"I'm not sure what happened to change you to the man you are now. But I want you to know that Jesus still loves you, is still holding out His hand of love toward you and waiting for you to come home. You have a home in heaven. Don't miss it. Don't miss *us*."

Violet sighed. "I would say more, but that's all that matters. I hope you don't hurt me, and I hope you can pause and think about what you're doing, for whom, and why. I hope you choose the right side and not the wrong side. Nevertheless, Pete, I love you, and whatever happens, I forgive you wholeheartedly. No matter what, you will make heaven."

He was silent for a while, eyes soft and brow contorted. Then the harsh glance he shot her as he rose to his feet and asked his guards to lift her up, was so different from her twin that it was almost like comparing soft bread and a rock. This Pete was cold and calculating. That left her to wonder what happened in that boarding school? Why had he returned home...heartless? She tried to find common ground with him, but each time, the ground kept shifting away.

When she thought they might've turned a corner—like at their dad's funeral when she had gleaned some of the kind-natured person he used to be—he changed and became harder and more distant.

Then a song pierced into Violet's heart with undeniable certainty and brought coolness to her mind. "Blessed Assurance" sang in her heart as Pete walked her out of the Cortexe Corp. main office building, toward the resident interns' building. It sang louder, even stanzas of the hymn she'd forgotten played back in her soul word for word. She felt her spirit gravitate toward the song, and her heart grew calm. Conflict surrounded her, but inside she had peace. She couldn't call the cops now, even if she wanted to. She couldn't change Pete's mind either.

When they walked outside, it was dark and quiet, likely the

wee hours of the morning. Darkness covered the horizon, meaning most people were asleep. Where was Mike? What was he doing at this hour? His phone had entered voicemail when she'd called this afternoon. He'd mentioned that, if he was sanctioned off the grid in preparation to take down The New Rulebook software, then he would be unreachable. She should have left a message for him.

Something to tell him that she loved him, that she appreciated him, that she would miss him. But if she did so, he would ask questions—questions she couldn't yet answer.

And she didn't want to see his heart broken. If Mike had even the slightest hint that she was in danger, at the hands of her brother, he would storm the Cortexe Corp. grounds—and he might get killed by Pete. She couldn't risk it. Tim was already in a coma because of her. She wasn't sending anyone else into danger. She would face this cross alone.

"Blessed Assurance" continued playing in her mind, even as Pete walked her up to a certain room and his guards forced the door opened.

They stood and observed as Pete questioned a young lady. Only when Violet was brought in full view with her did she recognize the lady. She'd asked her the previous day to place the journal in her car to assure its safety from Pete in case he searched her office.

Pete threatened the intern. But as he spoke, "Blessed Assurance" sang louder in her mind—almost as though the lyrics became physical and imprinted themselves on her heart.

A new sensation took over her...as though her body was still here on earth but her spirit was fully with God in heaven. The sounds she was hearing were new and unheard before—angels singing praises to the name of Jesus, a choir chorusing praises to God in unison, and her spirit sang "Blessed Assurance" to Him. And it felt as if she was singing it face to face to her Savior. The room got more chaotic, but Violet found it harder to focus on Pete's threats. His voice dimmed in to the background, and the song soared above it.

Finally, tired of witnessing his continuous barraging of the young lady, she said, "Listen to me, Pete. She's done nothing wrong. Leave her." She wasn't sure of her exact words, but they seemed to have riled Pete even worse. He seized her hand, said something cruel she couldn't hear above the voice of the heavenly choir, and handed her off to his guards.

They took her and led her out of the building. The minute they stepped outside, in the darkness of night, flashes of light began to work into her vision. She began to pray in the spirit, with her whole heart, and her whole body trembled as the words came out. "Father God, as long as I'm still in the flesh, I still have the right for intercession. Therefore, I plead with You, dear Heavenly Father once more. Save my brother. Save Pete, according to Your divine promise to me. I know You promised already, but I'm praying for there to be a performance of that which You have spoken. As You promised to me, dear Lord, please do."

They sat her down inside an SUV until dawn, and she dozed off a few times. The men made flurries of phone calls outside her earshot.

She prayed on and on until they strapped her in and drove to an unrecognized location—an abandoned building next to the road. It seemed as though her car had been towed to the location. They stopped behind it. She glanced around, but maybe because it was quite early in the morning, the street was deserted. "Take this package." They shoved something into her hand, and the envelope crinkled, but she didn't look at it. "We will drive you to this address, and someone will meet you there. One of our men will drive with you. But you will be in the front seat. Understood?"

She was too tired to argue. Everywhere hurt. Badly. "'Blessed Assurance, Jesus is mine. O what a foretaste of glory divine,'" she mumbled. Then she smiled, still hoping, searching for a possible means of escape. A weird sense of peace overrode any fear she might have had.

She felt herself get shoved into the car and buckled in. One guard drove, while another held a gun to her back. The man came to a speed hump too fast. The car jolted, thrusting her forward, and something drew her attention.

Desperate to try anything to help her escape, Violet startled. The jolt had dislodged the glove box improperly shut by the intern. Her journal tumbled out, the hard corner cutting into the top of her foot exposed in her pumps. She bent over, acted like she was coughing loudly, slid it under her jacket, and pinned it to her body with an arm.

Soon, the car parked when they arrived at a construction site at sunrise. "Get out. Go and deliver this package. Someone will be there to accept it from you." They drove her all this way to the middle of nowhere only to deliver a package? That couldn't be true. But their voice drew her back to the present. "Remember, we are watching you."

She accepted the flat envelope with her free hand and walked forward. She made a few turns and glanced back—could they still see her? Only the taillight of the car was clear. So, she surveyed the area. Maybe she could go ahead to make the delivery, then make a run for it?

As she neared the place, Violet chose to abandon their

delivery. She shoved their package underneath a cement block and moved forward. If anything was getting shipped, it would be her journal, with the destructive secret hidden inside it. Because, God willing, she would either destroy that software and protect the world or die trying. But, if she mailed the journal, wouldn't it end back up in Pete's hands? She bit her lip and prayed.

26

"Then we who are alive and remain shall be caught up together with them in the clouds to meet the Lord in the air. And thus we shall always be with the Lord." -1 Thessalonians 4:17

∾

Violet walked toward the main construction site. She had to find a place to hide her journal if mailing it was not an option. But she was already at the pickup destination and couldn't turn without attracting the attention of whoever was watching.

She approached the unfinished building and slowed, surprised to see somebody was already standing there, probably waiting for the delivery. The young lady appeared businesslike in her sleek leather jacket with her dark but straightened hair waving against the wind. Square shoulders that seemed able to bear more responsibility than that of a simple delivery stood as a contrast against the uncompleted building behind her. Was that resoluteness behind those warm brown eyes? Her dark skin glowed, and sincerity shone in wide eyes beneath full lashes needing no mascara.

If Pete sent this lady here to get her killed, the lady didn't fit the bill. She was too polished. Wasn't she? Violet observed the lady again and came to the same conclusion. Something was off.

But her brother could only have forced her to a place like this for one reason—to take her out. Shivering, she made up her mind to forgive Pete for whatever he might have arranged against her. Kicking her out of the company was the worst she'd thought he would do. But this...

She remained focused and refused to take offense. Now, she understood why God warned her. If she died holding a grudge against her brother, she would miss heaven. The vision had given her time—time to be angry, time to forgive Pete face to face, and time to prepare her heart for eternity—if things went that far. It was no use holding a grudge when she knew God was in control, even now. But Violet still hoped for a chance to escape, a chance to still live here, a chance to escape Pete's plans.

As she settled her gaze on the lady, and their eyes met, a bright light shone ahead. She thought it was a reflection of the daylight and the sunshine—but the sun shone from behind, not ahead, where the light originated. Then a chorus of singing voices followed. Then she heard the voice of the Lord instructing her, His voice even clearer now that it had been at the church. "Give her your journal, Violet."

Violet scanned the lady, unsure that she could trust her. "Why don't you shoot me first?"

But the chorus grew louder and louder. The voices were so beautiful that Violet was tempted to join them. The lady stared at her like she didn't understand. So, she wasn't the killer?

"Give her the journal. Now," the Lord instructed, His voice clearer once more.

So, Violet faced the lady fully. "They can see everything. Nothing is hidden from it." The lady frowned, scrunching her smooth forehead, and said something. But Violet could barely hear her. With the urge in her spirit, Violet hurried to complete her statement. "It's called The New Rulebook. They can see everything." She handed her journal over—her most precious possession, besides the locket bequeathed by her parents which she'd left at Tim's bedside so he could see it when he woke—in obedience to the Lord.

By now, the chorus was so loud.... Could the lady truly not hear them? The journal left her hands as the lady accepted it. A figure appeared before her, glowing in white, beyond the lady. He extended her a hand, and Violet blinked against the light surrounding her.

The chorus sang louder—deafening, but beautiful refrains. Having heard their song over and again, Violet could sing the lyrics now. She'd never heard words sung so beautifully anywhere. She reached out, accepted the hand of the figure that looked like an angel.

As soon as her hand melted into His, Violet felt swept off her feet by the power of the Holy Spirit. Every fiber of her being was hit with light shining from within. She could hardly describe it. The power of God permeated her pores, and she blinked again as more beings appeared, standing and bowing before the One holding her hand. That was when she realized —it was the Lord Jesus.

She heard a gasp, like it was from the lady she'd handed her journal, and tried to see, but the Lord held her hand. And her gaze. "Don't look down, Violet. Keep your eyes on Me."

So, she did. The glory she was seeing, the power she was swimming in, and the beauty she was surrounded in, were incomparable to anything she could set her gaze upon.

Her purse clattered to the ground, but she kept her eyes trained on the Lord. She was transitioning to glory—incomparable incorruptible glory.

Then the Lord reached out, and a golden crown appeared. He set the golden crown on her head and smiled. "Welcome home, My daughter. You served your Lord faithfully. Now, enter into His rest."

A slight pause followed. She scarcely resisted shutting her eyes, sure the intensity of light and glory before her was more than she could take. Glory upon glory showered over her.

"Violet," He, with fire-like light for eyes, looked at her, laying her soul bare before Him. "I heard your final whisper, your final intercession for your brother. Yes, Pete shall be saved," the Lord said, and his assurance bore the signature of certainty.

She knew it would be done, according to His Word.

Violet shut her eyes as The Lord settled the golden crown on her head. She had indeed left the earth, but she didn't ask Him how. She was here, with Him, for all eternity. And the Lord would keep His promise to her, and indeed Pete shall be saved. "Thank You," she whispered.

∽

JOHN HAD JUST ARRIVED AT THE CONSTRUCTION SITE WHERE HE

worked when he found one of the vents reported as blocked. "It's too early for this," he muttered as he walked toward the building. He'd thought they'd finished on this site, but apparently, something happened at the last minute. "Like it always does."

He beckoned one of the nearest workers, who had just arrived, to him. "Hey, Carlos, can you come with me? We need to climb high-rise Number 1 to take a look."

"Sure. Let me get my stuff." Carlos grabbed his tools.

John strode ahead of him, and he was grateful the elevators here were being fixed but were still up and running. Taking the stairs for the first half of the building last week had been rough.

When they reached the floor with the vent out, he sent Carlos to check it out. Trying to hurry the process, John traced the route of the air vent to see where the air stopped flowing. Maybe, if a piece of protective nylon was sucked in, he could take it out and be done with it.

The door to one of the completed offices was partly closed. But he'd instructed the site manager to have the men leave the doors open for easy perusal.

Frowning, he approached it, then froze. A man in black stood at a window with his back turned—and a rifle in his hand. John sucked in his breath and ducked behind a concrete wall. He held his breath and wished he had a way to warn Carlos, working in the room at the other end. John shuddered when the rifle fired a shot. He winced at the sound, hoping it didn't hit anyone.

He dashed back to the other end and warned Carlos about the shooter and led him to hide. While Carlos hid, John returned to the door. A second person with a gun ducked. There were two shooters after one person? His heart pounded in his chest. Then he prayed as Angel and Tim had taught him. He slid back fully inside the room, hid, and hoped he and Carlos would make it out alive.

Soon, hurried footsteps followed the shot, leading away from the floor where they were, and he exhaled. Whoever they were, they were leaving. But he had to protect both himself and Carlos. So they waited an additional half hour before venturing out. They glanced around, came out, and went down the building using the stairs.

As soon as their feet hit the first floor, he called the others, who hadn't come in to work yet, and dismissed his men for the day, then hurried to his truck. He thought about calling the police but stopped. Considering his past wrongful choices, if something bad happened, they would look at him as a suspect. He could only trust his sister to believe him. Thankfully, she was a cop and reaching her and explaining things to her was only a half hour drive away. He drove straight to the SSPD, intent upon telling his sister what he saw.

When he arrived at the SSPD, he turned off his truck and paused for a moment, sitting in the parking lot, wondering if he'd witnessed a murder. After all, he didn't see a victim, didn't hear a scream, and wasn't sure what he saw had meant. Maybe he'd made a mistake in coming here. He should've checked out the scene first to see if someone did get shot before rushing here. But he'd been too shocked and had only thought to protect his other employees. He confirmed with their office that his men were accounted for by the time he left and had all driven off in their vehicles.

But what if someone had been hurt? He shook his head and made up his mind. He would tell Angel what he'd seen. Then he'd leave it to her and the cops. At least, he had cleared the building before leaving the site. As he opened his door and swung one leg out, something hit him hard on the head. He tried to turn, but another blow landed on his back and a third hit his head. There was no time to fight back. He blacked out.

∽

ANGEL PEERED AT THE TIME ON THE WALL OF THE SSPD AND wondered why the morning felt long. She had had a restful couple of days since closing the murder case and couldn't have felt more accomplished. The grandma was in jail, and her surviving grandson was held for questioning. Apparently, this wasn't the first time they'd gotten their hands dirty. So many things were getting uncovered from their activities in the past twenty years. Some were too much for her ears to handle, so she simply moved on to her next case while another detective wrapped things up.

She checked the time. Too bad, she couldn't visit Tim at the hospital at lunchtime. She and Violet had alternated their schedules. She watched Tim for an hour over lunch, and Violet took the evening shift while Angel was busy. It worked well, and she was getting to know Violet better. Which made her wonder why Tim and Violet never became an item. She was glad Tim chose her, and apparently, judging from what officers had recovered from his pocket before he was wheeled unconscious into surgery, he had bought an engagement ring and would've proposed. Her chest tightening, she prayed she and Tim wouldn't lose their chance at love. She couldn't bear the thought of losing him, so she avoided such thoughts.

Angel walked over to the coffee machine, made a cup of coffee, and added some sugar and milk. She was walking back to her desk when Pierce drew to a stop. "Oh, I see John is here. Where is he?" He looked toward her office.

She frowned. "No, he's not."

"Yes, he is." He pointed outside. "His truck's outside. And he must be in a hurry to have left his driver's door open. Tell him I shut it for him."

Angel blinked. "Pierce, John is not here."

They glanced at each other.

"And he never leaves his truck door open." The cup slipped off her hands and hit the ground with a thud. The hot fluid poured over her boots, but she didn't care. Pierce ran ahead outside. As soon as they emerged, she could hardly breathe. Not out of a health situation, but out of fear for her brother.

They reached the truck, and with the hook of her cuffs, she pulled the unlocked door open. It swung to a standstill, and she surveyed the sight. "His bag is in the front passenger seat. The truck is still warm, so he was in here not too long ago. The key is in the ignition."

Something was wrong. She shivered.

"I'm going to get the captain," her partner said.

"Your keys, please." Her cruiser's keys were sitting on her desk, and she wouldn't waste time to go inside to get them.

"Here." He tossed his to her while running back inside, and she caught them.

Swinging around, she ran toward his cruiser. She dialed John's number, but it went straight to voicemail. Frustrated, she searched for the right key in the bundle. If someone had taken John, she hoped they were still close by. "Lord, please keep John alive. Please, Lord." She recalled the threat of the grandma sitting in jail. Were the woman's gang in-laws after her brother as punishment? Angel shoved the thought away and focused. John needed her, and she would not fail him.

Reaching Pierce's cruiser, she yanked the door and slid inside. It was cooler than John's, having had no human occupant for a few hours, so she rubbed her hands together to warm them up before sliding the keys into the ignition. She revved the engine and drove off the parking lot. She entered the traffic, lost as to where to go or where to search. So she started with the last place she knew he had been in contact with as they left home. She called his job with the number he had given her.

"Hello?" she said as soon as someone picked up. She scanned the streets, driving slowly and searching for signs of unusual activity.

"Hi. Thank you for calling Happy Home Builders Inc. How may I help you?"

Angel swerved to avoid a car that got too close, or maybe she got too close to them. She wasn't sure. "Yes, I'm Officer Angel Martinez. I'm trying to locate my brother, John. He works with your company."

"Oh, right, John. He dismissed his guys for the day and told one of them he was going to see his sister who is a cop. I'm guessing that's you."

"Yes, that's me." This wasn't good. "He got to the station, but no one has seen him. Do you know why he sent his men home?"

"One of the guys, Carlos, said John heard a gunshot on site, and they hid until the shooter was gone. So, he sent everyone home. Carlos didn't call the police because John was going there. Moreover, he said he saw nothing. But we have called the police to report the incident, and we were waiting to hear back from John. We had left him a voicemail as canceling the day's work is not our documented procedure."

And John likely knew that. So why did he choose to dismiss the workers, send them home without calling the cops, and then disappear in her parking lot?

Angel groaned inside. "What's the address for the construction site where this happened, please?"

They dictated the address, so she parked by the street and punched it into her navigating device. "Thank you." Driving as fast as she could, she called the station and updated them through the radio.

"I'm sending you backup now. And Pierce is coming with," the captain informed. "Please be careful."

"I will."

Angel called her siblings next, asking if any of them had heard from John. Their replies only worsened her worry. At the construction site, she surveyed the area from inside the car while waiting for backup. Calm surrounded the street, and nothing appeared out of place. Of course, she hadn't walked farther inward, but the captain would be incensed had she hopped out of the cruiser and headed to a possibly dangerous crime scene without backup.

Secondly, she knew her brother. John would not call his men to go home without a reason. Something scared him, and he didn't scare easy. To find where John had gone to or disappeared to, she needed to see proof of whether something happened here. Whatever scared him was here. Somewhere.

The wail of police sirens got her jumping out her cruiser, ready to go. She stepped down as Pierce emerged from a cruiser parked behind hers and walked over to meet up with her.

"Ready?" He had his weapon drawn, head lowered.

She drew hers as well and gave a nod. She led the way as they lowered their heads, trailed by other officers. Treading over leftover construction equipment and broken glass, pounding over concrete dust, and watching for the signal from the officers climbing the high-rise to provide cover, she turned a corner near an unfinished building. She saw a lady's feet on the ground peeking from the distance, and even before she saw the full form, she knew they were in for a long day. Did John see something happen here? Did it spook him?

She sighed and wished this new matter didn't hit this close to home. She swallowed harder, and as they came up on the body, she gasped and her knees buckled.

"No!" Not Tim's best friend, her friend, Violet. She spun, her eyes met Pierce's, and she passed out.

27

"And whoever compels you to go one mile, go with him two." – Matthew 5:41

∽

Tim tugged his eyes open. The first thing he saw was Violet's golden locket, the gift from her parents, where it hung off the foot of a bed he lay in. A smile stretched his cracked lips, and it hurt. Then he looked around. He was in a hospital. He felt as though he'd just woken up from a long sleep—but how long was he out? And why?

But he was not alone. A nurse in the room was busy attending to his IV. When she saw that he had woken up, she ran off and called the doctor.

"He's awake! He has woken out of his coma," she rang out as she disappeared through the door.

Coma? Tim frowned. He hadn't felt like someone in a coma,

just like he'd slept for a long time and was ready to wake up. But he had more than that on his mind. He had to see Violet and tell her about his strange dream—a dream about her.

Soon, a doctor entered the room, interrupted his thoughts, and checked his vitals. "What is your name?"

Tim remembered his name and address. But not what happened in the past year. The doctor asked about the last place he was and how he ended up in the hospital, but he couldn't recall.

"Don't allow that to bother you. Temporary amnesia is common when patients wake up from comas," the doctor assured him. "Give it time. It will all come to you."

They soon left him to rest before another interview to assess his mental state. Judging from the rawness he was feeling, he might not be leaving the hospital for a while.

Tim managed to lean up from his lying position for a sip of water the nurse had brought. Waking up from a coma, having missed so much news from the people he loved, was tough enough. But his experience just before he woke puzzled him more.

He'd seen Violet, but she looked different—radiant, standing at a beautiful distant gate. She smiled, and she glowed in light. He wanted to talk to her, ask her how she was in that place, where they were, and why she glowed and he didn't. But she'd swept past him to go inside, leaving him now at the gate.

Then he opened his eyes.

Had it just been a dream? He hoped so because it had felt so real. Once they completed his next medical check, he'd ask the nurse to help bring the hospital room's phone closer.

He had to call Violet and tell her what she saw. He had to hear her voice. Feeling like he was forgetting something or someone, he tried as hard as he could, but he couldn't recall what. He lay back down but didn't want to sleep again, in case he didn't wake up. The doctor had confirmed he'd been in a coma before a flurry of medical staff poked and prodded to their content.

While he contemplated, a nurse entered with a wary look.

He smiled at her. "You thought I'd be asleep again?" He shook his head. "Not for a while."

At his comment, she smiled back. "That crossed my mind. Are you comfortable? Do you need something to eat? You should be hungry."

He was, actually. But his thoughts were so busy he'd forgotten to ask for food. "Sure. I could use some food."

As she walked toward the door, she paused. "Oh, your girlfriend said to call her as soon as you wake. I'll call her shortly."

Tim frowned. His *girlfriend*? He had a girlfriend? He cleared his throat. "Do you mean Violet?" Maybe she'd finally come around to seeing him as more than a friend.

The nurse's platinum bob bounced as she shook her head. "No, she's not Violet. I don't think so." She blinked. "Oh, your memory."

"Right." He nodded. "I can't remember recent history, so if I have a girlfriend, please tell me about her before she gets here. I'd not like to shock her as soon as she walks in."

She smiled and reentered. Her glance trailed his to the locket. "I see someone left you a good luck piece."

"Would you mind handing it to me, please?" he asked and she obliged. "Thanks."

She perched on a chair and glanced at the door. "I have to make my other rounds, but for a man who just came back to the land of the living, I can spare a few minutes." She raised a finger. "Oh, give me a second." She dashed out of the room.

What had been so urgent?

Tim held Violet's locket. Reading the sticky note taped to it, and recognizing her handwriting, he grinned. *To my favorite digger, I left this so you'll know I came. See you when you wake soon. Cheers, Vi.*

Of course, she would leave something valuable of hers with him because she knew he understood how important the locket was to her.

The nurse returned, clutching something. She sat back down, and excitement glistened in her eyes. "Your girlfriend is a cop."

"A cop?" Tim swallowed past a tight throat. "How did I get comfortable enough to ask a *cop* out?"

She laughed but still hid what was in her hand. More curious, he raised himself up on one elbow to meet her eye to eye, but she just shook her head. "Well, you'll need to ask her when she gets here. But she's really nice."

"What does she look like? Do I have a cellphone?" Maybe he could see her picture on his phone.

Touching his arm, she drew his attention. "There's something important you should know in case someone already called her and she's on her way here." She placed a solid object into his hand. "She's seen this already, and she knows what is inside. You'll have to explain how you don't remember, but I'm sure she will understand."

Tim sat up as much as he could. He opened his palm and stared at the box in his hand. "Does this mean what I think it means?" When she didn't answer, he unclasped the box. And with trembling fingers removed the ring. A name—*her* name,

Angel—was engraved inside it, and he choked with emotion. He not only had a girlfriend, but he was going to propose—and *she* knew about it—and *he* didn't remember a day of their relationship. Tim eased the ring back, closed the box, and settled it under his pillow.

"She's got a great smile." The nurse described her, not seeing his turmoil. He refused to think of how his girlfriend—Angel, according to the ring's inscription—would react if she knew he didn't remember her. Would it end their relationship for good? Or at best, make things awkward since one had these memories and the other didn't? Her name must be a coincidence. He knew only one Angel, also a cop and good Christian. But she was his friend, not his girlfriend.

Midway through the nurse's description, the door flung open, and someone entered. The nurse's description matched the face of the person standing before him—but not the condition of her appearance.

"Angel?" he whispered, too shocked to say more. So, she was his girlfriend. Realization dawned amid confusion. He grasped to remember something—*anything*. But failed.

Dust clung to her police uniform. Tears matted her hair to the side of her face, a face reddened and puffy, almost obscuring her coffee-brown eyes. Angel may not look like a girlfriend this minute, but she was his friend, and she needed a hug. He reached out both arms, and her lips trembled as she took slow steps toward him. When she reached his bed, she crashed into his arms, and sobs racked her body.

What broke her down? But from the lady he had known her to be for many years—strong and protective of her siblings and society—he'd never seen anything break her down. His heart broke for whatever caused her such pain. He offered her the only thing he had—comfort. "Shhh. Let it all out. You're going to be all right."

When her sobs quieted, she raised her eyes and peered into his. Long dark lashes blinked at him—how beautiful those eyes were! But that thought quickly melted with her next words. "They took John." Her lips quivered. "They took my brother." She burrowed her head into his chest and wept again, and he knew now what could break her—anything happening to any one of her siblings.

But he didn't understand, and he didn't want to rattle her by sharing news of his memory loss. "What do you mean? Who took John? Who are they?"

"The people who kill—" She grew silent, and the nurse tapped her shoulder and motioned toward the door.

"Can I chat with you outside for a moment?" The nurse led the way.

Angel nodded, straightened, and followed her out.

When they returned moments later, Angel had changed. Stiff shoulders set above her straight spine, nothing like the trusting person who'd wept on him minutes earlier. Her gaze observed him as she stopped at the foot of the bed. "They say you don't remember anything from the past year?" It came out partially like a question and like a statement. "You don't remember....me as your girlfriend? Or us?"

"Yes." Somehow, he kept his voice calm. This was hard, harder than he'd thought it would be. He'd hoped to find time to collect his thoughts and try to remember before she arrived.

Her gaze faltered. "I'm sorry, then, for assuming that you knew. I was caught up in my grief and also in the joy of seeing you awake. I'm truly sorry if I embarrassed you."

"That we were in a relationship? You have no reason to

apologize. The fact that I don't remember now doesn't mean I won't ever remember." He pointed to the chair. "Please, sit. And let's talk. I really have to speak to Violet about something. I can provide you with her number if you have a phone. It's urgent, please."

She blinked those eyes at him again. Tears pooled in their brown depths again. Clenching her fists, she looked away. "I'm sorry."

He smiled, growing a bit impatient. "It's okay. We're going to chat about what happened to your brother. But, please, dial Violet. It won't take but a minute. I promise."

"This is too much."

Tim wasn't sure what she was referring to, but the nurse was nodding and crying too. What was going on?

She backed toward the door, shaking her head. "Listen, I'm glad you're awake, Tim. But I'm sorry, I need some time, and I have to go now. I'll try to be back tonight. Please don't sleep for too long again." She dashed out of the room like she was being chased, leaving Tim stunned and the nurse trailing her.

28

"Rejoice with those who rejoice, and weep with those who weep." – Romans 12:15

∼

Tim rotated the engagement ring loosely looped on his pinky finger and stared at the ceiling. Then he tapped his thumb on the bed alongside the seconds ticking by on the wall clock. It had been hours since Angel dashed out, leaving him confused and with his thoughts. So, he'd asked a nurse for a phone, then dialed Violet's number. It said the phone was switched off. The voicemail was full too so he couldn't leave a message. He called her office at Cortexe Corp., and it had been disconnected. He didn't see his cellphone anywhere in the room, so he'd have to find another way of contacting her later.

Why was everyone acting weird? He looped Violet's locket over his neck and forced his taut muscles to relax. Things were fine. All he had to do was breathe. Wherever his best friend was, she knew he was in the hospital. Surely, twenty-four hours would not pass before she got in touch with the medical team. Then he would talk to her.

An hour later, they served him a light soup with toasted bread and salad, and he'd eaten it gladly, feeling like he'd never eaten food before.

Full, he felt drowsy, but he fought sleep, determined to wait up for Angel. He prayed, read the Bible someone had left beside his pillow, and listened to the news. Then he flicked through several channels, finding nothing he liked to watch. He flicked through more stations, scrolled past reality shows, and soon, he landed on a local news channel displaying information about an art show in town during a commercial break.

It would be nice to take Violet there if she wasn't busy. He checked the date it was supposed to start. Since it was happening within a few days, he suspected his doctors might not clear him to leave by then yet. He was to be under observation for some time, especially since he was still suffering what they hoped to be short-term amnesia.

He was about to turn off the TV when BREAKING NEWS flashed on the screen. He blinked at the image, wondering why it was familiar. Then recognition hit, and the newscaster's words registered. "This victim was found murdered at a construction site. Suspects are currently being pursued by police, and we will bring you updates as we receive them. Anyone with information about this case should contact..."

The remote fell to the floor, and Tim's heart broke into uncountable pieces. "Vi?" His lips uttered her name, but he felt distant and far removed from the sound. He scrambled to reach the phone to dial the police to find out what happened, but the pain that hit his side kept him on the bed. No. Violet couldn't be dead. She couldn't have been murdered. He pounded his fist on the pillow. "Nooooo!" Pain swept over him and unleashed a storm of emotion.

He bowed himself over the bed and wept. The puzzle pieces began to fall into place. This was why Angel fled. She didn't want to break the news to him.

His best friend was gone forever. Who killed her? And why? He raised his eyes to the TV and wished the news away. Then he recalled his dream.

So, what he'd seen was real. Violet was dead and had gone to be with the Lord.

He grasped a fistful of the bedsheet. How was he supposed to live without his best friend to whom he never said goodbye?

Tim cried until he grew limp and couldn't shed a single tear. Just when he thought his heart couldn't take any more pain, the door opened. "Why didn't you tell me, Angel?" he spoke without looking. "You shouldn't have kept it from me. If you were in a relationship with me, you must know Violet and I were close."

A gentle tap on his shoulder had him looking up. A police officer looked at him with concern lining his brow. He rubbed the side of his head, leaving a peppering of gray hair standing askew. "I'm sorry for your loss. But I'm not Angel. And I have some sad news."

"I heard about Violet's death."

The man shook his head, and compassion clouded his gaze. He glanced at the TV. "We withheld the news, waiting for at least a day to break it to you. The nurse must have forgotten to remove the remote as instructed. You weren't supposed to find out like this, and for that I'm sorry."

Tim nodded, wiped his eyes, and sat up a little, his body struggling to accept his comments while his heart lay broken. "My memory loss isn't helping things either."

The man glanced at another officer who had just entered and whispered something in his ear. The elderly man frowned, then shifted his glance to Tim.

"What's wrong?" Tim held his breath.

The man was silent.

"Listen, you already kept Violet's death from me, and I had to find out in the most shocking way. Please, if something else happened, please tell me. I'm tired of getting shocked."

The man swallowed. "Angel was kidnapped on her way here an hour ago. The officer assigned to watch her house reported it when she left her house but didn't make it here as expected."

Tim twisted the sheets so tightly it ripped. He darted his gaze between the man and his colleague, searching for the hint of a joke. But he found none. "No. This isn't happening," he flatly said, then gulped. "I must still be in a coma. Wake me up when it's over." He slid down the bed, clenched the ring box, turned his cheek on the bed, and shut his eyes. There had to be a way out of this bad dream.

A tap on his arm had him turning around. He scowled at the cop. "I said wake me up when this dream is over! Vi is not dead. John and Angel are not missing."

"Listen to me, please."

But Tim was done hearing about one bit of bad news after another. Was he back here to find out he had two people he loved and then lost them at the same time? He uncurled himself, grief overwhelming him. He glanced up with tears looming in his eyes. "Am I the reason they're dead and missing?

Was there something I did wrong? Please let me die in their place."

The man squeezed his shoulder. "None of this was your fault. We can find her."

His ears perked.

"We need your help to save Angel. Before it's too late."

Tim wiped his eyes and managed to sit up. "I'm ready. Please tell me how I can help."

"We installed a device on the shoulder of her uniform due to a case she just completed where she was threatened. The device records sound and video and transmits them every twenty-four hours. Then it wipes clean and starts recording all over again. It's also equipped to transmit her location as long as it catches a whiff of some wireless signal nearby for about two minutes. We took this precautionary step hoping it wouldn't be needed but..."

Tim swallowed and tried not to imagine the pain Angel must be going through now. "What can I do?"

"The device downloads into a file, and we need you to give us the password she used so we can unlock it."

"In case you don't remember me, I'm Pierce Hollande, her partner." The other officer stepped close. "She said she'd used a passphrase you knew about should she be absent to log in. We'd created this weeks ago."

"But..." Tim swallowed. *Dear Lord, I don't remember!* "I don't even remember our relationship. This is unbelievable." *Lord, how can I be powerless when so much rests on me?*

The elderly man settled a hand on his arm. "I have just the right suggestion to help you remember. Go through your communications with her, and something will click. I believe it."

Not so confident, Tim was willing to try. "Sure." He shrugged. "I just need to find my phone."

∼

Angel winced from the ropes binding her hands before she sensed the cloth blindfolding her. "Argh." She tugged hard at the rope, but it didn't budge. She wriggled her body, and cold, firm steel pressed against her back. She remembered something she'd once learned, though she couldn't recall from where or whom.

There are three ways to get through a kidnapping. Confrontation, compliance, or provocation. Confront your enemy when you see an escape, comply when you don't, provoke them into a mistake and seize the opportunity.

But Angel didn't know who her kidnappers were. She hadn't seen their faces. She was barely conscious enough to see the truck had been a deep red color—nothing else. How could she allow herself to get kidnapped! She'd been so focused on getting to the hospital, seeing Tim, and asking him some questions to try to ginger his memory. She'd missed him so much it hurt, but also dreaded breaking the terrible news about Violet while she was still reeling from the discovery.

She'd also wished to apologize for her abrupt exit. Her emotions had been scattered, and she'd needed a place to pull herself together and not scare Tim back into a coma. Then a car had hit her cruiser, slamming it into oncoming traffic. Reeling, she was grabbed from a smoking vehicle, dumped into a truck, and bound by very strong hands. It happened so fast she could barely fight back, especially with the fuzziness of the accident blurring her vision. Then they knocked her out.

Now she had no idea how she got here. So, not only was her brother missing and Violet dead, she was in bondage, unable to find her brother. As it was, *she* needed to be found too. And Tim—the man she loved—saw her as no better than a friend. How much worse could her life become?

Did the SSPD know who took her or John? She wrestled her bonds once again, more worried for John than herself. He was a civilian and was not used to these situations. If she had a choice, she'd swap places for her brother. But she didn't, and worse, she'd been placed in the same situation without the swap. She practically growled her frustration.

The door squeaked open, and light warmed her face. She blinked away the harshness beneath her blindfold. Someone was there. She wanted them to speak so her recording device could pick up their voice. She hoped and prayed that the SSPD team would get the recording. "What do you want from me?"

Silence.

Something was tossed at her and landed against her hip. She groped for it, and her fingers closed in on a hard object. Next, someone untied one of her hands, then cuffed the other to a metal pole. "What do you wan—"

A hard slap left her cheek tingling. A salty taste hit her tongue, and she sucked in her breath. She probed the object in her hand—stale pizza? Then the door slammed shut.

Now in silence and surrounded by darkness, she flexed her free arm and ate the dry meal, but fear needled her spine. Whoever took her was not interested in negotiating. They were out to eliminate her. So, she prayed hard that the SSPD would find her in time—before these kidnappers killed her.

For three days, Tim barely slept. This time, it wasn't due to a coma, but due to grief. And the heartbreaking loss of those who mattered most to him.

"Tim, are you ready?" the SSPD captain asked. The man had been so polite that it calmed his worries. He'd hoped to remember something, but... nothing yet. So, they worked on his phone, searching for clues to download any file the device recorded. Someone accessed the system and hadn't seen anything show up yet. They needed the passcode for when something did enter.

Tim glanced at the intimate text messages once again. Had he truly revealed so much about himself and his past to Angel? Just scrolling through their email and text message and voicemail communication over the past several months, he found himself loving her afresh and smiling at the words he read.

That surprised him since he didn't remember their relationship. But her vulnerability toward him was born of his toward her and evidenced in every word.

The captain cleared his throat as Tim's fingers worked the cellphone. "Listen, this can't be easy for you. But you have to keep hope alive."

Tim nodded. "Of course."

"I have another bit of news."

"Oh?" Tim glanced up. "Okay."

"We've nailed the culprit behind Violet's death." The captain paused. "It was her brother, Pete."

Fury rose like a ball of fire inside Tim, and he struggled to jump down from the hospital bed. "I'll kill him!"

"Hey! Hold it, man. Tim!" The captain held him back.

But Tim would not stay still. It took three officers to get him to calm down after a few minutes. With his heart still breaking, he sobbed. "I knew he couldn't be trusted. She should've left. Why did she stay? *Whyyyy?*"

He clutched the side of the bed. Tears mingled with pain and set his heart on a vengeful path—but God stopped him—right inside his heart. He felt the rebuke of the Lord, even before he finished forming the thoughts and planning how to accomplish it. *You don't reward evil with evil, son.*

"He could've let her live. Why did he kill her?" he murmured in prayer, even as he reluctantly let go of the hate creeping up his heart. Pete would pay.

Let him go, son. Release him from your heart.

"No." Tim sobbed harder.

It was one thing for Pete to kill Violet and him not seek revenge. But forgiving him? No. That would be a very long way coming.

He lifted his gaze and met the captain's. "I want to go with you for his arrest."

But the captain, with gray-haired wisdom, seemingly saw through him and knew Tim wasn't making a clearheaded choice. "No, dear friend. You need to stay here. Get better, mourn Violet, and be ready to be reunited with Angel when we find her, because we must. I'm not sure an angry man is who she will like to see right now. You might not remember your relationship, but I saw you two together. You were perfect. And I don't want to see that ruined." The man drew close and tapped Tim's chest with a finger. "So, please, deal with the issues in here first. Then cool off and, when you're ready, be reunited with the world."

And with those words, he led his men out and left Tim with his thoughts, and with the Lord as he twirled Violet's locket he now wore over his neck on his fingers. He bit the edge of the locket, and something clicked in his mind. And he remembered. He remembered his last chat with Angel—and the passcode she'd shared—and he shouted from the room.

The door opened a fraction, and a nurse, face awash in fear, poked her head in. "Are you okay?"

He was smiling. "Please call the captain. I remember the password. Angel's password."

29

"*Your ears shall hear a Word behind you saying, 'This is the way, walk in it,'*" –Isaiah 30:21

~

Angel was sleeping when she heard the explosion. She jerked up from sleep as voices shouted. A round of gunfire exploded, and a vehicle started. Then the hum of an engine vibrated beneath her. She was tossed to one edge of the... container?...as it drove off sharply. Then a screeching turn followed, and chaos—with voices shouting, reverberated, and *sirens* were blaring! She scrambled to her knees, powered by adrenaline. Was it a rescue? Her head throbbed, and she could scarcely focus. She was still in her uniform—was it possible that...? She inched her bound hands to her side and exhaled the rush of hope. Nope, the only thing missing was her weapon belt, nothing else.

She cocked her head, trying to listen, to figure out what was happening. Soon, a loud pop shook the container, and the vehicle tumbled. Angel felt her belly float, then her head hit the hard floor. Another round of gunshots rang out, and everything went silent. Her head swam—*what* was going on?

Keys jingled outside. Then a door squealed open. Someone jumped inside. Their thudding boots lulled the platform on which she lay, and she shrieked.

"She's alive! Over here." Someone drew close, and a gentle hand touched her face. "I'm with the SSPD, Angel. You're going to be okay."

Those words felt foreign. She'd waited and hoped to hear them for three long and torturous days and had given up hope. Her lips began to tremble as someone cut the blindfold from her face and released her hands from the cuffs. She blinked as more men in her favorite attire—the SSPD uniform—climbed in and lifted her to her feet. Eager hands embraced her, and she sobbed into the arms of her captain.

She withdrew and searched his face. "John?" she croaked out.

The captain's brows furrowed. "No leads yet. We're still searching." He squeezed her hand. "We'll find him, Angel."

"I...wish you found...him first." She could barely speak, having eaten only a dry piece of pizza and drank one bottle of water for three days.

"Shhh." He wrapped her under his arm. "Let's get you home. Your love is waiting for you." He stepped back, and his men carried her and set her on a Gurney as her legs could barely stand. They bore her out of an RV, into a police van. Tim...she sighed, unable to form the beloved name. She could hardly wait to see him.

AFTER HER HOSPITAL DISCHARGE FOUR DAYS LATER, ANGEL WAS sure her heart would burst as she perched by Tim's hospital bed. When he clutched her hands and buried his face in them, she caught a whiff of his pleasant aftershave. Did he have someone bring his personal items from his house? He'd had a beard on him during his coma. But she appreciated the clean shave he now sported. "I remember, sweetheart. I remember everything." He lifted his gaze to hers, shook his head, and his dark Italian curls bounced. "I'm not sure if the deep emotions I felt when I heard that Pete had killed Violet triggered it. But I remembered telling her someone was after me. Then from there, it was like a movie playing on rewind. Everything came back."

"And?" Angel had feared their next level would be a breakup if he didn't remember. This news couldn't have come at a better time.

He kissed her hair, brought out a ring, and slid it onto her ring finger. The cushion-cut, platinum, diamond-encrusted ring shone and was snug in a perfect fit. Then he smiled. "And this. It doesn't fit onto my hand so I'd rather put it where it belongs." He toyed with a loose strand of her hair near her face.

She blinked, and his hand settled on hers again.

"Sorry, that wasn't a question. Will you marry me, Angel? I want to spend the rest of my life with you." His finger grazed the ring. "And I want to join your search for John. I won't rest until he's found." His honey-brown eyes searched her face as he sucked in his lower lip.

Angel swallowed then considered his proposal for a moment. For the past four days while she recovered, her colleagues had turned over every piece of information they had, and nothing had shaken loose about where John might be. On top of that, the doctors had strongly advised four more days of rest for her before she could actively join the search. But in her heart, at this minute, she knew she would commit to spending the rest of her life with Tim. No doubt about it. And although she wished the timing was better, and that John was home, she knew how close they had been to losing this chance at love for good. She and Tim were getting a miraculous second chance, and she wouldn't waste a moment of that. So, she replied.

"Yes." She wanted to jump and dance, but she hardly felt more than a little excited with her brother still missing, but her heart firmed resolute to find John. With Tim at her side, they would be a force for good and double their search effort.

Tim kissed her cheek. "Thank you. And sorry for the unconventional proposal," he gushed. "I will do it properly soon. I'll get down on one knee, the whole nine yards.... I just wished the circumstances were different." An exhale whooshed from him, and his shoulders relaxed.

To ease his concerns, she focused on their gratitude. "Things could've been worse, honey, so we won't live in regret. You're alive and awake from your coma. I was rescued from kidnappers—alive. We can be thankful. And yes, our focus will be the search for John going forward. And I'm glad to do it with you by my side."

His gaze traveled the length of her. Then he focused on her face again. "I'm glad they didn't hurt you. I don't know what I would've done losing Violet permanently, with John missing. And then losing you too?" He shook his head. "That would have spelled the end of me."

She rested her head on his chest and felt his heart beating strong, perfectly sure that was where she belonged. "Me too. I'm just worried about John."

He ran a hand along her back. "I'm also worried, sweetheart, but we can pray. God is in control. We search and find John—wherever he is. We're a team, so don't go off on this alone, okay?" He searched her face again, and this time, the anxious lines atop his forehead loosened.

Her heart joyed over the man who loved her afresh like never before. "I'm not going anywhere, Tim. I'll be by your side forever."

"I love you, Angel." He kissed her hair again and curved an arm around her shoulder, pulling her close.

Her heart bloomed hearing those words she never thought his lips would utter again. "I love you too, Tim. Now, let's go and find John. And we will succeed by God's grace, however long it takes. God will keep my brother alive."

Angel rolled Violet's locket hanging down his chest and resting near her face with a hand while her mind worked. "I have ideas of how we can get started with our search in addition to what the SSPD is doing. They're capable, but this is *my* brother. And we can't rest all of our hopes on them. We will do more, beyond what I can achieve through my job."

"Amen. I agree," Tim chimed—his voice sounding healthier and stronger—the opposite of the man who'd barely clung to life on this same bed, the man she hadn't been sure would come back to her again. Hearing him speak rang like a melody so sweet she didn't want to hear it end. And she knew that if God did this miracle, He would bring John home alive. She believed it with all her heart. And she was willing to thrust her fight where her treasure was.

Tim clasped her face in his hands and smiled, shining his pure, unfeigned love through every crinkle creasing his swoon-worthy eyes into hers. "My heart and hands are ready, my love. So, let's get started."

*THE END * CLICK HERE and read the next book in this series-THE SECRET HERITAGE. So exciting!

Find out how, when, and where Pete got saved in The New Rulebook Series. **CLICK HERE** and enjoy this gripping 9-book acclaimed series today and find out how two orphans grew to become the most powerful couple in the world.

NOTE TO THE READER

Thank you very much for reading **Whisper**, the first book in this exciting Christian romantic suspense series! I hope you enjoyed it. This is my note to introduce you to me as an author and why I'm writing these books.
First of all, Red is my first book, followed by After, which I also wrote at a very tough season of my life. A season where I saw no way out but leaned wholly on Jesus every day for hope and He saw me through to the other side.

Years ago, when I wrote Red, I was going through one of my most difficult seasons. The first draft on paper, was dotted with tear drops enough times to diffuse the ink. The attacks were so personal, and so severe that I considered quitting.

I couldn't understand why the more I wrote, the worse it became. Then, I heard the Lord saying to me, "Keep writing." I said, "But Lord, the attacks are too much. I can't write under attack." He said to me, "Keep writing." Everyday, God encouraged me.

So, even though it didn't make sense, I pressed on, still crying, still writing, heart still breaking, still not understanding why. I thought Red would be both my first and last book. Once I had Red fully professionally edited, and I pressed Publish, I ran away from writing for approximately six months (could've been longer than that). All I wanted at that stage, was to be a Political Science professor, not writing fiction of any kind. But God had better plans for my life.
As soon as Red was published, I got some breather from those attacks.

Guess what? When I started writing my second book, the attacks returned and intensified.

I saw a pattern. I wrote, I got attacked. I didn't write, and there was relative calm.
So, I knew by the Holy Spirit that I had a choice to make. The only way I could avoid those battles was by not writing.

But, you know how fiery the Word of the Lord is. It would burn a hole in my soul if I kept it in long enough :), a sweet fire that I was willing to submit to any battle to get the words out. So, I jumped back in, fully aware, fully ready for coming battles, and yes, fully scared too—and those battles have not stopped through all my books, twenty books in all to date. And I hope to write more by God's grace.

Everyday, I'm fighting one battle or another to get my words in, and to get these precious stories out to you—sick or well, full or not, comfortable or not, in whatever place I find myself—I'm pressing forward and upward toward the mark of His high calling.

Therefore, please realize that every book of mine you read has passed through the fire, tears, sacrifice, fierce battles, and much resistance to be born. So, when you read them, you're enjoying a product of much sacrifice and faith that only God could've made happen by Himself.

He helped me through many storms and got me to where I wrote this series. Right now, if you buy the whole series, I will give as much as possible to support orphans in need.

Will you support me? If you would, then...

CONTINUE READING, GET THE OTHER BOOKS TO SUPPORT me, and THANK YOU for your support!

∽

THE SECRET HERITAGE (SAMPLE)

"But if the spirit of Him who raised Jesus from the dead dwells in you, He who raised Christ from the dead will also give life to your mortal bodies through his Spirit Who dwells in you." Romans 8:11

∽

IN THE LAST YEAR OF THE TIMES WHEN LANZAROTE WAS STILL RULED by kings....

SOMEONE NUDGED SIERRA FERNANDO'S SHOULDER, SHOOK HER awake, and pressed a note into her hand. She blinked, still half asleep, and looked up at Mary, her fellow slave—a forced slave, but she wouldn't go there just yet—peering down.

"Shhh." Mary raised a finger to her lips. "It's a note for you. Read it."

Angling herself to catch a wave of the flickering oil lantern at the end of the female servants' quarters—an old rectangular wooden barn—she tilted the note, smoothing crumpled edges in her struggle to read it with sleepy eyes. Then the name scrawled at the edge chased sleep from her eyes.

The day was finally here. It was time to choose, and the man was involving her in his decision? Goodness.

She swallowed as Mary was turning to leave while Sierra still rubbed her eyes. "Wait, who gave this note to you?"

"Ache." The lone answer confirmed her fears. It was truly from the king.

Sierra's eyes widened, and she stifled a yawn. "What? Ache is here?" How did he get past the security guard who kept the slaves from running away? Unless the guard was in a drunken stupor.

"He is here. And he's waiting outside the door. He said for you to hurry." Mary nodded toward the note. "What did it say?"

Sierra couldn't tell Mary what it really meant, but she could mention what it literally said. "King Peralta has sent for me immediately. It says he has a...request to make."

Mary observed her from a distance, obviously expecting more information, but Sierra wasn't saying any more. Not until she spoke to the king face-to-face. Not until she was sure he meant his words to her yesterday afternoon in the palace garden under the blooming lilies. And not until she knew he wouldn't proceed to marry the lady-in-waiting as scheduled in twenty-four hours—a woman whom he clearly didn't love but was betrothed to, right before they met accidentally—in order to keep his throne. Until then, her answers would be as vague as the circumstances surrounding them. "That's it?" Mary probed.

"For now, yes. But please gather the others to pray for me while I'm gone. Things may change when I return. Have everyone be alert. I may ask him for our freedom. And in case the king helps us gain our freedom, somehow, I need you and everyone to be ready for our possible return to Spain."

A flicker of excitement glinted in Mary's gaze as a wide smile stretched her thin lips into sallow cheeks. "Okay, sister. And may God grant you favor in the king's sight."

"Amen." With that, Sierra swung her feet off the bunk bed, put on the best clothing she had, which was distant from what the ladies of the court wore, and slipped out of the servants' quarters. If the king's note tonight, one night before his arranged marriage, and his words to her yesterday were anything to go by, King Peralta might be facing the toughest personal choice he would make—the choice of who to marry—

and she was caught up in it by accident. An accident that started in the king's garden six months ago and led to love. But...would the king choose a slave over a princess?

∽

SIX MONTHS EARLIER...

The heat beat down on her head while dirt jammed deep beneath her fingernails. Hoe in hand, Sierra worked hard in the king's garden. The sight of the large, earthen water trough sitting on a rough-cut stone near the center of the garden tugged at her heart. But it was too far from her now. A sigh slipped through her chapped lips. If only she could scoop a cup to splash over her head and wet her tongue. It would've cooled her skin, if only for a moment. But her work couldn't be delayed if she would finish on time to leave with the others.

As the sun crested overhead an hour later, she wiped beads of sweat off her brow and, while singing a Hallelujah chorus under her breath, Sierra bent to dig up those stubborn weeds still hugging the roots of a turnip plant. She'd labored all day around the west side of King Peralta's garden, weeding through the flowers and had almost finished with her daily tasks. If she was lucky, the bruise sustained at the back of her hand when she'd pushed her hoe away from a blooming flower would be the only hurt she'd tend this evening.

"Work faster!" their master, keeper of the palace grounds, a man of very few words and an evil heart bellowed above her, jerking her eyes from the turnip to the weeds looming beyond the seemingly endless weeds.

She bent deep over them, hoe uprooting stubborn grass held down by caked earth. Then a scream resounded near the rose garden. She jumped to her feet before thinking through it, dropped her tools, turned left, and ran over there.

Her heart pounded as she wiped sandy hands on her apron while she ran. Was one of her friends in trouble?

Only after she saw King Peralta leaning over a figure did she remember—she was no longer a nurse in a small village in Spain, a village whose people were decimated by war. She was a missionary, caught in a shipwreck, and captured and forced into slavery on this island. Before she could beat a retreat, the king spun, and his eyes met hers with a plea, a look her nursing eyes readily recognized.

She'd heard that he daily came to the garden to walk among the circle of rose trees while ruminating in thought. But she didn't work on this side of the garden. Looking at him now, she saw a tall man with broad shoulders and a chiseled face who carried himself with dignity. He beckoned her with a wave, and gold bracelets jingled beyond the extended sleeve of his regal purple, gold-embroidered garment. "Can you help him?"

Sierra didn't answer, still wishing not to incur her master's wrath. Surely, she'd be punished with half a ration of meal for leaving her designated workplace simply because someone gave a scream for help. Obliging the king, she reached the fallen man, squatting as the king hunkered next to her. A musky scent of white lily, jasmine, and rose with a base of lavender floated into her nostrils from him—nothing like the sweaty smell she surely emitted. What a way to meet the king! Schooling her thoughts, she focused on the fallen man. "What happened?"

"He collapsed and fell." As the king supplied details, her nurse's training kicked in. She visually scanned the man for injuries and, seeing none, exhaled in relief. Then she tilted the man's chin and listened for breathing. She pressed a hand to his wrist.

"He has a weak pulse, but we must revive him. Please, send someone to fetch some cool water, a medicine kit, and a towel." As the king did so, she eased the man sideways and guided a hand to the back of his head, feeling for injuries. "Did his head hit the ground?" She didn't see a bruise of any kind.

The king shook his head. "I caught him before he did." No wonder the king had some mud on his shoes and sand splashed on his royal apparel. But he didn't seem to mind. His eyes were on the fallen man. "Please, what kind of knowledge do you have?"

"Since he didn't hit his head on the ground, he should be all right. Let's pray he comes around once I give him first-aid treatment." She folded the skirt of her long dress between her thighs and considered his question while she checked the man for any other injuries. How much could she reveal to the man who could speak one word and change her situation?

Or should *she* bring up her situation? Twice now, she and the other missionaries had petitioned the king's council for their freedom, narrating how they were traveling missionaries, forced into slavery by an agreement to save their lives after a shipwreck, but twice she was told their petition didn't meet the requirements to be presented to the king's council. But here, the man who could change all that squatted right next to her, and her stomach tightened, words pushing up from it, clogging her throat, her will alone scarcely holding back her need to scream her request. "I was a nurse in a village in Spain. Then I became a traveling missionary for Jesus Christ."

They brought her the water and the requested items then. "But—but you're a slave here?"

Her fingers clenched the water scoop as tightly as her wish for freedom urged her heart to say the truth. But, in this situation, was this the right time for such a revelation? In a way that will produce the result of freedom she so desired? No. She stuck to a simple reply. "Yes."

Meanwhile, vivid images of her life in Spain so long ago filled her mind—the colorful end-of-year ceremonial village dances, the friendly classes where she'd studied nursing, and the loving home where she'd grown up. Images strong enough to make her want to tell him how much her freedom meant, but she heard a Word in her heart.

Share the Word with him. Share in season and out of season.

Here? This was hardly the right circumstance to share the Gospel. Maybe she could ask for another chance when a man's life wasn't at risk. So, Sierra prayed. *Lord, please provide me with a better opportunity.* As she glanced up, caught by the intensity of the king's gaze, a frown creased his smooth face. So, she wondered, had he ever had mud on his body before now? Or did his royalty set him too far apart to see the pain of those who served at his command?

"How?" he pressed, handing her the towel.

Surprised, she accepted it. "It's a long story." She straightened, pretty sure that he wouldn't understand and willing herself only to focus on reviving the unconscious man. After taking a scoop of water, wetting the towel, and settling it on the man's forehead, she sprinkled some water on his head to cool his skin. Then she loosened the neckline of his clothing and checked his pulse again. "His pulse is still weak, but he's breathing." She couldn't simply watch a man die.

Then Sierra couldn't resist what she had to do. She knelt down, clasped the man's hand into her own, bowed her head, and prayed for him. All while acutely aware of the king's observance. Prayer completed, she opened her eyes, slipped out of her outer coat, raised the man's head, and placed her coat underneath. Her bare arms tingled with the searing heat, but she endured the burn. "I suspect the heat got to him. We need to give him some shade."

So the king rose, shed his purple robe, and settled it across two waist-high rose bushes blooming over them. That protected the fainted man's upper body from the direct sunlight. He hunkered beside her again. "Is that good?"

Sierra smiled and met his gaze as she also squatted. "Yes, that is great. He should revive soon, God willing. Let me wet the towel again." She grasped the damp towel, which was now warm, and dipped it into the bucket of cool water before placing it on the man's forehead. Their hands met over the man's head, and warmth enveloped her belly. Why was she having butterflies in her belly for this king whom she barely knew? But he was kind and generous and not at all what she thought of him from a distance.

A sneeze from the fainted man drew their attention. His eyelids popped open, and he blinked. "He's awake. Praise God." As the man struggled to rise, and she urged him to remain laid down on the ground, a few other men came and helped him lean to a sitting position. She offered him a cup of cool water. He sipped it, then spoke with a weak voice, thanking her for her help. Relieved that he was okay, Sierra rose to leave, if only to escape her unexpected warmth for the king. She had to clear her mind, and she needed some space to do so.

The king touched her arm. "Thank you, milady."

With his hand resting on her bare arm, she saw the red dot of a wound on his thumb. She grabbed his hand without thinking and inspected it. "Your majesty, you're wounded. Here, let me take a look." The healing kit, still on the ground near her feet, remained open so she took a cotton band and wiped the king's wound. "Maybe you took a cut from the rose thorns." Then she pressed and held it to stop the bleeding. And she covered the wound as she'd been taught.

Everything she knew about caring for the sick was coming back to her. When she was done, only then did she look up to find him watching her actions. His hand lingered on hers longer than she thought it would, and as she lifted her eyes to his, his gaze dropped to her lips. Color filled his cheeks and hers heated, and he inhaled sharply. She gasped, released his hand, and spun. "Your majesty, I should go."

Spinning, she bumped into her master. "The turnips are waiting to be weeded, Sierra," he scolded, then bowed to the king. "Sorry for anything she did wrong, your majesty."

But Sierra's thoughts were spinning. What had just happened? Could the king indeed be attracted to her? No. It couldn't be. It must be her imagination thanks to being under too much sunshine. Maybe she needed a drink of that cool water at the trough to clear a foggy mind.

But she turned again. And as she stared, enrapt, into his soft chocolate depths, she knew what she saw and experienced was real. So Sierra reminded herself of three facts.

He was a king, and she was a slave. And those ends never met without grave consequences.

Before she finished her thought, his voice rose above her head toward her master. "From today, let this woman work only in my rose garden. And do not send her elsewhere." She fully faced the king, whose gaze locked in with hers. "I'm sure she'll tend them well. Won't you, Sierra?"

Too stunned to speak, she pivoted on her heel. Their worlds might never meet, but this king was breaking down those barriers, without fear, like a wrecking ball with no chains. *END OF SAMPLE* Thank you for reading!

CONTINUE THE SECRET HERITAGE by clicking HERE

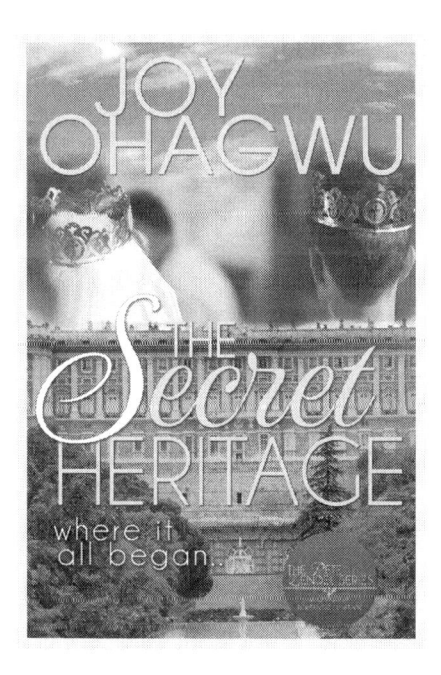

THIS BOOK REVEALS THE ZENDEL FAMILY HERITAGE DATING BACK 100 plus years. Read it now.

DESCRIPTION

Her courageous faith defied the odds. Her heroic design saved the world from a psychopath. Now an ancient family rivalry threatens it all...

***

It was bad enough for Violet Zendel that her twin brother hated her and avoided her like a plague because of her faith. When he became the CEO of their parents' company, she did everything she could to support his success. Then she planned a vacation to help bridge the gap between them and improve their relationship.

However, when the news about a shocking event reached her ears during the trip, it shook her to her core—and led to a trail of broken hearts. Violet saw no other option but to shift her focus from pursuing corporate achievements, to preserving her family members and their legacy. But that came at a very high cost. And in the process, she is challenged by riskier choices, which demonstrate in dangerous ways, that not everything was as it seemed.

Police Officer Angel Martinez was not a stranger to hard work. She had almost single-handedly guided her four siblings into adulthood and did not feel threatened when a murder case landed on her desk. Feeling confident about her ability to solve the murder, little did she know that some cases came with decades-old secrets that could tear apart the peace and unity of those she held dear. Can she solve this case without losing her life and that of her precious family members?

Tim Santiago loved his career as an Archeologist. He seldom walked past old things without stopping to admire them, and he yearned for his best friend, Violet, to gain an appreciation for his profession. When events at a funeral unleashed a storm of mysterious phone calls and a dangerous chase, he quickly agreed that some old things were better left buried. But when he suddenly lost someone dear to him—and was close to losing two more—he faced a critical choice about unearthing more secrets. Was he already too late?

What will happen to Violet, Angel, and Tim?

WHISPER is the full length prequel of the highly anticipated **PETE ZENDEL** Christian Romantic Suspense Series. **The Pete Zendel Series is a spin-off of The New Rulebook Series—a 9-book acclaimed series. If you have not read The New Rulebook Series, start here-**

ASIN- B076F5RT79

Read **WHISPER** now.

***

*This book is a spin-off of The New Rulebook Series. If you haven't read The New Rulebook Series, please do so as that will enhance your understanding of this series. Thank you!

BRIEF NOTE

Thank you so much for getting **WHISPER**, the first book of The Pete Zendel Christian Suspense Series! Whisper is a prequel, however, it is a full length novel.

I would like to give credit for the three lessons from Angel to John, which I paraphrased from something I heard being shared on my birthday this year (the fictional birthday, and my actual birthday was only a coincidence as I had likely written the scene much earlier). It was a young man who worked with Integrity music who was online on a livestream, and had played some worship songs on their Instagram handle on Feb 5, 2018. I was blessed by his music and message. I was writing Whisper that day, and the young man said these: "The Cross has the final Word. The name of JESUS is above that situation. God is good and in every situation I will praise Him." Those words spoke to me and I felt led by The LORD to include them in Whisper. It is the first and only time I've added any words from another person that were not expressly revealed to me by the LORD to any of my books, therefore, even though I don't know his name, I would like to give him credit regardless. Thank you.

Please expect **HUNTER**, the next book in this series soon, by God's grace. It promises to be as exciting! God bless you!

A REALLY COOL OPPORTUNITY

Join my VIP readers club to be the first to know as soon as my books are available for purchase here: http://www.joyohagwu.com/announcements.html

> Want to know when my next book releases?
> And to grab :
> * a free ebook (limited time offer)
> * Release day giveaways
> *Discounted prices
> * And so much more!
> Hit YES below and you're in!
> See you on the inside!

THEN JOIN MY VIP READERS CLUB

DISCLAIMER

This novel is entirely a work of fiction. As a fiction author, I have taken artistic liberty to create plausible experiences for my characters void of confirmed scenarios. Any resemblance to actual innovative developments in any scientific area is purely coincidental. My writing was thorough, and editing accurate; hence active depictions of any kind in this book are attributed to creativity for a great story. It was my pleasure sharing these stories with you! ALL glory to God.

Copyright First Edition © 2018
Joy Ohagwu

LifeFountainMedia

CHRISTIAN FICTION TWINED IN FAITH, HOPE, AND LOVE.
Life Fountain Books and Life Fountain Media logo are trademarks of Joy Ohagwu. Absence of ™ in connection with marks of Life Fountain Media or other parties does not indicate an absence of trademark protection of those marks.

All rights reserved. No part of this publication may be reproduced, stored in a retrieval system, or transmitted in any form or by any means—electronic, mechanical, photocopy, recording, or otherwise—without prior permission of the author, except as brief quotations in printed reviews.
This novel is a work of fiction. Names, characters, incidents, and dialogues are products of the author's imagination or are used fictitiously. Any resemblance or similarity to actual events or persons, living or dead, scenarios, or locales is entirely coincidental. This ebook is licensed for your enjoyment. Unauthorized sharing is prohibited. Please purchase your copy to read this story. Thank you. Christian Suspense 2. Christian Fiction 3. Contemporary Christian Romantic Suspense 4. Christian Romance 5 Faith 5. Fiction 6. Thrillers on Kindle 7. Mysteries and Suspense Thrillers on Kindle 8. Man-woman relationships 9. Family 10. Inspirational Religious Fiction 11. Contemporary Women's Fiction 12. Amazon Thrillers & Suspense 13. Clean & Wholesome Action-packed Christian Romantic Suspense 14. Romantic thriller 15. Contemporary Religious & Inspirational Fiction 16. Religion & Spirituality Inspirational Fiction

Except where otherwise stated, "Scripture taken from the New King James Version Bible®,

Copyright © 1982 by Thomas Nelson, Inc: Copyright © 1982 by Thomas Nelson, Inc. Used by permission. All rights reserved.

All glory to God
Printed in the United States of America

❋ Created with Vellum

VOLUME TWO

THE SECRET HERITAGE

*To **JESUS**- The King of Kings.
My Everlasting King of Glory.*

A CONTEMPORARY CHRISTIAN ROMANTIC SUSPENSE SERIES

Get Joy Ohagwu's starter Library for **FREE**. Details are at the end of this book.

Foundational Scripture

∽

"You shall also be a crown of glory in the hand of the Lord, and a royal diadem in the hand of your God."- Isaiah 62:3

FOREWORD

THE SECRET HERITAGE- A PETE ZENDEL SERIES NOVELLA

∼

DISCLAIMER

This book is a work of fiction and does not reflect the actual history, traditions, or culture of Lanzarote. Any similarities are coincidental and should be taken as such. The author has taken artistic liberties to create an enjoyable story.

∼

The Secret Heritage reveals The Zendel family heritage dating back 100-plus years before Pete Zendel was born. Enjoy the story!

1

∿

"But if the spirit of Him who raised Jesus from the dead dwells in you, He who raised Christ from the dead will also give life to your mortal bodies through his Spirit Who dwells in you." Romans 8:11

∿

In the last year of the times when Lanzarote was still ruled by kings....

Someone nudged Sierra Fernando's shoulder, shook her awake, and pressed a note into her hand. She blinked, still half asleep, and looked up at Mary, her fellow slave—a forced slave, but she wouldn't go there just yet—peering down.

"Shhh." Mary raised a finger to her lips. "It's a note for you. Read it."

Angling herself to catch a wave of the flickering oil lantern at the end of the female servants' quarters—an old rectangular wooden barn—she tilted the note, smoothing crumpled edges in her struggle to read it with sleepy eyes. Then the name scrawled at the edge chased sleep from her eyes.

The day was finally here. It was time to choose, and the man was involving her in his decision? Goodness.

She swallowed as Mary was turning to leave while Sierra still rubbed her eyes. "Wait, who gave this note to you?"

"Ache." The lone answer confirmed her fears. It was truly from the king.

Sierra's eyes widened, and she stifled a yawn. "What? Ache is here?" How did he get past the security guard who kept the slaves from running away? Unless the guard was in a drunken stupor.

"He is here. And he's waiting outside the door. He said for you to hurry." Mary nodded toward the note. "What did it say?"

Sierra couldn't tell Mary what it really meant, but she could mention what it literally said. "King Peralta has sent for me immediately. It says he has a...request to make."

Mary observed her from a distance, obviously expecting more information, but Sierra wasn't saying any more. Not until she spoke to the king face-to-face. Not until she was sure he meant his words to her yesterday afternoon in the palace garden under the blooming lilies. And not until she knew he wouldn't proceed to marry the lady-in-waiting as scheduled in twenty-four hours—a woman whom he clearly didn't love but was betrothed to, right before they met accidentally—in order to keep his throne. Until then, her answers would be as vague as the circumstances surrounding them. "That's it?" Mary probed.

"For now, yes. But please gather the others to pray for me while I'm gone. Things may change when I return. Have everyone be alert. I may ask him for our freedom. And in case the king helps us gain our freedom, somehow, I need you and everyone to be ready for our possible return to Spain."

A flicker of excitement glinted in Mary's gaze as a wide smile stretched her thin lips into sallow cheeks. "Okay, sister. And may God grant you favor in the king's sight."

"Amen." With that, Sierra swung her feet off the bunk bed, put on the best clothing she had, which was distant from what the ladies of the court wore, and slipped out of the servants' quarters. If the king's note tonight, one night before his arranged marriage, and his words to her yesterday were anything to go by, King Peralta might be facing the toughest personal choice he would make—the choice of who to marry—and she was caught up in it by accident. An accident that started in the king's garden six months ago and led to love. But...would the king choose a slave over a princess?

∽

SIX MONTHS EARLIER...

The heat beat down on her head while dirt jammed deep beneath her fingernails. Hoe in hand, Sierra worked hard in the king's garden. The sight of the large, earthen water trough sitting on a rough-cut stone near the center of the garden tugged at her heart. But it was too far from her now. A sigh slipped through her chapped lips. If only she could scoop a cup to splash over her head and wet her tongue. It would've cooled her skin, if only for a moment. But her work couldn't be delayed if she would finish on time to leave with the others.

As the sun crested overhead an hour later, she wiped beads of sweat off her brow and, while singing a Hallelujah chorus under her breath, Sierra bent to dig up those stubborn weeds still hugging the roots of a turnip plant. She'd labored all day around the west side of King Peralta's garden, weeding through the flowers and had almost finished with her daily tasks. If she was lucky, the bruise sustained at the back of her hand when she'd pushed her hoe away from a blooming flower would be the only hurt she'd tend this evening.

"Work faster!" their master, keeper of the palace grounds, a man of very few words and an evil heart bellowed above her, jerking her eyes from the turnip to the weeds looming beyond the seemingly endless weeds.

She bent deep over them, hoe uprooting stubborn grass held down by caked earth. Then a scream resounded near the rose garden. She jumped to her feet before thinking through it, dropped her tools, turned left, and ran over there.

Her heart pounded as she wiped sandy hands on her apron while she ran. Was one of her friends in trouble?

Only after she saw King Peralta leaning over a figure did she remember—she was no longer a nurse in a small village in Spain, a village whose people were decimated by war. She was a missionary, caught in a shipwreck, and captured and forced into slavery on this island. Before she could beat a retreat, the king spun, and his eyes met hers with a plea, a look her nursing eyes readily recognized.

She'd heard that he daily came to the garden to walk among the circle of rose trees while ruminating in thought. But she didn't work on this side of the garden. Looking at him now, she saw a tall man with broad shoulders and a chiseled face who carried himself with dignity. He beckoned her with a wave, and gold bracelets jingled beyond the extended sleeve of his regal purple, gold-embroidered garment. "Can you help him?"

Sierra didn't answer, still wishing not to incur her master's wrath. Surely, she'd be punished with half a ration of meal for leaving her designated workplace simply because someone gave a scream for help. Obliging the king, she reached the fallen man, squatting as the king hunkered next to her. A musky scent of white lily, jasmine, and rose with a base of lavender floated into her nostrils from him—nothing like the sweaty smell she surely emitted. What a way to meet the king! Schooling her thoughts, she focused on the fallen man. "What happened?"

"He collapsed and fell." As the king supplied details, her nurse's training kicked in. She visually scanned the man for injuries and, seeing none, exhaled in relief. Then she tilted the man's chin and listened for breathing. She pressed a hand to his wrist.

"He has a weak pulse, but we must revive him. Please, send someone to fetch some cool water, a medicine kit, and a towel." As the king did so, she eased the man sideways and guided a hand to the back of his head, feeling for injuries. "Did his head hit the ground?" She didn't see a bruise of any kind.

The king shook his head. "I caught him before he did." No wonder the king had some mud on his shoes and sand splashed on his royal apparel. But he didn't seem to mind. His eyes were on the fallen man. "Please, what kind of knowledge do you have?"

"Since he didn't hit his head on the ground, he should be all right. Let's pray he comes around once I give him first-aid treatment." She folded the skirt of her long dress between her thighs and considered his question while she checked the man for any other injuries. How much could she reveal to the man who could speak one word and change her situation?

Or should *she* bring up her situation? Twice now, she and the other missionaries had petitioned the king's council for their freedom, narrating how they were traveling missionaries, forced into slavery by an agreement to save their lives after a shipwreck, but twice she was told their petition didn't meet the requirements to be presented to the king's council. But here, the man who could change all that squatted right next to her, and her stomach tightened, words pushing up from it, clogging her throat, her will alone scarcely holding back her need to scream her request. "I was a nurse in a village in Spain. Then I became a traveling missionary for Jesus Christ."

They brought her the water and the requested items then. "But—but you're a slave here?"

Her fingers clenched the water scoop as tightly as her wish for freedom urged her heart to say the truth. But, in this situation, was this the right time for such a revelation? In a way that will produce the result of freedom she so desired? No. She stuck to a simple reply. "Yes."

Meanwhile, vivid images of her life in Spain so long ago filled her mind—the colorful end-of-year ceremonial village dances, the friendly classes where she'd studied nursing, and the loving home where she'd grown up. Images strong enough to make her want to tell him how much her freedom meant, but she heard a Word in her heart.

Share the Word with him. Share in season and out of season.

Here? This was hardly the right circumstance to share the Gospel. Maybe she could ask for another chance when a man's life wasn't at risk. So, Sierra prayed. *Lord, please provide me with a better opportunity.* As she glanced up, caught by the intensity of the king's gaze, a frown creased his smooth face. So, she wondered, had he ever had mud on his body before now? Or did his royalty set him too far apart to see the pain of those who served at his command?

"How?" he pressed, handing her the towel.

Surprised, she accepted it. "It's a long story." She straightened, pretty sure that he wouldn't understand and willing herself only to focus on reviving the unconscious man. After taking a scoop of water, wetting the towel, and settling it on the man's forehead, she sprinkled some water on his head to cool his skin. Then she loosened the neckline of his clothing and checked his pulse again. "His pulse is still weak, but he's breathing." She couldn't simply watch a man die.

Then Sierra couldn't resist what she had to do. She knelt down, clasped the man's hand into her own, bowed her head, and prayed for him. All while acutely aware of the king's observance. Prayer completed, she opened her eyes, slipped out of her outer coat, raised the man's head, and placed her coat underneath. Her bare arms tingled with the searing heat, but she endured the burn. "I suspect the heat got to him. We need to give him some shade."

So the king rose, shed his purple robe, and settled it across two waist-high rose bushes blooming over them. That protected the fainted man's upper body from the direct sunlight. He hunkered beside her again. "Is that good?"

Sierra smiled and met his gaze as she also squatted. "Yes, that is great. He should revive soon, God willing. Let me wet the towel again." She grasped the damp towel, which was now warm, and dipped it into the bucket of cool water before placing it on the man's forehead. Their hands met over the man's head, and warmth enveloped her belly. Why was she having butterflies in her belly for this king whom she barely knew? But he was kind and generous and not at all what she thought of him from a distance.

A sneeze from the fainted man drew their attention. His eyelids popped open, and he blinked. "He's awake. Praise God." As the man struggled to rise, and she urged him to remain laid down on the ground, a few other men came and helped him lean to a sitting position. She offered him a cup of cool water. He sipped it, then spoke with a weak voice, thanking her for her help. Relieved that he was okay, Sierra rose to leave, if only to escape her unexpected warmth for the king. She had to clear her mind, and she needed some space to do so.

The king touched her arm. "Thank you, milady."

With his hand resting on her bare arm, she saw the red dot of a wound on his thumb. She grabbed his hand without thinking and inspected it. "Your majesty, you're wounded. Here, let me take a look." The healing kit, still on the ground near her feet, remained open so she took a cotton band and wiped the king's wound. "Maybe you took a cut from the rose thorns." Then she pressed and held it to stop the bleeding. And she covered the wound as she'd been taught.

Everything she knew about caring for the sick was coming back to her. When she was done, only then did she look up to find him watching her actions. His hand lingered on hers longer than she thought it would, and as she lifted her eyes to his, his gaze dropped to her lips. Color filled his cheeks and hers heated, and he inhaled sharply. She gasped, released his hand, and spun. "Your majesty, I should go."

Spinning, she bumped into her master. "The turnips are

waiting to be weeded, Sierra," he scolded, then bowed to the king. "Sorry for anything she did wrong, your majesty."

But Sierra's thoughts were spinning. What had just happened? Could the king indeed be attracted to her? No. It couldn't be. It must be her imagination thanks to being under too much sunshine. Maybe she needed a drink of that cool water at the trough to clear a foggy mind.

But she turned again. And as she stared, enrapt, into his soft chocolate depths, she knew what she saw and experienced was real. So Sierra reminded herself of three facts.

He was a king, and she was a slave. And those ends never met without grave consequences.

Before she finished her thought, his voice rose above her head toward her master. "From today, let this woman work only in my rose garden. And do not send her elsewhere." She fully faced the king, whose gaze locked in with hers. "I'm sure she'll tend them well. Won't you, Sierra?"

Too stunned to speak, she pivoted on her heel. Their worlds might never meet, but this king was breaking down those barriers, without fear, like a wrecking ball with no chains.

∽

2

"Bread from Asher shall be rich, and he shall yield royal dainties." Genesis 49:20

∽

Sierra bent low and worked under the rose bushes, careful not to get fresh cuts. The thorns had been left to their own bidding by whoever cared for the rose garden previously, but she wouldn't let that pattern continue. She would give this garden her spin of excellence.

Pruning the rose bush gave her a reason not to wonder afresh why she hadn't seen the king since resuming her assignment. He had requested that she be posted here. But in the week since their chance encounter, not once had she sighted him. So...why did he disappear from what was said to be his favorite place?

Was it her fault? Of course, it had to be. If only she hadn't left her assignment for a scream...But she couldn't disregard a shout for help. Was she supposed to have shared the Word with him right away and seized that opportunity?

A sigh slipped through her lips. *Give me another chance, Lord Jesus, please.*

A low whistle sounded behind her. "What a perfect job you've done. The roses have come alive." The voice, laden with authority, needed no introduction to her ears—nor to her heart, which began a song of its own.

Yet she didn't turn, afraid that what she felt inside might show.

"I knew you were exceptional. Your hands are miraculous on my garden, I must say." King Peralta's voice blended with the spicy, rose-scented air, seeming to belong in this garden and in this place and time. "Thank you for accepting to tend my roses."

That got her to her feet, and she stood inches from the king who swung down from his horse and handed its reins to a palace guard, who led it away.

She exhaled before knowing she held her breath. "Your majesty, I don't know what to say." Wait, was this not the other chance she'd just prayed about?

"A 'thank you' would suffice. Or," he shrugged as he drew closer, "you can tell me how you ended up a slave like I asked the other day." He clutched a branch of the tree above her head and leaned against it, shielding his eyes from her direct gaze.

Sierra walked around to stand face-to-face with him. Then, remembering her manners, she genuflected. "My king, I will tell you, on one condition. If you allow me to share the Good News with you first."

"What good news?"

"The gift of salvation through Jesus Christ is called the

Good News, your majesty. Jesus is the One I pray to, and He died for our salvation. That is what I want to share with you."

"The reason why you prayed for the fainted man, you mean?"

Under the sharpness of his gaze, she somehow kept her poise and gave a slight nod. "Yes." As he studied her, she prayed urgently. *Lord, please make him know that I want nothing from him. I only want to see him saved.*

Then a smile lit his eyes and curved his lips, sending butterflies aflutter in her belly. Confused, she ducked away, intent on fulfilling the reason for her mission—sharing the Gospel.

As she bent to pick up her hoe and resume her work, a hand touched hers, and she spun. Kind eyes, softer than she'd ever seen them look at anyone else here looked back at her. She swallowed hard at the sincerity, the openness—and the unhidden admiration—staring back at her. "I will accept to listen to your Good News, daily even, if you will allow me to get to know you more…Sierra."

Maybe it was the way he said her name, almost like a gentle whisper of an unspoken firm promise, that led her to nod. "My king, I accept."

"Where can I learn more about the…Good News…for myself?" the king asked.

"There is a store in central Spain where your servants can buy you a book called the Bible. It is Holy Scripture, and as you read the New Testament, it tells you everything about Jesus Christ our Lord who came and died for our sins so that, through His death and resurrection, we might gain eternal life."

"Can I learn all about that in six months?" He crossed his arms, chin high, one foot tapping the cobblestone beneath it.

Was that a challenge? She was up to it. But…what was it

about six months' time...? Oh, he would marry the lady-in-waiting then. "Yes, you can learn it by then, my king. I will do my best to teach you all that I know before then." Of course, by then, the butterflies in her belly should've disappeared too.

He drew close, and the lavender scent from him again contrasted with her sweaty clothing. "I'll be here around noon every day, or as often as I can, to discuss with you." His gaze dropped to her lips again, and color filled his cheeks. "And hopefully, soon enough, I will hear your own story, Sierra."

"I will be here, your majesty." And she knew, with a smile, that this was the beginning—of something good and pure and special even if she couldn't call it love. No. She wouldn't dare think that far.

After all, what king would leave a princess to marry a slave?

Soon after he left, a servant of the king brought her three roses, some chocolate, and a bottle of wine, setting it among her workbasket.

She frowned. "Wait, are these for the king?" She pointed toward the gate. "He just left."

The servant shook her head. "No, milady. He sent these to you. To request your kind presence at his palace lunchroom tomorrow for one hour since it's Sunday and he will be busy with meetings and won't be in the garden. Your master has been informed of your coming absence. He says he'd see you there at noon for the...talk?" The female servant gawked at her, not knowing the talk meant the discussion of Scripture.

"Please tell the king I will be there tomorrow with a friend named Chimera."

The girl nodded and left. And all Sierra could do was stare at her back. Then a chuckle slipped through her lips and turned into a wide smile. *Thank You, Jesus.*

~

Present Day...

Six months was too long to seek an answer from one elusive woman. But first, he had to attend to the general of his army. "Why are you here?" His majesty, King Peralta of Lanzarote, adjusted his golden crown as he crossed the arched doorway and stood at the curve of his expansive balcony in Arrecife, the capital.

Under the full moonlight, he surveyed his kingdom, originally named *Tyterogaka*, with pride. His heart bonded itself with love for his people, yet settled heavy with the news he just received—news not nearly as personally troubling as the choice he had to make for his life.

Could he do what was necessary? If the worst happened on all fronts, was Africa close enough a sanctuary to flee to—or far enough from his potential pursuers—if he bucked the traditions upheld by preceding kings? Should he proceed with the arranged ceremony or not?

No king in one hundred years to date had rejected a lady-in-waiting as a bride. Once chosen by the council, she was guaranteed her place as queen. Usually, she was handpicked from a series of princess candidates and well vetted, so there was never a need to doubt her perfect status as a fitting candidate for queen.

Until now.

Until something changed, and now, his heart was speaking a very different language, a language far from tradition. No, if... if he followed his heart and the consequences ensued, he would travel up north, way up north—and cross The Gorge—the same gorge none in his kingdom had ever safely crossed.

But if he and his would-be queen made it across, that natural barrier would keep them safe—unless The Hunter was just as good.

King Peralta swallowed and shook his head before he realized it. No, he wouldn't think that far yet. He had to focus on right now. And this moment and the potential threat to his kingdom.

"Your majesty, we're hearing a rumor of an impending invasion from a foreign power." His army commander's voice drew him back, and he paused under a twined archway with spring lilies and hibiscus roped around its curve above in beauty—just as beautiful as the lady he'd charged with tending them. She was as perfect as they were, but not in the eyes of everyone else. And tonight was going to be the night to choose between the lady-in-waiting and her, except he wasn't ready to make a life-altering decision.

His gaze settled on the full-bearded warrior beside him. Commander Henry was as ruthless during war times as he was peaceable at home. When he'd fought beside him in the skirmish between Lanzarote and Tenerife two winters ago—a skirmish that lasted for three days and was resolved in mere minutes after both sides decided they'd lost enough men, then signed a peace treaty—one would never equate the Henry on the battlefield with the gentle man facing him now. But a worried frown creased his commander's brow. Hmmm, that wasn't good.

"Are you listening to me, your majesty?"

As the man's keen eyes searched King Peralta's face, Peralta knew he had to maintain focus to keep his private... matter...private, for the few hours remaining before dawn, before his engagement and wedding on the eve of his thirtieth birthday by law, to a woman he didn't love or want to marry.

Technically, he had twenty-four hours, including the full day of his birthday, but when this was planned one year ago, he chose to go with tradition and fulfil the law the day before. But not like this, and not to the person chosen for him without his input. Resistance lodged a lump in his throat, but again, he had to keep his mind on the current trouble. "I am. Continue, Henry."

A slight pause followed behind short and curly black hair that fell over gray eyes and shielded pensive thoughts from perusal, before ever-intuitive Henry resumed speaking. Henry clearly knew he was distracted, but King Peralta wasn't ready to discuss his matter yet. "They have conquered the other islands and could be headed to Tenerife. And soon, they'll reach Lanzarote. How shall we fight?"

Giving a curt nod, he resumed walking, in the hope of hiding his countenance from his most loyal subject. King Peralta liked how easily his citizens conversed in English, even when in his presence, especially those who knew his love for the English language. Had his father, the late king, not ventured to send him to Britain for more education, he would have missed an opportunity to observe the world. Thanks to that experience, he viewed the world differently, knowing that so much beyond Lanzarote awaited discovery—his discovery. "Do you have any proof of a threat? Any at all?"

"No..." Henry drew out the word thoughtfully. "Not one. That's why we're on alert but have done nothing else. We sent men out to investigate. But they could be a long time in coming back."

King Peralta's head dipped with a nod. Then he walked out

of the palace toward the garden with Henry following. "Good. Then let me know what else you find out. Send the palace guards to the ramparts to keep watch. Make sure our outer territories and ships' crews are alerted. And keep all of our men armed. I will speak with you again when you have more information."

"I will do so, your majesty." Another nod followed, and Commander Henry parted ways as King Peralta emerged at the entrance to his garden and Henry made a left turn toward the palace gate.

Once he was finally alone with his thoughts, King Peralta's lips curved with a smile as his stride slowed. The roses planted earlier had bloomed. An orchard stood at the center of the garden, and he was surrounded by a guava fruit tree, a large mango tree, and a pawpaw tree. At his request, in the last year, some benches lined the garden's edges to give the workers a place to sit and rest. Since a man collapsed while working here, he made sure it would never happen again.

But that wasn't why this place was so special.

This garden was where he'd learned about Jesus—and fallen secretly in love with the garden's overseer, a woman of great depth of insight. Sierra. Her name teased his thoughts.

He plucked a rose, smelled it, and inhaled its fresh aroma, shutting his eyes briefly. As lights from lanterns set on flat stones around the garden and blown with the wind danced with the night's shadows on the wall, a sigh escaped his lips. "Oh, my heart. Why did you fall in love?"

It would have been easier to go through tomorrow's ceremony if only his heart was not in love with anyone. It wasn't so with his parents, the late king and queen. His dad explained how he'd grown to love Peralta's mom after their marriage. But

Peralta hadn't wanted that. He'd wished for a choice to love, but knowing the law and customary expectations and the excitement that followed the process of choosing a bride, he couldn't bring himself to go against it without a reason—and for the love of his people. He didn't love anyone at the time and saw no reason to fight a law that wasn't against him. Except that, now, it was.

"My king."

At the feminine voice behind him, King Peralta whisked around. His shoulders slacked—a diminutive girl in black cotton curtseyed. The servant he'd assigned to attend to the lady-in-waiting blended to the dim light. "Simona? Is everything all right?"

Maybe his bride-to-be had changed her mind about the marriage? He swallowed as the slim figure shifted on her feet. Servants in the female quarters rarely came into his presence so that was likely the source of her discomfort.

"Milady asked for me to find out from you the color you prefer for the flowers in the new royal bedroom after the marriage ceremony."

King Peralta struggled to hide his disappointment. "Thank you, Simona. I will leave that choice to her judgement." He wasn't going to select flowers for a wedding he wasn't sure would happen if he listened to his heart.

Simona dipped her chin. "Milady says that, if you say this, then she will come to meet you tomorrow morning to be sure of your choices."

In other words, she'd noticed how he'd left too many decisions about the wedding to her and might be worried his heart wasn't in it.

It wasn't. But could he tell her so? *Now?* Will revealing how he felt about another woman cancel the marriage? Will she accept to walk away? Will *he* accept the possible life-altering legal consequences?

Too many questions to answer in one night. He swallowed. "That's fine. If so, I'll see her in the morning." He still couldn't refer to her yet as his lady, with the current state of his heart. "Thank you, Simona. Please, excuse me."

She bowed then scurried away, her hurried steps slapping a hollow echo against the paving stones.

A palace guard who must've trailed him at a distance from the palace drew near and, stilling her pace, escorted her away. As the echo faded, another guard showed up and stood with a sheathed dagger hanging off the side of his wine-red palace-guard uniform.

When the guard bowed, King Peralta acknowledged him with a nod, then spun and moved inward. The dual spiral garden beckoned him, its sweet fragrances wafting over from hibiscus flowers dancing on sturdy branches. He could sense every conversation he'd had here with Sierra, and every Scripture she taught him here was etched in his memory. Her smile and her laughter chased away every worry he came here with. He could step his shoes into the same place where she stood to pray before starting her work daily under the mango tree's shade, and all over this garden, her imprint of excellence remained.

A lion statue crowned the center, surrounded by a rectangular moat filled with water and bordered by red brick stones. She had stood here yesterday when he'd finally admitted his feelings for her, though he was sure she knew from her first day. Her reaction had stunned him. But desperate to be clear about her response, he'd sent Ache for her. Maybe, just maybe, speaking with her one more time would clear his mind and lead him to decide.

He could get taken in by the beauty around him—and the beauty of its keeper. But his heart grew heavy as he reached a decision. No matter what the law said, he couldn't marry a woman he didn't love when the one he loved was alive. But… could he face the grave consequences of such a choice, based on Lanzarote's custom?

∼

3

"But you are a chosen generation, a royal priesthood, a holy nation..." 1 Peter 2:9

∽

THE LADY-IN-WAITING'S REQUEST FOR A MORNING MEETING worsened the tough decision awaiting King Peralta. That shattered the little focus he'd had, bringing him face-to-face with the other side of the matter.

He felt too emotionally uncertain to come face-to-face with her now. If only he saw his beautiful Sierra...but Sierra had shooed his advances away and said he was not to speak with her about it again, citing their class differences—he, a king and she, lower than a servant. He knew what she meant. Any move by him could put them both in danger. But he had to marry someone tomorrow or lose his throne. If it wasn't the lady-in-waiting whom he didn't love, and it wasn't Sierra whom he couldn't marry, then who would it be?

He rubbed his neck, and the golden crown tilted slightly, so he righted it and made another round, pacing the garden while the palace guard trailed him. Three times, he'd strode in it to see if he could think his way through this. But, if the hourglass, which his nighttime servant had turned one more time at his request before leaving the palace was any indication, he was running out of time.

He sat on the stone-carved chair he'd occupied several times in the garden, but it didn't yield its usual comfort. Instead, it felt like sitting between a rock and a hard decision.

How long he sat there thinking, pondering, and waiting for some illuminating insight before a frog croak jerked his attention back to the present, he had no idea.

He swallowed, gripped the edge of the leather-skin-covered stone chair, and heaved a sigh. He might not know how Sierra would react, but he had to take a chance and make sure she knew how *he* felt. If he would do this, it had to be done now. No more delay. With that thought, he rose and navigated the garden, climbed the cobbled steps and returned to the palace.

∽

As soon as he reached his inner court, King Peralta swung aside his royal regalia, which was starting to slip down his shoulder, back upward. Then he turned. "Get me some water to drink, son. Then go to sleep."

Esposito, his night servant, a son to a member of the royal court, bowed, then walked away. King Peralta strode to the inner balcony surrounding the court and placed a hand on its cold marble. He glanced outside where the moon's tilted brilliance announced that the day he hoped not to need to face had come. Dawn closely approached now. His shoulders slacked, and he gripped the marble tighter, ignoring its dew-slickened dampness.

According to their law, he had to marry today or abdicate the throne tomorrow as the throne needed an heir after him.

But there was the snag—again.

With the law stipulating he had to marry the chosen lady, and with the said woman present in the palace grounds and likely sleeping in the reserved quarters, opposite the female servants, this may not go over so smoothly. The lady-in-waiting, possessing a fair beauty to inspire legends, displayed a keen intelligence.

She just wasn't his Sierra. How could he serve her such disappointing news of heartbreak when she had since been briefed on the royal etiquette and matters of the kingdom which she'd be in charge of? As it was, she was well on her way.

On her way to becoming *his* queen.

But what other choice did he have if he jilted her? Pain circulated around his chest at the thought of marrying a lady he did not love, and he could not imagine living the rest of his life with her by his side. He hated to think of living aloof and not committing his whole heart to her. He shook his head. If Sierra's Jesus—whom she'd led him to believe in—were standing next to him, He would not approve of such a lifetime of deception. King Peralta was sure of it.

He clasped his head in his hands. "Oh, Sierra!" The mention of her name tasted like sweet nectar. Shouldn't he be thinking of the lady he was about to marry? But his heart wouldn't let him. Sierra's oval face, square jaw, and long, dark, waist-length hair, usually hidden in a bun, filled his vision. Her smile was so bright it always sent his heart racing. It would usually glow behind the sweat beading her forehead due to her labor for his garden, under her master's hard hand. Her washed-out apron and muddied feet could not compare to the knowledge and wisdom hidden behind those hazelnut eyes. Earlier this year, he had offered to buy her from her master, but the man had flatly refused, saying she was his best hand-woman. Which was the biggest hurdle he faced. He couldn't marry Sierra by Lanzarote's law.

Because Sierra was a slave.

And her master's family were the keepers of the palace grounds, and the man's daughter was the lady-in-waiting.

King Peralta lowered his gaze and pressed his lips tightly. Why, oh why, were their worlds so far apart? Hard as he tried, bridging that divide, while remaining king, was impossible.

Yes, it was.

But their hearts had been intertwined so long that forgetting her was a mere wish. He lived for Sierra. For her smile. For the delight of her laughter…

He closed his eyes as a sweet memory flooded his mind.

His arms encircled her slender waist under the mango tree. But she brushed them away playfully, darting her gaze this way and that. Then she scowled, and it only made her high cheekbones more beautiful. "Your majesty, you shouldn't. If someone sees you too close to me, it could spark rumors."

He touched a hem of her skirt and toyed with the mud-stained lace. "If only you knew how much I want the whole world to see us. I want your heart, Sierra. All of it."

Sierra settled her hoe to a curve in the tree's base. "My king, I wish that was possible. But you know the law. I won't let you be hurt or ridiculed for my sake. So, I suggest you discount any ideas about us you might have." She shook her dark waves. "And you best not stare at me while I work either. Your kind heart keeps justice enforced in your kingdom, and we are grateful for you. You have to remain king. Our king. *That* is my priority."

Her words flew past his ear as his heart grew even more loving toward this woman who put his interests, and that of the kingdom, above her own. He extended her a bag containing some gowns wrapped into a roll and two changes of shoes, all covered with a scanty-looking, worn, feathered hat on top as a disguise. "Here. At least, allow me to clothe you in something better. I don't mind what you are wearing, but these would fare better on you. I could easily give you much better clothes than these, but they would raise eyebrows. Like you said, I can't take steps that would start rumors just yet. For now."

After a slight pause, she accepted them. "Your majesty, you didn't have to." Her gaze met his, and she bit her lower lip, a move that sent his heart into a flutter.

"Accept it as my thank you for the Scriptures you make time to share with me regularly."

"What do I tell my master about these gifts as he's sure to ask where these are from?"

He smiled. "Tell him they are my reward to you for saving a man's life. Because it's that too. I'd meant to reward you that week we met, but I realized my heart wanted more. Then I delayed and here we are." He took one step toward the gate then stopped. "Oh. But don't tell him about the bag of gold hidden in the pocket of one of the dresses. It's for you. Do with it whatever you like. He shouldn't take that from you. *That* is my real gift."

A gasp escaped her soft lips. Then she blinked. But before she could refuse or argue, he spun and, with a satisfied grin, exited the garden. The next time he saw Sierra was the following day as he rode his stallion in the garden and pretended to almost fall at a gallop while she worked those plants to beauty with lithe fingers. She'd gasped at his near-fall then raced to his side, buying them some time to talk privately. And his heart warmed at the sight of one of the gifted dresses on her. She looked as beautiful, as he knew she would, clad in the rose-flowered long gown with elbow-length cuffs.

He'd then guided the horse and led her outside the main garden, only to still when he found a pleasant surprise. Beyond the rose bushes, Sierra was growing a small vegetable garden for him behind the palace. It was close to the keeper's land, the fields where Sierra served on before coming to work in the palace garden. Her fingers grazed the ears of wheat on the keeper's field as though they, too, deserved to be loved.

Shaken back to the present by the sight of those very vegetables, now grown and clustered near where he stood, he had two choices—neither of which he liked. Marry the lady-in-waiting or lose the throne. Marry Sierra—if she was willing to take the risk—and get killed by The Hunter. The Hunter was empowered by Lanzarote's law to kill a king who married a serving slave. He stroked his jaw. But...what if Sierra became an ex-slave?

Marrying an ex-slave would make him to only lose the throne. Could The Hunter, whoever he was, be convinced to leave them be, if so? But the keeper of the grounds still would not release her to him, even as a slave.

Worse still, The Hunter had a hidden identity. No one knew who The Hunter was. In fact, if The Hunter had a clue of how much he loved Sierra, he would've slain him already—and the law would be on his side.

But, then, what would he do now? He could offer the keeper a reward for Sierra he can't refuse....

With his back to the door, he heard it open a crack and stiffened. How had the night servant returned when he was supposed to be gone? But as he spun fully and saw who stood there, he blinked, and his heart thudded in response.

She made it.

"Sierra? How did you...? You could be in trouble." He had expected her to reply to Ache, but the man must have let her come to him instead, which was even better than a written response. He'd only needed a word from her. Instead, he received the gift of her presence. *Thank You, God.* He moved to shield her with part of his royal garb, hiding her behind a draping purple curtain drawn together and running floor to ceiling. Her eyes glowed and his heart sank.

He knew. Something had to be wrong.

"Sierra?" he prodded, tipping her chin slightly.

He let his hand drop when she said nothing, then strode over to partly close the door to the inner court, asking his guard to stand outside it. Checking again to ensure they were alone, then wondering whether that was even a good idea at this time of the night before a wedding, he returned to her, using his arm to block the light from revealing her face. He tried to ignore how her nearness troubled his insides and made his heart beat rapidly, but he had to know how she made it out of the keeper's house.

∼

4

"For the Lord of Hosts will visit His flock, the house of Judah, and will make them as His royal horse in battle." Zechariah 10:3

∽

HE RESTRAINED HIMSELF FROM STANDING TOO CLOSE THIS TIME and scarcely resisted using a finger to tuck the stray dark lock behind her ear. Her breath came in quickly like she panted as she dipped her sweeping lashes. He felt his brows narrow.

Clearly, she'd been running. But did she run all the way to the palace—a very great distance from her master's dwelling—roughly ten miles from here by road? Or did she ride on a horse with Ache? As she lifted her gaze to his, her tears welled, glazing hazelnut eyes, and she gulped. His concern and love for her grew.

Sierra ventured a hand out tentatively. He stared at the slender fingers as though they reached for his heart instead, and it took only a moment before he received it, to bridge the gap between him and her, between royalty and slavery.

The calluses on her palm felt rough to his smooth one, and his heart turned inside him. He would wipe away her suffering if he could, but that choice was stolen from him by the law, a law which, if he contested now and his connection to Sierra was later discovered, would backfire greatly and surely raise eyebrows from members of the royal court who sought such occasion against previous kings. And here he was, being stopped at every turn. Was there a way out of this predicament, or should they give it up?

When she gulped again and drew his gaze downward, it brought his attention back to the elegant beauty camouflaged as a slave before him. "I–I have to know, your majesty," she breathed. Her brown eyes searched his face. As her hazelnut depths bore into his, he wondered, no matter what, *how* could he not love her? He couldn't. She was beautiful inside and out. She brought out the gentleness in him and made him yearn for the confidence she had in her Lord Jesus.

Although not born a slave, she was forced into servitude. And no one in the palace knew this, but him and her. She had confided in him almost one week ago, adding to his frustration with this situation. Even though he'd sought to know for six months, she shared the Word of God with him instead, stating it was more important than her status. But, last week, he'd refused to let her leave the garden. Then she revealed it all, leading to his present anguish of heart.

Sierra had told him that she was a captured missionary, along with thirteen others, long after she'd shared the Gospel with him and with a shaky voice. He hardly believed how she didn't say a word about her forced captivity for six months since meeting him, six months during which his garden strolls became the best part of his day because Sierra was in it.

Weeks of more conversation followed before he asked again about her prayers for the sick man. Then she shared even more about her faith. As he searched to know about Jesus, he discussed Him during his few minutes of privacy daily. Years ago, his search for truth had taken him northward, and having found nothing to quell the deep desire in his soul, he'd returned for his coronation when his father died.

Then Sierra came into his palace, into his life, and everything changed. Her beauty had drawn him, and her wisdom had kept him listening. When she'd dared to share Jesus for the first time on his daily trip to the outer gardens, he'd been stunned. First, by the boldness of this slave, and secondly, by the urgency of her words and how they seemed to start meeting the hunger in his heart. A hunger he'd assumed would never be quenched.

King Peralta had wished to challenge her tale of a virgin birth but had been too intrigued by the story. So, his curiosity had won. Then, as he listened to her narrate how Jesus of Nazareth was born and how he worked so many miracles, then died to save the world from sin, it rang true to him. He had no proof of her truth, but its realness reached deep down in him. Which was fine. Except that it didn't fit into the custom of Lanzarote.

He was a king over subjects who were ruled. The law was supreme in Lanzarote, and every member of the royal court would fight against his eliminating slavery. He would lose before he began. His culture stood against a society where everyone was equal. Such a concept was a threat to his kingdom and to his throne.

He could die.

So, he balked at part of her faithful words and stayed away from her as he sent a messenger to Spain to purchase a Bible. Upon his servant's return, he studied the New Testament and drew his own conclusions, seeing Sierra hadn't lied about anything.

So, a long while later, he returned to her side for more. Then they'd journeyed in words of faith until she'd led him to a remarkable place where his heart was ready to accept her Gospel of Jesus if she asked him to do so once more.

Her grip on his arm now drew him back. Seeing the crease in her smile, he studied her face again. "You want to know what, Sierra?"

"I want to know," she smiled a little shyly and bowed slightly, although her warm smile conflicted with their present scenario, "whether you choose to accept Jesus as your Lord and Savior, my king."

He contemplated her question. He'd thought she was thinking of what he was thinking, but apparently, her mind was somewhere else. Maybe he could push her on her refusal of him a little later... Relaxing, he equally smiled. "And I want to know, milady, if you accept my regard for you." He shook his head. "A no will not suffice for this waiting and hopeful heart."

She studied him beneath long lashes. Then her shoulders slacked. "I can't say, I mean...yes. How we feel about each other is not the problem. You know Lanzarote law. You know what will happen if..."

"Don't worry about what might lay ahead. Do you accept?" He had to know. If he was going to put everything at stake for the sake of his love for her, shouldn't he know if she accepted him?

Silence followed while she toyed with the knot of the flowing brown scarf looped off her neck and resting on her hip. His slight shake of his head had paused her words. At length, she replied, "Yes. I gladly accept your regard for me, my king."

Joy soared through him.

"But," the softness of her whisper rushed on, "your faith is a more urgent matter, your majesty." Her shoulders dropped further, and she exhaled, pressing a hand to her chest. "It matters most to me."

Elation raced through him as he faced the balcony with his back toward her. He clasped his hands together, a smile easing his worries. One major victory was his. He exhaled slowly.

She had accepted him. She knew he was scheduled to marry someone within a day, or more like today if the day had dawned. It took a lot of courage for her to utter those words.

Which led him to make up his own mind about her request. "My acceptance of Jesus will come at a cost."

He strode to his throne, eased his crown down on it, and spun. Then, returning to her, he pressed a hand to his chest. "Sierra, the cost for me will be unimaginable. Following Jesus means I will change the status of people, remove slavery, and possibly lose the throne or lose my life for that alone. This will be my greatest risk. Everyone will say I did this because I...I love you." He finally said the words his heart had long spoken for months now—to the right person—and he didn't care too much what the next minute brought. He would handle things as they came.

When Sierra sucked in her breath and color filled her cheeks, he enfolded her slender fingers in his, savoring the tenderness of her response as he held her gaze. "Do not fear, my love. I will find a way for us through this."

She hesitated as though still in shock, but then, gave a slow nod. "God will make a way for us. I know, my king. I mean, I know what stands at stake." So, she wasn't responding to his declaration of love yet.

He warmed inwardly. She was tough and a smart lady, but she had to know he loved her all this time.

He was sure of it. "Sierra..."

"My king." She shifted on her feet. "But would you rather know the truth about Jesus' sacrifice on the Cross for you and me, and then pretend it doesn't exist, so you can continue as you are?" A quick shake of her head sent more dark hair sweeping over her shoulder.

Suddenly, he imagined her wearing something royal, not the cotton clothes of servitude now obscuring her. She would be even more beautiful, and color heated his cheeks. But she pressed his hand encircling hers, and he looked into the hazelnut depths again.

Urgency filled her voice as she glanced toward the door, surely worried about someone walking in on them and what they might think. He wondered how she left her master's residence before daylight and without offering a reason to the keeper.

But Sierra was still speaking. "Remember, the apostles who died, and mostly, not at their preferred day or time. It was their sacrifice. And Jesus died for us all to begin with. That was His sacrifice. We all face a fight where our faith is proven. But we are winners through Christ." She sighed, her slim shoulders sinking beneath stiff cotton. "No one ever prays to get saved and face a fight soonest, but every case is different. Still, it is a choice you are not exempt from making. I know these things are not perfect, and I respect you as my king...but your eternal life is worth more than your throne, your majesty."

Fully convicted in his heart, he knew it was time. He paced back and forth, but there was little chance he would prevent the consequences from following his choice. Like a cascade of tipped dominos, once it started with one choice leading to the next and to the next, everything toppled.

So, he paused in front of her and took her hand again. "Sierra, I will accept Jesus now." He squared his shoulders. "And I will also accept whatever consequences might follow."

She inhaled sharply, beaming, and hope lit up her eyes as she clasped his other hand and led him in a quick prayer of salvation. "Dear Heavenly Father, I come to You in the name of Jesus, just as I am. I recognize that I am a sinner, I cannot save myself, and that I need Your salvation. Therefore, today, I choose to accept Jesus as my personal Lord and Savior. I believe Jesus died for me and shed His blood to cleanse me from sin. I repent of my sins, and I declare that from this day henceforth, I will follow Jesus forever. I am born again, and I receive Your gift of eternal life through Christ in Jesus' name. Amen." He repeated the words she said, sure of the impact they would have after his declaration and convinced that transformation had taken place inside him. Instant peace filled his soul, satiating the aching hunger there. His search had met his answer.

As she lifted her head, and they opened their happy, tear-filled eyes, she released one hand and pressed his other hand gently. "It is done. You are a Christian now, my king. And my brother in Christ. Congratulations," she added the last ever so softly.

"Thank you." If only he could wipe away the crease of worry still lining her forehead! Sierra nodded, and some tendrils of dark hair bounced over her shoulder, leading his heart to start a dance of its own. "I will do everything to protect you from harm."

"But I have another question, your majesty." Her sweeping lashes lowering, she withdrew her hand.

"Okay." He frowned, staring at his empty hand, regretting the loss of her touch. "I'm listening."

"Do you love her? The lady you are about to marry?"

It took him longer to answer. He waited until she looked up before smiling. "I'm sure you already know the answer to your question."

Her cheeks bloomed a deep shade, more lovely than the flowers she'd tended. "So, will you go ahead with the marriage?"

"To her? No." He shook his head, returned to his throne, and set the crown atop his head again, feeling the weight of its responsibility even more. "But to you—"

A palace guard strode in, cutting off his words.

The door groaned wider open, and the quick tilt of Sierra's head told him someone else had followed the guard in and further interrupted an important moment for them. But her piercing gasp—and her instinctive steps toward him—made King Peralta turn sharply. When he saw who was standing there, the way she darted her gaze between him and Sierra, then frowned, King Peralta knew this was about to be the longest night of his life.

The lady-in-waiting and her brother had entered.

5

"What shall we say to these things? If God be for us, who can be against us?" Romans 8:31

∽

"Sierra, please step to my right," King Peralta instructed, and she did so.

The lady-in-waiting slid past him, her blue coat flowing over the intricate, smooth black-and-blue marble as she brushed past Sierra without acknowledging her, their clothing a clear contrast. She paused at an arm's length and studied his countenance. Then she turned to Sierra. Maybe to confirm her suspicions? Sierra simply stood unwavering, her confidence impressing him.

"What can I do for you?" He was supposed to address her as milady, but he couldn't link the term together, implying her as his when he had declared his love to Sierra moments earlier.

But he also didn't expect a head-on collision with the raw reality after making a decision for Jesus and expressing his love for Sierra.

And now, he feared the lady-in-waiting would call attention to the presence of a lady in the king's inner court a night before his wedding.

But she didn't.

She simply stopped between them. "I decided to come tonight instead of in the morning, so we can make this official." Another pause followed. "Before tomorrow night when we'll need to do it in front of everyone."

He glanced at her then at Sierra. He exhaled slowly, allowing the escaping breath to temper his frustration toward her. "What are you talking about?" Could she not speak plainly?

When she walked closer, Sierra trailed her and stopped a few steps behind her, crossing her arms. None of them acknowledged the presence of her accompaniment, the lady-in-waiting's brother standing at the door, watching. Feeling the man's eyes on him, King Peralta didn't turn.

Instead, he trailed the movement of the woman he now knew for certain he would disappoint by dawn. How could he get his bad news to her without a major calamity befalling him? She sunk into the large seat beside his throne, and when he turned, Sierra cast one glance at the lady-in-waiting, then faced him, staying rooted where she stood.

"I came to find out whether you love me before I marry you, my king. I want to hear the truth, your majesty." She pressed a hand to her temple then cast a glance to Sierra. "Sierra, what are you doing here? Are the flowers in the garden ruined or something?" Some despise laced her tone.

Her brother spoke up then. "Why are you not in your servant's quarters?" Anger sharpened *his* tone. "Father wouldn't let you out of the house at this time."

Then, as Sierra opened her mouth to speak beneath an ashen face, an idea occurred to King Peralta, so he cleared his throat. "She's here to ask for her freedom. And I'm willing to grant it to her."

"But," the brother began speaking, "she's..."

This man's word would serve as substitute for his father's. King Peralta raised a finger. "For a hefty price of gold. I will purchase her freedom from you and your family."

The man fell quiet, drawing closer from the door. His shoes clicked on the marble and stopped behind his sister. "For how much?"

Greed glinted in his eyes. Perhaps it would stay there until they completed their transaction.

"Enough gold."

Both men stared at each other. Knowing the man was trying to figure out his intentions, King Peralta allowed nothing to slip from the stoic gaze he returned.

For the first time, he prayed on his own to Jesus. For Him to make it possible to free Sierra. *If I'm going to lose something, let it be just my throne. Please, my Lord.*

Finally, the man inclined a slow nod, then smiled and rubbed his palms together. "Okay."

King Peralta exhaled inwardly, then beckoned one of his palace guards, whispered instructions in his ear, and the guard nodded and left. "Your gold is on its way and will be delivered to you in the outer room, after which you may depart. Now, please leave us to finalize the details of the...wedding."

Seeming pleased, the man smacked his lips, and Sierra's

brow curved. But pretending he didn't notice, King Peralta turned to the lady-in-waiting, who gave Sierra a full sweeping glance as though seeing her for the first time. "Well, I've never seen the king give such a...gracious...pardon before." Her brother had already left the room.

But King Peralta had to tell her the truth. Whatever happened, he would detain her as long as possible until her anger subsided before alerting her family—after the gold had been delivered and Sierra's freedom guaranteed—that he would not marry their daughter.

But she fixed her gaze more intently on Sierra. "You must be special."

Sierra held her gaze mutely, lashes winging up over guileless eyes, chin firm, not high and haughty but not cowering and subservient either.

"You were always the best of my father's servants, so I can see how the king would want your service." The lady-in-waiting spun to him again, some impatience in her voice this time. "Like I had asked, your majesty, before we marry, please, do you love me? It is important to me."

He waited to catch Sierra's slight nod behind the lady. "I am sorry, but I don't. At least, not in the way necessary for marriage. So I don't think it is right for us to marry. Things changed recently, and I worried about how to proceed. You are lovely, and I'm sure there are more than enough eligible bachelors in Lanzarote, one of whom would catch your fancy."

Silence, then tension burst from her. "You'll turn me away, on my wedding day?" She drew closer near the throne, fisting her hands at her sides, and gasped. "How dare you humiliate me so?"

"I did not humiliate you. I simply answered your question.

You were chosen for me. I didn't choose you. Nevertheless, I wouldn't turn you down without a strong reason." King Peralta rose and stormed even closer, her head beneath his jaw, and dared her with a steely gaze. "Remember who you are speaking to."

She lowered her gaze, took a few steps back, and bowed. "My apologies, my king. I forgot my manners." She wrapped her arms around herself. "It's just…" she threw Sierra a quick glance, "when you're about to marry a great king, you want to be excited about it, but you can't for a very simple reason."

He didn't say a thing. He simply listened as she drew her conclusions.

"He doesn't love you. And you know it. Then you hope love can develop along the way. But I'm guessing that's not what you want."

Again, King Peralta remained silent.

Suddenly, she spun to Sierra, then glanced at him, and her eyes widened. Her jaw slackened, and he saw her throat move as she swallowed. "Is she the reason?" A frown pinched her high, smooth forehead—a forehead others had claimed was born to wear a crown. "Do you love her, your majesty?"

The secret was out.

He might as well admit it. "Yes. And if I could, I will marry her." From the corner of his eye, he saw Sierra gulp, but she said nothing. He was thinking as he went along and had little time to work through the consequences of the truth. But he loved Sierra and knew she strongly felt something for him. That was enough for them to build on while they figured out the rest.

"That was why you bought her from my family. To make her an ex-slave and avoid you and her getting killed."

"Yes." As smart as she was reputed to be, she was catching on fast.

"But, if you marry her, you will lose your throne. And my father may contend that you freed her to marry her."

"What your father knows is fine. He is a gentleman and will honor this agreement."

"There is a problem." She fell quiet, then spoke with sad eyes. "I don't love you either, so I'm not too disappointed that we won't marry. In fact, I came here hoping you would drop the idea. I just didn't want it said that the king rejected me."

"And I will make sure no one thinks such."

"I'm also worried about my father for two things. He said he was in debt, and he gave up some shipping interests because of what he sought to gain from you after our marriage in order to settle his debts. Which he won't be able to do now."

"I see." King Peralta stroked the small beard on his jaw. So, he was really about to be used as a wealth mine? Well, now, that won't happen.

∼

6

"Therefore do not fear them. For there is nothing covered that will not be revealed, and hidden that will not be made known." Matthew 10:26

∾

Silence settled over the room.

"What else worries you?" he asked.

The lady-in-waiting glanced at Sierra. "A few weeks ago, I heard from a good source that you might love someone else. I didn't believe it—it sounded too risky. But your guard made me swear to carry his secret to the grave. Seeing her here tonight, and the way you looked at her..." She shook her head. "I could never marry a man who loved someone else, even if he is my king, your majesty."

King Peralta let his shoulders drop, his cloak, as royally purple as the silver floor-to-ceiling curtains covering the wall behind his throne, sweeping lower over the tiles. Someone else knew his secret? Ache, the guard assigned to walk with him in the garden, might've suspected something. But he'd hoped the man would keep his confidence and tell no one. But then Ache must be the one who told the one person least likely to appreciate the news.

"I thought about it for some time, finding it hard having to choose whether to go on with the wedding or..." She swallowed hard once more while wrapping shaking arms tight around her middle. "To do otherwise, which would endanger you when people asked why. Coming here tonight to see you was tough, but I had to ask you for myself. I had to be sure. And now that I am, I don't know which is worse."

A gasp echoed from Sierra, but he maintained his calm. "So what did you choose, lady-in-waiting?"

"This is the toughest choice I'll ever make." Loosening her hold on herself, she pressed a hand to her chest. "I feel hurt, and I'm not sure what I would've done had I not had a hint about this before today." She looked at one then the other.

"I can assure you none of this was planned. I professed my love to Sierra moments before you entered, so I did not plan to disappoint you."

The lady-in-waiting was accomplished in Lanzarote law, as she'd mentioned to him before now, so she was aware of her rights and what damage would follow any revelation of what she now knew to be true about whom he loved and could potentially marry.

She rose, paced in front of him, and then, about a minute later, halted across from him after darting a glance to Sierra. "I hate to end up unmarried for years to come because I was scorned," she sighed, "but heavens forbid that I would ever stand in the way of true love."

King Peralta's worry climbed down a notch, but she still hadn't expressed what she *will* do, and that could be just as damaging. "And?" he pressed. His throne, his legacy—despite having grown the wealth of his subjects and alleviated the suffering of slave labor before he met Sierra—were on the line. Everything his fathers, previous kings of Lanzarote, did might be lost if things went wrong here.

Her shoulders slackened, her responsibility in the moment not lost on him. Had he loved her, she would have made a good queen. Her poise, despite the bad news, spoke of a woman who carried herself well and made good choices. She pushed back the golden frills on the sleeves of her fine, long, turquoise gown. "I won't inform my father until the wedding day passes." She spoke with finality.

"Thank you." Sierra rushed over then hugged her, and both ladies stayed embraced.

When they parted, the lady-in-waiting spoke to him again. "Still, it's the law for you to marry by your thirtieth birthday, so there has to be a wedding, whether you're ready or not." She eyed Sierra. "But I won't be your bride as chosen."

A shrug followed. "Royal history tells me that, occasionally, previous queens have married kings who didn't love them." She shook her head and gripped the armrest of his throne, her eyes boring into his with resolve. "But I cannot marry a king who loves someone else. You love Sierra with all your heart. I can see how much you both love each other just by the risk you took sharing this news in my presence, risking everything you are, including your life. And slicing myself in-between you two is a misery I will not put myself through, especially for a lifetime commitment."

Although sure he heard a sob escape Sierra's lips, he kept his gaze on the lady-in-waiting. He had to acknowledge the risk and embarrassment she took for his and Sierra's sakes. "Thank you." Expressing his gratitude, he clasped her hand resting inches from his. Then he released it, and she stepped away, standing aside with Sierra.

At her nod, he asked again, "What are we going to do now? Since I can't marry you." He spun toward Sierra, hating the suffering he'd surely put her through if he proposed. "And I can't marry the lady I love." He reached out a hand toward Sierra and felt his heart beckoning her even closer, now revealing to her for the first time in the presence of another the fullness of how he felt.

Her lush dark lashes dipped as she pressed one hand to still her trembling lips. A bruise, likely from yard work reddened the back of her hand, and he wished to kiss it and take her pain away. "O, my king." Her other hand settling on her heart, she whispered, "my love."

Those words soared with wings into his heart and matched his heartbeat toward her. He could sit no more, so he rose, climbed down the steps, and left his crown on his throne. He curled his fingers around her neck and drew in her earthy scent. How could she feel so earthy and so royal all at once? His heart traveled further in its love for Sierra, and he made up his mind.

He will marry Sierra, today, unfailingly. Sierra will be his queen, come what may.

With his mind fully made up, he embraced her. Ignoring the lady-in-waiting, who observed at a distance, he wrapped his arms around Sierra's slender waist and wished he could have it all. He wished to keep her safe, marry her, and retain his kingdom.

But those three could not coexist.

He would be forced to yield something, and he made up his mind—it wouldn't be Sierra. He leaned away from her, loosely holding her and wiping a lone tear from her sun-kissed cheeks. "I love you too much. I won't lose you," he croaked out.

"No. No, your majesty." She gulped, unshed tears filling her eyes as she gripped his royal robe, so far from her humble gown. "You can't lose your throne. You risk too much. I want you to stay safe, my king. Knowing you love me indeed is enough to last me a lifetime."

"No, Sierra. What is the use of loving you if I cannot have you?" He shook his head, and his hand clenched around her waist then relaxed. "I choose to love you. The risk is worth the reward. You are more valuable to me than things. Everything is replaceable. You are not. Please." He searched her face until her smile of acceptance settled his heart.

Sierra leaned her head on his chest, and he pressed it closer protectively. As long as he lived, he wouldn't allow anyone to hurt or denigrate her because she was a commoner. "So, what do we do now?" she asked.

"Well, you cannot risk The Hunter finding out. He will kill you. That is his job if you deviate from the written law," the lady-in-waiting reminded him.

"I have an idea," someone said, and they all jerked their eyes behind the king's throne. A guard emerged from the shadows of the silver silk sliding curtains which, blending with his uniform, must've hidden him. How long had he been there? Apparently, long enough.

King Peralta swung Sierra to his other side as the man placed a hand on the sword hilt.

While their gazes met and held, King Peralta's frown deepened. Was the guard about to "help" The Hunter finish him off? "An idea about what?"

Sierra squeezed his hand and edged out from behind him. "My king, don't fear. He is for us."

King Peralta felt his brows curve. "How?"

She stepped forward with her shoulders squared and her head held high. Without these humble clothes, no one could ever mistake Sierra for a slave. No one. A certain dignity declared her royalty. Her intelligence for matters of state the times when they had chatted in the garden were at par with those of his top advisors. Besides, thanks to Scripture, he knew she was royalty in Christ. "I witnessed to Ache as soon as we arrived and were taken by the keeper to be his servants. Ache is saved."

King Peralta glanced at him with a querying brow. "Ache?"

"She is saying the truth." The man—tall, bald, broad-shouldered, and sharp-eyed—offered a curt nod. "I am a Christian."

Ache darted a glance to the lady-in-waiting. "I shared with her that your heart was with another in case she saw that as a deal breaker. Usually, we allow the ladies-in-waiting to choose to remain in such cases, which most do, even if the king doesn't love them. It has been done in the past to prevent division in the kingdom. This time, she chose wisely from what I've heard her say here tonight." He glanced at Sierra. "But there are consequences."

Silence enveloped the room once more.

"Consequences I can help you escape." Ache paused and

clenched his jaw. "I am loyal to you, King Peralta, and won't allow you to be killed or overthrown."

Those were the most faithful words he'd heard from anyone. "What do you have in mind? Tell me the truth, your truth, and I won't be offended if it hurts." Giving a slight nod, King Peralta edged Sierra closer, as though having her closer to him ensured she was safe while they talked. After all, the events tonight had started with just the two of them, and as the audience grew, he felt a need to guard her personally.

"But I love Lanzarote, our people, and won't allow it to be without its rightful king."

"What do you propose?" The lady-in-waiting stepped forward, the soft rustle of her gown adding a layer of urgency to her words.

"King Peralta, you have to marry Sierra. Today. To keep the requirement by law. And in private, due to your circumstance, and I can arrange for that." Ache spun to Sierra. "I know you were not a slave, but a missionary forced into slavery. The keeper, her father," he tipped his head toward the lady-in-waiting, "is going to insist that you are a slave and that the king freed you to marry you, and he will try to kill the king."

He clasped her shoulder. "But, as the one man charged with protecting the king at all costs, I owe it to you both to ensure you are safe." His gaze crossed their faces, giving King Peralta a measure of assurance. "I will command my most trusted men to put things in motion for the marriage. The real marriage will happen while the gathering at the palace waits for the public wedding with the lady-in-waiting, which won't happen. You leave soon after the wedding. But there will only be one cause of delay, and according to our laws, that, I cannot waive."

"What would that be?" King Peralta sat up, clenching the arms of his throne.

"You will perform every ceremony to make Sierra your queen. That includes the consummation of marriage ceremony in the lower chambers, and we will wait for as long as it takes."

He hadn't thought of that requirement as he'd assumed, before now, that he would be marrying someone he didn't love. Now things had changed. "Oh." His cheeks warmed, but he couldn't care less about who saw his reaction as Sierra stiffened then relaxed against him. Surely, she, just like himself, would have preferred to take things slow, much slower than this. Having no choice, she handled the pressure well. "Okay."

Ache's throat bobbed. "After that, if we see that The Hunter is coming, you leave Lanzarote, you and your queen—until he gives up. Or never to return."

A hush fell over the room.

Ache resumed speaking, his voice deepening as though understanding the gravity of his words. "As a principal guard, I know a secret path for you to escape in an emergency to save the kingdom. And a secret escape ship is hidden, stocked with men and supplies all year round."

King Peralta exhaled and returned to the throne, the plan bringing some order and a certain level of morbid realization to his soul—he was leaving. Fleeing. "Yes, I know of them." Those secrets the kings and trusted advisors knew. His own father had drawn a map on a leather skin and taught him to memorize the escape tunnel. But he'd never dreamed he would need that knowledge—until now.

"As it is, only four of us know there won't be a public wedding ceremony. Let us use that to our advantage." Ache glanced at the lady-in-waiting. "But you have to leave as soon as you can." He nodded outward, beyond the balcony's view. "They will come to fetch you at dawn for the wedding preparations, and dawn is only hours away. Please play along and buy them time. Go." Ache bowed to him. "Please come with me."

Scanning the group, King Peralta shook his head. "Wait," he instructed the guard, who paused, and his armor clinked at the movement. "I can't just...leave Lanzarote. I love my people, Ache. I love Lanzarote. I have fought for my people, and I would die for them."

"Of that, there is no doubt." The guard drew close and knelt at the first step up to the throne. "You are the best king Lanzarote could ever pray to have, King Peralta. I have no fault with you, your majesty." Ache pressed his lips tightly. "But if you don't leave," his Adam's apple bobbed, "you won't be king by tomorrow night."

He pointed toward Sierra. "Even if Sierra wasn't regarded as a slave, a mere expression of interest in another woman after betrothal qualifies The Hunter to kill you—without notice—if he was to follow tradition strictly. A hunter did so three kings before you."

"At the time, he acted so he could also steal the king's land afterward," King Peralta countered, his jaw muscles grinding beneath his skin.

"True. But who could fault him? Your majesty, I'm on your side. But you are in love with a woman you cannot marry and also keep the throne at the same time, for as long as The Hunter lives. So, if you want your lineage to have the chance to reclaim your throne, you have to go, and go far away where The Hunter may not find you."

"But, if only we knew who The Hunter was, then maybe..." Sierra said.

The lady-in-waiting sighed. "He won't accept a plea. I know this for sure."

The Hunter's identity was guarded. No one, not even the king, knew who he was. So, King Peralta turned to the lady-in-waiting. "How are you so sure? Do you know who The Hunter is?"

Her lashes dipped, and she curled her arms around herself. "Yes. That is the problem." She shifted on her feet and further lowered her gaze. "Why do you think my family has been charged with keeping the palace grounds for generations?" Her gaze rotated between Sierra and him. Sierra gasped, but he held the lady's gaze, saying nothing, assuming nothing. Not until she finished. "If you marry Sierra, you have broken the law and engaged The Hunter. And he won't stop until you're both dead." She shook her head. "He won't."

Someone gasped, but he didn't look to see. "Who is it?" He needed an answer. "Who is The Hunter?"

Her head lifted, and her gaze touched on each of them. Then her shoulders fell. "My father is The Hunter."

7

"For there is nothing hidden from the king…" 2 Samuel 18:13

∼

King Peralta's mind spun with possible ways to avoid a conflict with the man following the lady-in-waiting's stunning revelation but found none. "Your father, the keeper?"

"My master?" Sierra whispered barely above a breath as she clutched the arm of his royal robe. "Oh no."

She turned to him. "I promised myself never to say anything against anyone. But this is not good. Her father, my master, was cruel to all his slaves and his servants," she swallowed, "including me."

At her words, anger burned within him. "I understand how harsh he can be. In addition, I know the man never gives up, and he refuses to lose."

The lady-in-waiting's silence resounded in concurrence to

Sierra's words. The man had always been quiet but observant on the occasions he interacted with King Peralta. Plus, the keeper had asked him for a favor recently, and he was yet to respond.

Concern lined her gaze, and as Sierra continued, all he wished to do was to smooth it away. "He is a determined man and has little to no kindness in him. He will kill you without pause."

She walked up to the throne, drew closer, and, cupping his face in her first show of affection, peered into his eyes. "I won't risk losing you, your majesty. Please," she pointed to the lady-in-waiting, "marry her, live, and reign." Sierra collapsed her head on him and sobbed softly into his shoulder, breaking his heart. "It will be my greatest sacrifice, but I will live out the rest of my days knowing you lived and ruled well." She looked up at him with a teary face. "I know you love me, O king, but I am not worthy of all this trouble. Plus, wherever I am, I will be praying for you. Please, my king."

But he dipped his head and kissed her teary cheeks. "Please, don't cry. There is always a way out."

She straightened. So, he countered her offer by turning to his faithful guard, a man sworn to protect him. "Can you do me a favor? Take my Sierra away from here to..." His tough words scorched his heart more than he'd expected, "somewhere safe, where she can live out her days, and I will make sure to keep The Hunter away from her. And I will stay unmarried for life."

She clung to him tightly. "But you can't keep your throne, and The Hunter will know by tomorrow night that something happened. He might still come after you, and then you will lose me, your throne, and possibly your life. Moreover," Sierra shook her head, gripped his hand, and another tear rolled down her cheek, "I won't leave you. I cannot allow you to stay behind, face this all alone, and not know whether The Hunter killed you. Not knowing alone could kill me." She pressed a hand to his chest, and he covered her hand with his own. "I would rather we both stay here, if so."

"Except I won't allow you both to die." The lady-in-waiting drew close. "People would blame me if you both got killed and there was no wedding. They would say it was because you refused me that I set you up. And I know my father, and everything Sierra said is true. He is determined, and you won't escape him in Lanzarote. Please, marry, then go. I will handle things here to keep it quiet as much as I can. Your God will keep you."

Saddened by the escalating events, King Peralta realized the choice was made for him. But day was breaking, so he pointed toward the door. "I have heard you all and will stay long enough to marry. Then we leave." He swallowed past the difficult words. "Thank you," he inclined his head to the lady-in-waiting, "for your understanding. May God reward you. Now, go, before a search commences for you."

She hugged Sierra and smiled. "Congratulations to you, Sierra. You will make a great queen." Then she left, leaving him wondering how such a sweet soul could have been born by the keeper, a hunter.

"Let us pray." He joined hands with Sierra and Ache as soon as the lady-in-waiting left. Studying Scripture since he obtained his Bible had taught him about the efficacy of prayer. "Lord Jesus, like I often heard Sierra pray in times past, please lead us this day in whatever comes before us."

He paused then, realizing he was praying his first public

prayer, but he had no choice and no time to reflect on what was happening.

It was happening.

He had to make choices, and none of them were appealing. "I love Sierra, and I will marry her, God willing. But there are consequences, grave consequences we need your help and grace to go through. Please guide us and protect us every step of the way. Shield us from The Hunter. Give us a way through this. And if I'm forced to leave my kingdom," his voice broke, "keep my people, preserve Lanzarote, and please let them know I love them. In Jesus' name. Amen. And long live Lanzarote."

"Amen. Long live Lanzarote," Sierra and Ache echoed, and a cock crowed outside.

"It is dawn. Let's go and get ready for your real wedding. I have a few people I can trust to fetch the queen's crown from the lady's residence and get it to the secret chambers where we will hold the ceremony. We have little time," Ache concurred with the cock's crow.

"Sorry, but with everything that has happened, I have to do something first." Sierra held King Peralta's hand. "I ran here last night to see whether you wished to marry the lady-in-waiting, knowing what you have expressed to me in recent times." She pointed to Ache. "He knew our story and so kindly smuggled me out. But it was the other slaves, back at The Hunter's house, who helped me escape."

Everyone spun to her as she pressed her lips tightly. "If my master, The Hunter, rises and sees me missing among his servants and later discovers that you purchased my freedom, that his daughter was rejected, and that we escaped, he will piece everything together," she swallowed, "and he will kill everyone who helped me escape. All the other servants." Her voice quivered and she turned. "But I can't let that happen. I have to set them free, and then we leave."

"I don't want you to go." He ground his jaw again, his hands fisting at his sides before he gave a brief nod. "I understand what you are saying, but if you must go, I'll go with you to ensure your safe return."

But Sierra shook her head. "No. Your presence can heighten the suspicion, and we might not make it to the wedding if he suspects anything beforehand. I will go alone. I must. For us."

When she looked into his eyes, a wonder pumped into his heart, for he saw no fear in hers. How was it that his queen was already behaving as one? "There's another reason why I can't leave them there. They are all fellow believers and missionaries like me. Like I'd told you, we arrived at this island seven years ago together, and we were young. Our boat had capsized, and we sought help. Then we encountered The Hunter who took us into his ship in exchange for our freedom."

Yes, he had heard this, but hearing it again now showed how vulnerable they must've been. "But instead of helping us and sending us on our merry way like travelers, he enslaved us in return. We had no choice then. If we hadn't said yes, we would have perished at sea. So, we became his slaves to this day. Although not born a slave, I was forced into it. I and my brothers and sisters in Christ."

That wonder that had pumped into his heart changed, heated, and throbbed as it spread through his veins, rang in his ears, and spurred his feet to action. No one traveling under his reign—a mere guest to his country—was supposed to be subjected to slavery. He would not have allowed what The Hunter had done, had he known about it before he met and fell in love with Sierra. But he couldn't exactly call out The Hunter at this precarious time.

Sierra gave his hands a squeeze, her steady gaze imploring his understanding. "I need to rescue my brothers and sisters. They need my help. I'm sure when I tell them what will have to happen, they will keep our secret safe forever with their last breath, your majesty."

But he wished to address what she had endured, what she had suffered. "I'm sorry for how you have been mistreated." He returned the tender pressure of her hands. "I do not condone nor support what was done to you, and I make no excuses for it. I would have ended your forced slavery if I knew about it before all this. But if I freed the rest now, it will also be misunderstood. With me, you are free and always will be. You owe no man anything. Please accept my apologies on behalf of me and my people."

Her gentle nod warmed his heart. "Thank you. Your apology is accepted, but it's not the time to consider all that now. They need my help. I have to go and return soonest. Please, stay safe. And wait for me. I will come back."

"You can go, Sierra." His heart twisted as he gave in—but what choice did a man have? Her desires were pure and noble, her intent obviously unstoppable. "But please allow me to send my guard to go with you to ensure that you return safely. You are now a member of this royal household under Ache's protection."

Reluctant to release her, he drew Sierra close, clasped her long, dark hair, and kissed her forehead, again inhaling the earthy scent that surrounded her. "I love you, Sierra. And I will keep you safe."

Who could help admiring her bravery? Not only had she

survived a shipwreck, but also she and her fellow survivors were forced into slavery. But all that didn't stop her from continuing her missionary work while serving her master. Sierra attempted and succeeded in converting a reigning king into becoming a Christian. And even now, while presented with a chance to escape, she chose to return to where she'd been bound, to go and save those still held in captivity.

His gaze perused her face, spotting the few beautiful freckles adorning her cheeks. "You are worthy of being my queen, Sierra. You have shown leadership, bravery, and although the world might not know this, I will make sure that our children will forever know what a remarkable mother they came from. I love you, my queen." He had just made the ultimate declaration by any king before marriage, a designation of future queenship, and he understood the impact of his words.

Releasing her, he turned to Ache. "Protect her as you would protect me. Do whatever is necessary to keep her safe and alive. Please, take another guard with you to go with her. But don't tell a soul what you are there for. Use my fastest horses to go to The Hunter's house, but stop some houses away and wait for her to travel the remaining distance by foot. Then, when she enters to get her people, you do not return to the palace without her and her fellow travelers. Understood?"

Ache's arms flexed with movement as his protective metal gauntlets shifted on his wrist. "My king, your secret is safe with me. I will do as you say." He bowed to Sierra, for the first time. "My queen, please follow me."

A lump rose in King Peralta's throat at Ache's acknowledgment of her new status. Though Sierra was still clad in servant wear, her status had changed in his eyes. She was the queen of the land. "Please return soonest, my love." He charged her, and she nodded as though her throat was constricted due to emotion.

This was the biggest risk he took in this situation, knowing it was possible that she may not return. But she was right. His presence without an explanation would raise questions. And any direct confrontation with The Hunter, especially with the prevailing marital twist he found himself in, would only lend credence to The Hunter's basis to eliminate him.

So King Peralta prayed again with all his heart, then awaited Sierra's return.

8

"Do not grant, O Lord, the desires of the wicked; Do not further his wicked scheme, lest they be exalted." Psalm 140: 8

∽

AT THE CRACK OF DAWN, QUEEN-TO-BE SIERRA CREPT BACK IN through the rear of the servants' lodge where dishes were stacked to be washed on large metal bowls, and she bypassed the secluded wooden stalls where they usually showered.

Adjusting to the change bestowed upon her in a few hours was like a dream. She'd gone from being Sierra, the committed single missionary seven years ago who would do anything to leave the confines of Spain, to a forced slave after a shipwreck.

And now, she was a queen—or she would be within a day.

If she was to be honest, she was scared. So scared that her hand, holding the wooden partition shielding her from being seen through the parted gates, shook. She tiptoed into the substandard living quarters she'd called home for years, nothing like her home as a young girl in Spain. And nothing like King Peralta's palace.

Seven years ago, when she and those other missionaries left Spain, eager to arrive in Africa to evangelize, she'd never thought they would be shipwrecked or be taken captive on this island.

But out there at sea, cold and without other options, survival was the utmost priority and witnessing to *any* people was her mission. Soon after they settled in to Lanzarote, she didn't leave her call to witness far behind, neither did the others. In every opportunity, they stepped out to witness to these islanders about Jesus. Some rejected them, but not everyone.

A tingle of joy shivered through her over what they had accomplished. So far, more than one hundred believers had accepted Jesus here, all secretly. Thirteen of those served in the palace, and Ache would likely recruit those to help them to set up the wedding—her wedding. As much as she trusted the king and knew he would die in her place if it came to it, she couldn't reveal their identities to him just yet.

Their safety depended on her and her team's silence, for now. Little by little, they had preached Jesus to many other slaves, led them to make the confession of faith, and baptized the few whom they could at the island's beach when they were sent to take something out to the keeper's ship. Dipping them in the slow stream of clear water by a brook and baptizing them in the name of the Father, Son, and Holy Spirit had felt exhilarating. Teaching each one the Word of God had been even better, including the king. He had been especially attentive, and the manner with which his gaze would vacillate between eager learning of His Word and physical admiration of her sometimes left warmth in her cheeks in its wake—a reaction which she stopped trying to hide by the third month of their interaction. Instead, she focused on giving him the Word as instructed by the Lord. So, she tore her thoughts from him now and focused on finding an opportunity to reenter the quarters before more people woke.

Her thoughts warmed when she remembered how one new Christian, who was a slave for another master, a friend to The Hunter, had recently talked to her about sharing the Gospel with his master who was getting a rough deal from his wife. He had hinted to her that his master was responding well to his discussions of Scripture.

However, a few days ago, he had shared that murmurings from other servants in the household caused him to be sent by his master's wife to work at the farms and no longer in the house, putting significant distance between him and his master. He had said she'd complained that her husband was changing and her nagging no longer bothered him, and she blamed his interactions with the slave as being responsible for it. So, Sierra had encouraged him and prayed for him. Before they parted ways, she managed to press a sheet into his hand written in Spanish with as much Scripture as she could recall from memory. She hadn't seen him again since, but from the reports she got, he was doing well in the faith.

Although glad to have the man she loved finally declare his love for her, Sierra longed to continue working to share the Gospel amongst the slaves. No other person would be willing to become a slave to reach them, and although she disliked the way she and her companions were thrust into these circumstances, she assumed the Lord must've allowed it, so she'd seized the chance.

But now, with her freedom guaranteed, and her safety only hours away, she hurt with knowing that she would be separated from the other missionaries. Yes, she would assist them with escaping The Hunter's house, but to keep her secret with the king safe, she could not allow even her friends to know about the most recent plan. They would need to go separate ways to prevent the king from being captured by The Hunter. A thought that caused her to swallow hard and made her to focus again on her reason for coming back here.

Just then, a hand pressed on her shoulder, and she jerked it off before she spun.

"Shhh. It's just me, Sierra," a male voice whispered. Chemira, a brother in Christ and fellow captive, swung around to face her. "The ladies told me why you were gone when I asked. You took too long. We were worried."

She seized his arm, drew him aside, and they both hid behind a low wooden gate whose base had rotted away due to constant rain. "You scared me." She leaned against the brick wall, thankful that the king's horse had ridden her here faster and that she reached the house sooner, buying her some much-needed time.

"Sorry, I didn't mean to."

"Are the others safe?" The sun had still not fully risen. *Thank You, God!*

"Yes, they are. He is not awake yet." Meaning, their master, now her former master, thanks to the king's ransoming of her. "Tell me how it went, and whether the risk you took was worth it."

She released his arm and leaned in, keeping her voice low. "It went well. In fact, better than I had hoped. I'm grateful you had asked me to go and witness to the king, *señor*. And to ask him directly to receive Christ. I was scared, but your encouragement pushed me. Ache led me all the way to the king's inner court. The rest of what happened is the reason I'm back here." She gave him all the details quickly. "You must tell no one. I am here to help set the others free. You know our master might punish anyone who is not found working in daylight or doing whatever he wants."

His eyes brightened. "That is a great testimony, Sierra. I'm so happy, praise God. We prayed as a group for you while you were gone."

"I was so surprised as I had no idea how things might turn out." She held his shoulder, allowing herself to lay down her concerns for a moment and to feel excited about the good news. "The king professed his love for me. And we are leaving, but we're taking a different way from you and everyone else. But whatever happens from here on, I want you to know one thing."

She exhaled. "The work of the Gospel is rarely done without being scattered abroad or going into difficult places and seasons. Those places are hard, uncomfortable, and not where we would want to be. But remember this, until we get to heaven, we stay in that place where we're planted, and we fight for His will, by His grace, because every single soul is worth leading to Christ."

"I know." Eyes crinkling in a smile, he patted her shoulder. "Why else would I have asked about the trip? I had to be sure if the king accepted Christ, and that is, of course, the best news of all." He curved a hand around her shoulder. "Let's go in before we're spotted. I'm not sure the master will be kind to seeing us out here. And we don't want to send you back to the king in bad shape when he finds out what we're up to. He might take out the wrath for his would-have-been-queen daughter on us."

"But we have the king on our side." Elation swelling within her, she rested her hand on his arm. "He received Jesus, Chemira. That gave me indescribable joy to hear my king sincerely confess those words of faith."

Her friend grinned widely. "And he bought your freedom, too, Sierra. You are no longer a slave." He patted her back with equal force as the ear-to-ear grin covering his face. "You are free, sister. Christ has secured your freedom, and He will do ours, too, at His time."

"Thank you." The joy bursting through her heart bubbled into words. "He called me his queen." She grazed a finger across her forehead where his kiss had been, and the memory warmed her soul. "It felt surreal. Queenship was not my intention when I went to him. I wanted him to receive Christ. And secondly, I simply wished to know how he felt about me. I just wanted to be with the man I loved, and if that meant becoming his queen, then that is fine with me."

She added, "As long as he loves me, which he does. It's just a whole other lifestyle I need to adjust to." Sierra shook herself back to the present and admonished herself to stay vigilant. She clutched the hem of her flowing, brown-flowered cotton gown with laces at the frills, the best dress she owned since arriving in Lanzarote—not one of those gifted her by the king as she'd wished to hear his response without prejudice or influence of any kind. "I have to go and wake the others before the master gets here. Perhaps, I may be able to rescue everyone."

"Let me get the four out of the men's quarters, and we will meet back here soon." Chemira cupped his hand over hers until she met his eyes. "Please be careful, sister. The Lord go with you.

I will rally back here in about one hour. But if we don't see you, we will move to the seaside where I will be waiting at the dock to secure a ship from our convert weeks ago. I'm sure he will give us a ship to travel on to save our lives. I know you're doing this because, if you go with the king and leave us behind, the master will come for our necks. And I appreciate your sacrifice."

His Adam's apple bobbed, and his eyes brimmed with resolve. "But be sure of this—I, and the others, will die before we give up any knowledge of you and the king's love or of your whereabouts after you escape. Your secret is safe with the Lord. Come this way."

He led her through a narrow path she'd never taken. Usually, she would spot anyone who appeared behind the large tree that shielded the path before they emerged. But today, she discovered it led to a back door and the open area where the servants laundered and dried clothing. Several clothes, already hand washed, hung on a line across the yard. Chemira made sure she stayed low until they reached the female quarters—the long, old, wooden barn holding several small rooms and a wide sleeping area. "Go inside and make sure you get to the laundry area, our meeting point today, or send the others to the dock if you can't come. Once I see them, I'll know you're safe."

"Thank you, Chemira," Sierra whispered. "I will tell the ladies and prepare their minds to escape as soon as we see an opportunity. No matter what happens to me, please go to the dock with the men and don't leave until the ladies arrive. I will head back to the palace and leave to somewhere secret with the king, after our wedding, so as not to implicate you. If this is our goodbye, please, keep the faith and know I will be praying for you."

His Adam's apple bobbed again as he swallowed. "Of course. And you too. The Lord keep you, Queen Sierra, and King Peralta safe. God be with you." A slight pause carried the heaviness of their hopes. "Please, be careful. And if I don't see you again on this earth, I will see you in heaven. I love you, sister. The Lord guide and protect you."

With a nod, Sierra entered the row of the female quarters. Many of her companions were up. Upon nearing the closest person, who was tying a girdle around her waist, likely getting ready for the day's work, Sierra gripped the lady's hand from behind. "Anna! I need to talk to everyone before the day starts. Gather everyone at my corner."

Anna gathered the other missionaries together. Typically, they held an early-morning prayer session, no matter how little time they had before the master entered, by himself, to give instructions to his security watch about where to have them work for that day. The security guard had once shot an arrow at someone who fled, killing the girl as a threat to the rest. That had been sufficient warning. But he had likely been gone all last night—so where was he?

Once everyone stood close and had formed a circle around her, she briefed them that they had to leave, then clasped the hands of those beside her. "I'm not allowed to tell you the details, but the Lord graced us with favor at the palace. We have protection, but we have to make our way out of this house first. Then our escort will guide you to safety where a boat will transport you to a ship and carry you safely away from this place, back to Spain." Pausing, she glanced at their eager faces, but no one spoke. They simply watched. "One more thing, after we leave here, I won't travel with you."

"Why?" Anna's high-pitched voice warbled in the dawn's stillness. "Where will you go?"

Sierra looked at each of them once again, wishing she could say more but knowing otherwise. "I don't know. I have to protect the interest of the palace even if I knew, so I cannot tell you where. Both for your safety and mine. But someone among you knows the details, and if you need to know, this person will tell you at the right time."

Again, she glanced at each of their faces, and a small smile formed. "We prayed each day for the Lord to make a way out for us. Now He has. And never could I have imagined that it will come this way."

She gripped a metal ring attached to one of the bunk beds, recalling how the keeper used it to restrain them when they first arrived. Night after night, she'd cried herself to sleep. As she looked at it now, its rusted hinges lost its grip of fear over her. It became an old piece of metal with worn black paint unable to keep her down or in bondage ever again—and nothing more. She continued with renewed confidence purring through her, "I will be with you in spirit. And please, pray for me as soon as you arrive in Spain. But please, for my sake, and that of those with me," her gaze perused their faces, "don't come looking for us. You will endanger our lives. Please, promise me."

Silence followed before one person nodded and a tear dropped down Anna's cheek. Being the youngest of the missionaries, the girl was like a sister to Sierra. She buried her head in Sierra's neck and sobbed. "I want to come with you! I will miss you."

Sierra comforted her until her sobs grew quiet. When she lifted her head, Sierra gazed at her lovely gray eyes and loved her heart like she would her own sister. "I love you, Anna. But I need to protect you. You will hear the truth at the right time. For now, get ready and let's go. Hurry, everyone."

With that, she dispersed them, and as soon as they were all ready to go, as though on a prompt, their master burst into the place and surveyed the room. He neared her, furious. "Sierra, the king says, you are free to leave." He sighed, as though in resignation. "Your freedom has been purchased." The flatness of his tone rolled into his eyes. He gazed at her then looked her over from head to toe with a sneer. "The king must've been in a good mood to buy your freedom. But, very soon, he will be my son-in-law." An evil laugh floated from him, and Sierra let out a whooshed breath when he turned away.

"What is everyone standing around doing?" he barked at the rest, a hand on his sword dangling off his side. "Get dressed and ready! You have work to do."

His guard entered. While hollow semicircles left deep purple around his eyes, his drawn face twisted with pain, and his legs wobbled as he leaned a hand against the wall as though to brace himself.

"Make sure they work the fields today from end to end. I saw weeds growing a few days ago," he waved at nothing in particular, "and some crops were not harvested. They all get done today." He pointed a finger downward. "No lazying around here."

Instead of responding, his security guard clutched his belly, fled the quarters, and emptied its contents on the ground.

Sierra resisted the urge to look at her friends. She prayed in her heart. The master had never been up this early. Why was he up now? Maybe his son had woken him to show him the gold for her ransom? Or could it be as a result of his daughter's presumed wedding? Thankfully, the fields her friends would work on were near the palace even if they played along. But the keeper kept a close eye on them and usually spent nearly the entire day there. Since he assumed his daughter was marrying the king today, maybe he wouldn't pay enough attention for them to slip away unnoticed?

She swallowed. Chemira must wonder what was delaying them as they were already supposed to be on their way. She had planned on tackling the guard by herself at whatever cost, if they chanced on him, or he on them, during their escape. Now, he was sick, but with their master here, this new twist only made things harder.

Just as she gave up hope, the door swung open behind their master, and someone entered. Sierra gasped—Ache? King Peralta's guard, who had ridden with her here, stood. His eyes searched the dimly-lit quarters, then settled on her. He might've been worried for her since she had not returned to the designated meeting point. Ache turned to her master, or rather, her master turned to see who had entered.

Upon his sighting Ache in his royal guard robe, the keeper's attitude warmed into a smile, however awkward. "His majesty's guard. To what do I owe this pleasure? What brings you to my humble house?" He rubbed his hands together, just as his son had done in the palace.

But Ache kept a measured glance on the man. "Sir, I came to inform you that, by nature of the king's marriage ceremony today, he has issued a decree that no slave be allowed to work today. They are all invited to the palace for the king's marriage ceremony. You may not contravene this law, which according to the king, is punishable by death. Everyone, old or young, sick or well, must come to the palace immediately."

"But..." Her master's smile died right then. "I have work planned for them."

"But..." Ache grinned. "You are in favor with the king obviously, as he requested you and your servants to be seated at the front of the wedding party. You get double compensation for the crops you supply to the king's court in one month's time as well. Do you still want your servants out in the field today, in contravention of the king's order?"

Was Ache making this up? Could he?

∼

9

"My servant...will set his throne above these stones that I have hidden." Jeremiah 43:10

~

Sierra could hardly believe her ears. Her fingers wound tightly around Anna's, who clutched them as though clinging to life. The room was so tense she could hear the sparks in silence and in the sharpened, staggered stance of both men as they measured each other.

One of them had to yield.

But she knew Ache, and she was sure that, with her new status, he would do anything to ensure her safety. And this dedicated guard would make sure she and everyone got out alive. He was taking a risk, a huge risk.

Gratitude she could not safely express, and tension due to the standoff, made her release Anna's hand and clutch her belly. In contrast, Sierra spun to find her friends smiling—toward her. Did they know her reason? Of course, they had been aware of her and King Peralta's friendship at the garden, considering how he talked to her almost daily. But she had told her whereabouts to only the two people who helped her sneak out to the palace last night.

With God's grace, her friends wouldn't ask her any questions, knowing how dangerous such questions were. Especially since her former master turned out to be The Hunter. He, of all persons, should be the last to know about her and the king. She just had to get through the time she needed to help these others gain their freedom.

Her master patted Ache's arm, added another evil laugh, then nodded. "Of course, I will comply." Exhales of relief echoed around the room as her own shoulders relaxed. That was close. "The king is a good man. I will have these ones cleaned up and ready." He waved dismissively at the missionaries-turned-slaves and his other servants lurking farther behind. "After all, it is my daughter who would soon be the queen of the land. Long live King Peralta." He pumped a fist in the air and squared his shoulders proudly.

Ache's eyes met hers, and she discretely nodded her gratitude as her greedy master made his way toward the door, giving his coat a slight tug of satisfaction. If the king had truly made the decree Ache implied, then he had sent another guard to relay the message and had chosen to spare her a battle with The Hunter—a seasoned warrior.

He was shielding her from afar, choosing rather to bring the battle to the palace, his own grounds where he had an advantage.

To acknowledge that their plan was still in play, she gave

Ache another nod before the door shut behind the men. Then she hurried the others to prepare for the marriage she knew would not hold, and she prayed that, by the end of this day, herself and the king and God's servants would make it out alive.

∼

AFTER TRAVELING WITH THE OTHERS TO ENSURE THEIR SAFE escort and arriving at the king's palace, Sierra separated from them. Being among the first to arrive, they settled into their designated seats but were briefed by her and Ache that they wouldn't be seated for long as they would be alerted to head to their escape ship. Then Ache disappeared when she was finished hugging Anna and the others. The men must've already gone to secure the ship since Chemira and the others hadn't been at the meeting point outside The Hunter's house.

As soon as the coast was clear, Sierra sneaked away and entered the palace through a back door, where a guard instantly accosted her, pulling her behind a curtain draped over an archway. "My queen." He inclined his head respectfully, his large callused hand still clamped over her wrist. So she knew he must've been sent by the king as her new status was a secret. "Please follow me."

Sierra strode with him into a wide courtyard, turned left, and emerged before an inner courtyard. She crossed the stoned path to the king's private residences. Her heart beat faster as the guard led her past some other guards who, arguing over a game they played, didn't see them cross the circular room to a hidden doorway into a yawning hallway.

After passing through a set of double doors with lions carved on them, they wound deeper, then made several turns, so many that she finally paused. "Wait. Where is the king? And where is Ache?"

He pointed forward. "Right ahead."

So this truly was the preparation for their escape—an escape already in motion. She prayed in her heart for divine guidance and protection for them as they passed doors decorated for wedding guests, the public wedding that would not hold.

At last, they entered a large room where Ache stood close to a window, holding a folded garment. As soon as he saw her, he crossed the room and hugged her. "You made it." He handed her the elegant garment. "Go into the adjacent room and shower quickly. Everything you need is in there. Then wear this so you don't stand out from the other ladies." He left the room, sealing her in with a deadbolt, as did the other guard, so she hurried into the adjacent room, seized the soap, and showered. Then she changed her clothing with little time to appreciate the updated attire, though she did fondle the cloth's supple softness. Then, leaving her servant clothes piled by the corner, she exited by another door and met him. He surveyed her. "Good. These are still lowly clothes not fit for you yet, but they will do for now. Let's go."

The blue pleated dress's bulky hem bounced around her ankles while its high neckline cut at her throat. Still, she stifled a smile, thinking of her enjoyment moments ago—it was better than anything she'd worn in recent times. Sierra patted his arm. "Where is the king? Is he all right?"

"He is." Ache pointed ahead. "We're going to him. But we must hurry."

So, she followed him. Another winding hallway led them through two more turns where servants performed daily duties.

No more wedding guests or standing guards. Just endless rooms and stretching balconies. Hurrying to keep up, she realized that he was pulling her away before everyone around them settled in and anyone noticed she'd left the public wedding seating.

But as they entered a chamber with stairs leading down a dark pathway, her feet slowed, and her worry rose. Her heart thudded, for literally, no one else was there. Just her and Ache. Even the other guard had left them at some point, at Ache's instruction. Fear crawled up her spine. "Where are you taking me? It's dark down here."

Ache halted beside her. Then he took her hand and hurried her along. "Do not fear. I'm taking you to safety." Even in the faint light from a window or two they passed, his features were sharp and his eyes alert. Did danger lurk nearby? "Taking you to the king." Of course, he was.

But it became even clearer now how much danger lay ahead of them. This choice to marry her and not The Hunter's daughter would cost the king literally…everything.

Sierra gulped, and again unworthiness rose in her belly. If only she could reverse the events now in motion! But, as they strode along, she asked herself one question.

If King Peralta was not king, would she go ahead to marry him? As she searched her heart, she knew the answer. Yes, she would marry this man even if he was a pauper. With her choice sealed, she followed Ache onward.

"Thank you for getting us to the palace without bloodshed."

"It's my duty, my queen. I had them send out a decree in the king's name to that effect as soon as I arrived at the palace so it is true." Still unused to being addressed as queen, she wanted to ask him simply to address her as Sierra. At least, until the wedding when it became official, but Ache hurried forward even faster. He halted at a window. "The sun is high, and the people would be expecting the wedding party to begin. We have to move faster. Come on."

"Okay." Sierra trailed him, adjusting to the clothing as it pinched a little tight around her armpits. They descended another set of steps winding around a pillar. Then he pushed a heavy door shut behind them.

They emerged at a roughly-cut opening, like the mouth of a cave but with smooth edges leading out into a massive room. He rolled a large flat stone against the opening, leaving them in nearly pitch dark until he struck something and lit up an oil lantern behind the door.

The room came alive.

The entire space was chiseled from rock, and a Lanzarote kingdom emblem of lions facing each other was carved into the rock wall. Dust had now clouded their entrance. Surely, this was the last stop. Sierra felt a frown dip her forehead. "Where is the king, Ache? You said we were going to meet him. But he's not here, and we are locked in."

Ache nodded to the right without answering. As her gaze followed his gesture, her shoulders loosened. Farther along the right wall, the light revealed a wooden door, a door Ache was already moving toward. Once they reached it, he paused. "This is a secret chamber known only to the king and two of his closest guards. The king is inside, but there are two more persons with him."

He cupped her shoulders and peered into her face. "Your life is about to change. You will no longer be Sierra when you exit this place." His hands dropped to his side, and his gauntlet clinked against his armor. "King Peralta is a powerful man, but once you marry him, you are his wife and a queen. So, we are about to commence the ceremony of marriage according to Lanzarote custom, and he asks that you trust him and do what I tell you to do now."

Nodding beyond a tight throat, Sierra searched Ache's face. Light flickered over features seeming as roughhewn as the stone around them—and just as solid and steadfast. She swallowed. "Yes. I will."

He pointed to the left side where some stones were stacked waist high, blocking something from view. "I will stand away from you, facing the wall while you move to the opposite side near those stones. Due to the sand and dust, you will wish to bathe once more. And I'm sorry that these provisions are not what we would like to provide for you as our queen. Behind those stones, you will find two buckets of water, some soap, royal vesture, and never-before-worn clothing as well as new shoes laid out for you. Please shower and dress up quickly. When you are done, let me know. Then we will enter the next room, and you will meet the king and the wedding audience."

∽

10

"The royal daughter is all glorious within the palace; her clothing is woven with gold." Psalm 45:13

∽

Without another word, and understanding the importance of this moment in the tapestry of her life and of the king's, Sierra did as instructed. She dodged getting rough cuts from the rock wall next to her, using one flat rock to separate her feet from the dusty ground. As she bathed, she breathed in and out to calm her heart. So much was happening so fast, but she admonished herself to be grateful, for things could have gone differently. *Thank You, my Lord.*

This had to be a closely guarded secret chamber beneath the palace. And yet, it was so quiet. How was it she didn't hear any noise of movement above them?

Did The Hunter know this place existed? Even worse,

would he pursue them? With no way to find out for now, she basked in pure elation for neither her, nor her friends, had suffered any harm during their escape from The Hunter's bondage.

"Oh, the king signed a letter sent to The Hunter along with a bag of gold, with the names of your companions as his exclusive wedding guests to be catered to inside the inner court. With that letter, they should be able to leave the palace through the back unnoticed. The guard who left us will see to it that they reach their waiting ship. He also provided them with two bags of gold and a letter with his seal on it, proclaiming them free citizens of Lanzarote, asking that they be allowed to board any ship without a fee and without being stopped all the way back to Spain."

"Oh, praise the Lord. Thank you for telling me." Her friends were safe and free? Her heart bubbled with joy, a little giggle slipping free—how long had it been since she had felt such release? "I am very grateful, and I will let him know that."

"It was likely his last act here as king." With those words, solemnity stood between them beyond the rocks separating them.

She dried her hair as much as she could and combed it with her fingers until it was barely damp. Then she let her hair down, a rarity, and it cascaded down her back in luscious waves. "I understand and appreciate his sacrifice and yours. Thank you for supporting us, Ache. You didn't have to."

Moments later, fully dressed up, she slid her feet into those new gold-rimmed white shoes and stifled a cry as they felt so good. She remembered the last time she wore shoes this good and not torn and tied-together sandals while working under a burning sun and cold rain as a slave.

It was back home in Spain on her seventeenth birthday. Her uncle, who was like a father to her, had bought her a special, red flowery dress with a pink finish at the edges. And a pair of lovely, shiny-black, pointed-toe heels. She had worn those shoes all that day even when her feet started blistering.

As she glanced down at the pair now hugging her feet, she gave thanks to God in her heart. Things were changing, and it wasn't all bad. She was entering another season of her life, a life of honor and responsibility. A life of godly marriage.

She would be served and also serve. She would be the strength and backbone of King Peralta wherever life took them. She would appreciate what he gave up to live with her for the rest of his life. She would be a queen not only in title but in deed. She bent over, picked up her former service shoes, and laid them atop the stack of stones. Another pair of flat shoes sat at the corner, and she picked them up and tucked them at the crook of her arm.

Sierra tugged at her royal wedding dress—a glowing white lace dress which rustled to her ankle—and she was satisfied with how well the dress fit. Did the king have any say in choosing this dress? Because only someone sure of her size could have gotten it right. But he'd gotten her gifted dresses right six months ago, at a time when they'd barely known each other.

She blushed at the thought. Then she put on a shimmering, golden coat over her wedding dress. Gold embroidered the rich purple royal linen, each exquisite thread catching the lantern light while she cinched a wide golden satin belt to match its golden trims. Running her hand over the coat, she knew it was very expensive and could only be reserved for a queen.

For her.

Excitement wove through her belly, and she prayed for her wedding to go as planned without a hitch.

Nevertheless, Sierra prepared her mind for whatever might lay ahead. Even if it wasn't a smooth escape or a perfect situation, God was with them. God had a hand in what was happening, and she prayed again for her friends to reach the ship and arrive in Spain safely without interception.

Then she prayed for her and for King Peralta. For the Lord to be the third person in their marriage and for their safety, even though it still felt like she was living a dream while unexpectedly becoming queen.

This elegant king—with broad shoulders, a kind heart, rich smile, short dark hair and curls that hugged his ears and tugged at her heart, a rich baritone voice with a slight drawl, and an intent gaze that seemed to rummage through one's soul and gorgeous lips that always seemed to be inviting her for a one-on-one meeting—loved her out of all the women in Lanzarote.

And she loved him, too, long before she allowed herself to accept that it had happened while thinking it would go nowhere.

But here she was, about to marry him.

A smile tugged at the corner of her lips. However things turned out, she was willing to take this risk for the man she loved. She slid on the dangling golden earrings someone had tucked into the shoes.

Spinning and leaving her last outfit inside one of the emptied buckets, she squared her shoulders and exhaled. "I'm ready."

Ache slowly spun, took one look, and his eyes rounded. His mouth dropped open, and he gasped as she drew near. "You are a perfect, beautiful queen indeed. And it took a wise king to search you out, just like the Bible says." A smile creased his eyes. "King Peralta could not have chosen a better wife." Sadness darkened his gaze. "I wish you didn't have to flee. The people have to know what a fitting queen you are."

"Thank you." She clutched the ensemble consciously, eager to go on and see the man her heart beat for.

Ache glanced away with a sorrowful look. "When I was guarding the king, I did listen to you two in the garden occasionally as you discussed Scripture, and I learned from there too. Soon enough, I knew he loved you even though you couldn't see it. As a secret Christian, I was blessed by your wisdom. So I went privately to ask about you to protect the king's interest. And I discovered you weren't a slave but were forced into slavery. How did you endure it for so long even when you were freeborn?"

A smile softened her lips, and she touched Ache's arm. "Slavery is a state of mind, just like freedom is a mindset. Someone can imprison your body, but you cannot let them imprison your mind. Moreover, you are free, once Christ says you are, from any kind of bondage."

She allowed her hand to drop from his and pressed it to still the butterflies in her stomach as she thought of her king. "I came to Lanzarote as a slave. So did my friends. But we turned it into an opportunity to witness for Jesus, knowing that all things worked for our good, while we petitioned for our freedom to the council. We had prayed prior to leaving Spain for God to send us to where the Word of God was lacking, so He did. We had thought it would be Africa, but I guess we were wrong. And whether we came here as slaves or as missionaries, that did not change what God commissioned us to do. Preach the Gospel of Jesus to every living creature, whether bound or free."

"I'm lost for words, Sierra." Ache stared at her. "You are more honorable and wiser than I thought you'd be."

"Ache, nothing happens to a genuine Christian outside of God's control. I know who I am in Christ, a divine royalty, and not even slavery can take that inner identity away from me. So I had faith that, if Jesus allowed me and the others to be enslaved, He would get us out by Himself, whether in this life or in the life to come. In the meantime, I did His work. I witnessed to both the slaves and masters of the land whenever I had a chance to do so."

Ache smiled. "And you performed excellently. So well that even King Peralta is now a Christian. Of course, he wasn't aware that, when he'd asked you yesterday in the garden whether you would marry him should he request such of you, he was overheard. He is an honorable man, so I was not surprised when he sent me to you for an answer. He would only have married the lady-in-waiting to preserve his kingdom had you turned him down. I'm glad you did not. I'm only surprised it took him this long to ask you."

"But haven't I made him lose it all if I marry him and we flee?" she inquired.

"No. The freedom to marry whomever you choose triumphs over the need to retain power. He—and you—made the right choice. Which would have been easier had there been no hunter in pursuit. And no age-thirty deadline for him to marry."

His voice cracked a bit. "When I heard him recite the statement of faith to accept Christ, something broke in me. I could see how much he loved you, so I swore to help you and the king live as free as possible. I'd lived my own life bound by fear for so long after losing my wife and son eight years ago."

Ache shook his head. "After all you have gone through, you deserve a happy life free from fear. And the king has shown incredible bravery by endangering his throne. My goal is to preserve his legacy and to protect his throne for his," he paused, "your, descendants until you return. It is a binding, sacred oath of honor. And I will keep it and so will my descendants until yours return and claim what is rightfully theirs. There will be no other king of Lanzarote after King Peralta until he returns. I will inform the kingdom that the king has gone to conquer other lands, and we will hold his throne until he returns."

Sierra frowned. "Isn't that false?"

A twinkle lightened his somber gaze. "No, my queen. You conquer lands when you preach the Gospel. May the Word of promise never leave your tongue. Please, let's go, if you're ready."

Without another word, he crossed the remaining space to the hidden wooden door. Ache set the lamp aside and lifted a heavy wooden rod wedged against the door. He landed it against the door three times, set it down against the rock wall, and lifted the oil lantern. Then he twisted and held the handle, and Sierra felt like her insides were the ones being turned.

Then Ache spun to her. "Are you ready? Once you enter that room, your life will change for good. There will be no going back, Sierra. You will be the queen of this land for life. This will be the last time I address you by name. Do you understand what this means?"

Excitement and caution warred in her heart.

Was she ready?

Could she handle the coming wave of consequences to awash over her?

What if the king changed his mind? It wasn't just to marry a king, but to marry one who gave up his throne for her sake and will be on the run for the rest of his life.

Sierra swallowed hard, understanding the full weight of this moment. "I was born ready, Ache. The Lord's will be done. And by God's grace, His mercy and defense, no life shall be lost today. In case we are forced to flee, please make sure the people know that the king loved them greatly and would have given his life for their sake."

Ache nodded, and the muscles on his broad chest flexed with his movement. Ache was definitely not a guard to be messed with. Blessedly, he was on their side. Being the one personally in charge of the king's safety, and supervising the other guards, came with heavy responsibility. "You have my word. Please, follow me."

As he pushed the door open, her insides twisted yet further, tightening into a knot. Anxious ripples wove around her belly with excitement as she stepped into a large regal room, as big as the inner room of the palace upstairs and nothing like the roughhewn room they were coming from.

Royal-blue tapestry decorated the walls and chairs, very much like the ones in the palace. A small group stood at the center, and she recognized everyone.

"Oh, thank God, you made it, Sierra." King Peralta took brisk steps toward her, enclosed her in a warm hug, and she buried her head in his shoulder and sobbed, emptying herself of tension she hadn't known she was carrying. "I was very worried for you, my love. I waited for so long, and I prayed like never before. Please don't cry."

When she finished shedding the load of tears that had weighed on her heart, Sierra lifted her head to those preparing around them.

"Chemira? What are you doing here? Aren't you supposed to secure and prepare a ship for the rest to escape?"

"I led him here before coming to get you," Ache informed her. When she inched up a brow, he added, "He has a sacred duty."

She released the king and faced Ache fully. "What is that?" Surely, nothing was more important than assisting the others escape.

"He will perform your wedding ceremony. I have someone who will settle the matter about getting your friends to the ship."

Oh! How had Ache thought of that? Sierra touched her shimmering dress and whispered so low in her throat she feared no one could hear her, "Thank you for everything, Ache."

The resourceful guard bowed a little. He seemed to have thought of everything they would need. "I serve at the pleasure of the king."

But someone else was there. Someone she didn't expect to see.

The lady-in-waiting.

Why?

11

"He who finds a wife, finds a good thing and obtains favor from the Lord." Proverbs 18:22

∽

When Sierra eyed her, the lady smiled. "I'm sure you're wondering what I'm doing here. This is awkward, but my presence is necessary for a new reason."

The king curved a hand around Sierra's waist possessively.

The lady-in-waiting eyed the move but continued, "I will draw a portrait of you both after the ceremony. I'm an expert painter, and I studied at the Royal Academy of Spain. And I can create a fast portrait and fill in the details when things settle down and nobody is searching for you two to kill anymore." Silence trailed her words. "I won't ruin your wedding, please. Although it's a bit awkward to stand as witness for the man you should be marrying while he weds someone else, please know that I'm happy for you."

The lady tapped a drawing pencil on her lap. "Like I said yesterday, I won't marry someone who loves somebody else. So, before my father realizes we're all missing and comes after you two, I suggest we proceed with this process."

Compassion warmed her chest for this lady who found herself in a peculiar situation. But Sierra hadn't planned on falling in love with the king. And surely, the king didn't intend to fall in love with her either. It simply happened, leaving them to deal with the outcome. She glided across the room, pausing before the lady who would have been her queen, the fullness of her heart spilling out in words. "I thank you for your magnanimity. The king was indeed yours by law, but you honored our love by releasing him from his commitment to marry you. And the Lord, my God Himself, will provide you a man of your own."

When the lady-in-waiting nodded, Sierra's nerves eased a bit.

"Please, let us get started." Ache waved a massive hand, at which everyone came into focus.

The king stood, put on his regal attire at the center of the room. Then he set his golden crown atop his head as the guard placed a smaller crown in his hand. He beckoned to Sierra, who drew closer, then stood opposite him, again feeling the weight of this moment.

"I will be one of the witnesses to your marriage." The lady-in-waiting stood adjacent to them, and they faced Chemira, who opened a worn Bible. "King Peralta, and, Sierra, I am here for the sole purpose to serve as a priest and officiate your wedding ceremony."

He nodded to Ache. "Ache informed me that, if you and the king left without marrying, it will be considered an elopement. Therefore, to preserve his throne, as required and mandated by Lanzarote law, on this day of his thirtieth birthday, he must be married. The marriage must be consummated now. Then you can both leave, and the throne will remain his upon his eventual return and to his descendants."

Whatever God has joined together let no man put asunder. Sierra stared at the king's hand clutching the crown. "I'm ready."

The lady-in-waiting offered her something wrapped in velvet. "The king gave me this ring one year ago. This is the ring that was to be for our wedding. You're the rightful owner. You might as well have it."

The king accepted it from her. "Thank you, milady. And, indeed, your magnanimity this day shall never be forgotten."

"I will make sure of it," Ache said with a twinkle in his eye. Was something going on between the lady-in-waiting and Ache? But this was not the time to ask, so Sierra focused on the king as her heart picked up speed. She was getting married—to a king. And this, *this* was beyond her wildest dreams. She inhaled deeply and smiled, while swirls of excitement turned in her belly at the coming commitment.

~

KING PERALTA HAD DREAMED OF THIS MOMENT, AND IT WAS finally here. He set the crown he had in his hand aside, accepted the ring from the lady-in-waiting, and took Sierra's hand in his. The roughness of her palm tore at his heart, and he swore to make the rest of her life as easy as he could. She had gone through a lot already, and he wished, above all things, that risking her life to escape with him had been unnecessary.

But they had no choice. "Sierra, you are the most beautiful woman I have ever seen. And your heart is even more beautiful. I love that I love you, and nothing I give up to marry you can equal your worth. You are a queen indeed."

A smile creased the corners of her eyes, and she swallowed then nodded behind what must be happy tears glistening over those beautiful freckles adorning her cheeks.

"I, King Peralta of Lanzarote, hereby request your hand in marriage. As is customary, it is necessary to receive your acceptance before a ceremony of marriage is performed. Do you accept my proposal of marriage, milady?" Finally, he could say the phrase without hesitation.

Sierra's throat bobbed. "Yes, King Peralta. I accept your proposal of marriage."

From the corner of his eye, he saw Ache stagger his stance and take a defensive position at the door, then urge the lady-in-waiting to move a few steps away from the couple, which she did. She pulled out a piece of cloth, placed it over a wooden board, and started drawing something, presumably, her first efforts on their portrait.

In front of King Peralta, Chemira lifted the Bible, read from the book of Matthew where Jesus had performed a miracle of turning water into wine at a wedding. Then he read another passage about the sanctity of marriage from the books of the Apostles. He set it down and began, "Do you, King Peralta, take Lady Sierra Fernando to be your lawfully wedded wife, to have and to hold, in sickness and in health, for richer or poorer, from this day forward, until death do you part?"

His heart warmed at the words he'd wished but never knew he would be lucky enough to hear. "Yes, I do."

Sierra slid the ring on his ring finger, and her beaming smile matched the thumping of his heart.

Chemira faced Sierra. "Do you Sierra Fernando, take King Peralta to be your lawfully wedded husband, to have and to hold, in sickness and in health, for richer or poorer, from this day forward, until death do you part?"

A nod dipped her delicate chin, her shining hair rippling with the motion. "Yes, I do." King Peralta slid a ring on her finger, raised it to his lips, and kissed it. They turned and faced the minister.

Chemira smiled. "By the power vested in me, I now pronounce you husband and wife. Sierra, you are no longer Sierra, but Queen Sierra Peralta of Lanzarote. King Peralta, you may kiss your bride. Congratulations."

King Peralta cupped her chin and gingerly planted a kiss on her lips, but he knew his job was not done. After kissing his bride, he parted from her and lifted the smaller golden crown, encrusted with precious stones—sapphires, amethysts, aquamarines, rubies, diamonds, and emeralds—from the nearby stool. "With my authority as the king of Lanzarote, and now husband to you, Sierra Peralta, I now pronounce you the queen of Lanzarote from this day forward. You shall be second only to my authority. I love you, my beloved queen." He set the crown on her head firmly and kissed her again, deeper this time.

Applause rang out, mixed in with wishes of congratulations.

"Please, sit, my queen. I need to paint your portrait," the former lady-in-waiting requested as Sierra occupied a stool with a blank canvass settled on the wall beyond it.

"Do we really need to do this?" Sierra asked as she was swept into an embrace by him—her husband.

The former lady-in-waiting nodded. "Yes, it is customary. However, due to the circumstances of this marriage, your portrait will be hidden in this chamber after...," she swallowed and darted her gaze at him then averted her eyes, "after the marriage is consummated today. It is the royal law. You cannot leave until that is done. Then you are free to go."

At the mention, Sierra's cheeks turned a deep shade. She nodded. "I'll sit then."

∼

12

"...For her worth is far above rubies." Proverbs 31:10

～

Sierra adjusted the crown encircling her head as King Peralta moved forward and uncovered a smooth stone seat. Ivory covered the armrest and gold encased the head while the floor in front of it had corals on the side. Only after he stepped, aside did she see it was a smaller replica of his throne upstairs.

He sat with confidence on his throne as only a rightful king would, and her heart twisted over what he was giving up for her sake. "Here, my queen. Please sit on my lap." The king held his hand out to her as an invitation. "Perhaps, it could make the painting go faster."

The former lady-in-waiting chuckled. "Not quite so, my king. However, I agree as it will help your queen relax so you can consummate the marriage and be on your way." She lifted her gaze to them. "May your God go with you and give you peace."

"Amen." This time, with her back turned to the others, Sierra saw that it was the king who blushed, but he maintained his poise. She sat on his lap, and while the former lady-in-waiting painted, the king whispered sweet words in her ear. Her grip on his hand tightened in response.

He told her what he thought the first time he saw her. How his heart had leapt when she'd first smiled at him. And how grateful he was that she was taking this journey of love. He shared his admiration of her attitude despite being thrust from simplicity into royalty. "I'm proud of how you have handled things so far. I promise, God willing, we will be fine. Trust His grace." He kissed her fully on her lips this time, much longer.

Eager to keep things on an even keel, when they parted, she thought ahead. "Will we be going up north or down south or perhaps to Spain?" she whispered in his ear, and his beard grazed her skin, leading her to blush yet again. "If we need to flee, where do we go and for how long?"

He curved a hand around her waist and whispered a sigh into her hair before answering. "Spain is risky. We need to go up north."

∽

KING PERALTA WATCHED SIERRA'S FACE FOR SIGNS OF WORRY AS she twisted and gazed into his eyes, and he felt like his love for her would swallow him whole.

"But it's colder, much colder up north. Isn't it better to go to Africa? How do we survive up north?" she asked.

But he could hardly resist. So he kissed her lips fully again, a kiss that left her breathless, before answering. "We'll go south first, to confuse anyone who tips off The Hunter. Then we'll turn and head northward." He curved one arm around her waist and drew her closer. "The Hunter wouldn't come looking that way." He tucked stray hair behind her ear, loving its silky feel between his fingers. He released a sigh at the freedom he now had to do something like this he'd wanted to do for her, but for so long, had not earned the right to. "I love you, my queen."

The lady-in-waiting cleared her throat. "Um, sorry to interrupt, my king and my queen, but I need you to remain still until I finish. Thank you." A twinkle sparkled in her eyes as she spoke. A twinkle which said she would, someday, want someone to hold her and love her like the king loved his queen.

King Peralta prayed in his heart that the Lord God would make someone so dear to love this lady with a large heart. And as his eyes settled on Ache, whose eyes were fixed on the lady-in-waiting, admiring her expert strokes while she painted, he wondered if that prayer might already be answered. Nevertheless, he and the queen stilled for the remainder of the session until their painter lifted her canvas with a satisfied smile.

"We're done," she announced. "I have my rough sketch. This should do. I know you both well enough to fill in the curves later." She cleared her throat and twisted to motion Ache while Chemira also stood. "We," she glanced at the rest of the party, "can wait outside the room so you can, um, do the needful. Knock three times on the door when you're done."

An acknowledging nod from King Peralta sent the trio on their way out of the room. He glanced around while he heard the door lock from outside behind them. Then Ache hit the heavy wooden log on the door thrice, announcing that they were clear to engage.

So, King Peralta spun, smiled at his wife, and drew her in. The moment he curved a hand around Sierra's neck and lowered his lips to hers, her soft responding whimper said all he needed to know to consummate their marriage.

She was ready for him.

∼

ONE HOUR LATER, AS HE LAY ON THE EXPANSIVE BED WITH QUEEN Sierra's tousled hair spread out on his chest, he knew his heart had chosen right. His heart beat only for Sierra. And he would do anything to ensure his wife was safe. "My love?"

"Yes, my king?" her soft voice replied beneath his chin.

"I think we should get ready to be on our way. Our lives are about to change. Remember everything, especially the secrets I've told you. Our royal secrets must be protected, and the riches of the royal treasury aboard our escape ship would be guarded at all times." He looped a locket with a key inside it around her neck. "In this locket is the key to the box containing the greatest riches of the royal treasury, passed down from many generations. If anything happens, keep this key safe." At her nod, he kissed her hair. "I will tell you the rest when we board the ship."

Unsure how to break the next news, he simply did so but trusted that she would understand. He tilted her chin to look up at him and barely resisted planting another kiss there. "The last thing I want to do is to thrust you out into danger soon after our marriage, but we have to leave to stay alive." He studied her eyes but, again, was glad to see no fear. "The Hunter would surely know by now that something is wrong. And when he finds you missing, and there is no wedding upstairs, he will suspect the truth."

She leaned up on his chest, planting lithe fingers on it. "I will get ready."

But he held her flat palm on his chest in place and stopped her from moving further. He gazed into her soft brown eyes as she wrapped a robe around herself, and he said with a firm voice. "I have to teach you a poem. It was handed down to me by my father and by his father. It's about the King and The Hunter." He paused, allowing the gravity to sink in. "You must teach it to our children, and they, to their children forever."

"Okay, but why?" She adjusted to rest beside his arm.

"If we are able to escape, The Hunter will give pursuit. And if he cannot find us, he will pursue our children and their lineage. He is sworn not to stop until we're dead." He stroked her hair, wishing he didn't have to say the next words. "And also because the other side of this poem is taught to the chosen Hunter's family. They teach it in secret to their children too."

"So, if he fails, his children will take over his pursuit?" At his nod, she sat up and crossed her legs. "I'm listening."

King Peralta recited it from memory. His father, the late king, had taught it to him almost daily in the garden and whenever they were alone. "The poem says:

'Long may you live, O King!

'Escape the Hunter when he comes

'His heart is dark, his dagger is cloaked, and his finger is cut

'He comes for Kings

'And none see him coming

'Escape the Hunter every way you can

'For the King is favored by God to live

'Shield the crown and protect the royal treasury

'Live among the orchards, vineyards, and garden of roses and blossom

'Fresh as the air, sweet as the berries, and refreshing as the rain

'Long may you live, O King!'"

The expressions shifted on his wife's face as she recited the poem, but determined to make sure she knew the words, he led her to recite the words over and again until he was satisfied. When she had a firm memory of it, they rehearsed their escape route again.

Then, when she made to rise, he drew her lower to himself and kissed her again. "I know we need to go, but be with me one more time, my queen."

She paused, smiled, then relented and allowed him to cover her with himself.

∽

13

"God is faithful...[He] will make the way of escape..." 1 Corinthians 10:13

∽

Another hour had passed before the king and queen emerged from the chamber to meet with the rest of their wedding party. As soon as they emerged, the group glanced at them.

He tightened his outer royal robe. "It is done. Our marriage is consummated."

Sierra blushed a deep color on her cheeks as his subjects bowed low to her.

"Long live, Queen Sierra," the former lady-in-waiting, who now stood quite close to Ache, holding the painting, genuflected. The others echoed her words.

Ache stepped forward, smiled to Queen Sierra, and bowed

to King Peralta. "We have to proceed to your ship. The other two guards whom I called to support us are waiting outside this chamber. They said The Hunter disappeared as soon as they left the inner court and he may know what is going on and might have a means to find us if he asks the right persons."

"Do you have all that we need?" King Peralta took hold of a dagger and set it inside his inner clothing beneath his royal robes. His wife, Sierra, nudged closer to him.

Ache pointed outside the rocky chamber's rolled stone. "Yes, my king. I went back to gather enough money to ensure your safe secret passage for a thousand miles and more. I also confirmed that Queen Sierra's friends' ship embarked for Spain. Two horses are aboard your ship for your crossing northward, if you so choose. I have included maps and guides as far as we know to travel, and I wrote letters stamped with your seal to allow for safe passage for you two. Everything has been sent to the ship awaiting your arrival with the queen. If your flight takes months, I would suggest you dock somewhere safe and settle there if the queen is with child to allow her time to deliver before you continue north. The weather will be harsh and not good for a woman with child. If possible, and if it does not risk your safety, send me word of your safe arrival and please make sure it bears your royal seal."

At King Peralta's nod, he added, "It's getting dark now, and the wedding party was dismissed, telling them you went off to conquer new lands."

"Did they believe you?" King Peralta couldn't help the doubtful lift to his brow, knowing that they only needed one person—The Hunter—to believe it and not to pursue them.

"Yes, almost everyone." Ache didn't need to say who. "Just

trust me and know you will be kept safe as much as is within my power."

The lady-in-waiting returned to their inner chamber. "If my father already knows, then I need to hide this painting now." She did and soon returned to them. "Why don't I go and find my father and try to convince him that all was well?"

"I won't be surprised if he doesn't believe you. I'm sure that, being the keeper of the palace grounds, he has informants and that he knows his way around the secret passageways."

King Peralta patted her arm. "Don't go. However, I appreciate your loyalty. Now, let's leave while there's been no bloodshed yet." He moved toward the outer entrance, curving an arm protectively around Sierra's waist.

Ache rolled back the stone, pulled a large block of wood from the door, and as they left, he sealed the doors.

King Peralta glanced behind him, cherishing all the memories created in those chambers. His marriage, the consummation of his marriage to the woman he loved, and the painting of them to preserve their legacy. *Lord Jesus, no matter what happens, may my descendants return here to see this place, even if we don't.* Everything he could have asked for had happened. *Thank You, Jesus, for our marriage. Thank You for Sierra. I am grateful.* He paused, took her hand, and asked, "Please pray for our protection."

∼

SIERRA NODDED, UNDERSTANDING THAT HER HUSBAND WAS allowing her to lead their spiritual lives, being a more mature Christian than him. But she knew that, as they journeyed from here, he would learn everything he could to take his rightful place of headship in their family. Comfort and convenience could be something they may leave behind, but she was not averse to hard work. She would blend in wherever they reached as long as they were safe.

"Dear Lord Jesus, You helped David slay the lion and the bear in the wilderness. And when he faced Goliath the Philistine, you helped David to overcome. You've conquered our lions and defeated our bears, and You have brought us to this point. Lord, please conquer every Goliath that might be headed our way. And please lead us to safety in Jesus' mighty name, amen. For You, Lord, are our Good Shepherd."

Soon, she concluded the prayers, and they moved outside. Every main door they passed, Ache turned and sealed it shut behind them, possibly to ensure no one went in there. They made a sharp turn, and he stopped. "The escape doors are that way, and I will go with you."

But the king shook his head. "You and the former lady-in-waiting will need to keep the kingdom running and keep things quiet. Stay here, Ache, and protect my people until I return."

Ache swallowed hard, took the king's hand, and wept over it. "Long live King Peralta," he choked out.

"Long live the king," Queen Sierra concurred. So did the others.

Ache assigned a guard to them. "He will go with you. Four others I assigned to travel with you on the ship are already aboard. They will protect you with their own lives, my king."

Sierra's shoulders relaxed. "Thank you very much, Ache. The king and I are grateful."

"Now, I will get you to the passage door. Farewell. May God keep and protect you."

"Amen," they chorused.

King Peralta took several steps toward the escape door, and Queen Sierra was walking in front of him. They reached it before they turned at a crackling sound. Queen Sierra opened the last door and saw Ache gasp as he bumped into someone.

Then he drew to a stop. He was still watching them from the fork where they parted, where the path had split right and left. The light he held shook when someone hit his cheek. Then it tumbled, hit the floor with a blaze, and he pulled his sword out.

"Ache!" she shouted, but they had seen who his attacker was as the king swept her behind him in a protective move.

"Go!" Ache shouted back to them, and the king pushed her out through the escape door while Ache tackled his attacker—a face she'd seen enough times in the dark to make out from afar.

It was The Hunter, clad in a warrior's clothing, with his face set as grimly as his mission.

While Ache and The Hunter fought, through the open doorway, Queen Sierra heard the former lady-in-waiting scream for her father to stop the attack, even as the king pulled her, the queen along, shut the escape door behind them, and they disappeared into the darkness of the escape tunnel.

She clutched his hand, prayed in her heart, and rehearsed the poem. One thing was clear. Until they reached the escape ship, they had only one person watching their backs now—God.

Their lifetime journey into the unknown had only begun, with The Hunter fast on their heels. To stay alive, they and their posterity would have to stay one step ahead of him—always.

And stay alive, they will.

THE END **CLICK HERE** and PREORDER **HUNTER**- the next in series at 50%OFF now

~

Have you read THE NEW RULEBOOK SERIES? If not, click HERE and enjoy this gripping 9-book acclaimed series today and find out how two orphans grew to become the most powerful couple in the world. **CLICK HERE** and enjoy it now! Read these before HUNTER releases to avoid some serious spoilers!

THEN JOIN MY VIP READERS CLUB HERE- http://www.joyohagwu.com/announcements.html -to know as soon as the next book releases.

ABOUT THE AUTHOR

By God's grace, Joy Ohagwu is an award-winning, bestselling Christian Fiction Author.

Follow her on these sites for news about instant giveaways and book updates.

A REALLY COOL OPPORTUNITY

JOIN MY VIP READERS CLUB to be the first to know when my books are discounted and available for purchase here: http://www.joyohagwu.com/announcements.html

> Want to know when my next book releases?
> And to grab:
> * a free ebook (limited time offer)
> * Release day giveaways
> *Discounted prices
> * And so much more!
> Hit YES below and you're in!
> See you on the inside!

THEN JOIN MY VIP READERS CLUB

FOLLOW AUTHOR JOY OHAGWU

∼

You can visit and follow my Amazon Author page with one click and enjoy my other available titles.

You can also follow me on

BOOKBUB

FACEBOOK

TWITTER

God bless you!

BIBLIOGRAPHY OF MY BOOKS

~

You can visit and follow my Amazon Author page with one click. And select your next read from my available titles.

RED-The New Rulebook Series #1
SNOWY PEAKS-The New Rulebook Series #2
THE WEDDING-The New Rulebook Series #3

VANISHED-The New Rulebook Series #4
RESCUED- The New Rulebook Series #5
DELIVERED- The New Rulebook Series #6
FREEDOM- The New Rulebook Series #7
REST- The New Rulebook Series #8
SUNSHINE- The New Rulebook Series #9

BIBLIOGRAPHY OF MY BOOKS 2

∼

UNCOMMON GROUND- Pleasant Hearts Series (Book 1)
UNBOUND HOPE- Pleasant Hearts Series (Book 2)
UNVEILED TRUTH- Pleasant Hearts Series (Book 3)
PREORDER

DECOY- Elliot-Kings Series (Book 1)

The New Rulebook Series Boxed Set- (Books 1-3)
The New Rulebook Series Boxed Set- (Books 4-6)
The New Rulebook Series Boxed Set- (Books 7-9)

Whisper- The Pete Zendel Series
The Secret Heritage- Pete Zendel Series Novella
Hunter- The Pete Zendel Series- Book 1
Christian Inspirational Titles:

<u>After Series (Book 1)</u>
<u>Jabez (After Series Novella)</u>
<u>After Series (Book 2)</u>
<u>After Series (Book 3)</u>

DESCRIPTION

A slave or a princess, which will he choose?
***

Shipwrecked and stranded at sea, Christian missionary Sierra Fernando had no choice other than to surrender her freedom. But when she arrives at the beautiful island of Lanzarote as a slave and stumbles into the king, she finds that slavery threatens more than her freedom—it threatens her life.

One year ago, King Peralta was sure his destiny as king of Lanzarote was fixed for him according to Lanzarote custom. He would marry the lady chosen for him by the council. Until he met Sierra and his choices shifted. With only twenty-four hours left, he must decide who to marry—a princess or a slave. One choice will lead to a life of misery. The other will end his reign—and possibly his life—and set off the dangerous Hunter after him forever. When time runs out, which bride will he choose?

Read The Secret Heritage today to find out. The Secret Heritage is a novella in the Pete Zendel Christian Suspense series, the next book after WHISPER. Reading WHISPER will improve your enjoyment of this series. Grab your copy of WHISPER by clicking here.

***

NEWS & NOTE TO THE READER

Thank you so much for getting **The Secret Heritage**, the second book of The Pete Zendel Christian Suspense Series! The Secret Heritage reveals The Zendel family heritage dating back 100-plus years before Pete Zendel was born. Whisper is the full-length prequel of this series, so please make sure to read it first. Please expect **HUNTER**, the next book in this series soon, by God's grace. It promises to be as exciting! God bless you!

A REALLY COOL OPPORTUNITY

Join my VIP readers club to be the first to know as soon as my books are available for purchase here: http://www.joyohagwu.com/announcements.html

> Want to know when my next book releases?
> And to grab :
> * a free ebook (limited time offer)
> * Release day giveaways
> *Discounted prices
> * And so much more!
> Hit YES below and you're in!
> See you on the inside!

THEN JOIN MY VIP READERS CLUB

DISCLAIMER

This novel is entirely a work of fiction. As a fiction author, I have taken artistic liberty to create plausible experiences for my characters void of confirmed scenarios. Any resemblance to actual innovative developments in any scientific area is purely coincidental. My writing was thorough, and editing accurate; hence active depictions of any kind in this book are attributed to creativity for a great story. It was my pleasure sharing these stories with you! ALL glory to God.

Copyright First Edition © 2018
Joy Ohagwu

LifeFountainMedia

CHRISTIAN FICTION TWINED IN FAITH, HOPE, AND LOVE.
Life Fountain Books and Life Fountain Media logo are trademarks of Joy Ohagwu. Absence of ™ in connection with marks of Life Fountain Media or other parties does not indicate an absence of trademark protection of those marks.

All rights reserved. No part of this publication may be reproduced, stored in a retrieval system, or transmitted in any form or by any means—electronic, mechanical, photocopy, recording, or otherwise—without prior permission of the author, except as brief quotations in printed reviews.
This novel is a work of fiction. Names, characters, incidents, and dialogues are products of the author's imagination or are used fictitiously. Any resemblance or similarity to actual events or persons, living or dead, scenarios, or locales is entirely coincidental. This ebook is licensed for your enjoyment. Unauthorized sharing is prohibited. Please purchase your copy to read this story. Thank you. Christian Suspense 2. Christian Fiction 3. Contemporary Christian Romantic Suspense 4. Christian Romance 5 Faith 5. Fiction

Except where otherwise stated, "Scripture taken from the New King James Version Bible®,

Copyright © 1982 by Thomas Nelson, Inc. Used by permission. All rights reserved.

All glory to God
Printed in the United States of America

❦ Created with Vellum

VOLUME THREE

HUNTER- THE PETE ZENDEL SERIES- BOOK 1

*To **JESUS**- The Only Living God.*

∽

Your Love for me leaves me speechless. I love You, my Lord. Eternity awaits.

A CONTEMPORARY CHRISTIAN ROMANTIC SUSPENSE SERIES

Get Joy Ohagwu's starter Library for **FREE**. Details are at the end of this book.

Foundational Scripture

∽

"For the vision is yet for an appointed time; but at the end it will speak, and it will not lie. Though it tarries, wait for it; Because it will surely come."- Isaiah 62:3

FOREWORD

HUNTER-
THE PETE ZENDEL SERIES -BOOK 1

∾

SERMONS COPYRIGHT
The sermons, messages, and exhortations in this book and series by the character of Pastor Pete Zendel, are original from the author, given to her by the Lord, and have never been preached before. Occasional quotations should be cited. Full delivery or share of any of these sermons requires a written permission from the author.
Thank you.

∾

DISCLAIMER

This book is a work of fiction and does not reflect the actual history, traditions, or cultures of any of the peoples represented. Any similarities are coincidental and should be taken as such. The author has taken artistic liberties to create an enjoyable story.

PROLOGUE

~

Malcolm Bridges found the moral code.

It had zero written on it.

Zero chances.

Zero nuances.

Zero trust.

And zero trespass.

Which was why the traveling party inching toward his Higher Grounds private mountain cabin hidden away between the thick woods and snow-capped mountains of Oakland, Maryland, looked suspicious—and their stubborn trek against the hilly up-climb piqued his curiosity.

"Good heavens." He scratched his long beard and wished he'd trimmed it for company. But no one had hiked here in the last four months. No. Not after their harsh winter. And certainly not after he'd posted the Road Closed: Private Property. Do Not Trespass sign at the fork into his private land, to ward off creeps.

And not after the media recently shared about a tourist who'd barely escaped getting mauled by a bear higher up on the mountain. That alone scared most people off and let him live here in seclusion, far from everyone and any possible drama.

Yet, clearly, some people either loved the snow too much or were as stubborn as he was and couldn't resist the alluring peaks. But how did they find his hidden cabin? Did they follow him from his recent grocery store run at the closest town? His hometown of Snowy Peaks neighbored Oakland, and even they knew to keep off his cabin or risk a rough welcome. He tugged at his beard. His great-grandfather built this cabin, and it had been in his family ever since. No matter how far each traveled, they always returned here to spend their later years. All he needed was a good truck to go to town and back.

Today, his rugged truck had made the long ride in good time, and he'd seen no visitor on the path before he'd made the turn into here. Did they see his truck and follow? But how could they have seen him in the busy landscape, unless they were desperate and in need of shelter?

But...Shelter from what? They sported no serious hiking gear—one clutched a walking stick and another had sleeping bags strapped to his backpack—so were they really hikers?

He wasn't sure.

A church bell rang from the distance winding down to the clustered town in the valley below, ringing out his personal reminder to feed the dogs before hunger turned their barks into growls.

Like it or not, he was sure of one thing—those people were headed in this direction—to his cabin tucked into the lush grove of pines, surrounded by nothing but snow and bordered by mountains.

And he'd need to reach a decision as to whether to provide a warm welcome or a harsh get-out-of-here greeting. And with each step drawing them closer, time was running out.

But, if he remembered right, the last time a team of strangers arrived in his hometown of Snowy Peaks uninvited, he'd been a little boy and a witness to the havoc and near wipeout of the town by a certain Pete Zendel, a name the town made sure no one forgot. But this was Oakland.

Beyond the travelers, snow still painted the landscape white, and with several more feet piled below the surface, everywhere was sure to stay white for some time.

His gaze caught the dark shadow of one of them stomping forward faster, and he groaned. "Decisions, decisions."

Nevertheless, the people crept annoyingly closer. Either they didn't read the sign or they'd ignored it, which ticked his anger. For just one second, he toyed with the idea of sending out his hunting dogs for a rough welcome. Those scary beasts usually put the right amount of fear in any intruder to turn them back toward the road, with their running feet flapping against the back of their heads if the snow didn't slow them down.

He raised his binoculars, chewing on the idea.

But he didn't do it. Something held him back. Instead, gripping his binoculars tighter, he observed them through the cracked window, careful not to allow its wooden edges to swing fully outward, but open just enough so he could see them and they couldn't see him. Something about the way they moved spoke purpose. And that made him even more cautious. Maybe he could hear them out first....

"One, two, three..." He counted the winter-dressed party under his breath. Ten people in all, although one looked quite young and another one behind him was likely female.

"Hmmm." Usually, mountain climbers in the dead of winter traveled here in small parties of four or five at most. But these people were twice that number. It appeared they came for more than a hike.

Who were they?

Why were they here?

And why wasn't he taking action already, like he usually would? He never took this long before to do something. It was usually, sight intruders, send the dogs. And get them off his grounds. But... *something* kept him rooted.

As they came closer, he saw some unusual gear on them—large printed maps rolled into one's backpack, thick armbands, and purple badges attached to their hips—so he lowered the binoculars and settled them onto his lap.

His curiosity won. Swinging to grab his mug and take a sip of his hot-but-quickly-becoming-iced coffee, he set it down just in time to pick up his binoculars again. He had to figure this out. He had to reach a decision before they arrived at his doorstep.

Would he welcome them or turn them away? He tapped his feet on the wooden cabin floor.

The first person was now close enough to the cabin, his black hiking stick leading the way. He could shout out to them. So he closed the window, rounded to the door, cracked it open, and peered out. "Who are you?" He cupped a hand against his mouth and hollered. "What do you want? This is private property. No trespassing."

The first man halted, cast a glance toward the rest of his party still a ways off, and faced him again. "Ed," he shouted.

A cool breath ushered his next words. "Ed who?"

"Zendel. Ed Zendel. Sorry for trespassing. We come in peace." His voice sounded young, but his last name had done him in.

Air whooshed out of him. Did he say...*Zendel*?

No way.

He blinked, clenched his fists, and blood rushed into his ears. He managed to shuffle his feet backward into the house. Without another word, he turned around, slammed the door shut, and chose the latter option.

Malcolm went into his living room, picked up his house phone, and called the sheriff.

Then, without hesitation, he set his hungry pack of hunting dogs loose on them.

1

"Shall the prey be taken from the mighty, or the captives of the righteous be delivered? But thus says the Lord: 'Even the captives of the mighty shall be taken away, and the prey of the terrible be delivered; for I will contend with him who contends with you...'"- Isaiah 49:24-25

A FEW WEEKS EARLIER...

"Where did you keep my tie, woman?" The bulky-framed, golden-brown-haired, hunk-of-a-man asked.

Stephanie Martinez drew the comforter close to her face with trembling fingers and pinched her eyes closed, pretending not to hear him, pretending she couldn't still smell him in the bed.

"Didn't I say you should hang it with the suit? But now I'm

getting ready for work, and it's not there," he bellowed, his voice rising several pitches higher.

She shut her eyes tighter, loathing the day already and dreading what she knew was coming. Today will be another regular morning with him—filled with his rage-powered, cuss-filled perambulation in their bedroom.

But today will also be the last time that will happen.

Her heart pounded loudly in her chest as she remembered her escape plan. And even louder when the stomp of his shoes echoed past the bed as she counted the time remaining for her to rise. She peeled one eyelid open wide enough to see the clock and his lowered figure, searching through the clothes she'd meticulously hung in their closet. The tie was right in front of him—if his anger cooled down enough for him to see it.

She shut her eye and exhaled long. Only thirty more minutes. Then she'd leave Alaska for good, never to return.

The city of Fairbanks was good to her. The man she was caught up with in it was not. But, at the time they met four years ago, she'd wished to be like everyone. And to live like everyone, without boundaries. And to "have a man" at any cost. Now, the cost had become so high her life was the only price she hadn't yet paid in this relationship. And now, she was done living in fear. Never again.

Not after today. Not ever again.

Still gripping the comforter as his voice rose higher and the cuss words started coming in a faster stream, she did the one thing she hadn't done in these four years—she prayed desperately. *Dear God, if You would keep me safe and help me escape, I will never leave You again. I won't choose sin over You anymore. I will serve You, in any way You want, for the rest of my life. Please, Jesus, rescue me.*

She tried to ignore how she walked away from her faith in Jesus four years ago when she'd been angry at God for allowing her brother, John, to get kidnapped. She'd hoped, prayed, and joined her sister, Angel, and her other siblings, Hughes and Grace, searching for John—to no avail nineteen plus years to date. So, she'd quit believing.

But she couldn't keep anger buried in her heart anymore. Today, she realized her need for help from on high, from someone greater than her current threat—her soon-to-be ex-boyfriend. If the system couldn't help her and she couldn't help herself, from experience, she knew God *would* help her.

Thankfully, she typically left for work an hour after he did, so he shouldn't suspect why she was still in bed. If she could, she'd stay here. Otherwise, something might slip if she was preparing while he was.

Just then, rough hands flung the protective comforters off her body. A blast of cold air hit her skin, and her eyelids flew open. Despite the working in house heater, winter's brutal chill sent shivers tingling over her skin.

Shielding her face with her arms from the impending assault she was used to taking by now—a hot slap, a rough jerking awake, or an object thrown at her while she cowered or, perhaps, struggled to catch fitful sleep—she counted the seconds until the first hit arrived. Calling for outside help in the past had done her no good. It only worsened the situation.

He was a cop and had blamed her injuries last time on a skiing accident they'd been on. No one believed her over him. He was the perfect man outside but had grown into a menace inside, to stop her from leaving him. Escape was her only choice before she ended up dead. "Get up, I say. Why are you still sleeping on a bed you don't own at this time of the day? Everyone else is awake. Come on out and find my tie." He stalked back to the closet, expecting her to follow.

At other times, she would comply just to keep the peace. This time, defiance rose in her belly and poured out in a quiet prayer through trembling lips as she drew up her knees to herself. Stephanie curled her arms around her knees and bowed her head. "Jesus, please save me," she prayed. "I can't deal with this man anymore. Please get me out of here, Lord." Thankful her posture muffled her words, she kept going. "I'm coming home to You right now. Back to the faith where freedom is real and unpretentious. Back to Your love which is genuine and unfeigned. To where I can spread my wings and fly with no one clipping them because it got in their way." She pressed a hand to still her lips, then whispered to the ears of the One who heard even whispered words, "My Lord Jesus, I'm coming back to You."

"Didn't you hear me, woman? Come get my tie!" Rage shook his voice, but she didn't move. "I'll come over there and…" He threatened with a string of words that made her cringe, but she stayed in place as a strange comfort she'd not had before enclosed over her heart like a shawl and the fear of him melted away.

After he stopped speaking, she coolly replied, still not looking directly at him. "I placed it on the pink hanger so it can stand out for you. I made sure it hung next to your uniform, which I also ironed. If you saw the uniform, then your tie is right next to it. But you didn't bother to look for it where it should be, did you? Yelling at me felt better."

She braced for it—the physical assault. Instead, he swung

around, fished out the tie, and threaded it around his neck. In relief, she slid back down and lay to sleep, or at least, try to, even when she knew all she could see right now was the minute hand telling her she had twenty-four minutes to rise. First on her agenda was to verify today's arrival of her car with the transporters shipping it—with her most important possessions locked in its trunk—to their dock at Olney, Maryland.

For all her boyfriend knew, her car was out for repairs for the past week, which it had truly been for about twenty minutes, before she completed the shipping paperwork and sent it on its way. Now, she just waited for him to leave. Once he did, she could go.

A few minutes after she laid down, a tap jostled her shoulder, and she jerked away from it.

Her boyfriend lowered his head close to her face and gave her a cold stare. "Today is the very last time you will ever speak to me the way you did, you hear me? If you try it once again, you won't be able to see the consequences of your words." He drawled his next words out. "Do we understand each other?"

Things she could say hurtled through her mind.

Yes, today is the last time you will abuse me.

No, I won't be here to see any consequences from you ever again.

Yes, what I said was true.

Yes, it took courage to say what I said now, and nothing you do would stop me from speaking the truth.

Could she compromise her whole plan for a hit at his ego?

No. Instead, she straightened. She could endure this spiteful verbiage one last time. "Of course. You're perfectly understood. If you'll excuse me, I have to rest up."

She turned away and settled into the comforters. Then she

closed her eyes. Soon, he left the house, but she held her breath until the outer door shut downstairs and his car left the driveway. She darted her gaze to the clock.

Ten minutes to go.

She ran barefoot to the shower and bathed as fast as she could. Next, she called the Greyhound bus station to confirm their departure, said to be in about two hours. Then she dressed up. Grabbing her purse, she paused at the door, then returned inside. She snatched up a notepad and scribbled on it:

Hi,

I know you will wonder where I am. I have left you. You and I are over. We were over a long time ago. You know that. I will no longer tolerate being abused. I called the cops last time, but you wiggled your way out, blaming the stuff you did on my skiing accident. I'm done looking for outside support. Again, it's over, and I left you of my own accord. I am not missing. Do not try to look for me. I'm done. Thank you for the good times. I forgive you for the bad and horrible times. If you come after me, I can assure you of this—the cops and Federal authorities will be waiting. Goodbye.

Steph.

Stephanie snapped a picture of the note in case he altered something afterward. Then she held it to the center of the dining table with a saltshaker where he'd see it. She glanced around one last time.

She crossed to her picture with him on the wall. She extracted it from the frame then tore it up and poured the pieces into the kitchen trash. *Lord, I tear up the painful, bitter past I've had here. May it not follow me to my next destination.*

Then she clasped her purse as her taxi pulled up outside. Leaving the spare keys he'd given her when she'd moved in, next to the note, she also left everything else behind—her clothes, shoes, and jewelry he had bought for her, and the engagement ring he'd refused to take back—and she fled for her life.

Climbing into that taxi felt like home. It brought her to the shipping dock where she confirmed that her vehicle had shipped and would arrive as scheduled. She'd specifically requested they leave her things in the trunk, and they'd graciously agreed, only charging her a little extra after searching through the bags. Her degrees, certificates, awards, and everything of value was in there. If she used postal services, her boyfriend might use it to track her destination, so she risked no chances of that happening. Shipping them in her car was safer.

She called another taxi and rode it to the Greyhound station. But when her stomach growled, she had the driver stop at a Subway shop one street over. It was also an alternate stop just in case her boyfriend tracked the taxi to their destination. Reaching the counter, Stephanie bought her ticket for Anchorage. Then she changed her mind.

He had resources. And the bus was a slow means of escaping a man capable of finding her within hours. So, she left her ticket at the counter and chose to fly. Thankfully, her taxi had already left. After calling yet another, she rode to the airport and purchased a flight ticket to Seattle, the next available flight, left within the hour.

Then she sat and waited, her heart thudding, her breath

laboring, her mind spinning, contemplating what had happened so far. And she prayed for her boyfriend not to find out she'd fled until she escaped the state. A man like him could fabricate something to force her to legally stay. But getting her back from another state would be harder. She could hardly remember praying this much in recent times. But, for a faith she'd known and loved so well, everything was coming back like second nature, and it felt great. Still, a few thoughts nagged at her.

It could go bad.

He might find her.

She might be forced to go back.

Gripping her winter coat with gloved hands, she shivered. More than the weather sent prickles of ice through her veins. For the first time since leaving the house, she struggled with the possibility of what he might accuse her of.

Falsely, of course. But it would be his word against hers, and he *was* the law around here. Nobody would believe her. Dating and marrying law enforcement was good, unless the person was bad. Then their power became a snare no one could help you out of. It was a good thing that her sister was loving and a good cop. And it was bad that her boyfriend was a cop, and nothing good could be said about him. But Stephanie was done being ensnared. If the cost of leaving him was uncertainty, then it was far better than the certainty of the misery of living with him.

With her mind made up, she dialed her sister, Angel, whom she hadn't called in a long time.

As soon as Angel picked up, her loving voice floated over the phone. "Hi, Steph Bear."

Hearing someone call her by her childhood nickname almost had her bursting into tears.

Her sister loved her.

Her family loved her.

But she left their love because it was pure and the path she'd chosen was not.

Now, she was more than ready to be embraced by that Christian love again, and this time around, for good. "Hi, Angel. It's good to hear your voice again." Some static crackled. Then police radio chatter droned through. So her sister was at work.

"I could say the same," Angel said with a slightly hushed voice. "I called you last month and left a number of voice messages."

"I know." She sucked in her lower lip.

"Last week when I'd called, I'd gotten such a cryptic response, I figured you weren't in the mood to talk."

Quite true. She had sounded cryptic. "I'm sorry, sis. I wasn't trying to be harsh. I was in a…situation, and I couldn't see past my pain."

"Oh." Angel paused. "It leaves me wondering what has been up with you."

"Let's just say it's easy to throw away one's faith when the world tells you it's useless—until you face a storm where you realize the only way out is the God you threw off your boat on land." A sigh slipped loose. "I'm truly sorry for being out of touch all this while. Please forgive me."

"Of course, sure. What kind of situation are we talking about?"

Sure, her sister would pick up on that. Any threat to her siblings, she instinctively took personally. "It's an issue about my boyfriend. I'm headed to your place on short notice, but I'd planned to take two days to arrive in Maryland."

"Really? It doesn't take two days to get from Alaska to Maryland. Why the runaround?" Someone said something hurriedly to Angel at her end, and she replied, asking for another minute. Then she returned to Stephanie. "Is the man that dangerous? Did he hurt you?"

She wasn't going to answer the second question, so she settled on the first one. "Well, I can't explain over the phone. But he's potentially dangerous, and he didn't know I was leaving him." A sigh slipped through. "Sorry, there is a lot I haven't told you, including how the relationship started."

"You don't say. Yes, there is. I don't know what's been going on with you until now. I didn't even know you had a boyfriend, let alone a dangerous one. Come on home, and we'll talk when you get here. Our doors are wide open. I love you. Be careful and keep me posted at every stop in your journey."

"I love you too, Angel. Thanks for having my back. I will keep in touch. See you."

After she hung up, she called her brother Hughes in North Carolina, and her sister Grace, who just like her, barely ever called, and briefly told them of the situation.

When Stephanie finished talking, Grace was alarmed, but Hughes was not. Instead, he was angry that she'd stayed with a man who would hurt her, but she wasn't ready to argue, so she let him off the phone. He didn't come home often, and neither did Grace these days.

Of all their siblings, Angel was the one whose door was always open. No matter how much they messed up, she'd always welcome them like a mother.

Angel was their God-sent, well, angel, who took up the

responsibility of parenting them after their parents were gone. Their parents would be proud of all Angel accomplished for them, and for the first time in her adult life, Stephanie intentionally prayed God's blessings on her elder sister.

Soon, her flight's boarding gate was announced and repeated, and as she picked up her purse and small hand luggage, she gave God thanks that her boyfriend had not called in to check on her. She hoped it stayed that way until she was airborne.

When she was finished going through security checks, she boarded the plane. A tight seat enclosed between two people had never felt more comfortable. Other times, she'd complain about how much smaller the economy seats were getting. But today, this seat was her channel to freedom, and she could've been sitting on a palatial love seat for all she cared. Pulling her long, dark hair into a tight bun, she set her purse in-between her legs.

Again, she prayed for a safe flight.

"Ladies and gentlemen, please strap on your seatbelts. We are about to take off. Switch off all devices..." Those words sounded like a heavenly call. She texted Angel.

I'm about to take off from Fairbanks. Will land in Seattle next. Turning my phone off.

A quick reply followed. *Okay. Praying.*

She chuckled. *Thanks. I appreciate your prayers, sis. I need them.*

She pressed the power button on her phone, then relaxed against the seat as the plane took off and lifted skyward, every move, powering her flight toward freedom.

Thank You, my Lord Jesus, for getting me safely out.

Now, she just had to stay out for good—and arrive safely.

~

As soon as Police Officer Angel Martinez Santiago got off the phone, she slid it into the back pocket of her uniform, jumped into her police cruiser, and hurried toward her waiting team. After hours of wading through rush-hour traffic, from the affluent part of town to the ghettos, she arrived near Grown-Up Dorm Living—a cluster of bungalows where residents rented rooms and shared other facilities. Sliding into her designated parking space at the Seven-Eleven where her team had gathered, she grabbed her radio and jumped down, fully clad in tactical gear. From here, they'd walk approximately half a mile to this individual's registered address. "Thank you, Captain, for letting me take that call before we take down the suspect. My sister was on the line and needed help."

Static crackled from the other end. "Copy that. You're welcome. After God, family comes first. Let's get on with our mission."

Angel slid on her biohazard goggles, disarmed her gun's safety, and led the team of four into the slum neighborhood bungalow. Everything seemed calm, but, around here, appearances could be deceiving. Gunfire sometimes rattled the seeming quiet and led to gang wars. A number of officers lost their lives in unexpected crossfires while patrolling. But if the person who could lead her to her missing brother was here, she was going in, with or without support. All of the warmest leads they'd chased for John's kidnapping had led them here, and she wouldn't leave without answers.

The man in question was said to have been seen with someone who looked like John across state lines, shortly after he disappeared.

But staying focused was hard when her sister was having issues too. Now, she'd broken up the mission twice to communicate and had standing permission from the captain to answer her sister. Emotions warred in her heart. How could Stephanie have allowed herself to get caught up with a dangerous and determined man? Why didn't she tell her anything about this until it became a safety issue? Didn't Stephanie trust her?

Angel pressed her lips tightly, wading through the narrow hallway into a row of rented rooms in the house. Her phone pinged with a text message from Stephanie, letting her know she had landed. So, Angel typed a quick reply and pocketed the phone.

Attempting to keep her mind on this mission, she glanced past an open doorway and was about to move on when something on the TV paused her steps—Stephanie's face on the screen.

2

"For the Lord will plead their cause, and plunder the soul of those who plunder them." Proverbs 22:23

SHAKEN AWAKE BY THE PLANE'S DESCENT, STEPHANIE CLENCHED her hands into fists, then exhaled. She'd made it. Out of the state. Away from him.

She had fallen asleep, probably due to not sleeping much last night. But as soon as the plane touched down, she smiled for the first time.

She was in Seattle.

Tiredness clung to her joints, and hunger pangs bit her belly. Only then did she remember she hadn't eaten the sub-sandwich still in her purse. So after she bought her flight ticket to Baltimore, with two hours to wait before takeoff, she settled on a lounge seat and pulled the food out of her purse. Biting into the sandwich, she sucked in a stray onion and allowed the tangy salad dressing to coat her tongue. Sipping some water, she set her purse down and relaxed.

Remembering her promise to update her sister, she shot Angel a quick text. *I've landed in Seattle, and I've got two hours before I board the next flight to Maryland. Please keep praying. See you.*

In the same manner as before, Angel replied fast. *Thank God. I'm praying.*

After finishing her meal, Stephanie tossed the wrapper in a trash can. Then she strolled to an airport shop to buy a bottle of drinking water. After paying for the water and uncapping the bottle, she took a sip and placed it on the counter to tuck her debit card into her purse. In passing, she glanced up at the wall-mounted black-and-white TV. Breaking news splashed across the screen, and her face stared back against the garish all-caps of a single word—*MISSING*.

~

STEPHANIE GASPED. HER BOYFRIEND…

He must've caught on. And declared her missing. But didn't he see her note? She scrambled to fish out her phone from her purse. Her screen lock displayed a text message from him.

I will find you, woman. You can't run far in this town. Huh. He thought she was still in Fairbanks? Or at worst, somewhere in Alaska? She figured he must be searching everywhere for her. But she noticed something else. His text message gave no indication that she was missing. And if he did see her note, then he'd hidden it from the world. Her ringing phone jerked her back. She blinked at the number, gripping the phone harder.

It was him. So, she did the next thing she knew how. She

rejected his call, then blocked his number. But not before a second text followed. *You can't outrun me, Steph. Watch out.*

On a whim, she turned in time to hear the newscaster say, "Anyone with information regarding Stephanie Martinez's whereabouts should contact this number." The number was printed on the screen.

Good.

Stephanie took down the number and tapped out a text message. *I'm not missing. I'm fleeing an abusive boyfriend. Please take my image off the news as he is trying to use you to locate me. For details, check the Fairbanks Police records. Thanks.*

That should be enough.

Only after she sent the text, she realized they could call her phone now. "Oh no." But it was too late.

Her phone chirped with a response from the tip line number.

Can we call you? We have to confirm that you're okay before we remove your face from the news.

She texted back—*Yes.*

Soon, her phone rang. "Hi, this is Channel 7 News. We learned you're missing, but you say you're okay. Can you confirm this?"

"Hi, yes, I'm Stephanie Martinez and I'm not missing. I left my boyfriend today because he's abusive, and I'm fleeing to my family. Please cancel the missing person's report. I left him a note at home letting him know I'm not missing. And please don't share any information about my whereabouts to him."

"We can understand your situation, but can you send us something…a video, an image, or anything to prove first that you are Stephanie Martinez and second that you're not saying this under duress?"

Stephanie thought about it. "I'll jump onto my social media feed for a live session. That should be ample proof."

"Good enough."

As soon as she hung up, she logged onto one of her social media accounts, and backing a blank, white wall, she went live. "I'm going live to let everyone know I'm okay. I left my boyfriend and I'm not missing. I'm safe and I'm traveling right now. I will make contact with law enforcement as soon as I arrive at my destination to confirm my safe arrival. Once again, any assertions that I'm missing are lies. Thank you all for your concern, and God bless you."

People she didn't know were connected to the livestream, and a thousand more than her one hundred friends were watching. Soon, her live video replayed over the TV before her. People were commenting, wishing her a safe arrival at her destination. Others left comments applauding her for leaving an abusive relationship and wishing her luck. More comments scrolled through saying she was a hero for not waiting to end up as a statistic.

Tears welled up her eyes. This was genuine love from people she'd never met. This was God showing her that, not only was He for her, He was welcoming her back with open arms and using His own creation to wrap arms of love and comfort around her.

Thank You. She opened her heart, her whole heart this time —not because she wanted help for escape or a way out of somewhere uncomfortable, but just surrendering to the One Whose love was eternal—to Jesus. *I surrender my all to You, my Lord Jesus. Take it all, no holds barred.*

Almost as soon as she finished praying, her departure gate was announced. She texted Angel about the false news her ex was spreading. And also about the call with the media. Then she let Angel know he'd threatened to find her and said she knew he meant it.

Never mind anyone's threats. Place your trust in God and come home. Anyone threatening you will have to pass through me.

At Angel's words, confidence surged into her heart.

What a sister she had!

When it was time to board, she texted Angel again, letting her know her next destination was Maryland. Her car should be waiting for pickup upon her arrival as indicated on the shipping documents. So she'd pick it to drive with her stuff inside, to her sister's place.

Several hours later, when she reached the BWI Airport, despite the chill, she exhaled long and blew warm breath into the cool air. No, this was not as cold as Alaska. But it was home. God got her home just like she'd prayed.

When she lifted her eyes to heaven, gratitude warmed her heart as she left the airport in a taxi to Olney, Maryland to get her gray Nissan.

3

"Therefore, judge nothing before the time, until the Lord comes, who will both bring to light the hidden things of darkness and reveal the counsels of the hearts." 1 Corinthians 4:5

After speaking with her sister, Angel moved stealthily down the hallway, toward the unit marked Unit 7, at the end. She'd first taken the time to inhale and exhale and mentally focus on the mission. Handling dual emergencies was stretching her attention to the max, but she wouldn't have it any other way. Neither this mission nor her sister could wait. Life was happening, and she could roll with the punches.

However, one thing was clear—if Stephanie knew she was on an active mission, she'd stop updating her, so she refrained from yielding that information.

"Remember, we're after information. Nothing more." She

spun and reminded her team, who acknowledged her with a nod.

"Copy that."

She rapped on the door. "Police. Open up."

A rattle sounded on the other side, then a squeal—like someone shouting to another person.

She rammed on the door with her shoulder, and its weak hinges gave way. She stepped into the crammed room. One person hid something with a blanket while another—whose appearance matched their person of interest—scaled the window. "Police! Stop!" She lowered her weapon, sprinted across the room, caught his arm clinging to the window, and swung him back inside. They both landed on the carpet, and she pivoted and pinned him to the ground. "Stop fighting."

The bearded man stopped wriggling and scowled.

"What do you want?" he demanded in a gruff voice. "Does living in a poor neighborhood mean I get harassed by police?"

"We're here for what might be a quick chat if you cooperate. I chased you because you ran. If you promise to cooperate, my fellow officers and I won't have to get rough with you." Angel loosened her hands on him and cuffed him instead. "I'm cuffing you as a precaution, not as an arrest. If you answer our questions, we'll let you go, unless you lie. Are you going to cooperate?"

Hesitating, he elbowed himself into a sitting position, then nodded. "Yeah." His brows curved. "Depending on what cooperation means."

She raised him to his feet and, with a second officer's help, sat him on a chair. "We'll see about that in a minute, shall we not?"

"What do you want?" He eyed her, then blinked at the slightly parted window over which an officer stood guard.

"Information. Some years ago, you were spotted across state lines with this man." She brandished John's photo, and the man's face showed he remembered something as he pinched his lips then relaxed his face again. "We want to know where he is."

He shrugged, looked away, and growled. "I don't know where he is."

"But you recognize him." She said it as a matter of fact. "Why don't you tell me how and where and who else was involved?"

"I don't know anything."

Her hands flew to the back of his neck, and she jerked his collar back and blew out words through clenched teeth into his ears. "Listen to me, if you think I'm here to play, you have another thing coming, because I will make sure you end up in the worst prison in the country where taking a dump will be a luxury. Now, tell me where he is!"

"It wasn't me. I was only a driver." The shock of her reaction melted his resistance. "Francis hired me to drive them there."

Well, they were getting somewhere. "Where is 'there,' and who is Francis?"

He was silent.

"You want to talk, trust me. I won't be patient with you," she warned.

"He's not the talking type."

"Who?"

"Francis. He works with the best, I mean, the worst." He exhaled, and the garlic in his breath stung her nostrils. "You can't find him, ma'am."

"Trust me, I will." In her earlier desperation, she still clutched to his collar. Stepping back, she freed his shirt and straightened.

"But, even if you do, he won't talk."

"Leave that to me. What's his number?" She could run a trace on it and get some background. Details like who he called around the time John went missing, and afterward, would be insightful.

"I've got to grab my phone from my back pocket."

She stared at him in warning. "Don't try anything funny. I'll un-cuff you."

Angel unsnapped the cuffs, and an officer stood behind him as he removed his cellphone and called out the details. She jotted the number down. "Does Francis have a last name?"

He shook his head. "I don't know his last name, ma'am. Nobody does. We just called him Francis."

"Fine. When was the last time you talked to him?"

"Many years ago. I can't remember."

She notated that. "Where did you meet him for this job?" Maybe they could investigate archived city security camera footage.

"A gas station in Rockville Pike."

"Which one?"

"Shell by the Laundromat."

She knew where it was. But it was so far from the construction site where John worked. "Then what?"

"Then I drove them to a BP gas station on Rhode Island Avenue, dropped them off, and left. I don't know anything after that."

"Good. We'll be in touch, and if you remember anything else, call this number." She left a card on a cluttered wooden, round table near the door and walked out, determined to shake some clues loose from Francis.

∼

When Angel returned to her office at the SSPD, Silver Stone Police Department, she started digging for more information. Francis had a prior record and disappeared a couple of years ago. Hard as she looked, she couldn't pin down his current address.

Her partner, Pierce, strolled through the door. "How's it going? Did you find anything useful in the raid?"

"We did. Not much, but a clue could be hidden in the details."

"Sounds like a success then. Some raids get you nada."

She chuckled, glad that she could smile, and the stress of the entire day eased a little. "You can say that again."

"I'll be glad to help in any way I can." He drew closer and braced a hand on the back of her chair as he peeked over her shoulder to eye her screen.

"Actually, that would be great. Can you help run a few checks on this phone number? You might find something in connection to John's kidnapping. I'll get more help for us to speed things up." She grabbed the phone and called in for support from their technical team, who took the number.

"Of course. What do you need?"

"I'm searching the records for recent calls and looking through information for the past ten years. It's a lot to go through. So I need someone who will go through the records for the ten years prior. Twenty years to date is the time period we're scrutinizing. Something must come out of this. I need a win."

"Sure. I'll be on it in my office and will call if I have any questions. Ping me if something comes up at your end, and I'll do the same as I have my entire afternoon free to devote to this. I'm sure the captain won't mind."

"Thank you so much, buddy."

He smiled. "Hey, I like John, too, and want him to come home."

Her throat tightened. "I know you do." When he left, she shelved her memories of her brother aside and focused on seeking a means to bring him home.

∼

CLIMBING INTO HER TRUCK AT THE END OF HER DAY, ANGEL WAS tired. She leaned her head against the driver's seat and stared at the roof. "I went through eleven thousand phone call records for this man today, spanning ten years, and yet, I have nothing. Not a single shred of evidence in them could possibly lead me to John."

Frustration climbed up her heart, and all she could do to keep from screaming at the top of her lungs, was to pray. "Lord Jesus, how long? How long will I search and find nothing? Twenty long years have gone by, and I don't know where else to look. How come it's John who went missing and not me?"

Tears stung her eyes. "Lord, last Sunday the pastor said deep grief produces deep grace, but I don't want this anymore. This is too hard. The SSPD's resources to support this investigation have almost run out. The number of staff supporting me have been cut in half and assigned to other tasks. The captain supports our finding John, but everyone expects me to give up. I can see it in their eyes. Everyone feels it's too late—twenty years is too long to still be hoping that he's alive. Are they right?"

She clung to the steering wheel. "Should I give up? Am I being unrealistic?" Those tears flowed down. "Somewhere deep inside, I know John is still alive. If he is dead, please let me know. If he's alive, please bring him home."

She swiped the tears off her cheeks as someone tapped on the window. Pierce leaned down to her window.

"Hey." She sniffed.

He observed her for a moment. "Um, I found something. Come back inside."

They made straight for his office where he pointed to a chair and she didn't wait for a verbal invitation. She slid right into it. "What have you got?"

He whipped his monitor around. "What are you looking at?"

She peered at the Excel document. "A spreadsheet."

He swung it back to himself. "Sorry, I meant the information in it. Let me explain. That could be faster."

Beyond his shoulder, the sun was already setting. Her sister would've arrived in Maryland and could be headed to her place. She hoped to be home, showered, changed into casual clothing, and looking less depressed. "Okay."

"Well, I was running the information, and it was simply too many phone calls to track. So, I modified my search to two criteria—numbers he called regularly and numbers he called less than three times. The regular numbers show us his daily patterns, while the less-than-three-times numbers show us those he could have high-stakes dealings with. Just a hunch.

And guess what?" He cracked a grin. "This should give you some hope."

She sat up. "What?"

"One of the numbers he'd called twice triggered something in our database. So I cross-referenced it with other cases."

"Okay." She shifted in her seat.

"A number he'd called the day John died, he also called the day the then-candidate Robert Towers was almost killed."

"You mean the former President Towers? Our former SSPD captain?"

His jaw set. His eyes hardened. Determination and admiration tightened his features with a pride in SSPD accomplishments and a resolve to live up to those who'd gone before them—both feelings she knew well. "The very same. The man he called was the one who killed Violet Zendel and had attempted to kill President Towers. He was killed at the scene. We matched his records. Voice, phone details, and travel information on both occurrences match the ones we found on Francis."

"Francis is dangerous."

"He is. He stops at nothing to get his way, and he works with—"

"The worst of the worst, according to his...friend." She referenced their earlier questioned source. "How do we find Francis?"

"We let the numbers take a trek. I ran several queries but found nothing." He scratched his jaw, then smiled wider—hopefully, a good sign. Chasing a guy who worked with a dead assassin wasn't something she'd expected, but it now explained why they couldn't find anything. They were dealing with professionals, very dangerous ones she'd prefer never to have anything to do with.

"So, what do we do?"

He lifted a finger. "But there was this one address where he went around this time every year. Calls registered from the cell tower there for about a month, and then he'd disappear once more."

"I'm guessing that's where he lies low?"

Pierce nodded. "I'm thinking the same thing. So, I've informed the captain, and we have his go-ahead to track the place down."

"When?" Never mind her exhaustion. She wasn't letting go of this new lead. "I want to get this guy and hear what he knows."

"I do too. However, we have to do this carefully and be well informed before we proceed. I need to locate a new phone number for him as this one looks like he uses it occasionally these days. We also need to scout the said location to make sure he still frequents the place and is there right now. We can't take chances with him running."

"Excellent. What do you need me to do?" She massaged her stiff shoulders.

"Go home. Get some rest, and I'll call you as soon as I have a new phone number. The captain and I agreed to send a team tonight to see if the suspect is on location. If we get these things done between now and this time tomorrow, we'll go there in two days. That should also give you enough time to sort out the matter with your sister."

"Thank you very much, Pierce. I appreciate all of your support. Please call me as soon as you have an update. You just made my day."

He gave her a side hug as she rose and led her out, walking her to her vehicle. "I know how hard this is for you. We all do.

Hopefully, this new lead refreshes your hope. Don't give up. John wouldn't want you to, and neither do we. We are praying for you."

Her heart warmed at his words as they reached her vehicle and she unlocked it. "That means a lot. I'll call the captain to express my gratitude."

"He left to see President Towers. Meanwhile, he'll be back tomorrow, and you can thank him in person."

"Great. Thanks, buddy."

"Don't mention it. Good night."

As she started the car, she felt refreshed. Smiling and raising her eyes to heaven a second time, she said the opposite of the words she'd prayed earlier. "Thank You, Lord Jesus—for restoring my faith and hope for John. I give You thanks."

Then she drove home, showered, and awaited Stephanie and details of why she fled from Alaska.

4

"I acknowledged my sin to You, and my iniquity I have not hidden. I said, 'I will confess my transgressions to the Lord,' and You forgave the iniquity of my sin." Psalm 32:5

"I'M SURE HE'S COMING AFTER ME."

Dusk settling in, Angel looked up past her younger sister, Stephanie, to her car in the driveway and sensed a crinkle on her forehead. It wasn't Stephanie's presence that alarmed her. "Come inside." She wouldn't query her out on the balcony.

Stephanie followed her into her Odenton, Maryland home, past remnants of former civilizations. Angel's husband, Tim, a former archeologist, had partially given up his passion for traveling and digging up ancient things in order to start a missing persons' nonprofit organization annexed to a private investigative team owned by famous actor Liberty Stone.

Angel once interviewed Liberty as a crime suspect, but

they'd grown close and become friends since she solved the case. Matter of fact, she'd visited the Fortitude Homes Estate a number of times. She and Tim even held their wedding reception there. Tim still lectured part-time during the winter and summer at the university but spent most of his daily hours at the nonprofit.

Celebrity Liberty Stone's involvement surprised Angel.

Everyone knew of Liberty's love for guns, and Liberty understood Angel's dislike for them despite being a cop. But Angel was shocked when Liberty stepped forward to support them, and accepting her offer wasn't hard.

After their wedding, Liberty championed their cause and started the Looking Glass PI agency when Angel planned to quit her job as a cop to join the search, without a police badge, if things went slow.

But both Tim and Liberty had strongly objected, insisting that she could better assist in the SSPD. So, against her wishes then, she'd stayed. But now, she was glad she did. All the support she could ever want came from her fellow officers who saw how hard she worked on every case that ever landed on her desk and were as committed to finding John as she was. Today, against all odds, they'd made some progress. Then this situation with her sister developed.

Was Stephanie going to be okay? Even with sketchy details, she could put out a restraining order against the man in question if he came after her. But Stephanie didn't say who he was, so Angel couldn't assume anything yet.

Plush carpet softening their steps, she led the way into the living room, then waited for Stephanie to speak up. On impulse, while Stephanie sank onto the cream couch and tucked her feet beneath her like a child in trouble, Angel strode to the window to ensure there was no imminent danger outside. "Who is after you, Steph? Your same boyfriend? Have you reported it to the police?"

Standing carefully beside a shelf displaying Tim's exquisite and vibrant Ethiopian baskets, Angel peered out through the lime-green curtains to what initially caught her attention. "And why does it look like you carried all your stuff and stashed it in that car of yours? Is the situation that bad?"

Stephanie gulped and nodded. "It is." Beneath her disheveled bun, her eyes had bags under them. When she began crying, sobs shook her shoulders behind the peach-colored sweater.

Shifting her stance by the window, Angel wasn't sure whether to push for an answer or console her. She crossed to her side and hugged Stephanie. If the threat was imminent, Stephanie would say so. "I'm sorry, Steph Bear. Can you tell me what's going on?"

Stephanie had closed like a book after John went missing. Getting her to say anything was like snatching candy from the mouth of a hungry kid.

It was impossible.

The only time she engaged Angel, Tim, or any of her siblings in discussion was when any clues or developments arose about John's disappearance. Otherwise, she didn't talk much. Angel prayed this time that, whatever had happened, Stephanie would speak up. She appreciated the openness Stephanie had shown on her way here and prayed it remained.

After what seemed like five minutes, Stephanie sobered up enough to lift her head. "Yes, it's him." Loosening her hair off a bun and sweeping long, dark curls off her face, she swiped the hair aside and looked into Angel's eyes. "I told him to leave, but he wouldn't go. So I chose to leave him several times, but he convinced me to stay."

Angel let her hand drop to Stephanie's own. "Who are we talking about? What's his name?"

"Sorry." Snuggling deeper into the couch, Stephanie pulled over a handwoven throw blanket, its pinks and oranges and purples as vivid as the baskets and a sharp contrast to her pallid features. She tossed her rubber band onto the retro, bronze, square table that Tim had brought home from Brazil anchored to a small water dispenser. "I forgot you don't know him. He's Richard, my ex. He gave me an engagement ring, and I told him I wasn't interested. I liked him before things went bad, but long before I met him, I'd chosen I wouldn't marry someone who's not a Christian. But I couldn't say it was because he wasn't a Christian. That didn't matter to him. I'd told him I wanted out of the relationship, but he disagreed and said we could work things out."

"Wait, so this...Richard you're in a relationship with, he proposed to you and you said no? And he's after you, to hurt you?" Although trying not to project impatience, she needed details in case she had to act fast on her sister's behalf. Being a cop made her know situations developed quickly, especially emotional ones.

Stephanie nodded, slowly. "We were in love at the time. I mean, when we first met, he was so funny and a really cool guy. I liked him." She shrugged. "So I figured it didn't hurt having him around, and we exchanged numbers. Little by little, a relationship started." When Stephanie glanced up, color lit her cheeks. "Then he kissed me, and well, the rest is history."

At least, she was talking. "So, what is the 'rest'?"

"We...um," Stephanie withdrew her hand and folded them

on her lap. She dug the toe of her flat-heeled, brown, knee-high boots, across the cream carpet, scuffing the weave backward. "Listen, I know you won't approve of these things. But John had gone missing, and that alone had wrecked me."

"It wrecked us all."

Those words seemed to spur her on. "I was so devastated, and I wanted a friend. I managed on my own for a while, but I needed someone to talk to, someone who wasn't in the same kind of pain. Someone who wasn't family."

"So..." Angel prodded. *Please, God...What has this girl done?*

"I, um, moved in with Richard. We lived together for years." With her shoe, she smoothed the smudge from the carpet, sitting in silence until she gave a little shrug—more a helpless gesture than an I-don't-care kind. "Like I said, as a Christian, I know you won't approve, but I did what I thought I had to do because I enjoyed his company."

Of course, the text message had given her a hint, but hearing it in person took the air out of her lungs. Angel swallowed everything she wished to yell at Stephanie.

You knew better.

You're also a Christian.

I wanted you to talk to me.

We all did.

I can't believe you trusted an outsider more than me, your sister...

On and on her mind spewed more suggestions, but she silenced them to help the woman sitting in front of her. A broken woman, running from fear, and uncertain of her acceptance by God. The past was done. It happened. But the person that little sister she'd loved caring for—was sitting here now, emotionally wounded and scarred and unable to fix herself.

Angel couldn't fix her either. But with certainty, she knew

Jesus could—*if* Angel pointed Stephanie to Him and displayed Christian forgiveness, instead of expressing her anger. "What happened?"

Stephanie frowned at the reaction—or lack of it—waited a moment like she expected Angel to lose her cool—but when Angel said nothing else, her sister continued. "He asked me if I wished to move to a new place together. I said no. At first, he was nice. But then, he began staying out late, partying, and drinking."

Her throat bobbed. "When I'd ask him where he'd been, he'd say it was none of my business. I called him so many nights past midnight, and he wouldn't pick up his phone. Some nights, when he got home, I smelled alcohol on him."

Soft, dark hair slipped over her shoulders as Stephanie lowered her head. "Then it hit me." She stood and walked over to the window. "I'd made a mistake. I had to figure out how to walk back from it. From him."

After tracing her finger along the intricate upper points of a large, silver Ethiopian cross—a treasure Tim had thought he'd lost, she leaned against the wall, crossed her legs loosely, and sighed. "So one night when he came home late, as usual, I suggested, once again, that we go our separate ways. Richard snapped." She unfurled her legs. "I said I was tired of looking out for him at night, wondering whether he was okay."

She curled her arms around herself protectively. "Richard said I should stop projecting my missing brother's case on him. That he wouldn't go missing any time soon. I said he had to tell me where we were going because I wasn't sure our relationship had a direction."

"And what did he say?" Angel asked, standing too.

"He said I wanted a ring. That that was all the stunt was

about." Stephanie lifted achingly sad eyes and poured all their pain and hurt into Angel until Angel felt the regret etched in their gaze. "But I didn't. I really didn't. I just wanted to see how I could untangle my life and start over. The only way I saw to show my determination was by taking that step and moving forward without him in my plans."

Cocking her head, Angel watched her for a moment. "Stephanie, I believe you. But I wish you had talked to me when all this was going on, back when everything first started. We're now at the stage where we're wiping spilled milk. But, please," Angel gestured with her hand, "continue. I can't help you without knowing the facts."

A quick nod dipped Stephanie's delicate chin. "So, I gave him some distance, even though we were still living together. I stayed out late, too, and only came back to the apartment at night to sleep. Then during the weekends, I went to the park early in the morning." She paused. "I also started going to church again on Sunday. I listened to the minister's preaching, and well, I knew I was living wrong. I knew I shouldn't live with a man I'm not married to. So I chose to leave. But since Richard had gone to a three-day conference, I stayed in the apartment alone and waited until he returned to let him know I had gotten my own place."

"How did he react?" Angel prayed, whoever this Richard was, that he would leave her sister alone.

"I'd never seen him so angry before. He drove off and returned with a diamond engagement ring, which he tried to force into my hand. I refused, and he...he slapped me."

"What? He laid his hand on you?" Anger roiled inside her, and her hands gripped the back of the couch.

"Yes. So I called the police, and he was arrested and charged with domestic violence. And I moved out that same day without telling him where."

"Good." Anger settled to a simmer.

"But it only made things worse. He came after me at my job, threatening to 'destroy' me for ruining his name, for giving him a criminal record. But I told him he was the one who'd hit me. I never asked for it. Almost as soon as he left, security requested to search my office. I obliged, and they emerged with a small quantity of cocaine in a pouch." When Angel gasped, Stephanie rushed on. "They weren't mine, Angel. They weren't! I've done a lot of things I'm not proud of—a lot of things you taught me not to do—but I'd never taken drugs. I denied ever taking drugs and said it could've been planted, but they insisted on a drug test."

"What was the test result?" Angel held her breath.

"Negative. I had no drugs in my system, so I was cleared. But I got scared. So I took some days of leave to figure things out. At least he didn't know where I lived, and I figured if I went back and forth to work daily, he'd either follow me or have me followed."

"That was smart." What would've been smarter was not to enter the situation in the first place. But Angel kept that thought to herself. We all made mistakes. What was important was how we came out of them, not if we went in. After all, God sent His only begotten Son to die for our sins, not because we would never sin, but because we needed rescuing when we did.

She should've pushed Stephanie to communicate back then. She could've dropped a clue. But, then again, prying open a closed book could be impossible. Only desperation made her open up now.

"At the end of the seven days' leave, I asked my supervisor to approve me to work remotely so Richard wouldn't know where I was. When she approved my request, I junked the old PC I'd used when Richard and I lived together. Then I ordered a new one online."

"And you were okay?"

"I was. But then, because of you and everyone who is family, I didn't change my phone number. Although I'd blocked his number, he used temporary numbers and hidden IDs to threaten me. He said he'd find me and make me pay. He'd lost his job and claimed it was all my fault." She wrung her delicate hands like a wet towel. "It was a nightmare."

Silence filled the house as Angel absorbed this. How long had she been unaware that her sister was in trouble? Had her total commitment to finding John made her not notice?

Or had combining that to her job's demands taken her time and made her not pay as much attention?

How could she allow her mind to be so occupied?

She should have noticed.

There should've been signs.

And she shouldn't have missed them.

"I stayed indoors a lot, afraid to come outside." Stephanie rubbed her arms. "The police had issued a restraining order against him, but he wasn't harassing me in person, he was pestering me with phone calls. Then I went inactive on social media and deleted all of our photos together. That only infuriated him more. He sent tweets, emails, and subliminally threatening private messages."

"Those are harder to track and tame." Angel knew that.

"I know. So I went solely to communicating by email. Yet he didn't stop."

"He's obsessed with you, Steph. My goodness." Angel wasn't

sure she wished to hear more. But she had to. Knowing the facts and feeling the shock now meant she wouldn't have to do so later.

"Now, I believe that. I didn't at first. I thought he was just sick with a broken heart."

"He's sick with a broken mind too. Anyone who would threaten someone they claim to love in such a manner is dead to decency." Struggling to contain her anger, Angel filled her lungs with calming breaths, for Stephanie's sake. The girl had to get her words out before something caused her to close that book again. Because if she'd contained all of this for months, and probably years, then closing up again might be for good this time.

"I felt so vulnerable. He was popular. People loved him, and if I went public, they'd throw their stones at me and not his way." Stephanie sucked in her lip, and her face fell. "I felt worthless. But, thank God, I'd gone back to church, because the message series the pastor preached for five weeks changed my perspective. I started taking small walks around my new neighborhood, although the fear of seeing Richard never fully went away. I took calls from people in church when they called to welcome me to their online group. I found that I could sit in the park outside without feeling unsafe. Then I could smile again."

Stephanie sank deeper into the couch, and her shoulders slumped, although the stress curves around her cheeks relaxed a little. "All that time, I couldn't bring myself to tell you. I'm so sorry to crash this on you now. I just didn't know where to start. Plus, I never thought things would get as bad as they did when I first entered this relationship. So I needed to start healing before breaking the news to you. Then, just as I was getting ready to, he showed up at my doorstep."

5

"So rend your heart, and not your garments; return to the Lord your God, for He is gracious and merciful, slow to anger, and of great kindness; and He relents from doing harm." Joel 2:13

"He found out where you lived?" Angel asked.

"Yes." Closing her eyes, Stephanie rested her head against the back of the couch as a long, slow breath passed her lungs. "Through the post office."

"Oh. Who would've thought of that?" A frown tightened Angel's lips. This was getting dangerous. A man this desperate to ruin Stephanie wouldn't give up easily.

"He'd trailed returned mail there and saw the forwarding address label so he took a screenshot and texted it to my phone as I was opening the door."

Angel covered her mouth, not sure she wished to hear what happened next.

"He stormed my apartment and demanded that I go to the cops to clear his name so he could get his job back. I refused. Then he raised his hand to hit me, but remember Liberty taught me the basics of self-defense that one time in her Fortitude Homes Estate, right?"

Angel rubbed her throbbing temples. "I recall you telling me. I was too busy preparing for my wedding then." Tim had volunteered to accompany Stephanie as a family member to keep an eye on her.

"So I kicked him hard. He doubled over, and when he reached to punch me, I ran to the door and pushed the emergency services speed dial button I'd installed all around the house. That move likely saved my life. I fled out the door and rapped on my neighbor's house. I remained with her until the cops arrived."

Angel's exhale whooshed as she felt blood flee her face. "Okay, you had such a close call, and you didn't call me? Steph? You know I love you and will shield you. Whoever comes after you has to pass through me. You knew that."

Stephanie's gaze lowered, and every inch of the sweet little girl she used to be, called out to Angel's heart. "I'm sorry, sis. I should have called you." She raised her gaze. "I'm really, truly sorry. I thought I could handle it. I also didn't want you to be disappointed with my life choices. I figured if I fixed the problem, there'd be nothing for you to clean up. I guess I was wrong."

"Yes, you were." Angel sighed and allowed her anger to ebb away. "And you're forgiven." She felt her shoulders slack. "Now, can we make a deal not to keep such secrets again? I would rather not have to do this again. A stitch in time..."

Stephanie nodded, then hugged her, sinking her head to

Angel's neck and wrapping her arms around for a good squeeze. "Thank you so much. You're the best big sister, and I don't know where I'd be without you. I love you."

Angel managed to speak beyond the squeeze. "I love you too, darling. Now, tell me the rest so I can make a decision about what agencies to call to ensure your safety, okay?"

They parted and sat across from each other on the couch. Angel brought up her leg and crossed her knees.

"So, after he promised to let me be, he was released. They were lenient because he was one of their own. And he stopped calling me for about three months. I didn't know his job at the sheriff's office had taken him back. He was on a three-month probation. When the probation ended, he took a new position within the department. He had access to their system, and little did I know, that was just to find me. I had moved to another part of town, but I left no forwarding address for obvious reasons."

"Right. If he'd found you that way, he'd use that means again."

"He wasn't past trying something funny, so I took protective measures. I'd also changed my job to another firm that closely worked with my former job."

"Was that when you told me you got a new job last Christmas and didn't say why you left the old one?"

Stephanie had been tightlipped then. Now Angel understood why.

"You'd said you tracked down another informant for John's kidnapping, and I hadn't wished to draw you away. Your attention to finding John was my priority. My problems came secondary."

Angel sat up and set her elbows on her knees. "Every issue

any one of us has is primary to me. I love you as much as I love John and will fight for you just as hard."

"Thanks, sis." Stephanie exhaled long. "Then around March, I started seeing a car drive around my place a couple of times at night. By April, another car was making the rounds around the same time of night, this time, a black sedan. Initially, I thought they were hired security. Then in June, the management sent around a memo—they were *about* to hire a security firm for the complex. Then I knew I was being followed."

"What did you do? Did you call the police?"

"No." Stephanie pursed her lips. "I figured now I had a serious stalker, and he was ready to do anything to exact revenge for our breakup." She blinked. "When I confronted the driver, he came out. It was Richard."

"You never confront a stalker, Steph. I taught you that."

"But I was tired of running. I also didn't want to call the cops and have him get away with anything. No one else cared enough to stalk me but him so I'd guessed it was Richard."

"What happened?"

"He didn't react like I'd expected. He fell to his knees and begged me to take him back. He said he was a changed man."

Her curls shook along with her head. "I refused."

Angel exhaled. Good girl.

"Then," she swallowed hard, "he took his gun and said he'd kill himself if I rejected him. That his life was over and that I was all he had."

Angel inhaled sharply and clutched her chest.

"In his eyes, I saw he meant it, so I moved back in with him. I know it was a terrible thing to do now, but at the time, it made sense. Giving people second chances and all."

"You never give second chances to a life destroyer, Steph. Jesus was his second chance, not you. You never, ever repeat that? Do you hear me?" This time, as her voice pitched higher, Angel didn't care.

And Stephanie could only nod.

"Continue."

"I went to work one day, and when I came back late, he was angry. I tried to explain, but instead of listening, he hit me. I told him I'd leave. Then he threatened me. With the intricate plan he'd made, I knew going to the cops was a waste of time. So I planned, and two weeks later, I ran, after I resigned from my job. I informed them I was going away for a while and wouldn't be able to only take leave. I shipped my car with my stuff and made sure he wasn't aware of it." She wiped a tear. "Today was the day I left and never looked back. He was the worst mistake I've ever made, and I'm so sorry to bring all this to your doorstep."

"You never should've taken him back."

"I know now. But at the time, I didn't want someone's blood on my hands. I felt like it was the Christian thing to do."

"The Christian thing to do would be to send him to the church for help, not to move in. You move in when you're married."

"Right. I also figured that part out after a chat with our pastor there. Losing John pushed me to a place where I was scared of losing people close to me. I studied the Bible, on the advice of my pastor, and saw a lot I had done wrong. What a complete mess. The only way to start over was to leave, so I made a complete break and came here. I'm back to Maryland for good. Thankfully, Richard doesn't know anything about you, only about John since I had leaned on him for comfort."

Angel frowned. It was too easy for someone living in close quarters to find out information. "I wouldn't take any chances."

Stephanie smiled—her first since she arrived—and her face lit up. "I know you won't. That's why I came. If someone wanted me hurt, or worse, I'm safest around you. Of course, I know God is my protection, but I trust your judgment." She sucked in her lower lip again. "Considering how badly I messed things up already, and have been unable to fix it, I don't trust myself to fix this either."

"God fixes us all and fixes our situations, too, Steph. I can't fix you, and I won't ever take the place of God in your life. But I am prepared to do what is necessary to ensure your safety and ours."

"Thanks."

"Let me call the SSPD. They'll send over an officer to take your statement. Tell them everything you told me. If you recall the names of the cops you worked with over there, include their information. Also, tell them everything you know about Richard so they can run a detailed background check. If he was determined enough to find you last time, he'll likely come here."

When Stephanie gulped, Angel placed a calming hand on her shoulder and swept back some of her hair. "But you know what? We'll be ready and waiting."

Soon, Angel called the station and briefed them on what was needed without going into details. Her boss confirmed that they'd send someone.

As soon as she hung up, she prepared a quick sandwich and set it before Stephanie. "I'm not sure you've had something to eat, so gobble up before they arrive."

"Thanks. I wasn't thinking about food until my stomach

growled a minute ago. Come to think of it, the last time I ate was a Subway sandwich for breakfast." Stephanie dug into it, taking a bite before Angel was finished turning.

"I'm going to call my husband to let him know you're here. He must still be at work or at our nonprofit. He's so dedicated he works every single day except Sundays, tracking every possible lead."

"He's consistent," Stephanie said between bites. "And a good man too." A sad glance crossed her face as though she was thinking about her choices with Richard.

"Yes, Tim is a God-sent. We'll get you through this, and at God's time, you'll meet a man who will love you just as you are and bring you joy and no trouble."

"I'm definitely not looking for a man in the near future. If I'm able to survive this, I'll stay celibate."

Angel wished to let her know she didn't have to stay where she was right now, but getting through something caused by a human being would make it tough to want to enter scenarios that could potentially lead to something similar. She'd run for dear life too.

"I'm sure you'll reconsider at the right time. For now, as soon as you're done eating, if the cops haven't arrived, we'll go bring your things inside. I'd rather have your vehicle parked in the backyard, not in the front-facing garage."

Stephanie nodded. "Okay."

Then Angel went upstairs to inform Tim that their lives were about to change—again.

6

"If one of your brethren becomes poor, and falls into poverty among you, then you shall help him, like a stranger or a sojourner, that he may live with you." Leviticus 25:35

When Tim arrived home and saw Angel and Stephanie moving things into the house, he knew the problem was bigger than he'd been told. Angel had been noticeably careful in choosing her words when she'd used Stephanie's pet name, Steph Bear, to let him know her sister had come. But she'd also said Stephanie might stay for a while. The boxes and suitcases suggested her stay would be longer than "a while."

But, instead of asking questions, he set his briefcase on the front porch and joined them. He carried the heavier things and placed what he thought could be personal items in one of their two basement guest rooms where she'd be staying.

When they finished, his wife drove Stephanie's car to the backyard, mentioning something about her safety.

That piqued his interest.

Once she came inside, Stephanie apologized for coming without notice. She said she'd come to her sister's place for refuge. "If you'd rather I stay in a hotel, I won't mind. I don't want to inconvenience you."

Tim shook his head. "Listen, Steph, you're family, and you're welcome to stay as long as you need. What matters is that you are safe."

Soon, an SSPD officer arrived to interview Stephanie and she requested that Tim stay with Angel to hear what happened. What he heard left him wondering how his sister-in-law could keep it all to herself.

But he also understood her predicament. Having lived through his best friend, Violet Zendel, dying at the hand of her twin brother many years back, he hadn't been sure he'd ever trust anybody again. Seeing John, his brother-in-law, go missing and being unable to find him had dealt another blow.

Now, Steph was being chased by an ex-boyfriend. How were they supposed to react?

When she was finished giving her statement, the officer took Stephanie to the SSPD to sign documents and to provide photocopies of her ID and for processing her new restraining order in case Richard chose to show up. The officer also promised to get in touch with officers in Alaska to cooperate across state lines.

Tim waited until they left before sitting down for a meal and for a conversation with his wife. "Babe, I'm proud of you."

Angel smiled as she put down the beans she was picking

through in a square tray for soup in her Crock-Pot. "About what?"

"How you didn't explode at Steph. I fully expected you to blow your lid. But from the way she said she told you about it, it seemed you held it together."

Her nod and smile confirmed his guess. "It was hard. Very. In fact, I prayed for God to help me not to explode. I also reminded myself—based on my experience as a police officer—that people never think things will go as far as they eventually do. And once you haven't informed your family during those seemingly insignificant starts, it's tough to land a bomb of painful truths on them. That leads to enough pain to go around, but sometimes, it's the only path to peace of mind. In a way, it's a form of restitution." She shrugged. "If you're the family, on the other hand, the shock is the first thing you experience, then the pain. And it's easy to get stuck there. I've seen many family members hold a grudge. I didn't want us going there. So, I forgave fast, and I prayed my feelings would catch up."

"I'm sure that's true. I am still struggling to contain my disappointment, and I'm not related to her by blood. However, I care about her and would protect her. So I can only imagine how you feel. Practically speaking, we need to think about how we can upgrade our security."

Angel nodded as he finished his meal. He had hoped to take her out for a date night tonight, but with Stephanie's situation, he scrapped the idea for another day. "I can order some security monitors, cameras, and proximity alarms beyond the home security alarms we already have. Hopefully, those should arrive in the next day or two. I'll need your help in setting them up though."

He wiped his mouth with a napkin as she took his empty plate away. "Thank you, honey." She strode to the kitchen and set the plate into the sink, then returned while he stretched out his legs beneath the table and winked. "I'll be sure to plan for that. I'm not as good in handiwork that isn't antiquated. That's your expertise around here." Her smile rewarded his compliment. "However, I can sure tag along to set them up."

"I'll appreciate your help." She tapped his arm and settled into the seat next to his. "How are we going to handle Stephanie's spiritual relationship? She said she's going to church now, but I'm not sure whether her spiritual walk with God is back on track. I'd hesitate to make any assumptions. We need to be with one accord on this."

"I agree." He braced his elbows on the table and steepled his hands before his chin. As an archeologist, he never let the larger picture distract him. One tiny section of earth could disclose so much, and his passion revolved around the people the past revealed—yes, the cultures were important, but so was each individual's history. One thing he knew... "Many come to God when they're in trouble. It doesn't really mean they repented or genuinely converted. We have to wait. Give her time but love her in truth. In the meantime, we can invite her to join us to go to church on Sundays, but maintain our private prayers as a couple while we pray for her too. Then watch to see how things go. But we can only do what a human being can do—believe the best and pray for her."

"Good idea. Thank you, wise guy. I'm so glad I married you, Tim. Before, I figured these questions out alone and, given my perspective of someone too close to a matter, chances are that not all my choices were the best."

"I'm glad to be a blessing to you. That's what a husband is

supposed to be." He curved a hand around her shoulder and kissed her.

An hour later, after they had both done the dishes and cleared the kitchen, she put the beans in the Crock-Pot for the next day, since she was going to work very early the next morning.

Tim sat at the kitchen table, and Angel started making popcorn. They usually snacked on it while they shared about their day. Once it was ready, she poured the delicacy into a large bowl, set some aside for Stephanie, and joined Tim in eating theirs.

After all these years, time hadn't changed her, neither had the forced absence of her brother. For that, he was grateful. There were frustrating times, but they were never enough to knock her off center.

He massaged his neck and sighed. "I took your advice and went to the DA's office. I met with someone who knew about John's case, and I tried to see if they'd grant me access to records about one of the guys at John's construction site to see if he knew anything. But they revealed that such information isn't public. Since he had something in his file as a minor, the case was sealed."

"Can they unseal it? Do we get an order from a judge?"

Tim wished he could say yes. "They say that's not going to happen."

The front door opened, and Stephanie shuffled into the kitchen. Hesitation creased her features as she glanced between him and his wife. "Hey." She hugged her sister and nodded to Tim.

"I'm exhausted." She covered a yawn as her purse's strap slid down her shoulder and she caught it. "Do you mind if I go downstairs and take a shower? I'm staying in the basement, right?"

A nod trailed her question. "Yes, I prepared the basement for you and changed the sheets." Angel shrugged. "No, we don't mind at all. Just make sure you let us know if you need anything, all right?" As Stephanie began walking away, Angel called to her. "Oh, and if you want to make a phone call, I'd prefer if you didn't use your phone. Use mine or Tim's, for safety's sake."

She nodded. "Sure."

Tim scooped a fluffy handful and popped a few kernels into his mouth. He soon told Angel everything about his day, and when they finished, she turned down the Crock-Pot to the lowest setting before they retired.

But he'd forgotten to re-arm the security after Stephanie had returned.

And so had Angel.

∽

JUST AFTER THREE IN THE MORNING, ANGEL GROGGILY PICKED UP the call jarring her ears. "Hello?" Her own gruffy voice alarmed even her. She peeked at the caller ID. "Pierce? Is everything okay?"

"Sorry to wake you, but we got something."

That had her sitting up in bed and swiping hair off her face. "Really? Praise God. I'm all ears."

"We not only have a number for Francis, but we've also confirmed that the suspect is on location. We could move on him today?"

"Yes. It works."

"I want to move quickly. If he even suspected we were looking into him, I bet he'd run. Surprise is our biggest advantage here."

"Cool. I'll be ready in an hour and meet you at the station. Did you notify the captain?"

"He's already at the SSPD getting ready for us."

"He doesn't sleep, does he? What a leader." She admired the kind of leadership they were blessed with. The SSPD got handed a blessing with the late captain, who'd trained Captain Towers. And now President Towers had trained Captain Charlie Bailey, their current captain well in leadership too. "All right. We'll see you there."

"Great."

She briefed her husband, who nodded. "I'll be praying. Remember, this is a dangerous mission. Don't be careless. Keep me posted throughout the day. I'll see you later." He leaned over and kissed her.

"See you, love." Angel departed home as quickly as she could, still partly wishing for some rest. Darkness surrounded her as most people were still sleeping. Her heavy eyelids kept drooping as she drove to the station and met up with the tactical team.

Many already sported full tactical gear. Inside, she suited up too. As she emerged, she prayed this mission would be successful.

This was it.

There were no more leads after this.

It dead-ends from here, and she prayed something would shake loose from Francis to lead her to John.

"Everyone, you know what is at stake here. I know two decades doesn't leave much wiggle room for hope, but we cannot give up. We must go into this fully expecting to find some evidence of John Martinez's whereabouts," the captain admonished. "Any questions?"

"No," Angel responded. "And thank you all for staying with our family on this. We are grateful for your sacrifice."

He patted her shoulder. "We're all family, Angel." He let her shoulder go. "Let's move out, everyone. Godspeed."

7

"Even to your old age...I will carry you! I have made, and I will bear; Even I will carry, and will deliver you." Isaiah 46:4

Angel studied the house on the edge of Lake Street and Union Boulevard then ducked behind her police cruiser. Still the wee hours of the morning, the street was empty and the house quiet and dark. After making sure they surrounded the house and covered all exits, they followed the captain's instructions to make contact with the suspect by phone.

She heard him cuss at the officer and warn him not to call or he'd open fire.

They called in SWAT for backup, now convinced that he was armed and dangerous.

Then she called this time, and asked about John while promising to work out a deal if he cooperated. But he'd shot through the window, sending them ducking and ending the phone call.

Right now, four hours later, flashing lights from other police cruisers and SWAT trucks cascaded around her view in the dawning light. It was about seven a.m., and crouching between an ancient van and her cruiser, Angel brushed sweat back from her temples. She knew what today was, and how important it was to capture this witness alive—if he would stop waving a gun every half hour, taunting them to shoot.

She ground her teeth as pebbles cut into her knees, and the acrid scent of rust and oil clogged her senses.

He knew they wouldn't shoot. He had to know they were after information—information he was severely rebelling against releasing. The captain chose to wait him out. At one point or another, he'd lose his guard, and they'd get him.

So, it had turned into a twelve-hour waiting game. Near three p.m., she called her husband. "Hey. Sorry, I've been busy." Tim would've checked with her office about her whereabouts when she'd missed their lunch date.

"Yes, I figured. I'm still praying. How are you holding up?"

She couldn't stifle the sigh. "Seriously? I'm tired. I need a breakthrough in this case. I've tried and pushed and searched—well, this is it. I don't know how I'll proceed if this doesn't work out. I really don't. Keep praying."

"I will, but I'll come by in case you need the support."

She laughed. "Um, as much as I love you, I'd say no. This is an active scene and coming here may endanger you and others trying to protect you. Though I appreciate the offer."

"I'm coming, end of story. I won't let you face the end alone. If it pans out, I'll be there to celebrate. If it doesn't, I'll be there either way. I'll wait at a coffee shop or somewhere close but not too close. Let me know where, okay? Then focus."

"Sure. Love you." The captain was saying something, so she cut the call.

"We're going in," he informed her, to which she nodded.

"You think that's safe?"

"We have no choice. We'd rather intercept him while we still can."

She felt her head bob. "Okay." Since she wasn't one of the officers going in, she gave her support from outside. Soon, a handful of officers surrounded the house and entered a cracked basement window obscured by rosebushes. She and those outside kept his attention on them.

For her sake—or rather for the sake of her missing brother—she hoped the officers breaching the basement succeeded in. She strode to the captain and tapped on his shoulder. "Why didn't you send me in?"

She needed serious convincing to wait out here while others went in.

"You're too close to it. You could blow this chance. I'd rather you wait out here. When he comes out, you can query him to your heart's content."

"Fine." Though she hardly felt fine, she accepted his position.

Soon they got the signal they were waiting for. The cops flashed a torchlight from the basement.

They were successfully in.

Oh, God, please let them get this guy.

John had to be found.

John needed to come home.

She'd waited twenty long years, and the final link was within reach.

He was the ultimate connection to new information. So many others' hope might've thinned out. But not hers. No. She would fight to find John. If he was dead, then she'd find his body and give him a befitting burial. But nothing—absolutely nothing—had stopped her from seeking him.

And nothing will.

"Sir, we're climbing the stairs now up to the suite," the officers whispered over the secure radio channel. Apparently, the suspect linked onto the police radio so the SSPD switched to a secure channel while keeping useless chatter going on the regular one. The guy was skilled and stubborn. But they were more so. And they planned to take him down without a violent assault.

"Sure, guys." The captain lowered himself from sight. "Go up and be safe. Radio back when you capture him. We need a live capture. Do you copy?"

"Copy that," the officers responded as the soft tap of shoes going up steps punctuated their reply.

Angel focused on the moments ahead.

Listening, waiting, and praying.

It felt like hours had passed, though it could've been only minutes before the voices broke the silence. The radio lit up with shouts and barked orders.

"Stand down! Police! I say—stand down!"

Angel clenched her gun clasped between her knees where she was hunkered outside her cruiser and prayed in earnest. Beyond the rosebushes, what could've been the spark of gunfire darted through the curtains.

She held her breath and stood still. Too much hung in the balance.

More shouts followed, thudding sounds, and then silence.

"What's happening?" She eased up and peered above her cruiser's window.

Moments later, a group emerged—the same officers who had entered now led a man out in cuffs. Shaggy hair, a rough beard, and old fatigues added to his unkempt appearance. He bled from his arm. Even though with no other visible wound, he seemed to be losing his vision as he stumbled.

"Watch out!" the captain shouted.

But the man was going down. He stumbled forward, then slammed his head against the concrete as officers rushed to stop the fall. But it was too late. The man had passed out.

Angel raced forward. "Do you know what happened?" She paused where he'd fallen, her frustration rising just an inch above the calm composure she'd struggled to maintain. "He was fine when he walked out."

Then she saw it. A needlepoint darkened the curve of his elbow. "He gave himself a shot. He might have," she glanced up in dismay, her strength leaving her, "killed himself. Call an ambulance! Quick!"

No way would she allow him to die.

No.

She collapsed on both knees and pressed her ear close to his mouth.

There was no breath.

Frustration wrapped around her mind. "Come back alive!"

She pounded on his chest with her fist, letting out all the anger pent up inside.

This was supposed to work.

He was supposed to give them information.

He was the last link to finding John—and he likely knew it. If they found him, they found John. But he just blew it up in their faces doing the unthinkable.

She crouched low, bent over him, and wished she could do something. Heaviness clouded her heart, and tears tore through her eyelids.

She wasn't sure whose arms pulled her to her feet and away.

But the next thing she knew, hands urged her forward as she tumbled toward and into her cruiser, and she released all the pain.

More tears cascaded. More frustration leaked in wetness over her heated cheeks and dropped over her crying lips. Her words blended with groans and let off sounds that echoed the pain of her loss.

So, Angel let go.

She cried like she had never cried before. She allowed herself to feel, for the first time, all the feelings she held back since John went missing—the loss, the pain, the fear, the hopelessness, the unknowing, and finally, the doubt of his return, and the hole that left.

Finally, she prayed in her heart when words wouldn't come.

If he was dead, she mourned his loss. But that feeling she couldn't explain came again with hope, as a tiny sliver, that he was alive, somewhere, waiting to be found.

Waiting to come home. But could she dare to hope again for John?

She sobbed even more.

She used to wonder what it would be like to see him marry. Start a family and have little ones, just like she once planned to have. She wished for him to see Stephanie and the others. To enjoy life and time with her.

Was that a lost dream?

Was her own loss supposed to be permanent?

What did God's plan have at this point-of-no-return?

"What now, God? What do I do?" There had to be a way to go forward, but she saw none.

Was there a way now? Was it too late?

Was she going to carry this unfulfilled hope around her soul, an unclosed wound, for the rest of her life? Nursing a loss she'd never know if it was really a loss or a pending restoration?

How could she move forward?

Was there a "moving forward" in this? Or was she stuck in this spot of loss and unknowing for life?

Did John hold onto his faith? Did he give up when things got hopeless?

A gulp seized her throat as the coroner transferred the suspect's body onto a gurney.

"My Redeemer lives," she muttered through trembling lips. "I don't understand this at all, but I know my Redeemer lives." Did John...did John take that way out? Or could he hold on, trust God wherever he was, day in and day out, knowing—whether he was reunited with his family or not—the Strength of Israel never failed anyone who trusts wholly in Him?

"My Redeemer lives. In me. In my situation. He lives." She lifted up her voice to let out another wail. If she was missing this long, she wasn't sure her strength would carry her in faith.

"Oh, God." She lifted up her teary eyes to heaven, clenching the steering wheel with both hands then setting her chin against it. "Can I still hope? I'm tired of waiting. Of not knowing. It's gut-wrenching. Please help me. I'm done. There are no more leads."

More tears racked her body.

Soon, someone rapped on the window, and when she looked up, her husband was there. Tim said nothing.

He simply opened the car door, scooped her up with one hand around her shoulder and the other wrapped around her legs, and carried her out of the driver's seat. He leaned over, opened the back of his truck parked next to hers, and settled her inside, laying her head down gently. Then he looked her in the eye. "I've got you. I'm with you in this, and I'm taking you home, love. Okay?"

A moment's hesitation was all it took before she nodded. She had no words left.

He said something to her captain, who shook Tim's hand before he climbed into the driver's seat, and rolled up the window then drove off. He turned up the calming song of hope already playing in his truck, and Angel wasn't sure when she gave in to a peace that surrounded her, a peace her wounded soul couldn't fathom.

Then she closed her eyes, and sleep overtook her.

8

"And we know that all things work together for good to those who love God, to those who are the called according to His purpose." Romans 8:28

For the next two days, Angel stayed home.

She could've gone to the station. Or called to see what updates anyone had, but she didn't even step out of her bedroom except to grab coffee before Stephanie woke up. She ordered takeout for lunch and ate whatever Tim placed in front of her for dinner.

In zombie mode, Angel moved with no agenda. Somehow, the lentil soup she'd set on the Crock-Pot two days earlier was still left so she had it with some bread for dinner, alongside Tim's salad.

On the third day, she didn't see Stephanie around.

Stephanie's ex still hadn't shown up. Maybe he'd given up searching.

Missing her time with God, Angel decided to do her morning devotion. She sat on her brown leather bedside ottoman and crossed her legs on it. As she read from the New Testament, a smile curved her lips. That morning's devotion centered on Jesus raising Lazarus, who'd been dead for three days. She'd been dead to the world, too, so the Scripture applied appropriately. Next, she prayed to God to heal her heart and help her resume her life.

She picked up her phone and called Tim. "Hi, honey. How's your day?"

His chuckle vibrated through the phone. "Well, it's going well now that you've called. Making a phone call is one good step in the right direction. How are you, my love? Do you think you may be able to rejoin society anytime soon? Your colleagues called a couple of times asking about you."

She'd forgotten how caring the SSPD was. They wouldn't leave her to wet her pillow with tears without wrapping their arms of support around her. "Oh my. I should have called them to let them know I'm okay and that my amazing husband is taking good care of me."

His calming laughter sailed through the airwaves. "Oh well, I'm doing the best I can. I pumped my fist in the air when you didn't throw up after eating my pitiful meals. I counted those as small wins. I'm glad you've cheered up enough to tease me. How do you feel about going to the office, maybe tomorrow? If they see you're fine—your second family, the SSPD, that is—they'll worry less."

"Sure, I can go there tomorrow. They're really our second family, aren't they?"

"Ha. You try telling them they're not. Who cares about Tim the archeologist? They just want to know how 'their sister' is doing." He feigned a funny voice. "So, I want to get out of their way."

"You're part of the way to me so you can't really get out, Tim." She stretched her feet out on the ottoman and rested her head against the throw blanket across the back of the couch as she peered at his treasured silver cross on the wall. "And when did you become a comedian, feigning voices and all?" Sunlight glinted on the cross as if reflecting heaven's glory, and she sighed. "I love you, Tim."

"I love you, too, Angel. I'll see you soon."

"Bye." When she hung up the call, she felt better. Her heart warmed. So many people cared enough to bother her husband until they saw her. She'd go to the office the next day. Maybe by then, she'd have the emotional strength to face the dead-end of the search for John.

～

Angel returned home from work exhausted. She'd been welcomed back with applause and more hugs than she expected.

"We won't stop looking for John, partner," Pierce comforted her.

"Don't give up," Captain Bailey encouraged.

Everyone was very kind, but at that place inside, she struggled to believe them. Not because she didn't trust God. But because she wasn't sure which way God's will led. She still remained hopeful, even if she saw no way forward. She'd show up to work every day and keep shining the light on the path for other people in need.

When she entered the house around eight p.m., everything was quiet, and so she stilled in the foyer. "Honey, where are you?"

Some tooting horn sounded out in the street. The weather had warmed considerably, and an ice cream truck's tinkling ditty lured kids to buy iced treats. When no one answered, she kicked off her shoes and set her purse and weapons belt on the dining table.

Minutes later, the front door opened, and Tim strode in with bags in both hands. He kicked the front door shut and settled his armload on the dining table. "I was out getting some groceries. Then I noticed we may need a toolkit to put up the proximity alerts you ordered, so I'm going back out to the hardware store. Stephanie should be at home, I think. She didn't say she was going anywhere." He kissed her then turned toward the door.

"Okay, I'll go check for her. But first, I'll put this stuff in the kitchen. Love you. Bye." When he left, Angel carried the groceries to the kitchen.

When she arrived, she stilled, her every muscle freezing even as her heartbeat picked up speed. She eased the bags to the counter. "Stephanie? Are you okay?"

She rounded to where her sister sat at the center of the kitchen floor, her legs spread wide, a large tray between them. Stephanie was eating what could've been a tenth slice of chocolate cake. A half-drunk juice bottle rested by her left, and a cake-smeared cutting knife lay next to it.

Stephanie set the plate down and massaged her rounded belly. "Ah." She belched. "That felt good."

Angel leaned over and curved a hand around her shoulder, ignoring where chocolate from Stephanie's hair was staining her police uniform—meaning another trip to the dry cleaner's. "Steph Bear, I know this situation must be tough to get over. But you can't eat it away. Do you want to talk about this or...?"

Stephanie's curls bounced. "No, I'm fine. Now, I am, really." She broke out into a full-throated laugh, confusing Angel more. Then she nodded toward the kitchen stool. "Please, sit."

Although wishing for a hot bath, a warm meal, and a cozy bed, Angel forced herself to sit. If her sister needed her, she'd be here for her—for the emotional breakdowns and for offering advice and prayers too. "Okay."

Stephanie picked up the fork and tapped the tray. "When I lived with Richard, I couldn't eat chocolate cake, at all." She swirled her fork through gooey chocolate goodness, mixing a perfect bite of cake and frosting. "I mean, he was so allergic to cocoa that if he inhaled it in his breath, he'd break out and choke. It caught his breath so hard I denied myself chocolate cake, which," she tapped on her chest, "you know how much I love. But," she threw her hands in the air, "I gave it up for love. A love that ended up hurting me more than it blessed me." Painful laughter trailed her words.

Angel now understood, and a smile broke out on her lips.

"See, since it's over, I've never felt at peace long enough to discover the things I once enjoyed. But, here? Today?" She dipped the fork into the tray and scooped another round. "I found peace." Stephanie ate it then smacked her lips, although it was clear she'd had enough. This had become more revenge eating than actual hunger. "Your house is peaceful, sis. It truly is, and I pray not to bring any trouble here. Matter of fact, I will get a place of my own soon so I can start over."

"I'm not asking you to go. You can stay."

But Stephanie shook her head. "I love you too much to hang around your marital home. I know how inconveniencing it is to have a third wheel around."

"You're not a third wheel. You're family."

A sad smile tilted Stephanie's thin lips. "Sometimes, extended family makes the worst third wheels. Seriously, I won't stay long. But I appreciate you welcoming me with open arms."

"And, now, that's why you ate half of a large chocolate cake, all by yourself?" Gentle rebuke deepened Angel's tone.

"Oh yeah. And I am not regretting it one bit." They both laughed. "I've deprived myself far too long for a man who never deserved it. I may regret this later, but it feels so good right now. Care to join me?"

And Angel would've accepted, but a sad memory stopped her. Many years ago, on her birthday, she and John—her missing brother—had shared a sweet moment in the kitchen over a lovely cake he'd gotten her for her birthday. He'd made great effort to celebrate with her, and the words of gratitude he'd said over her role in his life stayed forever etched in her memory.

And now, he was gone.

She couldn't relive that experience in a related way without going into tears, and that wouldn't help Stephanie, who was still hurting and healing from her own past. "I think I'll pass, thanks. But a warm shower will definitely do me a world of good."

"Okay then. I'll clean up after myself when I'm done. And I'll put away the groceries. You go get some rest. Goodnight."

"Goodnight, my dear," Angel answered as she left the

kitchen, wondering if she'd sleep tonight or spend it praying for Stephanie.

9

"And God will wipe away every tear from their eyes; there shall be no more death, nor sorrow, nor crying. There shall be no more pain, for the former things have passed away." Revelation 21:4

A SCREAM WOKE ANGEL.

She jerked upright.

Blinking against the dark night, she turned in the faint light to Tim sleeping peacefully.

Was that a dream?

She was halfway to laying back down when another scream jolted her to her feet. Scrambling for her gun, she woke Tim with a hard pat. But he was already rousing.

She shuffled into her bedroom slippers but could only find one slipper. Without time to search for the second one, she slipped the first off. "I'll check on Stephanie. Call the police, tell them I'm armed, and to send backup."

With those words, she slung a robe over her nightgown, then tiptoed into the hallway, her gun leading the way.

Allowing the nightlight plugged outside their room to guide her, she descended the steps. Cool wood chilled her toes and groaned on the last step. There, she unlatched the gun's safety and pointed the barrel downward.

Then something stirred toward the kitchen like the creaking of a door. With no shoes on and being lightly dressed, she dreaded leaving the house. But the kitchen door screeched open, so she had to go to the back of the house.

The kitchen door swung shut as she reached it, and a blast of chilly air hit her face when she stepped outside. Wet mud smeared her feet, and with fear crawling up her spine, adrenaline kicked in. Someone had tracked mud into the house, and it wasn't those living in it.

Beyond where she'd hidden Stephanie's car next to the woods shielding their home from the highway, Stephanie's voice trembled. "Richard, le–let me go."

Another stifled scream propelled Angel's shoeless feet toward her sister's voice. "Steph. I'm coming for you! Hang on."

With nothing more than the natural light, it was tough to see. But Angel trailed their voices and Stephanie's muffled screams with trained ears. She prayed Tim had called the cops and that they were on their way. She needed backup as the path was winding and she groped her way, bare feet slowing her progress.

Tall tree branches caught her nightgown, and this deep into the wooded path, she could hardly see anything. With the road still far ahead, she gave a shot in the air to elicit a reaction.

The suspect cursed loudly, and she tracked his voice.

Closing in, she shot into the air again. He answered with a shot in her direction, to which she ducked.

Dear God, please keep Stephanie alive.

Soft grunts and scrambled shuffles rustled ahead, as a scuffle between them ensued. "Kick me again, and I'll shoot you, Stephanie. Now, move."

Angel turned her attention toward his voice, and her feet followed.

She was on their tail. "Steph, duck!" A moment later, she shot and hit something. The man gave a loud groan and shot back.

Good. She'd hit him and slowed him down. But she still needed backup. Angel hid behind a tree as another scuffle ensued.

Then Stephanie screamed, "Angel! Help me!"

Angel rounded to the other side of the tree with cuts on her feet from stones and fallen branches and her nightgown's hem now muddy.

She chased them until their shadows against faint light from the road showed their full forms. Closer now, she shot at him again, and they ducked. "Let her go, Richard," Angel warned. "This is a warning, but I promise you—I'll shoot to kill next time if you do not release Stephanie. Let her go now."

As they emerged, Richard swapped Stephanie to his side and used her as his human shield. Angel could not risk hitting Stephanie.

So, despite the pain searing through her feet, she pursued without firing another shot just as the wail of sirens grew close. *Praise God.*

They darted around a corner, and she nearly lost sight of them. Calls to her resounded far behind them.

"Over here!" she shouted, though she didn't—couldn't—stop. Any miss would mean Richard would get away—with Stephanie. She couldn't lose another sibling.

No.

John was already missing. She would fight to get Stephanie back now.

Here.

And now.

She raced forward, pointing her gun and wishing for a chance to take him down. The road was now in clear view. As she rounded the bend, a pickup truck idled.

His getaway car.

"Richard! Don't move! Police!"

Ignoring her, he ran down the jagged, stony ravine and raced across the road. He held Stephanie so close she would hit either if she aimed at him.

So, she did the next best thing.

She shot his arm, the one gripping Stephanie, and he dropped her to the ground as his head disappeared and he climbed into the truck. She shot at his arm again as he tried to drag Stephanie in by her feet.

By now, Angel had crossed the road too. She raced for him as he swung his left leg into the truck and slammed the door shut.

Angel fired more shots at the truck, beyond where Stephanie lay, but he got away.

She set the gun on the ground and fell on her knees. "Arghhh!" Why did he get away? "I almost had him."

SSPD officers arrived. They carried Stephanie up and wrapped her with a blanket, her body quaking and scarcely covered beneath a torn nightgown, her feet muddy and bleeding.

A throbbing pulsed up Angel's legs from her bruised feet, and blood darkened the asphalt. The stones and rocks must have cut through her skin.

"I can't believe he got away," she cried out. "He was too close to Stephanie so I couldn't shoot him again, but I hit his arm."

But the captain patted her shoulder. "You did great for a barefoot chase in the middle of the night with no backup, Officer Martinez. And your sister is alive and safe. That is what counts. We'll find his blood somewhere here." The captain squatted low and observed something like dark stains. "Plus, you gave us enough evidence to prove the assailant's presence here—his blood on the scene." He pointed at something else she couldn't see. "Once DNA confirmation is obtained, it should provide sufficient grounds for an arrest. Great job. Now, let's tend to your feet and get you some blankets."

Angel spun and hugged Stephanie, who limped up to her. "Thanks for coming after me, Angel."

"Are you okay? Did he hurt you?" She clasped her baby sister's face and held her close. "I couldn't lose you, Steph Bear."

Stephanie shook her head. "No, he didn't hurt me. I don't know how he entered the house. I was asleep, and suddenly, someone clamped a cloth over my face."

"Goodness. I think Tim disarmed the security so he could install the proximity alarms then forgot to re-arm it."

"Maybe. He was still working on it when I finished clearing the kitchen."

"I'm sorry this happened just as you were getting over him."

Stephanie nodded under her sister's arms. "From his scent, I knew it was him. He forced me out of bed, and I screamed."

"That must've been the first scream I heard."

"He took me upstairs and led me to the kitchen. I dug a hand into the trash bin, scooped enough chocolate cake, and mashed it on his face, so he hit me and I screamed."

"The second scream that got me out of the bedroom."

An officer near them jotted down notes.

"So, he led me out the back door and toward the woods, but he couldn't go fast enough."

"Why?"

"He started reacting to the chocolate. He was struggling to breathe. At one point, he was hyperventilating. That's why you heard us when you came out."

"I'm glad you ate that chocolate. It helped save your life. I thank God for His mercy." Angel hugged her closer, and a cry left her throat as she wrapped up everything precious into her arms. "I couldn't lose you too. My heart can't take it."

Stephanie clung just as tightly. "I know. I couldn't lose you. Not after John."

A number of officers took Angel aside while they attended to Stephanie. She gave them her official statement while Angel's feet were being treated beside the road, which was now closed as a crime scene, the scant late-night traffic being diverted to other roads.

She offered thanksgiving to God for saving her sister's life. *God, thank You. Thank You so much. Lord Jesus, I know You love me. I cannot lose my family members anymore. Please.*

As she endured the sting of the alcohol prep pads disinfecting her wounds, some officers gathered around Richard's blood. Crime-scene experts preserved samples. Soon, the team finished collecting statements, from her, Stephanie, and Tim, who joined them, concerned about her feet.

Somehow, Stephanie's feet, protected by now-tattered slippers, weren't as badly injured as hers.

"Looks like you'll be bedbound for a while." Tim's frown showed his displeasure at her hurt. "I should have gone ahead and chased him down."

Angel held his shoulder. "You love me, but you're not a cop. I wouldn't put you in a place of danger when I'm better trained to handle it. You did the best any civilian can do, which was to call in more help." She hoped her smile eased his concern.

Soon, the three of them were shepherded into a police cruiser, and Angel was assisted with a stretcher to stop her from walking. There, they raised Angel's feet over the collapsed front seat. The paramedic, who had arrived much later, placed bandages around the wounds. He gave her instructions to keep off her feet for five days.

"I have to pursue this guy. We need to catch him," Angel protested. "Keeping off my feet means staying home. I'd rather go to work on crutches."

"I'll get you some," Tim offered. "But you'll stay home for at least three days. You can work from home, right?"

"Yes, she can," her captain said. "You're free to work from home all week, Angel. I know you won't agree to stay idle. But you have one job for the next five days—to keep those feet off the ground. I'll make sure you're updated on this case and John's."

Angel gulped. "Thank you, sir."

When the cruiser drove them home, the officer driving them came around and opened the door. Tim got out. Then Stephanie. But Tim didn't wait for a stretcher.

He drew up close to her and offered his hand, with a smile. "Babe, can I carry you inside instead?"

She blinked then smiled. "Well, if I'm not too heavy."

He shook his head. "Never."

Since they got married, he'd only carried her across the threshold twice—on their wedding day, and when they bought this home. Today, however, seeing how he lived up to his role as her husband, caring enough to carry her when she was hurting, refreshed her.

Tim lifted her off the seat, and she swung her arms around his neck. He curved his other hand behind her knees and carried her up the flight of steps onto the porch while the officer held the door open. Stephanie clutched the ruined nightgown Angel had left the house with, while a blanket covered her shoulders. As they entered, he strode up the steps to the bedroom and nestled her on their bed with her legs extended. Then he covered her with a comforter. After kissing her lips, he smiled. "I love you, honey. Now, get some sleep while I make sure Stephanie settles in downstairs. Then I'll see the officers out. I'll be back soon to help you clean up then change the muddied sheets."

Overwhelmed with gratitude, Angel sank against the pillows, downy comfort no comparison to his love. When had she ever had someone care for her like this? She'd always been caring for others, looking out for them. But to have Tim love her indeed like he was, took her breath away. God gave her whom she needed as a husband, an ever-intuitive man, who'd go to any length to protect and provide for her and guide her faith walk. "I love you, too, Tim. What you've done tonight means a lot to me. I won't forget it."

He nodded, then turned down the lights. "I have my phone with me, but I'll lock up the house, arm the security alarm, and be back soon." Tim had his flaws, but he was perfect for her. He was what she needed. God gave her a man to complete her.

As he shut the door behind him, she buried her head in her pillow and wept to God— this time, in gratitude.

10

"With the pure You will show Yourself pure; and with the devious You will show Yourself shrewd." Psalm 18:26

ONE WEEK LATER, ANGEL HAD BEEN ABLE TO GO TO WORK BUT felt tired of leaning against the crutches Tim and her partner had insisted she use for one more day. So, she left early at two p.m.

When she reached home, a call from her captain surprised her. "Sir, am I hearing you correctly?" Angel pressed the phone closer to her ears. Could this be really true? "You saw the suspect, Richard, on a speedway headed in our direction? What do we do now?"

He cleared his throat. "We changed our strategy. We'll allow him to think Stephanie has left your place and moved out. And we'll make sure he sees her leave in her car. Then we'll stage her entering a hotel and say out loud what room she's checking into when we give her a prompt."

"Okay...?"

"Hear me out. As soon as she reaches the designated floor, our officers will escort her out through the emergency exit. Then a female officer, wearing her same type of clothing and similar to her in appearance, will take her place. When he breaks in, she and the other officers will apprehend him. You know the drill. Judging from his growing rap sheet, he'll likely be locked away for as long as she's alive."

"Would Stephanie agree to this? I mean, I can ask her, but—"

"She already did. I spoke to her before calling you. Getting her consent before sharing with anyone, including you, was important."

"Then I'll go along. How soon are we putting this plan into effect?"

"Considering he's already on his way, I'd say she should gather enough stuff to convince someone she's moving. Four pieces of empty luggage will fill the car. We already have an officer en route to supply her with a comms device so she follows our guidance." A slight pause punctuated his words. "Angel, I know you love your sister, but this doesn't put her in any significant danger. My instinct says he wants to attack her only in a place where he can get her alone. We won't let that happen. While you're at home, we'll stay with her. At a distance, of course. But we'll have eyes on her at every minute. We'll jump in if anything seems off."

"And if he aims to shoot?"

"We'll shoot him first."

"Then, you have my go. God be with you and protect everyone."

"Amen. And thank you." As soon as the captain left the call, she dialed Stephanie. Having a boss who was a believer and close friends with the former President, also her former captain Robert Towers, was immensely freeing. She knew his heart was right and he had a focus on bringing justice with fairness to his community. Charlie was Asian, and yet he bonded with her and the others on a faith level that transcended racial lines, and it never interfered with how they did their jobs professionally and worked with those who weren't Christians. The department held no division among them based on race or skin color, or even culture. Captain Towers had been a champion of that.

"Hey, Steph?"

"Hi. Did you get a call from your people?"

Angel chuckled. "My people, huh?"

Stephanie laughed. "Yes, your cop people. You guys are just...different. You act like everybody else, smile like everybody else, but when danger shows up, you transform. I almost couldn't recognize you last night." Despite her previous laugh, something somber and reflective dulled her voice.

"Do you want to come upstairs to talk about it? I mean, it's not like I can move too much," Angel confessed as she kicked off her shoes, stretching her legs out on the couch, crutches braced on the ottoman with the throw blanket covering her from knees down. "I think I've done my share of walking for the day."

"Of course. After all, it's mostly my fault you're stuck up in bed." Ruffling sounded, promising Stephanie was on her way. Minutes later, Stephanie emerged. "Hey, sis." She drew close, kissed her cheek, and sunk into a chair facing the couch.

Tim had sat there this morning and read Scripture to her while the rising sun cast light into the living room, and they'd prayed afterward. It had been so calming considering the rough night they'd had days ago with the intruder.

"You know, I'm really sorry you were hurt. I wish that wasn't the case. I wish there was a way to reverse the pain."

"Stephanie, what's a few bruises to your life? I would've been horrified to stay put while you got hurt by a dangerous man. Never apologize for something that ends in a testimony."

Stephanie curled a hand around herself. "I was scared. I honestly thought he would shoot and kill me. He seemed only intent on getting me. What was he thinking?"

"That he could get you back. And if he can't convince you to go along with him, then he'd most likely kill you."

Stephanie gasped. "Why didn't he just kill me, then?"

Angel sighed. "People like him want to have their way. I've seen this a lot. They try to bend your will first. Then resistance leads them to kill." She paused when Stephanie shuddered. Then Angel leaned forward, the throw blanket easing slightly off. "He will try to get you alone again, just like the captain said. But, even though you may seem alone, the SSPD will be within distance." That seemed to calm her. "And, most importantly, God will be with you, even closer than they are. Be unafraid."

Stephanie nodded, then smiled. "Okay."

"God's got you this far. He will fully expose all that this man had planned and bring him to justice and you to safety, okay?"

A slow nod followed. "Thanks, I'll keep that in mind. I also appreciate how hard you fought for me that night. He almost took me away. He would've succeeded had you not fought for my life. You are my hero, sis. Everything I wanted in a big sister, you are, and so much more."

She hugged Angel, but Angel was fighting the tears choking her. This mirrored her conversation with John right before he went missing—a memory she'd held close and never shared with anyone, not even Tim. *Lord Jesus, please don't let this be a repeat.* She prayed desperately to God. *Let the cycle of loss in my family be broken. Please, my God. I need my family complete, safe, and together in one accord.*

Stephanie's phone rang. From her responses, it had to be the SSPD. "Yes, I'll have the luggage in the car soon. I'm fully dressed in the outfit you sent over. See you then."

As she got off the call, Angel decided that, when Stephanie left for this mission, Angel would be more than a spectator. She'd intercede for a successful mission for Stephanie—a civilian with no combat experience—to return home safe and sound and free of her stalker.

When Stephanie rose, Angel detained her with a hand. "Please be careful. Come back alive. You hear me?"

Stephanie swallowed hard, then nodded. "I will, God willing. Living in fear of one man and watching my back every day I step outside, has to end now. I'll see you later."

As Stephanie left, Angel plugged in her devices to charge and drew her phone close, after ensuring she had easy access to the laptop. She signed on to work and was fully informed with what was going on with Stephanie. All the preparation chatter over the radio felt pretty regular as she placed the laptop on her lap—until she heard the dreaded words, "He's there. He's arrived. Go, Stephanie."

Angel swallowed a gulp. If only she could swap places with Stephanie. Had it been her, she wasn't sure she could contain herself enough to play along, and even if she did, knowing he was just around the corner would be hard.

"He's watching you, Stephanie. Don't look around. But continue loading the car. One more suitcase, and you drive to the destination."

Surely, they added that bit of info for her since she couldn't really go to look out the window. Even if she could, she'd be too cautious to expose herself to the suspect and tip him off. But why *did* the man pursue her sister so hard? If he was simply after her because she walked away, that was odd. If he wished to exact revenge, then why watch her and try to get her alone? Was there some unfinished business they didn't know about?

Thirty minutes passed before another update. "Enter the hotel lobby but leave your purse in the vehicle. An officer is posed as an employee at the check-in counter. He will wave you over and keep you with him, asking you general questions until the suspect parks his vehicle and shows up inside."

A soft murmur came through as Stephanie accepted the officer's instructions.

And Angel prayed under her breath.

Soon, another officer said, "Okay. Please be alert. He has entered the lobby and located you. He is within hearing distance. You must say your room number and repeat it twice so he hears. And don't look back. Go to the elevators, take one up, and the officer holding the reserved elevator will ensure he doesn't enter the same elevator as you. Good luck. We'll be waiting upstairs."

Since Angel couldn't hear Stephanie's reply, she prayed that her sister followed the instructions. Only the man's actions would say whether it worked or not.

Soon enough, another update followed, and this time, Angel was clutching the edge of her laptop with tense fingers.

"She's en route to the hotel room. The suspect has entered the elevator."

Angel's heart was pounding, pumping blood quickly through her head until it whooshed in her ears. Another set of conversations crackled on the radio. "Stephanie says she wants to enter the room. She wants to confront him."

"Angel would object, and so do I," the captain warned. "Tell her to stick to the plan."

"She refused," the officer replied. "She says she wants to find out why he's after her. We ran out of time, so I couldn't stop her. She has entered the hotel room, along with her duplicate."

What was as close to cussing as she'd ever heard from the captain echoed through the radio. "All right, he's coming out of the elevator, and it's too late to change so I'll inform the guys who were waiting to receive her in the emergency stairwell to hang back. Tell the female officer to stay in the room, and stay out of sight but ready to shoot if he tries anything. Make sure she records everything as planned, both video and audio. Understood?"

"Yes, sir."

"And let's see if Angel won't kill me for this. She's like family." Being an SSPD officer, she'd enjoyed visiting her captain's family on a few occasions and enjoying their food and Christian music.

But she also wasn't the kind to visit too much so she'd kept as much distance with him as with everybody else. Now, Charlie was speaking for her exactly how she would, were she there in person. This was indeed her family.

But things were happening too fast for her or anyone to intervene. She simply hoped Stephanie knew what she was doing. Confronting a desperate man could turn deadly, a risk she wouldn't have let her take. *Father God, please don't let Stephanie die or get hurt. I know she doesn't realize how dangerous her choice right now is, but please protect her from the consequences.*

"The suspect has entered the room, uninvited," the captain supplied.

Other officers fell silent, but Angel felt her insides constrict.

She wished to be there.

She wanted to protect Stephanie.

Steph, always the stubborn one, insisted on going her own way. She seldom allowed someone to help her. She had softened a bit in the past years, but the instinct to do her thing was always in her.

As Angel waited, she called Tim and updated him. He said he was praying along. "How are your feet? Any better?"

"It still feels like I walked on sharp stones a week ago." She stretched them out in front of her, with a few bandages still wrapped around her smallest toe, and nestled them on the foot of the couch. "But I'll give it one more day of rest."

"Is there any sign of infection? Are the bruises healing?"

"Yes, they are, thank God. If they feel worse, I'm glad to go see a doctor. I'll need to get back to tracking Stephanie's case. Please keep praying."

"I will. God will lead her home safe to us, in Jesus' name. Keep me posted via text."

"Sure." As Angel hung up, the tension eased a bit in her belly. Right now, should be the time when she'd be the most anxious. She was no longer hearing what was going on in the hotel room. There were no updates. All she hung upon was her trust in God.

That He would give Stephanie wisdom.

That He will protect her.

That He would save her life.

She wanted nothing more than these three things. Everything else was superfluous.

The radio buzzed alive. "Officers, move in! The suspect has been apprehended when he tried to force Miss Martinez to sign life insurance claims forms. It seems he would've killed her then."

11

"No weapon formed against you shall prosper, and every tongue which rises against you in judgment, you shall condemn. This is the heritage of the servants of the Lord." Isaiah 54:17

Angel clasped her chest. "How do you know?" She broke her silence.

"Because we searched his car while he was in the room. He's got an empty body bag, a shovel, and other items for digging as well as duct tape and a map to a dumpsite in Greensburg. He had plans, and they were not good ones."

Angel gulped. "Is he in cuffs yet? How is Stephanie?"

Silence trailed her words, then an answer. "She's shaken."

"But she's alive and unharmed," another officer added.

"We're driving her to the station. A team's collecting evidence from the suspect's car," another chimed. "We're done here."

"Great." Angel whooshed an exhale. "Thank God. And thank you, guys."

She fell back on the couch just before another officer gasped. "Goodness! The car blew up just as we left."

"Copy that," the captain said. "He used a trigger in his back pocket he could manipulate with cuffed hands behind his back. It has been retrieved from him, and he's being searched for any other dangerous items."

"Is anyone hurt?" Angel inquired.

"No, we're all safe," the captain confirmed.

She was grateful as she saw how close she was to losing her sister. Questions crossed her mind.

Like, did Richard plan to die with Stephanie?

Or kill her and use her to collect life insurance?

Or force her to leave with him? The possibilities were endless. But for right now, she could simply thank God that Stephanie was alive, safe, and headed home. And the man who pursued her across state lines was in custody and would likely stay locked up.

Soon, she called Tim and updated him. She also informed their other siblings. She'd called them today and updated them on her story but informed them not to worry. So Angel provided them all with an update, explaining that the suspect had been apprehended and Stephanie would live a free life. She was so happy she could hardly contain herself. *Dear God, please let this whole experience pull Stephanie closer to You. Let her see that Your love for her drew her to a place where she found the right kind of support. Let her know true peace.*

As she finished praying, her phone rang.

"Hey, Steph, are you okay? I tracked everything until you entered the hotel room. What happened?"

"He came to the room, and I knew. Just stopping him from chasing me wasn't enough for me. I wanted to know why. If not, he could track me down again when he was released from prison. I wanted to end his pursuit. So I chose to be in the line of danger. I know you wouldn't have approved, but I did what I felt in my gut would bring a permanent solution."

"I'm listening." Angel would never approve of what Stephanie had done, but this was not the time to argue.

"He said he'd missed me. So I asked him what he wanted and why he tracked me down. I also told him I wished he would stay away from me. Had he not hit me, I would never have called the cops. I let him know his actions led him into trouble, and he could not and should not blame me."

"And?"

"He asked if we could start afresh. Then he apologized but said we should leave immediately. That he had plans for us." A tremor laced Stephanie's voice.

"What was your response?"

"I said there was nothing to start over. I was done with him. He became angry. He said that whatever happens after then was all my fault. And that he was unwilling to live without me. He brandished some forms and said I should've signed these the week I left. That he needed my signature. I didn't glance at them. I simply said no. We were done. There was no 'us' anymore and goodbye."

"Good." Angel sighed.

"Then he lost it. He kicked down the plant on the table, and it shattered. Then he hurled something at me. I'm not sure what. He yelled, 'I'll kill you!' But the officer in the room apprehended him. Thank God for shielding me from harm. He really did have plans for me."

"Yes, death plans. Those were life insurance forms he was trying to get you to sign. Please head home once you're done, okay?"

"Oh wow. Sure, sis." A slight pause followed. "Do you mind praying a short prayer for me just to thank God for helping me make it out alive? Like, right now?"

A spool of joy weaved through Angel's heart. "Of course. Are you ready?"

"Yes. I am."

"Father God, we thank You. We bless You. We are grateful to You for saving Stephanie's life today. Things could've gone awry, but by Your special grace and mercy, she made it out alive. And now, we have come to give You thanks. Thank You for answering our prayers. Thank You for defending Your daughter in a place we could not reach. Thank You for Your hedge of protection around her. For not allowing her to stay in an unsafe place. For making her reach out for help. For making her move away from clear danger. For returning her to Yourself. As we go forward, lead her in Your way and Your perfect will for her life. And may Your name alone be glorified. In Jesus' most powerful name, we pray."

"Amen," Stephanie echoed. Sincerity rang in that one word. "I'll be home soon. Then I'll stop by this church whose message sprang up on my newsfeed this morning. They have Bible study tonight. The pastor is someone with a past as scary as mine, from what I read online, and his words reached my heart in a new way. I'm going there in person to thank God for saving my life today."

Elation swept through Angel. God was, indeed, answering her and Tim's prayers. Stephanie was changing of her own accord, for good. "That sounds perfect. See you soon, my dear."

When she hung up, Angel bowed her head. In the two weeks since Stephanie showed up—scared, hurting, and fleeing danger—this was the one moment Angel allowed herself to truly exhale and be free.

The responsibility of being the eldest meant she bore everyone's pain, loss, joy, and accomplishments. None of those occasions happened without her feeling each of those emotions fully and completely. Had something happened to end Stephanie's life, it could've been the straw that broke her. She couldn't stand losing someone else. "Thank You, my Lord Jesus. You alone know my heart toward my siblings. How I have loved them without reservation. You know the pain I would feel should I lose another one. I am utterly grateful for how You saved Stephanie today. If she didn't praise You, I would. If she didn't thank You, I would. If she didn't return the glory for what You did, I most certainly would. You lead us out and bring us in. You keep and shield my family." She swallowed and said the next words, which were much harder than the first. "And even if Stephanie had died today, even if John never makes it home, even if You did none of what You did, I will still thank You. I would still glorify You, albeit in tears. Thank You, my mighty Savior, in Jesus' most powerful name, amen."

When she lifted her head, Tim stood by the door. "Amen." He smiled. "I had to come home early to check on you and to see that Steph was fine."

Angel leaned forward as he kissed her. "Yes, she's fine. Matter of fact, she's on her way home."

"Great." He took off his jacket. Then he helped her upstairs to their bedroom, and she eased herself onto the bed.

"Then she says, later today, she's headed to a new church.

They're having Bible study, which she's joining tonight, and also going to thank God for saving her life."

Tim's brow lifted. "She is?" His smile grew. "Good. Thank God."

"I know. Thank God. He is answering us much faster than we anticipated."

He sat at the edge of the bed. "Definitely. He is. Did she say the name of the church? Maybe I can do an online search on them to find out more."

"No, not yet. I'll ask her when she gets here."

"Or we can text her. I want to know ahead of time so we'll know if it's a good environment. I'm sure all churches are considered good, but it never hurts to verify."

"Hmmm. Well, she did mention the pastor had a bad past. So, I might want to check. I'm sure it's fine, and I support her going anywhere she feels welcome where the Word of God is truly being preached. But, like you said, we should be especially cautious considering she's in a vulnerable place today. I wouldn't want anything happening to ultimately draw her away from Christ."

Angel shot her sister a text. *What's the name of the church you mentioned? I'd like to check them out online.*

Soon, a response came. *Sure, sis! It's the Living Faith Bible Church. The pastor is Pete Zendel. Let me know what you find...but, either way, I'm still going.*

"Ha." Angel smiled. *Stubborn Steph. Fine with me. See you soon.*

"She said it's the Living Faith Bible Church."

"Where? How come I've never heard of them?" Tim shrugged. "Could be a new church. What's the pastor's name?"

Just then, realization dawned. Between her former captain,

Robert Towers, and his wife's case from many years ago and Tim's history with Violet Zendel, Angel gasped. "Oh no."

Tim frowned. "What's the matter?"

She shook her head. "You won't approve of this church. I'm sure of it. I just put two and two together, and I know who the pastor is. Oh yeah, he's got a horrific past for real."

Tim took her phone and read the text message. The phone fell from his hand, and he rose. "Pete? He's a...pastor?" His voice rose, and color hit his cheeks. "Incredible. Now, you tell Steph not to step a foot in that church! He's a liar! He can't be a Christian."

Tim gripped the locket around his neck—belonging to his best friend, the late Violet Zendel—and glared at her, something he'd not once done before. "This is why! He killed Violet. Faking salvation was his get-out-of-jail-free card. He's a liar. I know it." He pointed toward the phone. "And I won't let Stephanie anywhere near him. He's taken enough people from me."

With those words, he stormed out of the room.

Clearly, what Angel thought had been dead and buried, was merely waiting for the right season to manifest.

Tim was still hurt, angry, and hadn't forgiven Pete. And as far as she was concerned, that was going to change.

So, she texted Stephanie back. *We're going there with you.*

Her quick reply pinged back. *To the new church? Really? That's great! Wait, are you going as my chaperones or what? I don't need police escort.*

No. We're going there as a family. Let's just say my husband and the church's pastor have a bit of a...past to iron out. It's been far too long.

Stephanie replied just as quickly. *Sounds good then.*

Angel replied, *Love you.*

Then, she proceeded to text Tim, saying she was going to Pete's church with Stephanie and he was welcome to come along. That drew him back to the room—fast.

"How can you get there when you can't walk?" He slammed his hands on his hips and glowered at her from the doorway.

"You'll help me like before, won't you?" she replied oh-so-sweetly.

"Oh, Angel, don't play coy with me. You know I wouldn't go there, and I won't let you go there without help either." A sigh slipped through. "Fine. I'll take you and sit with you. Just as a helper."

Her smile widened. "Awesome. Thank you, honey." Then she started praying.

This would be more than a Bible study for sure.

Or one for the books.

12

"As one whom his mother comforts, so will I comfort you..." Isaiah 66:13

Pete Zendel, senior pastor of the Living Faith Bible Church, and founder of the esteemed Zendel Security Institute, opened the door of their master bedroom's bathroom and stopped when he saw his wife, Patricia, seated on the closed toilet seat. Her shoulders shook as her face was buried between her arms.

Alarm shot through him. "Honey, what's the problem?"

She glanced up at him with puffy eyes then shook her head. Without a word, he knew.

They'd lost the baby.

Pain, heartbreak, and confusion warped through his soul. "No," he whispered, placing a hand on her slouched shoulder.

She nodded, then burst into more tears.

She swiped dampness off her cheeks. "We...lost...him...last...night." She inhaled a shuddered breath and met his eyes. Her heartbreak shot through his soul. They'd prayed, hoped, and waited. And finally, she'd taken in. They were so happy that, three months in, they'd bought all the baby stuff, just waiting for their son, Emmanuel, to arrive.

Pete's legs grew weak, and he managed to squat. "I'm sorry, my love. So, so sorry." He wasn't a man to cry. He could hardly remember the last time he did. But, just then, heartbreak gushed out in liquid form. Grief wrapped around his soul and gave it a wrenching squeeze. His cheeks grew wet against his wife's as they mourned the loss of their son. "Emmanuel," he whispered between thick breaths, "we love you. We miss you. Rest in the bosom of the Lord."

After what felt like an eternity, an alarm sounded from his phone inside the bedroom. Someone was waiting.

Actually, a whole church was waiting.

He'd been holding the weekday Bible study since his pastor who typically did it was away. It started in thirty minutes. Matter of fact, people would already be seated in the church.

"I'll cancel the Bible study." Surely, Patricia heard the alarm too.

Her hair tickled his chin as she raised her head against him. "No."

"No? I want to be here with you. I can't leave you to face this alone, Pat. This is our loss."

"No, Pete." She sniffed. "I need you, but someone in that church needs you more. I'll have you for the rest of the day. They have you for only two hours. Go." She touched his arm. "I want you to go. The Lord will comfort me. Use our grief as fuel. Preach with everything you've got."

"How am I supposed to preach about God's faithfulness when I just lost a child?" Pete choked, barely able to get his words out. "How?"

She pressed a hand against her lips to hold back emotion. "The same way Jesus endured the Cross and the shame, for both our sakes without knowing for sure that we'd accept His gift of salvation. Go, Pete. Do what God called you to do."

Pete rose, unsure of what strength propelled him into the bedroom, out of the house and to his car. He simply knew that, within twenty minutes, he was inside his church and clutching a Bible, standing before at least one thousand people of his twelve-thousand congregation without the words to say.

Somewhere between leaving his house and reaching the church, everything he planned to say evaporated.

His heart was bleeding.

His soul was aching.

And his faith was being tested.

And Pete was not enjoying it at all. All he wished for was a wall he could punch his frustrations out on. Instead, God gave him hearts and eyes looking at him, hopeful he had received something from the Lord to share.

Pete stood up from his seat, leafed through his Bible, and thankfully, found his notes. "Good evening."

"Good evening, pastor," the church replied. He glanced at his deputy and longed to ask the man to take over. Instead, heeding his wife's advice, Pete cleared his throat and whispered to himself, "You can do this. The strength of the Lord is made perfect in weakness. I have joy in all circumstances."

Inhaling a deep breath, Pete proceeded to the altar when the needling in his spine began.

Something was wrong.

The many years of tranquility they'd enjoyed in Silver Stone had not waned his sense of security. Even more, the police and security guards he now trained several times a year maintained his security readiness and ensured he didn't get complacent. At all.

But this? This felt different.

Like he was supposed to know something was coming, but he found himself scrambling, thanks to a grieved mind. Yet he stood there, battling the overwhelming desire to mourn with his wife. His heart breaking, he stood there with a sermon to deliver.

But the needling wouldn't stop.

Pressure was coming at him on all sides. He just lost his child. He had to preach within an hour of discovering his loss. And now, something like a security threat lurked around here?

He swallowed hard. But he knew his wife. If he went home, she'd insist he return and deliver his message. She prioritized God's Word and His will above hers. So Pete sighed and exhaled, drawing grace from above and strength he didn't possess.

Now wasn't the time to allow distractions of worry about security threats.

After all, nothing out of the ordinary ever happened on Bible study days. Time to study God's word.

Taking the steps up the newly expanded altar, and despite his worn knees grinding against the movement, he climbed, then paused at the top step and scanned the audience.

Still, the needling wouldn't stop.

So Pete ran his usual visual check.

Checked the doors.

Scanned the security monitor.

Observed for sudden moves and anybody out-of-sync with expected church behavior—not that his church was a regular church, or that there was an expected behavior—but "weird" always stood out.

Those things he'd trained his men to do, he now did. But, yet, everything seemed fine on the surface.

With a quiet sigh, he proceeded to the podium and settled his Bible. When he lifted his head, his gaze caught his wife, sweet Patricia, striding in quietly as God's grace lightened up her beautifully framed face. She managed to come here at such a time as this? His heart warming, he nodded to her. She acknowledged him with a wave and slid into a seat in the front row beside the other pastors. There was only one reason she came, to ensure he didn't bail on this assignment. But what was special about tonight that his world had to come crashing for him to preach a simple Bible study?

As soon as Pete cleared his throat and accepted the microphone from the worship leader who had just rounded up and left everyone still in the spirit of worship, the needling grew stronger.

He had an odd combination of being a pastor and leading a security institute, partly due to his past. He couldn't change the evil he'd done, but he could utilize those former skills to frame a better future. And he knew when to trust his guts and believe a challenge was headed his way.

But he was ready. If something was coming, he could use the resources at his disposal now.

He exhaled slowly and pushed the small button beneath the podium on the left side, triggering a precautionary full scan of the church and institute's databases and the campus perimeter for the detection of any digital malware, security threat, or unlawful physical weapon. The last time they'd done this was when former US President Robert Towers had attended their church for the final time. These security facilities remained there should he ever visit the church again, though he'd moved to a lovely farm with his wife, Ruby.

Since his last visit to Living Faith, only periodic security checks were required to stay up to date. But, with the inconsistencies and recent anomalies in their latest reports, he'd planned to do a full sweep, and since it took a full hour, this would be completed by the time he'd finished his message.

Even though Pete saw no physical threat, he started the scan, preferring to be safely wrong, than be dangerously wrong.

A rare smile slipped through his lips, more an attempt to get himself present and in the moment than any happiness. He trusted God to work out even all of this for his and Patricia's good. "Praise the Lord." He leafed through his Bible.

Some of the over one-thousand persons present responded, noting the prolonged silence before Pete had spoken. He smiled again. His church knew him well. They knew he was having a tough day.

He eyed them, then smiled broadly to assuage any concerns, and leaned forward. "I said if you're happy to be alive, praise, praise, praise the Lord!"

"Halleluiah!" a more spirited response echoed off the walls.

He nodded in satisfaction, using the praise to mock his grief. If the devil thought he could get him to stop praising God due to the loss of his unborn son, that was never going to happen. "Now, that's much better. Let us pray.

"Before we pray, let me say this. Many people expect ministers to preach out of a comfortable place, but usually, that's not the case. Today—in fact, this moment—is anything but comfortable for my family, and yet I stand before you to minister the word. It is solely God's grace at work." Inhaling, he inclined his head and gripped the edges of the podium. "Father in heaven, I thank You for this day. Thank You for bringing us together for another beautiful time in Your Holy Presence. I know You have a word for someone here this evening. May Your anointing flow through me, teach us through me, and may the words I speak be Yours and not mine. Please speak to us individually and collectively as only a father would, in Jesus' mighty name. And we say an...?"

"Amen," the church replied eagerly.

Pete appreciated once again both the large twelve-thousand-seater auditorium and the newer microphone carrying his voice so easily across the audience.

But as a preacher, him shouting never meant he had a weak microphone. Rather, the words shuttered like a fire in his heart bursting forth, leading to his louder expressions while sharing the Word even while knowing deep down that a better microphone wouldn't stop that.

He cleared his throat. "May we open our Bibles to Genesis chapter 39 verse 1." Expectation wove through him at the product of the two-years-of-labor series he was about to start.

But first, he had to start.

He leafed to the right Scripture. "Can someone volunteer to read for us?"

A lady in the middle raised her hand then stood and accepted a microphone from an usher. "'Now, Joseph had been taken down to Egypt. And Potiphar, an officer of Pharaoh, captain...'"

But the minute she started reading, Pete's belly twisted, as though being tied up in knots.

Change the message.

He heard the Spirit of God speak in his heart.

"What?" he lowered the microphone, turned his back to the audience, and asked God.

I have a different message for you to deliver.

"What?" He tried to ignore that he had asked the same question twice, while wanting to scream out at God, "But they are already reading this Scripture, Lord. We worked hard, and You gave me this message about Joseph. I spent *two* years digging for this treasure. So, You want me to change the message right at the altar, *now*?" A huff followed. He wasn't one to pretend with God.

Change the message, Pete.

If he was alone with God in prayer, a whole lot of facial expressions and more objection would've followed.

Instead, Pete sighed as his shoulders sank. "Change the message to what?" He might have rolled his eyes a little, but he wasn't going to think about it so as not to offend God any further. "I have nothing else prepared, Lord. Or....You want me to...wing it?" Ha. After a decade-plus of preaching, he was going to wing it for the first time.

Open your mouth. I will give you what to say. Trust Me.

He spun, lifted the microphone, and spoke into it, cutting off the woman who'd been reading the given Scripture. "This is about to get interesting."

The whole church went silent.

Pete just lost his child and made it to church on a limping faith.

He was barely holding it together to preach and couldn't get over the awareness of a threat.

Now, he was going to preach something different, without

knowing what?

"This is one interesting Bible study. I haven't had this happen, ever. But...Well, the Lord wants the message changed. So, I'm winging it, and I hope you'll stick with me. We'll have fun on the Lord's time."

Applause broke out, and the woman who'd been reading earlier reclaimed her seat.

Stilling the pain throbbing through his heart, he swallowed hard and glanced where his wife sat. Her eyes had never left him. She rose, walked up to the altar, and leaned in toward him. "Are you okay?"

In her thirty-plus years of church attendance, this was one of the few times she came up to the altar without being invited to speak. In fact, this was the first time she came up while he ministered. She clearly knew he was struggling.

"We just lost our baby, so I'm just standing here by faith."

She squeezed his hand. "You can do it, Pete. God is here, and I'm here."

He nodded. "Security-wise, I'm a little worried. So, I triggered a full scan but..." He drew in a deep breath. "Would you mind checking with the security team? Tell them this is just a routine scan."

With a nod, she stepped down. The moment her feet touched the last step, the Lord dropped a message into his spirit —almost like an instant download. Detail by detail, every step Patricia took toward her seat, he followed the Word as it was served on a platter to his heart.

By the time she reached her seat and turned to face him, he could recite the message by heart. A small smile stretched his lips, and an exhale whooshed. *Thank You, Lord Jesus.*

The Joseph message series could wait. He had studied

rather the Holy Spirit had taught him several lessons in that story to last a lifetime—and he was very eager to share it with his church family someday. But he would obey the Lord. That Word took two years of sitting at His feet to receive, but today was not the day to deliver it.

Pete bowed his head once again. "Lord, as I minister, please minister to us and let Your word land on fertile ground. Handle every concern of our hearts, in Jesus' mighty name, amen."

He lifted his gaze and began, already feeling the power of the Holy Spirit pulsing through him, a contrast to the uncertainty of an unprepared sermon. "Our new lesson for today is titled, 'The Word Is Your Ark.' Please turn your Bibles to Genesis 6 verse 13."

13

"I am the Lord your God, Who brought you out of the land of Egypt; open your mouth wide, and I will fill it." Psalm 81:10

PETE ZENDEL PACED THE ALTAR AS THE SAINTS WAITED. Nervousness twisted his stomach, even while expectancy pumped through his heart.

Nervousness, because he had never winged a sermon. And expectancy, because what the Holy Spirit deposited into his heart was spectacular, if he could deliver it the way he received it. "In Genesis chapter 6 verse 13, God pronounced the end of the world as they knew it and said that, due to man's wickedness on the earth, destruction was scheduled for them." He struck a listening pose, curving a hand behind his ear. "Then God said to Noah, 'Build an ark.'" He settled his hand to his side. "God never gives you an end, without a new beginning.

But you need to prepare before you can come into that new beginning. How?"

"Well, if I was Noah, I'd be frank with God." He straightened and pushed back a coming smile. "That is impossible. I can't build an ark. I'm not young anymore. I'm not in my twenties, and seriously, I'm not sure there's any more fun for me to have here. Heaven is looking like a good prospect right about now."

A few laughed from the front row. "But God rarely prepares you for yourself. He prepares you for the future generations who need what you plant today to provide shelter for them tomorrow. God thinks eternal, while we think here-and-now. It's easy to think things moved smooth-as-silk from God giving Noah the instruction, to Noah building the ark, to the flood happening."

He scanned his audience. "Not so, my friends. It's never as simple or smooth as it seems. Let's bring this home, shall we?" He stepped down so he was standing on the first step, barely an arm's length above those who were seated closest. "Listen very closely. You'll need more than your pens for this. You'll need your attentive hearts, and if you allow it, it will change how you see and relate with God and man forever."

In his heart, the message was already transforming him. "If you were Noah and God gave you such an instruction today, let me break out a contemporary scenario for how this plays out, and maybe by the time I'm done, you'll see this story through a more practical lens." Then he settled into the message.

"Noah woke up one day, and God told him to build an ark. So, he seized his ax, walked deep into the woods, and began hitting the base of the first good tree he saw. The Bible never said he was a carpenter, first and foremost. But he saw a good tree and put his ax to it." He sat on the step when his knees grumbled against his constant movement. "Thunk. Thunk. Thunk."

Pete spun his gaze toward the other side of the church. "Imagine an old man swiping an ax with his little strength to a tree. His wife arrived and asked him, 'Honey, what are you doing?' And Noah swiped sweat off his brow and answered her, 'God said I should build an ark. He is about to destroy this world due to their sin.'"

Pete rose, dusted off the back of his pants, and approached the altar. "Well, she did hear that the man heard voices and said it was God. But this time, she must've thought he'd truly lost it." Laughter echoed. "She cried all the way home about how her husband could lose his mind at their empty-nest stage. She figured it had to be his age. Then she called her kids to go plead with their dad to leave the forest and return to his day job of being Grandpa Noah. They still had bills to pay, mouths to feed, and a mortgage. If Noah wished to cut trees, he needed to cut the type to make some money with. That kind, they could use in abundance." More laughter followed.

Pete smiled, feeling God washing his sorrow away. His heart skipped a happy beat as he saw Patricia, his wife, laughing too. "But something about God's command urges you on even when those around you don't understand. For example, something like God asking you to go into full-time ministry just when your career took off. Or God asking you to volunteer at a homeless shelter when affording a nanny for your three-year-old was above your paycheck. Or even God asking you to start a business when you've got a bad credit history from your teenage years that responsible adulthood couldn't wipe off. How do you go about it?" He symbolized an ax with his hand. "Give it one *thunk* at a time."

He rubbed his clean-shaven jaw. "Then the following day, against the advice of his wife and sons, Noah returned to the forest. Off he went, targeting another good tree with a hard trunk, and he hewed at its base. This time, his wife, his sons, and their wives came to beg him as a family intervention."

The church laughed again.

"In today's world, you'll hear stuff like, please stop sharing gospel tracks on the street so you don't lose your job. Please stop sharing about Jesus with people, just stop....hewing at that tree. Live like everyone else, and the days will take care of themselves. Leave helping out at the homeless shelter, and the government or someone else will take care of those people. Leave the orphans, widows, the unemployed, sick, injured, drunk, those high on drugs, people bound by rage, sinners, atheists, and rapists and murderers. It's over for them so let them follow their natural course. But, in your heart, God called you to hew at that tree of resistance until it falls."

Another round of applause and a whistle followed.

He placed a bookmark on the passage. "None of what I'm describing is in the Bible, but I'm contextualizing this so you get to see how much resistance Noah must have faced, and you can run a parallel to how much you will face. Today, the 'ark' God calls you to build might be different, but God is still calling men, women, children, and youth to 'build' today. And whatever your 'ark' is, you won't have it any easier than Noah did, so please follow me. I promise you, this is leading to somewhere good."

He wasn't too preoccupied to see the warm smile spreading

across his wife's face. Was she really smiling amid the pain? He drew strength from that. He also didn't miss the flash of the red beacon saying the full security scan was in progress. Twelve more red beacons flashing softly at the back of the auditorium would signal a successful scan with no threats detected.

"But Noah continued hewing. By the end of the first week, his family saw his determination. When he got home, he still loved on his wife, asked his kids how they were doing, and cared about their wives' wellbeing. Somehow, his family saw that Noah wasn't crazy. Then, let's say about three months in, they realized he was growing tired but still got up daily to obey God. Realizing his drive, curious about his work, and hoping to end the process faster, they all join in to help. Maybe by the time the last tree was felled, he'd regain his senses. You see, if Noah stopped at the one-month mark due to lack of support, he would never have built the ark. You need to take your eyes off whoever is clapping for you or booing at you while you are obeying God. If God said, 'Go,' you go and do not look back."

More applause and cheers lauded his words.

He returned to the first step. "But again, Noah pressed forward and continued gathering all the materials, despite his community's response. He had a plan from God and followed it diligently. He ignored the mockers, the haters, the attackers, the gossips, the backbiters, the saboteurs...are any of these ringing a bell about your situations?" Many people nodded. "Did you think people or the enemy would leave you alone to obey God?"

He shook his head. "No, no he would not. He will use people, situations, circumstances, lack, and even abundance to throw stumbling blocks in your way. They will come. But you have one job to do. Jump over them, walk sideways away from them, slip past them, overcome them, and keep going. God didn't promise Noah a lack of obstacles. He promised a completion, and you have the same promise from God. If—*if*—you are sure God sent you, then He will help you get there by Himself. So, when you arrive, you will be sure of one thing—it was not by your power, nor by your might. It was Jesus who graced you for completion. Are we all on the same page?"

Nods and shouts of yes! trailed his question.

"Good. Now, Noah worked on this ark for years, and all he said to himself when he got up every morning was this: 'God asked me to build an ark. I'm getting up today to build the ark.' Daily, he reminded himself of Who gave the instruction, and then he followed it. He didn't think or talk about his naysayers or critics, which you could be sure were abundant."

He tapped on the podium. "Hear from God. Obey God." He paused and let it sink in. "In our day, the way information spreads, God might not give you a 'why' before you obey like He gave Noah so you don't encounter more resistance than necessary. Moreover, the reasons can be His so He can be God and we can be men. If we knew all of the 'whys,' we still may not obey, so why not go ahead and do what he asked first, then find out why when you're done. Faith first, proof last—amen?"

"Amen." Rousing applause followed. To his surprise, people were scribbling over their notes, and he made a mental note to get a recording of this message as he didn't know half of what God was delivering through his lips and needed it for himself too later.

Even Patricia sat at the edge of her seat, listening with rapt attention. "So, as Noah saw his family working beside him, building with him, you can be sure his faith and his confidence grew. Sometimes, God withholds help at the start to steady the legs of your faith, and after your faith has gained firmness in Christ alone, then He sends you help to 'grow' your faith. Faith can't grow without a firm foundation. And its foundation must be total trust and confidence in Jesus Christ."

Applause rang out as the second beacon shone.

14

"Ask, and it will be given to you; seek, and you will find; knock, and it will be opened to you." Matthew 7:7

Pete continued, "Now, the day came when the ark was completed. And this symbolizes when you've jumped through all the hoops of resistance, gotten through all the attacks while you were building, and exhausted yourself and, perhaps, your faith. You've reached the goal. You've completed the task God gave you. Sometimes, it took God to quell the doubt that rose in your heart, wondering if you heard Him right. Wondering if your friends were right and you shouldn't have gone out on a limb because 'God said' such and such to you. Wishing you could see the end product of all the sweat, labor, and sowing but knowing the only way to see the fruits was to plant the seed by faith, trusting God for a harvest. When you arrive 'there' at that place of completion, you ask yourself, 'So, what next?'"

Sinking down to the top step, he sighed. "I've asked myself that question. So many times since starting this ministry. I've been challenged by the world to prove that I'm not the wicked man I once was. I've shrunk under the weight of the responsibility of giving hope to ex-convicts while the public cast doubt on the validity of my own salvation. You think it's easy to do this and run a prison ministry, and preside over a security institute in the same place where my reputation was tarnished?"

Pete pressed a hand against his chest. "No. Matter of fact, it has been one of the hardest things I've ever done. Do you know how easy it is to slip into a super-private life, devoid of public criticism, and live happily ever after? It tempts me sometimes to retire and avoid the public glare, but the Lord has not asked me to quit, so I will keep going. I know Who called me. I know Who anointed me. And I know His love. That is all that matters. My story does not have to be your story. My path may differ from your path. But, no matter where it leads, if God is the One leading you, and not your desire for publicity or the love of the crowd, you will complete your 'ark' despite any and all opposition."

A longer applause trailed his heartfelt words. More hands were scribbling notes now.

"Let's return to Noah. When God asks you to 'build,' He is asking you to prepare for something. Which means, something is coming which you need to be ready for. That 'ark' is your readiness." He paced the altar as the fourth beacon lit up. "In Genesis chapter 6 verse 20 to 21, God asked Noah to take animals and all foods into the ark. Imagine what the people thought as Noah went shopping daily to buy seeds of every kind. A little bit of this and a little bit of that. People might wonder if he was starting an agricultural business after cutting all the trees." A couple of people laughed. "As God takes you to different places in life to teach you a little bit of this and a little bit of that, even you will sometimes ask God, 'Did I really need all that?' I mean why on earth would you fit in a potato, a bird, and a fly together, and call it God's will? But, remember, things that may seem unrelated to you, are perfectly aligned in God's eyes. And the next part gets all of us. Without exception."

Pete rotated so he stood at the center. "In verse 22, it said that Noah did according to all, all that God commanded him. In our world today, full of distractions, most of us hear a Word from God, we start to do it. Then, our favorite TV show comes on, and we suspend God's matter. Our friends come visiting for the weekend, and our quiet time is replaced by gossip time. Our bills pile up, and our tithes and offering get deleted. Our doctor said we have a disease without a cure, and we assume incurable by man translates into incurable by God. We measure ourselves by our own standards. God's standard is complete, total trust. His heart is with those who fully go with Him all the way, not some of the way. When God asks you to do something—and I'm speaking to myself too—do it *all* the way. Don't stop halfway or pause where you've seen others celebrate success and start celebrating success. You can celebrate progress but know you still have some ways to go and make sure you get there. Go all the way. Obey fully. Trust completely. Go with God's instruction all the way."

Nods followed, as did the fast pens writing across the notepads—as did the seventh beacon light-up. Five more to go.

"You will know in your heart when you have fully obeyed God because you will have peace, total peace. You would have done everything in your power, leaving nothing within your control undone. God sees your heart. Even when man might think you didn't do it all the way, as long as God says you did, you have. Quit beating yourself up with man's standard and accept God's standard for yourself."

Applause trailed him again, louder this time.

"When you have reached the end, then the true test begins." He paused until all eyes were on him. "You see, the real test wasn't whether Noah had faith in God. At first, it seemed so. But it really wasn't. The real test—the test we ignore, the most important test of all—comes at the end of your obedience."

He curled his arms as the Words circled around his heart in truth. "The real test is of the validity of God's Word. It's a test of whether God and His Word are true and can be depended upon. It's a test of whether one can build their lives, faiths, and future on a God they cannot see, and yet Who controls all they see. It's God's test before man's eyes."

Godly silence enveloped the room. Pete pointed forward. "It's a test of whether you can allow God to show off His power in your life, using your life as His platform. His instruction to you is the preparation. Your obedience is the sacrifice. The flood is His proof of His power.

"God said to Noah, take everything and every one of your family into the ark. And he did. Then God shut the door. Again, God shut the door. Noah's job was done. He built the ark. Went into it. Then God shut the door. God will shield you once you obey Him. Fully. He will shield you from destruction. He will protect you. But then, here is the second important point of this message. Are you ready?"

"Yes!" The church was excited now.

"Great. Imagine how Noah felt when the first drop of rain

hit the roof? Imagine how he felt when more rain followed. Imagine his wife, sons, and his sons' wives surrounding him. Imagine how their eyes told their story of going from unbelief to relief that they had gotten on board and supported him? Then imagine how he must have felt when the ark tilted this way and that way as the water rose, then it groaned. Imagine his confidence in his watertight obedience to the Word of God that made Noah sure that the water wouldn't seep in? Think of him smiling at his nervous wife when the ark shifted, then righted and stood above the waters while others cried out and drowned outside the ark? Remember, the Lord shut the door, so no one can open it, not even Noah. What was evil could not enter a boat of faith. You have a chance now, to go with God in faith. But if you toss your faith, you jettison your ark. Will you trust God?"

"Yes!"

"It's not going to be easy. So, are you sure?"

"Yes!" echoed again.

"Secondly, and just as importantly, what Noah and his family were standing on was not an ark. They were standing on the Word of God, which Noah had obeyed. If Noah had thrown away that godly command, there would be no ark to stay safe, warm, and dry in. Noah and his family floated above the destructive flood on the Word of God, not an ark. The ark was God's idea." Some whistled. "The Word built the ark—the ark is the Word of God. Whoever runs into this ark shall be saved. That ark is still floating and ready for you today. Will you take shelter in Jesus and be shielded from destruction? If you will like to do so, let me pray for you."

Some people stepped forward, and Pete delightfully led them in a prayer of salvation. And as they returned to their seats, the tenth beacon had lit up. Two more. "The second group I'd like to pray for are those to whom God gave an instruction. But for one reason or the other, you have obeyed half-heartedly. You started your obedience. Then you stopped or got distracted or fainted or chose to walk away. I am in that group, so I'm no better."

He paused. "I need to repent too. I need to focus on God too. I have not gone all the way due to fear about people's reaction. I started the institute but kept it small-scale when God wanted a bigger dream. I need this prayer as much as you do. Let us pray together because finishing the instruction brings the fulfillment of God's promise."

Pete shook his head. "No obedience, no promise. Or the promise could be there, we may even see it, but we won't possess it. There is no regret worse than such. I don't want that to be my story. I want to obey God fully, sit in that place where He commanded me to be, and inherit His portion for my life. I want His ark in exchange for my tent. His promise in exchange for my struggle. His peace in exchange for my reasons. His strength in place of my weakness. And His Word validated in my life. I'm offering Jesus this life to use as His platform. I'm seizing His instruction as my sacrifice. I want His all, so I'm throwing my whole heart into obeying His instruction. Who else wants this?"

Pete was already on his knees as Patricia swept forward and joined him there, and their hands linked together. So, did the others—the worship team, the ministers, the ushers, those in their seats—everyone. No seat was left with an occupant. Together, they cried out to God in repentance and for the grace to obey all the way and claim the promise.

Minutes later, when they were done, he led them in a

concluding prayer. "Father God, today we come to You in repentance. We are sorry for not fully obeying You. Your 'ark' concerning our lives needs to be built, and we have prepared our hearts now. We are ready. We will obey your command and build our 'ark,' and we will not stop until we hear Your voice saying, 'Well done.' Thank You, Lord Jesus, because Your grace is already available. We walk on Your Word, receive Your grace, and we press on despite any challenge to come. We will obey. We will build the ark. And we will praise You at the end. Thank You, God, in Jesus' name we pray."

"Amen." A few remained praying while most returned to their seats as Pete handed the microphone over, feeling totally spent and spiritually reinvigorated at the same time. God didn't let him down but came through with a message that blessed everyone, including him.

As he reached his seat and one of the other pastors wrapped up the evening service, he glanced up.

The twelfth beacon—the final security check for his own office computer—did not come on. Instead, it blinked repeatedly, and his heart skipped a corresponding beat.

They had a problem.

A serious security breach had occurred. He had to get to the institute fast. He exited the church through the side doors. He narrowed the turn through the private exit, then climbed the stairs toward his office. He'd barely entered the secure building complex hallway when the alarm sounded. Pete, and everyone there got shuttered in.

Only a critical breach was engineered to do so. He swallowed a gulp and offered a quick prayer. A loud wail took over the space, and he raced toward his office as the lights blinked again. Then the whole space went dark. "Alert the security company! Let them send someone now."

He raced into his office, shut the computers down, and waited for external help.

15

"Judge not, and you shall not be judged. Condemn not, and you shall not be condemned. Forgive, and you will be forgiven." Luke 6:37

Angel was sure she would explode when she got home that night. Tim stayed silent throughout the message and the altar call. But what got to Angel's heart, what had her ready to shout the roof down, was Stephanie. She thought she knew her sister. But when the message heated up with the pastor's vivid descriptions of what obstacles Noah must've faced while obeying God's command to build the ark, her response was indescribable.

Stephanie sang in tones she hadn't heard before. She lay out on the floor at the end of the message and was the first to respond to the altar call. Even though the message completely absorbed Angel, she saw how Tim's look changed from anger and a tight face to a relaxed expression, more surprised than angry. "Well, I'm not sure how you all feel, but that was some study of Scripture!"

She set her purse down on the couch, green leather nestling against the vibrant throw blanket, as Tim locked the door and armed the security.

Stephanie whistled low. "Talk about digging in. The man did not hold back at all." She swallowed. "I heard the Word of God tonight, and I was more than richly blessed. But do you know what convinced me to go forward for that altar call?"

Angel and Tim glanced at her.

"What?" Angel asked since Tim was still tongue-tied.

"The man. The preacher. He is a broken man. He looks like someone who has really done a lot of bad stuff but has been brought low by God to a place of surrender. Like he said, he didn't plan to preach this message. God simply laid it on him."

Stephanie held Angel's hand. "I saw a man, who had authority, willing to struggle through the unknown. Ready to say, 'yes, Lord,' even when he didn't know what to speak. Ready to trust God for his next words while addressing thousands." She nodded. "If I were in his shoes, the uncertainty alone would kill me if the humiliation didn't. So I made up my mind."

She glanced between both of them. "If God can use a man that damaged, God can use me too. If he can trust God, despite his past, I can trust Jesus completely too. And if uncertainty about his message didn't deter him, I won't allow uncertainty about my future to keep me from serving God wholeheartedly." She rubbed her arms, crinkling up her white blouse. "So it wasn't his message that changed me, it was the vessel I could see God himself had transformed. I am a new person tonight, and I will grow in my faith."

Angel hugged her and barely held her tears back. Could

God really be answering their prayers? Then she thought something else. Would God bring John back after these many years, or was that miracle too late to hope for? She wouldn't stop searching. But after such a long time, her faith that John was still alive was starting to wane. She struggled to hold on to hope by the miracle in Stephanie unfolding before her eyes. "I'm so glad to hear this. I love you so very much. I support your journey, and I know God will lead you into His plan, not yours, for your life. Let's keep trusting Him."

If God could deal with Stephanie this way, God could help her wobbling faith for John stand firmly too.

Stephanie took some steps toward the basement. "Oh, I'd like to start looking for a place of my own so I can allow you both some privacy. Now that the danger is gone, I can pick up my life and trust God moving forward."

"That won't be a problem. But you should know that you are fully welcome here." Tim spoke his first words.

Stephanie smiled. "Thank you. Oh, and I'll be attending this new church regularly."

Tim fell silent once again.

"And I hope you change your mind about the pastor, Tim," Stephanie added.

"I've got nothing against him," Tim protested.

"Right," Angel said.

"Exactly." Stephanie laughed as her back disappeared behind the door to the basement.

As Tim helped Angel upstairs to their room, she was sure the silence was bothering even him. But if Tim wasn't in a place to forgive Pete fully, she wouldn't force him.

But she also wouldn't deny how she thoroughly enjoyed the Word that was shared today, and if she ever went again, she would enjoy the service. She'd learned—since John's conversion to Christ through Tim—not to pattern God. Not to expect exactly how God would do things, but instead to trust God and to obey His Word. And if she heard anything tonight that she could apply, it would be that she had to choose to trust God enough to walk on His Word and believe God had John's best interest at heart—no matter what.

She wished she could kneel, but since that wasn't an option due to her healing injuries, she lowered her head, after Tim helped her into the bed, to pray. "Father God, thank You for tonight. You changed my plans for the evening and led us to a place of conversion and consecration for Stephanie."

Soft carpet rustled against his slacks as Tim drew closer, and judging from the angle from where he clasped his hand with hers, he was kneeling down.

"God, we thank You for saving Stephanie's soul. Thank You for arresting her tonight and for using an unlikely vessel to bring her comfort. We are very grateful."

"Yes, Lord."

"We ask that You help our faith concerning John." She chose to be open and vulnerable. "I choose to trust You and to believe that, no matter how hopeless it now seems, You have a great purpose for John whatever his condition is right now. We pray, once more that, if John is in trouble, please send him help. If he is held against his will, please set him free. If he is hurt, please get him help and heal him. If he has lost hope, like we sometimes have, please restore his hope like you've restored ours." A strange peace settled on her heart the more she prayed. Surely, Tim sensed it, too, as he stood on his feet.

"Father, I know that, with man, circumstances may be impossible for us to hope that John is still alive now. Too many years have gone by. All stones have been unturned. Yet nothing has led us to him. So, we pray, dear God of heaven and earth Who sees that which we cannot see, Who reaches where our eyes cannot observe, that You do a miracle now and take all the glory."

"Yes, please, Father. We need You," Tim cried in prayer. Their hearts, joined as one, bare before God.

"Please God, show us mercy. Save John, Lord. Save him and lead him home to us. No one can say at this point that they did it. You alone do this, please, God. And You alone take all the glory. This we pray in Jesus' mighty name."

"Amen," Tim echoed. "And, Lord Jesus, please help me to forgive Pete fully and completely." His voice trembled as he collapsed on his knees. "He took someone precious from me. Seeing him and hearing him speak today amplified the pain of loss. I miss Violet. Help me to choose to forgive Pete. I need Your grace. To see him as who You've made him to be today, not the man he was. To stop judging a man You forgave and called as Your own. To believe in his ministry and even to support it in the future. In Jesus' mighty name, amen."

"Amen, including for whatever role he played in John going missing. We forgive him, Lord," Angel quietly added, grateful to see her husband baring his all to God too.

Without much further conversation, he climbed into bed beside her, and they fell asleep with more peace inside than she'd felt in a long time. God was in control. God was in charge, and all she had to do tonight was—sleep.

∽

THE LIGHT SHONE INSIDE PETE'S OFFICE AND ILLUMINATED THE

warm-colored interior and revealed the beauty of those floor-to-ceiling lilac curtains Patricia had chosen, as he strode toward it. The red emergency lights had come on in the hallway and guided him toward his office.

"Pastor." A voice paused him as he squeezed the knob, so he let go of the handle. His assistant who had been with him since he was a young man faced him with a grim look beyond the pimples on his face. "It's bad." He reflected light off the tablet in his hand. "Really bad."

But Pete wouldn't allow fear to rule the situation. "How so? Show me everything."

They strode into his office.

The young man followed, pausing so Pete could let him through the door then shut it behind him. "Well, it started at six this morning." The man sank into a black leather chair across from Pete. Having been at an online conference all day, Pete hadn't been in the building.

"Then, what happened?" Pete occupied his seat, the weight of responsibility it brought settling on him like a prepared robe. He'd handled many situations since founding this security institute and, not once, had they faced an all-out security situation.

Until now.

All three floors were fitted with security apparatuses enough to keep a president safe. Because they had a former president as a guest a couple of times. His daughter, the former first daughter, Ritz Towers, now Bailey, and her husband, Jaden Bailey, were church members. She had to be kept safe, not just because she was a daughter of his friend. But because she was also politically relevant. He took the safety of all his church members seriously as well as the members of the institute.

Now, this situation was new ground. And a new challenge he'd overcome. "Did you assess the situation? Run tests? I set off the test from the altar while preaching. I had a burden in my soul, stopped, and knew something had to be wrong. So I started the security scan."

Simon nodded. "I saw that. I'm glad you did because I was waiting for you to get here before starting a scan. So you jumped ahead and helped me isolate the source."

Pete blinked. "You saw the source? That's highly unusual. They're typically masked."

He nodded again, handing Pete the tablet he'd been working with his fingers. "Yes, but not this time. That's because the source..." He lifted his head and met Pete's measured gaze and next words with a hard stare, "is from here. Within the institute."

Surely, Pete hadn't heard right. "Did you say, from *within* the institute?"

Someone attacked his computer from inside his team?

A slow nod confirmed the bad news. "Yes."

"How so?"

The young man pointed to the tablet. "The security scan that didn't complete?" Pete didn't respond. He simply stared. "It was linked to a malware which bounced from the systems in the north end of this building to your computer."

"Why don't we search for the specific system and isolate it? We can get that granular, can't we?"

"Sadly, we cannot. It was disconnected. Before I could locate the specific PC, it was pulled from the network."

Pete's belly churned. "Which means there's a human accomplice."

"Right. And that is the only reason I'm asking that we

involve the external security company now. For starters, we may be headed toward a larger threat. This could be a test run. We need outside help."

Pete felt his face grow dark, even though he couldn't see it. "Especially since we have a threat from within."

"Agreed."

He lifted the receiver, dialed the number he'd hoped he'd never need to call, and put a request in. The respondent informed him they were dispatching someone onsite to assess the situation. After hanging up the call, Pete turned. During the days when people came to the church from all walks of life and backgrounds and he hadn't gotten used to so much diversity yet, he'd been cautious and wary of stereotypes.

But then, the people surprised him. They were accommodating, kind, and courteous—even those yet to receive Jesus Christ. So he relaxed and never had cause to suspect anyone's behavior.

Until today.

How could he fish out the traitor from a staff of three hundred or from clients numbering four thousand in three weeks? During their security awareness conference, largely attended by law enforcement from around the world, it was impossible to spot who could be planning to do them harm. But he wasn't going to jump too far ahead. One step at a time. "Let's wait for the security personnel. Then we proceed. It might just be a glitch." Believing the best but not unaware of the possible threat, Pete chose to consider all the options.

"Right. I'll try to share that optimism." And with that and a sad smile, his assistant left, and Pete prayed that, whatever the threat was, it was fished out in time and that it was from no one he trusted.

A threat was one thing. A threat by an insider—especially when he'd opened himself up to the people to teach and train them both spiritually at the church and physically on security preparedness at the institute—was a level of betrayal of trust he wasn't sure he had the stomach to overcome.

He reached out and turned off the building alarm, allowing free movement again. If the threat was directed to his computer alone, he wouldn't inconvenience others. Maybe, the security firm could tackle this problem and fix it.

Because, maybe, just maybe, this was the last straw that could break his back.

16

"The horse is prepared for the day of battle, but deliverance is of the Lord." Proverbs 21:31

A LADY CLAD IN BLACK-ON-BLACK JEANS AND TEES WITH THE NAME International Security printed on her chest arrived one hour later and circled to Pete's desk. "Sir, you reported a security threat to your systems?"

She spread out an array of digital tools, which she inserted and uploaded into his system, being the master switch, with which she conducted a quick but detailed scan of the entire network. As soon as she finished, she looked up with a puzzled glance. "You said there was a breach?" She pointed ahead. "I scanned everything digital in this building, and I can't see any evidence. Are you sure?"

Pete turned from her to his assistant. "I wasn't dreaming up the instance of the twelfth light not coming on, was I? Or the system breach you'd spotted?"

His assistant raised his brows at the lady. "No, sir. You and I had first-hand evidence of the breach. Maybe we should involve the SSPD. We even have some of their men and women coming here in three weeks. They can assist us."

"Coming for the conference," the lady said in a surprisingly sunken voice.

Pete turned up an eyelid. "You are aware of our conference?" Come to think of it, he'd never seen her before.

With a slight incline of her head, she turned toward his assistant. "I am. Or," a halfhearted shrug followed, "I'd tried to register, but I was told you were full. Your training is topnotch, and I'd admired it from the outside looking in so I'd hoped to cinch a spot. I guess it was not to be."

Pete wasn't sure what to say. Here he was trying to sort out why someone tried to take out his systems, or steal information, and this lady came complimenting him?

A small smile tightened his lips. "Well, if I was doing so well, I wouldn't have been facing a security breach. Someone caught us napping, and I won't allow that to happen again. If you say you see nothing, please feel free to leave. Like my assistant suggested, we will call the SSPD, because we did see something and it has to be investigated."

Silence trailed his words as she packed her gear into a tall, square pocketbook. "Well, if you'd like, I could walk with your assistant to the other side of the institute. I can try to give a more detailed assessment in that area since you had a hub there. If I find nothing, then you can call the SSPD. It's one more thing to try."

Pete looked at his assistant, who nodded. "Sure. Will you escort her to the hub, please?"

With a wave of his hand, Simon gestured for her to precede him. "Yes, sir."

"Of course, if you find anything, circle back here and let me know. I'll be in this office until I find out what had happened."

Her slower nod followed. Then she exited.

An hour later, both returned to his office.

"Sir, we found nothing. It was as though nothing had happened," his assistant said.

Pete turned to the lady. "Thanks for coming. I think we're done here."

"Sure." She smiled. "Have a great day and feel free to call us if you think of anything else."

Once she'd left, he picked up the phone and dialed. "Hey, Charlie. I need your help. Someone breached my computer today, and we can't see who it is. We think it's an insider threat, and I need your candid assessment."

"Ugh. Our team is out for two weeks on training. Mind if I send someone in about three weeks? Is that too late?"

"No. It's perfect. Thank you, buddy."

"My pleasure. God bless you."

Pete hung up, then picked up his keys, locked up his office, and went to console his wife on the loss of their child—with no more distractions.

∽

Three weeks after the eventful Bible study visit to the Living Faith Bible Church, Angel returned home early to help Stephanie pack. Stephanie had found a place not too far from their house but not too distant from the SSPD either, which allowed her to visit Angel and Tim, but also to stop by the station in a hop should she need to see her sister.

Many moons ago, Stephanie had sworn to leave town and never come back. But something about the place someone came from always called to them no matter how far they went. Home was always home.

Today, Stephanie was as happy as a bird. She sang in low tunes as they carried her stuff to the moving truck and not in her car, which was out for repairs. She'd be going to court in a matter of weeks for the hearings and sentencing of her ex-boyfriend. She wanted to get a job in her career but felt God was leading her in a new direction.

True to her word, she'd been to church every Wednesday for Bible study and every Sunday for church. She attended a wedding ceremony and introduced some new friends to Angel.

Angel was glad to see her sister smiling more and relaxing even more. Seeing her out and about with people, and even going to the grocery store without fear of danger, was such a relief. Judging from what Stephanie had told her, she was discovering life afresh. She was healing emotionally.

Also, both of them had started talking about John more. Reliving old memories and going through old photos. These three weeks provided an incredible bonding time. As she tucked in the last piece of luggage—luggage which included everything she'd left behind and had shipped from Alaska—and Stephanie readied to climb into the truck, Angel leaned over and hugged her. "I love you, Steph Bear. Make sure you let me know if you ever need anything, okay? I'm only a phone call away."

Stephanie gave a brilliant smile. "Of course. I will. Thank

you and thanks to Tim for the way you both took me in and hosted me. I really appreciate your hospitality and love. And thanks again for helping to save my life. You are a wonderful sister, and I'll miss you terribly. I have to go now before we miss my two-hour window for returning the truck. I don't want to pay any extra fees."

Angel laughed and released her. "Sure. Take good care of yourself and do stop by for a visit."

"Okay. Bye." Stephanie climbed in, and as the truck drove away, Angel stood motionless, wishing she could keep this new Stephanie around much longer, but knowing she had to let her go so she could move into what God had planned for her life.

"God, my Father, please keep Your daughter in Christ. Don't allow the enemy to steal her from Your hand ever again, Lord Jesus." Then Angel returned inside, intent to focus her attention once more on the search for their missing brother.

⁓

As Stephanie Martinez watched her sister from the moving truck's rear-view mirror, she dipped her head and offered a prayer. "Lord Jesus, our journey of faith begins. I have no penny to my name, and the money I have, I used to rent this new place, according to the instruction You laid on my heart to move. I also need to afford to pay the next rent within thirty days or I will have no place to live." She peeped heavenward. "If Noah walked on the water of Your Word, so will I. I have stepped out in faith according to Your will and purpose. Please honor my faith. In Jesus' mighty name, amen."

Faith she couldn't explain flooded her heart—God had heard her. She nearly trembled leaving the known to enter the unknown. A place in her life she'd been too scared to go to. An extreme that defined everything she wished not to face. But she knew how easy it was to get comfortable living with Angel and Tim, just like she'd grown comfortable with Richard. She leaned on people, period. And it was time she learned to lean on God. So she fought her instincts and moved out of Angel and Tim's place as soon as she was sure she could sleep alone without any nightmare of Richard bursting into her bedroom.

Also, she valued privacy, both hers and others'. Angel and Tim would never ask her to leave their home, but they'd surely rather be free not to host anyone. As would any couple who had individually and together been through what both of them had gone through in life. So, without imminent danger to her life, Stephanie chose to move. To stand on her own two feet and to learn—hard and unpredictable as it would be—how to lean only on God and on His Word.

That day, as she left Living Faith Bible Church, she knew she'd found a new spiritual home. God had led her there and given her a Word, and she was walking on it. And the Word would guide her to a large place, so she trusted God.

Almost as soon as the truck arrived, she stepped aside to let the men move her stuff inside. By the end of the hour, she drove to the truck rental and returned the truck. Then she settled in to pray, ate some pizza she'd bought in the grocery store's freezer section, and played some Christian music. With no furniture to boast of, she danced to God in her living room's open space, thanking Him for this journey and expressing everything she felt. Then she went to sleep on a camp bed she set up at the center of the living room.

17

"For there is nothing hidden which will not be revealed, nor has anything been kept secret but that it should come to light." Mark 4:22

PETE SAT IN HIS OFFICE, RETURNING PHONE CALLS WHEN THE SSPD team arrived. During the past three weeks, he'd reported to Captain Charlie Bailey what occurred the night he led Bible study. They had one face-to-face meeting, then a follow-up conversation where Charlie had checked out his system and found nothing. But, unlike the security company, he believed something had happened three weeks earlier.

They just had to find out what.

"Guys, thanks for coming." Pete smiled at the one lady on the five-person team. "And you too, Ladi." Slender, with light-brown skin complexion, and curly hair, she appeared of East African descent. No one knew how powerfully Ladi, a children's church pastor here, could preach. He'd been highly impressed when he'd listened in on one occasion where she taught the children the Word. Seeing her out of her uniform, no one would know she was a cop. It was as though she shed each personality, faced whatever responsibility God placed in front of her, and met the requirements everywhere she went.

Today, however, she was here as part of the team to find out what was happening to his system.

"Have you called anyone else to look at this?" Ladi swung around his desk, and respectfully, he stepped aside. Two of the guys accompanied her while the other two set out their equipment.

Pete shook his head. "I called our hired security company the night it happened. The lady they sent concluded she saw nothing. I didn't see a need to request a second visit since nothing else occurred." Pete scratched the little hair left on his head. "I don't know what it could've been. If there hadn't been witnesses, I would've thought I'd dreamt the entire thing up. But I saw it happen from the church and it was real. Something happened. I need your help to get to the bottom of it."

Mark, the team lead, nodded. "Of course. We will go back to all the action on your system seventy-two hours prior to the attack. If anything crawled through this system, including the battery level, we'll find it."

"Thank you. I'll hang back and work from my assistant's system while I wait."

Pete went over to the church members' records he'd intended to organize. He filed the records waiting for attention. Then he called some who'd requested prayer and personally called everyone who'd attended the church for the first time in those three weeks, welcoming them and praying for them. He was grateful to see how many were from the iconic Bible study

—the night God took over the message. His fingers hovering over the keyboard, he paused, struck by a lady named Stephanie. She said she came for the first time that night and that the message touched her heart. But what touched her the most, she said, was his brokenness. She recommitted her life to Jesus and was walking on His Word, which He'd given her. From her description of her response to the message, Pete vaguely recalled who he thought she might've been, but he couldn't be sure since he and Patricia were also smitten by the Word and had fallen on their faces in prayer.

Many miracles of salvation were wrought by one single act of obedience to God's command. That day wasn't just another Bible study—it was *God's* Bible study. The Word visited them Himself and transformed lives in a way only He could.

Two hours later, Ladi approached him, a frown curving her hazel eyes. "Pastor, we found something."

Pete rose, but she impressed on him to sit as three of her colleagues surrounded them and another was calling something in to the SSPD, requesting that more team members be sent over.

"You might want to sit for this one."

"What is it? What's wrong?" He dropped back down, pressing his hands on both sides of the seat. He wasn't a man to get anxious. But uncertainty took up space in his heart, and his fingers gripped the seat. "Tell me, Ladi. I can handle it by God's grace."

Mark sunk into the opposite chair facing him. "Sir, it wasn't a malware. Not exactly."

"What was it then?"

He and Ladi exchanged glances. "It's personal. It's about your family."

"What about my family?"

"The messages came in over a thirty-hour period. They came in letters, buried inside coded language. When the last message entered, it triggered a system shutdown that mimicked malware behavior and your system correctly responded. But, like we said, this wasn't malware. It's not even spear-phishing. It's a direct message."

"A message? What does it say?" He pushed on the armrests, growing impatient. "Just spill it guys."

"I'd rather show you. Please, come with me." Ladi led him around his desk to his computer, and he approached it like it was a strange object. She pointed to the screen. "Here is the message, sir. It's in different font sizes for disguise, but it says what we see it saying."

Pete read, and he gulped.

DO YOU KNOW YOUR REAL LAST NAME? DO YOU KNOW WHO YOU ARE, PETE?

"What is that supposed to mean?"

They eyed him. "That's what we're asking. Is there something you don't know about your family? Something in your history you're not aware of?"

"No." He was sure. There was nothing he didn't know and no home of his family's he wasn't thoroughly familiar with... except the cabin. He'd avoided it for years. It was Violet's favorite place, and her memories haunted him there. "I don't think so."

Mark eyed him. "What led you from no, to I don't think so?"

Pete sighed. "We have a cabin in a scenic locale where our family typically went on holiday when I was growing up. It was my sister's favorite place before she passed. I haven't gone there because I had Violet's things moved there and hadn't wished to face those memories."

The team glanced at one another. "Well, it seems someone knows something about you that you don't," Mark said. "I'd advise you to catch up on what they know before it turns into some serious leverage."

A thought occurred to him. "I just remembered something. Before Violet died, she'd said someone had been harassing her with phone calls after she sang our family's favorite poem at our dad's funeral. The calls stopped after a while, but maybe there's a connection?"

Ladi gripped the back of his chair. "I'd say it's worth checking out."

"Maybe I should take my wife's advice and go to the cabin with her. I need to close that loop. It's my own walking on the Word."

Eyes soft, Ladi touched his arm. Having been at that eventful Bible study, she'd understand. "Like Noah. Definitely do it. We'll send a member of the team with you on standby in case you find something. And if you don't, we'd suggest you keep searching. Something prompted someone to attack your system in order to send this message. Let's save them the trouble, find out the information, and protect you and it first. Before they reach it."

"Of course, I'll do so."

"Meanwhile, our team will dig into your family's background in available public records, with your permission, of course, and see what we can find."

"You have my permission. Thank you."

With those words, the team left, and he remained seated, staring at his screen. What in his family's history would cause someone to attack his system for historical information? Well, he knew one person—his late sister's best friend, Tim—who was good at digging up old stuff, and with this guy's help, whatever had to be uncovered, would be.

But, first, he had to see if Tim would talk to him. He loosed his grip on the armrests. There was only one way to find out.

18

"I will instruct you and teach you in the way you should go; I will guide you with My Eye." Psalm 32:8

SETTLING HIS BACK AGAINST THE COLD CONCRETE FORMING THE wall for his bed, John Martinez could hardly endure another painful moan from the girl curled in a fetal position with a hand on her belly in the bunk across the room. A slim, silk, brown curtain torn with holes from years of being flapped either way separated him from where she lay.

But he couldn't escape the room—a former grain storage warehouse—shaped just like the other five in the compound and surrounded by a high wall with 24/7 security watch.

Not while being held against his will for almost twenty years.

But, as he pushed the light blanket covering his feet, a compassionate word slipped out his lips before he could help it.

"It might help if you lay on your belly. I wish I can do more, but I can't, Bree." And knowing that hurt. "After all, what do I know? I'm just a guy. Sorry."

If only he could do something to help her...As he listened across the room month after month separated from the females, watching them as their assigned guard, Bree lay in pain for almost a full week every time her period came close. It was nearly as hard as being in captivity for all of them. The only reason they hadn't done away with her was because he convinced the handlers she could cook.

Another painful moan came from her, and John cast a glance in her direction. He caught a glimpse of her curved form when the curtain flapped. Small, with a tender frame like she would break, Bree was mentally strong. She'd arrived in the last four months, later than the others, but she'd been more vulnerable then. Vulnerable to dismenoria, an illness coming from within her. She would vomit, and curve in pain for days when her period neared and for days afterward, while he covered her kitchen duties to avoid any punishments for her.

Except today, when something revolted in his heart more than usual.

She had to get help before she became anemic, if she wasn't already. If left to him, he'd ask that she be sent to a hospital for treatment in his place. He'd serve out whatever term she owed the men who ran this human trafficking organization—even though he knew how dangerous they were. He'd pleaded with them to allow his family to ransom him, but they'd refused, telling John his case was different. He was the ransom for a debt the assassin who sold him had paid. Rather than killing him, the man used him to pay a debt. So, John was to stay until he died or they killed him—whichever happened first.

Frustration had birthed anger, and then resignation. Day after day, he sought a means to escape, and night after night, escape eluded him.

But during his bedtime devotion in his bunk last night, right before he fell asleep, a Scripture had pressed on his heart. Tonight, however, he was strangely at peace.

"I am the Lord your God, Who led you out of Egypt. Out of the land of bondage and out of the house of slavery..."

He recalled memorizing the entire verse years ago in his older sister Angel's house before his kidnapping. Yet he had not thought about it for a long time. But having not seriously paid attention to it then, he didn't know why it would come into his heart now.

Last night, he'd virtually tossed about all night struggling to sleep on the thin foam mattress separating his body from the hard metal springs. Every time he snagged some sleep, the Scripture came back. He'd finally slept off around early dawn. Rising so he could manage to pray a bit before they were interrupted by the usual physical checks for weapons or communication devices, he'd seen the girls clad in the school uniform disguises the men typically moved them in, in an attempt to avoid suspicion. Things had gone as usual throughout the day, although many of the girls from other units were piled into trucks and moved earlier. But he hadn't thought too much about it—until now.

With a loud squeak, the door burst open. Then someone entered, panting.

Dakota stumbled forward. The third person being held here, she said she'd been snatched off her front door when she stepped out to grab a gallon of milk from a deliveryman.

Physically speaking, she was the opposite of Bree. She burst with energy, had only been sick a few times, and didn't complain. Right now, excitement gleamed in her eyes and flared her nostrils. "Guys!" She cast a glance back and shut the door, then lowered her voice. "I found a way out. A way of escape." Still panting, she rotated glances between him and Bree but must've been disappointed when neither exhibited her excitement.

"Tell me about it," John managed to mutter. At least, she deserved to be heard.

A slow, less enthusiastic nod later, Dakota flapped the dividing curtain aside. "I heard the men talking in Spanish—remember, I said this place might be in Mexico? Anyway, I saw them having an argument. Then some of them were leaving fast in trucks. One said something to another to hurry up, the Americans were on to them. See, there's a gate on the left wall behind this structure."

Structure, right. She could hardly call where they were a building. It looked more like detached units of five bungalows surrounded by a high wall. He'd passed that back wall many times while guarding one or two girls assigned to him to watch while they farmed the garden. He'd seen them carve steps into the blocks, wishing for an escape. But the walls were too high. The girls couldn't scale it, even though it was mere meters behind the unit where they were housed.

"I know where you're talking about."

"So, the gate is usually locked with chains looped around it and a..."

"A heavy padlock securing it," John hurried her along. "You may want to skip going over what we already know before we are interrupted."

Another nod followed. "Right. Sorry." Bree's painful moan

cut Dakota off for a moment. "I saw that gate open, and no one was guarding it."

"Could be a trap."

"But why, then, would the chain be dangling off the hinge after the trucks left? The gate is open. Like, right now." Dakota brought him news from the outside when she'd arrived, once she realized he was on their side. But this tale was hard to believe. She eyed Bree, then him. "We can stay here until they decide we're no longer useful, sell us girls, and kill you, John. Or we can take a chance and make it out of the gate. Now."

Silence fell over them.

He might as well say it. They were all thinking it. "There was some talk about an explosive device attached to the back gate. It'll blow if anyone tries to run through."

"Right." She nodded, her short red curls shaking vigorously. "I've heard that too. But they opened the gate and left it open, so it must be deactivated."

John still waited for Bree to reply. She uncoiled herself slightly, tipping her face their way. Then her voice came so low both he and Dakota leaned toward her. "If you see a chance, take it. Leave me here. I cannot get up, let alone, run." Dark curls matted around her puffy eyes, and his heart ached for her pain.

"You can try, Dakota." John wasn't ready to consider that escape was actually possible. Dakota could be imagining things and wishing for an escape instead? Either way, he'd not leave Bree, the last girl left in his care, behind.

"Why would you stay, John?" Bree frowned at him, unfurling herself just a bit more. "Let's be practical. If three of us stay, we could die. If you both escape, that leaves only me. I don't have the strength to fight." She sniffed. "John, please, don't waste this chance because of me. I wouldn't wait up for you if I could flee."

A solemn silence followed between loud voices from outside.

"I appreciate all you have done for me, John. But it's time to leave me to God's care. God might be the One creating this chance for you, you never know. After all, among everyone here, you know too much for them to keep you alive. You trust God, don't you?"

How could such a soft voice cut into his resolve? John ground his teeth together. "I trust God. But I'm not leaving you." He nodded to Dakota. "If you see an opportunity, go ahead. Escape. Then send help for us, okay?"

Dakota hesitated, glanced at Bree, and slumped slightly. Resignation tightened her features until her freckles spread and blurred. She leaned over and hugged Bree. "I'll miss you, girl." Her voice cracked as she straightened and swiped what must be sweaty palms on her washed-out, rugged jeans. "John, come on. Let's go before this opportunity closes."

But John didn't move. He simply shook his head.

It made sense to go, if there really was a chance. But something made him hesitate, and Bree was a big part of it.

If Dakota saw an escape, she could be speaking the truth.

If he succeeded, he could see his sisters again.

He might smell home once more.

But his feet wouldn't budge. So, while he was indecisive, Dakota stepped back outside. The door shut behind her, and he counted the seconds.

Each second felt like hours. A minute passed.

Then two minutes.

Then five.

Bree had stopped moaning. She was probably holding her breath. He was too. For Dakota's safety.

"You think she made it?" Bree finally broke the silence after an eternity, which could've been minutes.

He wasn't sure what to say. Did Dakota succeed? There'd been no explosion. No scuffle. No sound out of the ordinary.

"You should go, John." Bree twisted herself almost to a sitting position and reached out a shaking hand his way, every bit of her posture imploring him. "Really. You're better off out there, getting me help than staying bound with me. They likely think we'd never attempt an escape so they don't guard us too closely. But this is your chance." She leaned up, and shafts of sunlight highlighted the purple under her puffy eyes. "You can help me best by escaping. Give it a shot, John. Please."

He remembered the Scripture again. The one that had given him a sleepless night. He thought of Angel, Stephanie, and his other siblings. He missed them so much that his heart ached. He pushed his feet underneath him. "Only if you're sure." How he hated leaving her alone here!

A weak smile tipped her pallid lips. "Yes, I am. Go." She waved a hand toward him, and that propelled him to his feet. He squeezed the door open and stepped out into the compound. At the far left, stood the kidnapper's mansion. John had never met the mysterious man. He'd only heard of him. Unusually dark for this time of the night, it did appear as though no one was in there.

John climbed down the few steps, turned left, and turned another left toward the back of his unit. He knew these grounds and could navigate them with no torchlight.

Before him, afar off, was the back gate that should be open, according to Dakota. He visually scanned the surrounding area.

The few guards to his right weren't paying attention. Something on a monitor had their attention, and a loud argument was going on. They looked like they would soon go too. What was going on?

John exhaled, then spun, and beyond where he stood, the gate now had a chain hanging loosely around it. He marched toward it, praying that, if it was ever open, it was still open.

But, when he reached the gate, his shoulders sloped, and his heartbeat thudded dull, his hopes dashed. Clearly, the gate had been open since the chains were much looser than they typically were. In fact, he couldn't recall seeing it opened or loose before. Dakota had been right—the gate had been opened. And it appeared she had escaped, unknown to the guards. He was happy for her. But once they noticed she was gone, they'd have his neck. Now he had to keep going.

But as he turned, two guards gestured at him and began marching in his direction, beckoning the others with a loud shout.

John knew he was all but a dead man.

They wouldn't let him back in. And he couldn't go back out.

His heart picked up speed and beat as hard as their feet pounded on the cemented ground. *God, please help me.* He darted his gaze this way and that, unsure of what to do.

He thought of Bree. He could die, but he couldn't let her be killed because of him. He had to escape somehow. It was too late to pretend that wasn't his intention.

The guards were getting closer.

John shut his eyes and muttered the last words he cherished —the words that had kept him alive and hopeful for two decades—words taught to him by his sister. "God is good. Jesus' name is greater than every situation. And Jesus has the final say." Repeating those words to himself nightly made his situation bearable. But now, it had to open his way out of life in confinement. He'd played by the rules his captors set, but time in captivity was a ticking bomb. One day, they'd grow tired of having him around and take him out.

Unfortunately, that day had arrived.

He opened his eyes, expecting to see the guards upon him. Instead, they halted like something was pausing—no, slowing—their movement.

Go, John. Now. God has made a way.

He heard it in his heart and knew it was God.

"But...where?"

He spun around frantically. Where! The guards began approaching, and his chest constricted. In their hurry, they'd left their guns in their stall. One of them ran back to go get them.

Then John spotted a low point in the fencing. Sand from the garden had been piled high close to the wall, probably by the girls who worked there the day before. If he reached that corner, he could scale it. But it was almost a quarter of a mile away from where he stood.

It was too far. And he imagined, still too tall to scale.

Wasn't it? But he had no time to figure it out as his feet, propelled by desperation, began moving toward it.

He knew. The only way he could scale the wall was if, and only if, he gathered enough speed. As he ran, he flung his steps farther to gather momentum. If this worked, he could end up with enough bruises on the other side.

If it didn't and he landed on the fence itself, broken bones would definitely be in his future.

But there was no going back.

Huffing and puffing while hearing shouts behind him, he cast one last glance behind.

The guards were almost upon him.

"Argh!" John spurred himself forward with his last ounce of strength, thinking of Angel, Stephanie, and Bree.

He had to scale the wall. Not trying was worse than failing.

"Jesus!" he shouted a prayer and a name he'd come to trust. With everything in him, he leaped upward, slung his feet high and over, then threw his body forward and twisted into a turn, like an Olympic vaulter, while hoping, wishing, and praying he made it. A tug by one of the guards on his shirttail nearly caught him on the wall. But narrowly, by a hair's breath, the man missed.

John landed with a thud on rough bushes on the other side and rolled to a stop. The stench of urine and animal dung filled his nostrils. He twisted, groaned in pain, and gripped his shoulder. He struggled to his feet in the dark, barely making out the horizon.

Blinking twice as shouts thundered from the other side, while chains from afar were being tugged to open the side gate, his eyes widened in shock.

"Goodness." He'd made it, with God's help alone, because the fence towered above him. "Thank You, Jesus," he muttered with trembling lips while his heart yet pounded and adrenaline still pulsed through him. He had no spare shoes, no clothing except the ones on his back, and no water or food. But he was free—for the first time in twenty years.

But he had no time to celebrate. Gripping his throbbing shoulder, he wound his way deep through the woods, groping the trees with his hands and moving as fast as he dared. He made every effort to cover his tracks. Whenever his shoes landed on muddy soil, he yanked vegetation and cast over it.

He prayed for God to lead him as he had no idea where he was or where he was going or how close those chasing him were. He reached a grove of thick bushes and knew he was lost. Having no desire to go back, no idea of how to go forward, and no strength to proceed, he feared being in the thick forest alone at night, knowing the men chasing him would likely catch him if he stopped to rest.

But his shoes had worn out long before now and were now mired in mud. His shoulder also throbbed badly. Thorns had torn at his skin. Heat in the air burned his face as though it had been daylight. John hoped he'd find a path somewhere.

He resisted the urge to call for help, so his pursuers wouldn't easily track him down. For all he knew, they were also lost on another side of the thick foliage. John quietly sang "Amazing Grace" to keep himself awake, grateful that he hadn't died.

If heaven made a way out, God would make a way for help to reach him. He descended toward a valley, past a cluster of tall trees, knowing he had no strength to climb the peak. The trees thinned out the lower he went. His ears were greeted with a welcome sound as the rush of water beckoned, and he hurried his feet toward it. Tiredness wore his limbs out, but he pushed forward. He had to find help. He had to.

A stream of clear water rippled before him, moonlight catching in twinkles, and even though the water was ankle deep, he fell into it and rolled himself in it, splashing coolness into as many parts of him as he could. Life returned to him as he lapped it up, without being sure of its hygiene, and he drank until he could drink no more. He sat on a rough stone, resting his aching feet in the stream to allow the water to wash them continuously. It stung at first but soon soothed his wounds.

John forced himself to rise rather than risk falling asleep. He had to keep moving. He soaked a few leaves from a tree by the banks of the stream, mashed them on his feet like balm, and drank more water. Then, groaning in pain with each step, he plodded along a narrow path, leaving the water, toward an unknown destination where city lights blinked.

Voices rumbled through the woods just then, and he hid behind a tree, careful not to break a twig or make a sound. Frog croaks and owl hoots filled the night air. The voices passed him moving toward the way he had come. Exhaling long, he resumed walking opposite to their direction and toward the city lights seemingly a lifetime away.

After what must've been an hour, John emerged at a footpath. Trees spread wide branches overhead while fallen leaves decaying on the trail suggested it hadn't been traveled in a long time. Exhausted, he could barely tell where next to plant his feet, yet he trudged on. His shoulders slumped, and his eyes begged to close. He groaned in pain as his throat dried up and his tongue stuck to the roof of his mouth. He stumbled over a tree root and fell. "Argh." Managing to rise again, he clambered forward.

Was he in Mexico like Dakota speculated? The music their captors had played in the compound suggested so. But looking around him now in the faint light—and hearing those who'd passed speak English—he was almost sure he was still in a part of the United States. Of course, he couldn't be absolutely sure. Determined to continue until he found a house, a human being, a car, or a road, he urged his feet forward beyond their willingness to continue.

After what seemed like forever, he glimpsed what might've been a passenger sedan parked haphazardly. At this point, his feet bled badly, his eyes glazed over, and he slumped at the base of a tree, unable to move. Then he saw what a man standing near the car was about to do—and he gasped.

19

"For as the Father raises the dead and gives life to them, even so the Son gives life to whom He will." John 5:21

Dr. Ahmed Diaz pinned the mouth of the pistol in his trembling hand under his jaw. *Shoot.* But he lingered as sweat trickled down his forehead.

I have to do this.

No, you don't.

He'd been going like this for almost a half-hour. Both thoughts warred in his mind as he'd left his hospital night shift and drove to the nearby woods to end his life. He hadn't intended for the patient to die. The nurses had missed including her allergens in her patient chart, and when treated for a regular infection, she reacted violently and died.

He'd also not known the patient was the hospital registrar's mother. Or that it would cost him his job now. This was his last shift, they'd said. He was to be on administrative leave. They'd conduct an investigation and get back to him, the official statement said. The unofficial statement? Dr. Wycloff had sworn to make him pay, life for life, for killing his mother. He'd all but promised to kill Ahmed. So Ahmed would be lucky not to get locked up. Knowing the family he hailed from, that was unacceptable. So he'd chosen to save them all the trouble and take care of the problem—him. He'd take himself out of the equation and all would be fine. Or so he thought....

Don't take a life you didn't give.

It was something his mom usually said when she visited the hospital. A way of asking him to be careful when treating patients. But right now, the thought appeared out of nowhere. She wasn't a big fan of his career. She'd wished for him to become an aerospace engineer, so a doctor was beneath her plans.

He'd disappointed everyone in his life, so why was he not doing this already? What held him back?

He positioned the gun more firmly, then shut his eyes. But the conflicting thoughts still fought each other. So he let his hand drop, buried his head in his hands, and wept as he leaned against the trunk of an old tree. "Will anybody miss me?" He pounded the tree until his hands hurt. "I'm useless. I couldn't even be a good doctor. Nobody cares about me. I'm a waste of space." He continued saying the things he thought to himself. On and on he went until he had nothing left to say.

Desperate to escape the darkness, he shifted on his feet when an owl hooted. Why did he come to the woods? He could've done this in his home.

If he killed himself here, people would know he was gone, but how long would it be before his body was discovered?

Would his mom understand the news after Alzheimer's had taken up residence in her mind and shut her off from him for ten years? But he hadn't said goodbye to her. No, he couldn't think about his mom. That would only weaken his resolve.

The gun shook against his jaw as his feet edged closer to the clearing he'd determined was the best spot.

The best spot to take his life.

But...Could he do this? A bird chirped as something slid off a tree branch and landed on the ground, and he shrieked. He couldn't see what the object was. A few leaves settled on his shoulder. His memories warmed as the movement reminded him of his mom taking him to the zoo in DC. He'd been a small boy. A leaf had settled on his shoulder, just like now, and as he was about to dust it off, his mom took both of his shoulders in her hand and whispered in his ear. "Leave it there. It's a sign of life."

Why were all these memories surging to the surface now?

The gun trembled in his hands even more as tears covered his vision. The life he had was not his own. How could he imagine taking it away?

But...But...He'd chosen to end his life for more than what occurred at the hospital tonight. The mix-up at the hospital was simply the end of his endurance.

He was an Iraq veteran.

Ahmed couldn't endure another night of jerking up from sleep and pointing a loaded gun in the air in the middle of his bedroom, thinking he was still on the battlefront in Iraq. He couldn't jump or run for cover every time a loud truck roared past. He couldn't sleep with another human being in the same room and not be a physical danger to them. Not after he'd nearly strangled his last girlfriend and woke up soon enough for her to escape his tight grip. He'd seen the fear in her eyes as she'd hurriedly packed her stuff and left. That was twelve months ago. And his pleas for her to give him another chance had been ignored.

So, she'd left, with most of his hopes for a life partner falling along behind her. Now, he was sure. He would never be married. He would never have an intimate relationship. And he'd begun thinking he might as well end his life. After serving his country with honor, what else remained to look forward to with a broken body and a traumatized mind? And now, add to that, an ended career in medicine?

Many years had gone by and his retirement from the military had not retired the trauma of being one of the first American boots on the ground for a foreign war, and everything that came along with it. Most of his buddies had died there. He couldn't explain why he survived. He'd heard about others taking this...way out of the trauma called PTSD. But he'd never thought he would consider it.

Therapists and doctors had failed him, yet cost him thousands of dollars. Yet there he was—about to exit life the way he detested.

But his mom's voice wouldn't leave him be, drawing him into their past once more. "I've got a lot of dreams for you, my son. To be a soldier, a man of honor." His mom's soft voice echoed in his mind as did her vigorous nod. "Yes," she'd observed his young face with hopeful eyes and trailed a finger across his cheek, "I'm sure you'll be a great engineer with your sharp eyes, kind heart, and careful hands. You will help a lot of people."

And she'd been right. He'd gone on to be a soldier first, then returned, went to medical school, and became a doctor.

Right now, they claimed he was one of the best doctors at the hospital. Until this happened. But no one there knew his secret issues—that sleep warred with his war memories, leaving his nights full of fitful, danger-filled sleep. No, he couldn't return to his old life. They could use any other doctor to replace him.

No. I can't do this for another night. A dizzy spell hit his head and had him clutching the tree.

It was time to end it.

He swallowed hard, pinned the gun harder until it ground against his jawbone. Then, he released the safety. He felt for the trigger, shut his eyes, and readied his mind, but his mom's face stayed at the front as the leaf fell from his shoulder to the ground.

A leaf is a sign of life.

Life is a gift from God.

You can't take what you didn't give.

You will help a lot of people.

"No." Ahmed covered his ears in a futile attempt to block a voice so native to him as the first voice he ever heard. Her voice seemed to care less about his impending act and weaved through him stronger than his will to do what he wished.

He blinked hard and glanced up at the moonless sky.

He just had to get a grip and get it done. Sweat broke out on his forehead once more.

A voice broke through his thoughts. "You're not useless. God loves you."

It sounded so weak Ahmed was sure he was hearing his own voice.

"It appears you've let everyone use you but the God Who

made you. Give Him a chance to show you what you were made for."

No, he wasn't dreaming. Someone else was here—and listening to him the whole time. In the woods? At this time of night?

"Please help me. Get me to a hospital. I need help. If they find me, they will kill me." The voice sounded even weaker. But it sent him spinning.

Ahmed trailed the voice to the tree next to the one he'd been up against. A form lay there braced against the trunk. A man. Exhausted or in pain. "Who are you and what are you doing here?"

"I can ask you the same thing."

Ahmed swallowed and hid the gun behind his back.

"I was kidnapped from Silver Stone, Maryland, about twenty years ago. I escaped, and I need to get out of here. Please take me to a hosp..."

The man was losing consciousness.

Ahmed's medical training kicked in. "Wait, what's your name?" He tossed the gun aside, probed the man's neck, and lifted him off the ground with a grunt. His pulse was weak, his body wet and trembling all over.

"John." He managed to say. "John...Jesus loves you, and He sent me here for you. Don't kill yourself, my friend."

Then he passed out.

Ahmed wasn't sure what to do. He simply saw himself doing. He'd process the man's words later. He carried the man to his car, lay him at the back of the car, and shut the door. He was returning for his gun when approaching voices grumbled through the woods. "Who's there?"

A shot in his direction sent him rounding the vehicle,

sliding into the driver's seat, and racing toward the hospital he'd sworn never to return to. A man's life was in danger and he would save this man before he figured out what to do with his own.

"Hang in there! I'm taking you to the hospital." He hoped his words made it to the man's subconscious. "Jesus, if You sent this man my way, save his life." Ahmed wasn't sure why he said that, but it was the closest thing to prayer he'd ever voiced.

And he hoped this man's God answered him—for his own sake.

20

"'For My thoughts are not your thoughts, nor are your ways My ways,' says the Lord." Isaiah 55:8

Around two a.m., Stephanie's phone rang. Blinking, she stared at the caller ID. Angel? So she fumbled to pick up the call. "Angel? Are you okay?" She rubbed the sleep still itching her eyes. Her first night in her new place came with its share of inconvenient bedding.

"You need to come to the station. They found someone they think is John."

Her ears rang. "What? What did you say, Angel?"

She had to be dreaming. It must be the springs of the camp bed making her dream.

"They found who they think is John, and you, me, and Tim need to fly over to identify him and bring along our IDs and proof of our relationship with him. Hurry, I'll explain later."

Stephanie didn't need to hear more. She hung up the call, dropped to her knees for a quick prayer of thanks, and called a taxi to the SSPD.

∽

Angel could hardly believe the call.

They'd found John.

Her ears rang as the captain briefed her on John's condition when she rushed over to the SSPD. After hearing a list of health issues—his blood sugar was low, he was admitted unconscious, and he had physical injuries—she asked him, "But he's alive?"

"He is. He's being monitored for signs of any mental distress, but beside the memory loss, which is expected due to the extreme dehydration he encountered during his trek, he should be back to normal within days."

Angel exhaled long. It was hard. Staring at the lanky image in the police photo, she'd almost said it wasn't John. But those eyes, those lips, ears, and posture were impossible to miss or to confuse with anyone else's. He was definitely John—older, more mature—and scared, which was highly unusual. But she had him back. At least, he was breathing. He was alive.

Thank God!

Everything else was fixable. It would take time, but she'd adapt. Whatever kind of support—physical, emotional, professional, spiritual, and medical—she would give. As would her other family members.

"How far are we from where he is? How was he found? By who? Is someone after him? Was he still being chased?" She wasn't giving the man room to answer. She just wanted all of the information. She wanted to hug John and not let him go ever again. Her precious brother was alive. She would count her blessings.

"He's in Yuma, Arizona. Do you wish to go there? He'll be transported back to Maryland," her captain asked just as Stephanie joined them.

"Yes. We'll go wherever he is. A night away is far too long."

The captain observed her.

"Until you've been away from someone you love this long, you'll never understand the hunger for reunion. I don't care where John is, even if he's on the moon. Wherever he is, we're flying there. Tonight. Please, give us the hospital's address." She swallowed, flushing. "Sir."

"Fine." He printed out an information sheet and handed it to her. "I'll be here waiting for your return if it is indeed your brother, so keep me up to speed. I'm sending an officer with you, in case something goes wrong and so we the SSPD have all the facts."

"Sure. That's fine." Angel hugged Stephanie. "Here's the images we were sent. He's in Yuma, Arizona, and we're flying over there. Can you come?"

She sobbed on her sister's shoulder. "Of course. I'll call the others to meet us there if they can. This can only be God."

Angel could only agree. "I had so much peace lately against all odds. It confused me. But the past weeks, I chose to trust God, no matter the outcome. And here we are."

"I am so happy, sis. Let's go." Stephanie literally dragged her out of there, and as they were leaving the SSPD, they were booking their flights to Yuma on their mobile devices. They still needed the local police to verify their identities and relationship to John and confirm his identity. She was completely willing to jump through any hoops to get her brother back. Who she'd seen was him. She had no doubt about it.

21

"When Joseph saw Benjamin [his brother] with them, he said to the steward of his house, 'Take these men to my home, and slaughter an animal and make ready; for these men will dine with me at noon.'"
Genesis 43:16

ANGEL, TIM, AND STEPHANIE AND THE UNIFORMED SSPD officer arrived at the Dulles Airport around three a.m. They boarded a flight to Arizona, and Stephanie led them in prayer for a safe and uneventful journey. As they landed in Arizona, the only thing on Angel's mind was how John would receive them. He probably wouldn't recognize them. And she had encountered a devastating situation involving memory loss before—with Tim.

This time, though, her mind was slightly more prepared. Knowing ahead of time eased the discomfort. But she also wondered whether she could keep back from reaching out to John when she saw him. Telling her mind to remain neutral was one. But being overcome with love for her brother when she saw him was something else, enough to make her lose her cool.

So, she prayed for wisdom instead. For God to grant her the grace to know how to react in a way that wouldn't strain an already strained relationship.

She also thought of things from John's perspective. He was alone, probably scared, and not trusting anyone.

St. Mary's Hospital was their destination, and as soon as they arrived, police officers escorted them to the room where John was being treated. They were briefed on the way. "Do you have your IDs with you?" one officer asked. "We're not letting anyone through without an ID check. Three reporters already came through here requesting access and were denied."

Angel stiffened, alarm shooting through her. "We have our IDs. Did you let the media in to see him?"

He shook his bald head, which shone against the reflection of the overhead fluorescent lighting. "We didn't. Not until we verify his identity. We were only able to match him using the missing persons database based on information from the man, a doctor, who'd found him."

"Good."

They arrived at a secluded room. A doctor was leaving through the double doors while a nurse was entering.

Someone with a clipboard and a gruff voice, obviously an officer, stopped them at the outer door. "I suspect you're the presumed family members, huh?" He eyed them.

"We are the real family members. My name is Officer Angel

Martinez Santiago, with the SSPD." She pointed to her right. "I have with me here, Officer Roman, and my husband, Professor Tim Santiago, and my sister, Stephanie. Our other siblings may fly in." She offered the officer her badge as ID. "We've waited almost twenty years for this day. Please let us through."

Either her ID checked out, or her plea worked. Because he stepped aside, bowed a little, and opened the door. "Another officer in the outer room will verify you when you go in. Be mindful the patient does not recognize anyone yet, so don't expect hugs and kisses."

"I appreciate the heads up." If only she'd had those warnings and reminders when Tim lost his memory, maybe they wouldn't have had several issues. But, now, she wasn't sure she could handle a brother who couldn't recognize her. After all this time, she had lots of questions.

Like, who took him? Why? What happened to him? Where was he taken to? What had gone on these many years? Why and how was he able to be here?

All those questions parked in her mind as she led the team inside the inner room. A glass window encased the actual room where John was. A nurse was administering something, possibly IV fluid, to his arm. She caught a glance of his ruffled hair, and her heart pounded in her chest.

She'd been so sure it was John that she never thought of how she'd feel if she walked into that room and it wasn't him. How would she handle it? She'd raised her whole family's hopes, and they'd flown here with her. Was that a mistake? Should she dial their expectations back a little?

Too late to second guess now. She was sure. Yes, that had been John. Those images didn't lie. And, if she got into that room and saw someone else, she could console herself for not discounting this opportunity.

"Ma'am, can you provide me with your home address, including the zip code for verification, please?" the officer's voice drew her back. "Also, please provide what personal information you have for the patient so we can confirm with our database."

"Personal information, like...?" Stephanie asked behind Angel.

Tim took Angel's hand and gave it a supportive squeeze. Surely, he remembered how her reaction had gone from excitement when he'd been found many years ago to crushed when she realized he no longer remembered their relationship. He was showing her that he was in this with her, no matter how it turned out. Was he feeling the same doubt she'd had?

"Birth date or eye color or preferred food. Things like that."

They supplied the information.

"Great. It checked out with what we have on file. Please proceed. Remember, we only verified this information with the missing persons' information for John Martinez. If the man in there says he's not John after he regains his memory and it turns out to be so, we'll cut off your access. Do you understand?"

"We do. Now, can we please go in?" Tim urged, apparently also growing impatient. He had chaired the search effort for John all these years, pursuing every lead, searching every file, documenting everything that might lead them to him no matter how small, giving her and her siblings hope, holding her when she cried for her brother. Now was not the time to lecture them about rules and regulations.

It was time to reunite.

As soon as the door opened, time froze for Angel.

She stepped inside, and cool air enveloped her. The ticking of a hospital monitor punctuated the sudden silence. Her eyes took in everything—the clock on the wall, the soiled clothing in a clear plastic bag labeled as Evidence, the cracked, mud-caked shoes beside them, and she swallowed hard.

Just as she was settling her glance at the man on the bed, he spoke through cracked lips, and her eyes confirmed that this was her brother. "You look like me."

His first words to her in two decades. She choked, and her feet felt like jelly. But Stephanie flew past her and wrapped John in a hug, weeping on him.

As Angel's legs gave way, Tim caught her. "John?" she croaked with a weak voice. His eyes met hers, though without certain recognition. His voice was steady, though without excitement, and his hand held Stephanie as he glanced at Angel. At least, he let Stephanie hug him even without readily returning the hug.

There was this...distance the information gap of his memory loss created. How she abhorred that. Why did all of her good moments get stolen from her? Seeing Tim in that hospital many years ago had been so peaceful. But the memory loss had ruined it. Now, seeing John here was everything she had prayed for, yet it lacked the joy it should've given, thanks to the same issue.

But she could see him trying his best to accommodate how he must expect them to feel.

This wasn't the reunion she'd pictured with hugs, joyous tears, flashing cameras, and Welcome-Home balloons.

Right then, Angel made a choice.

John was alive.

John was in front of her, and she would not allow the enemy to steal her joy.

So, while Stephanie still sobbed, she moved forward and wrapped her arms around her brother. Shutting her eyes, she let herself appreciate the miracle of his return. "Thank You, my Lord Jesus. You returned John to us, against all odds. You are indeed the God with the final say." She gripped his shirt and broke out in sobs.

The sleepless nights left wondering, the days passed in a daze, the comforting words from people soothed little more than the surface of their loss, the days of pasting posters and wondering whether it was a waste of time—all that weighed on her now. "Lord, thank You, for You've had the final Word here." Another sob escaped. This time, because she remembered she'd last said these words to John on her birthday those many years ago, just before he disappeared. "Jesus, thank You because You are Lord above every situation." She gasped, picturing all the work ahead to support John in getting his memory back and his life, and wondering just how hard that journey would be. She swiped a tear before the next words shocked her and had her jerking her head upright.

"And thank You, my Lord Jesus, because you are good," John said. That was the third statement she'd taught him that fateful night.

She jumped to her feet, eyes wide. "You remembered. That night..." Her tongue froze. This couldn't be happening.

Stephanie lifted off John, unsure about what was happening. She stepped aside, but Angel had her eyes fixed on John's face. His face was already breaking into a smile—accompanied by a vigorous nod. "On your birthday. Yes, Angel, I remember, sis. I remember you all now. Oh, God." His fingers gripped the sheets in both excitement and fear—the same fear she'd seen in that image shared with them in Maryland.

"I remember everything." He raised his hands toward her. "Those three statements you taught me that night saved my life and my faith. You have no idea." He reached out his arms, both of them toward her in an open invitation—the one she'd dreamed of having—her perfect reunion with her long-lost brother. And she ran into them and hugged him tight. They both cried and sobbed until they were spent.

She lifted her head, then called for the SSPD officer who'd come with them to come inside. "You need to take his statement. He remembers everything now."

The officer blinked, as confused as she'd expect him to be by the suddenness of the memory regain, but there was no time to explain. Whatever was behind the fear in her brother's eyes, she would deal with it for good first, then celebrate later. Since he recognized her now, her heart was at peace.

"Wait, what are the three statements?" Stephanie asked. "I was so happy to see him I didn't hear what all you said."

"I'd like to know too," Tim confessed.

Whatever was powerful enough to return a man's memory, she'd be curious to know too. So Angel smiled, then nodded to her brother. "Want to tell them or should I?"

"For ten bucks each, yes," John joked.

"Oh, he's coming back all right!" Tim punched his arm, and he winced, so Tim massaged it a bit. "Sorry, buddy. I forgot. It was a reflex action."

"I've missed you too, Tim." John glanced at Tim, then Angel. "Are you two...?"

"Married. Yes, we are. Long story," she supplied.

A cloud settled over his eyes. "I missed your wedding."

"But you're alive and here now. That's what counts." Tim laid his hand on John's shoulder.

A nod followed from John as he grew somber. "The three statements Angel taught me as we ate cake on her birthday are these—One, Jesus has the final Word. Two, Jesus is Lord over every situation. Three, God is good. I've held onto this treasure through," he swallowed, "very dark days, and they led me back home."

"Thanks for sharing." Tim patted John's shoulder as Stephanie typed the words out on her phone and set it inside her pocket.

"Can we give a prayer of thanksgiving for this miracle, as a family, and thank God that, right before our eyes, John regained his memory?" Angel struggled to speak through an aching throat.

"Yes." A sparkle lit John's eye, but the sad glaze remained.

Angel sank to her knees, as did the others, and they gathered around the bed, joining their hands together. "Father in heaven, we come to You today with our hearts filled with thanksgiving. No man could have predicted John would return, let alone return to us alive today. I promised to thank You the moment we found John, so I'm doing that now. Thank You, Lord Jesus, for working this miracle. The days and journey ahead might be tough, but You're tougher. It might be rough, but You'll outlast them. You have already given us the best gift —John—and whatever comes next, we trust You to handle. Please, lead us, guide us, and as we return home together, may Your peace and grace return with us, in Jesus' most powerful name, amen."

"Amen," John and everyone else echoed, so did their applause.

They squatted, sat on the handle of the hospital seat, or perched near the window as the SSPD officer, the Arizona Police, and a representative from the district attorney's office took John's testimony of the past two decades of his life.

After hearing stunning revelations, after much tears had flowed and all eyes were so reddened they could hardly leave without dark glasses to hide them, they went downstairs to the front of the hospital to announce John had been found, without showing his face, while a tactical team departed to the location John described. He'd requested they rescue the girl he'd promised to get help for.

"Someone needs to come with us," John further requested. "The doctor who found me."

Angel blinked. "I don't understand." Was he needing a doctor? "I'm sure qualified doctors in Maryland can provide the right care you need." She wasn't being specific as she wasn't sure what his need was.

He shook his head. "He's not coming as a doctor. He's, well, a friend. I can't tell you everything now. I just want him around me. Please."

When Angel glanced at Tim, he nodded. "We have enough room in our place for two guests since Stephanie vacated the basement and everything a visitor might need is still in there."

Angel didn't mind John bringing a friend along. She just wasn't sure about a man she knew nothing about. She was struggling to let John know that, due to the line of her work, she wasn't eager to trust people at first sight. But she also didn't want him to feel estranged. "Fine. As long as he's someone you can vouch for. You know how I feel about allowing strangers into our lives."

He chuckled. "There's the ever-protective sister I know." His eyes misted, and his Adam's apple bobbed. "Goodness, I've missed you." He turned to Stephanie too. "I thought I'd never see any of you again. I was…" He lost his words and looked away as a man approached.

Tall, lanky, with dark Middle-Eastern curls, and a bit of an accent, he flashed a wide smile. He fist bumped with John. "Congrats, man. I heard you got your memory back when your family showed up."

"Yes, I did." John smiled again—still a little wobbly, but a beautiful smile that beamed into her heart and burned her eyes with tears.

"So, did they scare you good or love you good to shake things back in place?" The guy was funny, and Angel didn't miss how admirably her sister, Stephanie, observed the man—and studied him from head to toe.

"Look at them. Do they look scary to you, huh?" John teased.

Seeing his sense of humor return took the edge off her concerns. She'd wondered whether whatever happened was bad enough to change him, and it likely did. But him handling it with grace was commendable. So, she stepped up.

"Um, John said you're coming with us. Is that so?"

The stranger glanced at them. His gaze traveled the length of Stephanie in clear admiration. Then he eyed John. "I didn't know you meant it when you made the offer." He gulped.

"The things you told me earlier to help jog my memory about how we met, well, I remember—everything." Both men seemed to communicate without words what exactly John remembered. "Here is your chance for a new beginning. I was sent to you. Are you claiming this chance or throwing it away?"

"You need happy people, not me. I can't help you."

"I saw you before you saw me there. I heard your words. You need a friend as much as I need someone who isn't family to talk to sometimes. Please, come. We'll give each other mutual support."

Lowering his face, the man stayed silent. Something darkened his already dark, downcast eyes even as his lips pinched white at the corners.

"You said you had no friend. No one who cared. You saved my life. Let me be that friend. Allow me to care, to be your brother. To be your family, just like my siblings are family to me. Come with me. You already quit like you'd said you would, right?"

Angel could only wonder what John knew to make him want this man around. Eyeing him, she itched to run a thorough background check before John invited him over—as she did with everyone regardless of race or origin.

"Yes, I did. I couldn't explain to them why." His shoulders slacked.

"I know," John said. "So, will you come? If not right away, I can give you our address so you can get yourself sorted out here and then come to Maryland."

He glanced at each of them. "I truly appreciate the offer, but allow me to wrap things up here first. Settle some stuff, and I should be there in about a week."

Smiling, John nodded. "Good deal. See you."

Angel supplied her home address and wrote the man's name down. She wasn't sure whether John told him she was a cop or how he might feel about living with one, depending on his issues. She would query John once she got a chance.

They parted ways with the doctor, and she led them to the rental car to take them to the airport. Then she called her other siblings and asked them to head to Maryland instead. Then, they headed home to a new, unpredictable, but very grateful life.

22

"For I know the thoughts that I think toward you, says the Lord, thoughts of peace and not of evil, to give you a future and a hope." Jeremiah 29:11

ARRIVING IN MARYLAND, THE GROUP PROCEEDED TO THE SSPD. There, so many officers and their church friends had gathered, and Angel understood why. John's return was rare. Seeing someone, a grown man, go missing and return after about twenty years was rare.

How did he survive?

What did he go through that had not been in the official reports?

From her experience as a cop, she knew sometimes people in John's condition remembered more details after their official reports. She urged John to call the SSPD and report anything else he remembered. They were still speaking with well-wishers when the captain drew her and John aside.

"We've been able to capture the compound where you were held. A sick young woman named Bree was airlifted to the hospital. Other than her, the place was deserted. However, investigators are combing the area for witnesses or suspects."

"They were already leaving when I escaped. Something spooked them," John said. "They heard law enforcement was coming. I wonder how that happened."

"It's got to be the man we intercepted. He must have sent a message before he died."

The captain nodded. "And in doing so, he instead set off the perfect situation for John to escape."

"Nothing else would've spurred such an action except a tip-off of sudden capture. I wonder how they stayed undetected for so long."

"Tree cover. The heavily wooded area masked the five buildings. Secondly, they made it look like a girl's school with uniforms scattered around the residences and teachers' curriculum on the wall. It wouldn't look suspicious like that."

"Wow. I'm glad we got them."

"Me too." The captain turned to John. "Have you any idea about the identities of the girls you mentioned?"

John's eyes sheened, but he held her captain's gaze. "I kept a record of every girl who passed through my unit. I asked their names, age, and state of origin. Then I noted it in a sheet of paper I stored in a tripled Ziploc bag with a pencil and hid in my back pocket. As they started searching us more, I rolled it then sewed it into the right leg of my jeans, the pair I wore when I fled. It should still be in there."

The captain spread his arm and hugged John tightly then let him go. "What you did was very brave. It could've gotten you killed. I will have the Arizona police extract your sheet. Then we will inform their families. They will be very grateful."

"About how many girls are we talking about?"

"Roughly five hundred over the past twenty years."

Angel clutched her belly. "Do you know where they were taken to?"

John shook his head. "I have no way of knowing. Sorry, sis."

She touched his arm. "I understand. Thank you for what you have done."

"Our community appreciates you, John," the captain added. "I have to go and follow up now. I'll be in touch."

Angel walked John back to their well-wishers, still in awe of how God had used John. But she also wished to know how his faith survived when hers for his return wobbled so often. She'd hoped to be stronger, but the trial was too much for her to take. She'd wished for more faith but ultimately trusted in God for whatever outcome. And she was grateful that, even at those times when her own strength had failed her, she got to such a place where trusting in God alone was the only option available to her.

If not, she might not have been as grateful now.

When they were finished there, they returned to her house, where her other siblings—Hughes and Grace—had arrived and were eager to see John. Their reunion was as sweet and tear-filled as hers and Stephanie's had been. They all huddled in a prayer of thanksgiving again while Tim ordered food. After they'd eaten, John was taken to the hospital to have his blood drawn for additional tests as recommended by the doctors in

Arizona. Then, as they returned to her house, Stephanie said she would spend the night there. She would return to her apartment the following day while John remained with Angel.

That night, Angel felt like hiring professional security staff to guard the house. She had this urge to protect what she once lost and would never lose again. So much so that sleeping felt like a luxury she could ill-afford.

Being responsible for her siblings meant everywhere she was, they were at the top of her mind. There was no dad or mom for them, or her, anymore. There was just her. So she stepped up every single day to think ahead.

The ordered food arrived, and John asked for a warm bath. He still had significant scratches on his arms and back, and based on her recent experience chasing down Stephanie's ex through the woods, she knew how badly those hurt. So she urged him to stay off his feet. But deep, healed scars also criss-crossed on his back, knees, and on the side of his neck. And none of them asked how or why.

There'd be time to ask later. John asked to go to sleep soon after eating, and Tim showed him to his room. She was thankful they could accommodate him in one of the two basement rooms. There was a spare bedroom upstairs, but Stephanie would sleep there before returning to her apartment. Her other siblings had chatted with John and were going back to their states of residence the following day, with promises to live-video chat daily through her and Tim's phones until John got his.

Angel sent up a prayer for her brother. As a cop, she understood the impact of trauma. It could wreck emotions to a state that was hard to recover. She was glad John was up and about. But what about his emotional state?

This was his first day as a free man. It will be his first night of freedom in a very long time. Would it go smoothly, or would it be an indication of how bumpy their family's lives were about to become?

23

"After this I awoke and looked around, and my sleep was sweet to me." Jeremiah 31:26

Around one a.m., Angel heard a scream.

"I'm checking on John." Jumping to her feet and retrieving the gun she now kept close since Stephanie's kidnapping, she raced out of her bedroom. Flashing her cellphone's light as she tiptoed, she reached the door, pushed it open, and descended into the basement.

At the first of two bedrooms, she shoved it open, flipped on the light, and froze. "John?"

John was curled in a ball in the middle of the bed, looking vulnerable, his head bent. "I am a hunter. I am a hunter. I am a hunter," he whispered. He looked up at her, glassy eyes confirming her fears. John was an emotional wreck in need of help. She'd seen that look before and vowed to get him all the help she could afford.

"I woke you, didn't I?" He swiped a tear as Tim entered and stopped near the door, and Angel lowered her gun then set it aside on a dresser.

She settled a hand on John's shoulder. "Yes, you did. But are you okay?" Her heart twisted at the look in his eyes. Like, did you expect me to be okay after what I've been through? He didn't say the words. He didn't need to.

Tim drew close. He perched on the bed near her. "What can we do? We're your family, and we're here for you."

Stephanie, still asleep upstairs, likely had her earbuds on, sleeping while listening to music. Which meant if something happened, she wouldn't hear it.

"Wait, what did you mean, when you said, 'I am a hunter'?" Angel had to assess how bad things were.

He glanced at both of them. Then he fell silent.

"John? Talk to me? I'm your sister. Tim is your close friend, and we love you. You can open up to us, and everything you say will be held in complete confidence. I promise."

As he lifted his gaze, his Adam's apple bobbed.

"The day before I was kidnapped..." He leaned against the headrest and exhaled long. "Please do not block the light. I need to see it. The glow helps calm me."

"All right." Tim shifted to allow him full view of the standing lamp across the room.

"Please continue, John. Tell us more," Angel urged.

"Sorry, I had a nightmare. I thought I was back at the compound. It felt so real." His voice weakened.

Then he inhaled a shaky breath and fell silent again.

"John?" Angel softly prompted.

Those tear-filled eyes fixed on her, and he gulped.

"About the hunter. I need to know what that is." Concerned about her brother, she wanted to be sure he wasn't a danger to himself or others. When he said things like "the hunter," she needed to verify he wasn't really "hunting" anything or anyone.

John crossed his arms. "Before I was kidnapped, that was the last sermon I heard the pastor preach. It spoke to me in such a personal way—like it was God saying it to me directly. I had never heard that before."

"A sermon?" Angel couldn't remember any such sermon. But, even if she'd heard it, it'd been about twenty years now. She couldn't recall anything from back then.

"Yes, a Bible Study message. It was titled, 'Being A Hunter.'"

Angel exhaled. So did Tim, she noticed. Well, at first, she'd been afraid John had been brainwashed into becoming a killer by hunting people. Angel was already worrying about how he could be remanded in a psych ward if care wasn't taken. But it seemed he wasn't crazy.

She also didn't expect it to have any reference to the church.

Now, he was talking about a message from church?

John shifted to Tim. "You went with me. Don't you remember?"

Quiet, Tim furrowed his brow. Then he shook his head. "Sorry, man, I don't recall. What was the message about?"

"It said we were made by God to be hunters."

"Who is a hunter?" Angel asked.

"A hunter is someone who eagerly observes, watches, anticipates, and does not delay to take advantage of an opportunity God provides. Once God opens a door to reveal His perfect will, that person seizes it. They don't wait. That is a hunter for God's will. During the message, he said God doesn't usually orchestrate bad things to happen to us, but if and when they do, God can turn it around for our good if we seek out His will in the storm. Things may not be rosy, but you will find the seed of God's will buried in the dirt of trial."

"How did this apply to you?" Tim sank deeper into the mattress, relaxing, even as Angel's heartbeat settled and her own breathing evened out.

John exhaled. "My kidnapping and eventual use for a debt's ransom was a bad thing. Being held against my will day after day with no way of escape was horrifying. But I'm grateful for all the girls I shared Jesus with in there who would never have put their trust in Him. All because of that sermon. I chose to stop seeing myself as a victim but as a seed. I appreciate the opportunity to save Ahmed, my friend, from committing suicide. He'd be a dead man, a statistic of another dead veteran through suicide, had I not been there. God loves me and would not have allowed these things to happen if He wouldn't bring something good out of them." He wiped his cheek, as did Angel. John's words were cutting deep into her heart. "I longed to see you, but I was a man on God's mission wherever I found myself, whether captive or free. I dug deep into those girls' shattered hearts as they passed through—afraid and uncertain about their future—and I planted the seeds of hope in Christ in their hearts. I might be broken as a result of my pain, but I was broken by life and empowered by God for His divine purpose."

"How did you survive, John? Very many people would've died long before now." Angel ached to brush that shock of hair off his forehead as if he were still a boy in her care. "We prayed and prayed, searched everywhere, and even I started losing hope of ever finding you alive." She crossed her arms to keep from reaching out, perhaps embarrassing him. "What did others not do, that you did? I know God ultimately has the power to save one's life, but how did you cope?"

When John smiled, his eyes lit up. "But I already answered you."

"What is the answer?"

"I missed it too," Tim confessed.

"The hunter. I am a hunter. I said that to myself as often as I breathed in air. I can't die before my divine purpose for being born is fulfilled. That is how I survived. That is where my hope was anchored. And everything that happens in between, leads me toward that purpose whether intentional or not. Like you taught me, Jesus has the final Word."

"That He does, and I might do well to remember it more often." A frown pinched her forehead. "You haven't explained how that made you a hunter."

"See, as the pastor preached it, after salvation God sent us out as hunters. He said hunters in Christ are those who are out for divine purpose. He said Jesus came primarily to seek and save the lost. Seeking is hunting. He sought out the broken, the sick, the mentally ill, the broke, the rich-without-God, the dead-before-their-time, the unbelieving. He hunted them, fished them out, and brought them into the sheepfold of faith."

"Ooookay," Angel drawled out.

"When I sat there in that place, angry, defeated, and feeling powerless, I thought about whether I had read anywhere in Scripture where people who trusted God were held in bondage or found themselves in a place they didn't want to be. And I remembered yes, I had."

"Who?" Tim asked. "I recall a couple."

"Yes, but only one occasion did I remember those people being reluctant to leave after the prison doors were open."

John's eyes lit up. "It's amazing what the Holy Spirit would teach you in the most unlikely places. He taught me in the place where I needed the lesson the most—in a hard place."

"What's the lesson?"

"Remember the Scripture I'd mentioned?"

"Yes?" Angel curled her arms. This had better be going somewhere, or she would be calling the hospital to help her brother.

"Paul and Silas were in jail, locked up, and stuck between guards. There was no way out for them, just like there was no way out for me. They praised God, and He shook the foundations of the prison, then opened the gates all the way out to the main entrance. But guess what? They didn't leave. They were hunters, Angel. They knew God didn't allow them to go through all the pain, the public beating, and humiliation just so He could shake the jail, open the door, and let them go. God sent them on a hunting assignment. They were not leaving jail until their assignment was done. Even in chains, I serve the Lord."

Angel gawked at Tim. "Um, that's a revelation. I never saw it that way before."

"See, the jailor arrived and thought they had fled, and he was about to commit suicide. Just like the good doctor was about to commit suicide when we met."

She unfurled her arms slowly. It was making sense, the kind of sense that came with premonition. Angel didn't want that kind of sense. Her brother had just reached home, and any talk of God's plan and God's will in a difficult way was something she may find tough to swallow. "I'm listening."

John smiled. "God doesn't hunt in pretty places, sis. What we fear is what He steps right into the middle of. The cross wasn't pretty, but Jesus hung on it because He is the ultimate hunter. A Hunter for souls. To save us, redeem us, and reconcile us to Himself," he explained. "Pastor said we ought to be hunters too. Hunting for God's will in every dark situation, hunting for His purpose for every suffering. Seeing how He is making things work for our good. Trusting that He will see us through even when we don't understand and would rather not be in it. Spotting the little places He uses us to make a difference when all we want is to escape. Spotting those in captivity who would never see His love had God not allowed us to be cast into captivity with them, like Apostle Paul. Then he said something that also stuck with me all these years."

"What?"

"He said you suffer with those you love. You sit there and suffer with them. You don't hurry. You don't complain. You stay there, suck it up, and bear their pain. It will be uncomfortable, but that's what hunters do. You don't hurry, you stay, you dwell. If God can endure sticking with us through decades of sin until we come to repentance, we can endure a decade of hardship in our lives to see God's purpose work itself out through us. The result will be beautiful. So, I stayed. And prayed and stuck it out. Had I seen a way to escape, I would've taken it, but I didn't. So I stayed, did what I could to remain alive, waiting, seeking God's purpose in that dark place. Hunting for God's perfect will." John sighed. "And it came the day I escaped. It came in the form of a man, out in the woods, in the middle of the night, ready to kill himself."

John raked his fingers through his now sweaty hair. "Nobody else was there. If I was not there, he'd be dead. I'm a Hunter for God's purpose, and when I spot an opportunity even when I'm in pain, I seize it. So, I did. Ahmed got me to the hospital. He was my purpose in that moment, and now, I'll show him the way to The Way. The ultimate Hunter, and I'll trust Jesus to work in his heart and to finish the job He alone started."

Angel stared at him. She thought she was a good Christian —until now. Apparently, John had outgrown her in captivity, with no church, pastor, or congregation. God became His teacher, and she was more than willing to stoop low and learn. "Wow. I'm still listening."

"I'm taking mental notes, John." Tim crossed his arms and leaned back. "These are lessons learned by experience. They're no longer sermons. They've become woven into the fabric of your heart and are now part of who you are. For the record, I'm impressed with the work Jesus did in you, in isolation."

"It's funny because you might not like what I'm about to say next."

They didn't respond.

"Paul and Silas waited for the jailor and intercepted his attempted suicide. That—*that*—was their mission that night. They had gone through all that to allow God to demonstrate to the jailor that God does not value physical freedom more than He values spiritual freedom. The jailor was God's mission. They ultimately—because of that singular interception against suicide—led an entire family to salvation in Jesus Christ."

John grew quiet. "You have no idea how many times I reminded myself about that passage in Scripture. How many things it helped me endure and overcome. I knew there was a reason God allowed me to be taken captive. There was a reason I found myself caught in deep and dark grips of wicked men. I saw many die at their hands for a simple error. And whatever was God's purpose, however God could use my captivity for my good, I wished to be ready."

"I must confess to you, I don't think that would've been my reaction." Angel rubbed shivers from her arms. "No. I'm a fighter. Now, I need to learn how to be a fighter in the right place and a hunter in the right circumstance."

John shifted and refocused on them, appearing calmer than when they'd walked in. "I am a hunter for God's perfect plan, I reminded myself often. Up until I escaped, I wondered whether that was possible. Until I lay, exhausted at the base of a tree in the bushes and heard a man reciting his last words to himself, prepared to take his own life."

"I hate suicide." John swallowed and gripped her arm. "Suicide is a thief. When people reach crossroads, instead of them turning to Jesus, the enemy prepares suicide and presents it as a viable alternative. But something that takes away your ability to choose a 'next' step is not viable and is not a choice."

He let her arm go. "Even though I was exhausted and wondering how long my eyes would stay open in the woods, when I saw Ahmed with the gun, I had a job to do. Everything in the last decade and half led me to those woods, to that night and to help save that man's life. I remembered Paul, and I remembered Silas and the jailor they saved from suicide, and I remembered that I am a hunter for God's perfect will even if I was breathing my last."

His eyes met hers and held her gaze. "So I seized the chance. That was why I invited him here to stay with us in a healthy environment. And I'm sorry for not hinting about this to you both earlier. But I intend to shine the light of Jesus into this one life and pray for him until he sees the Light so darkness does not come for him again. I hope you will support me. I know I may have these difficult nightmares. But I put Jesus in front of my problem, and I trust that He Who brought me this far will keep me, heal me. And even if He doesn't, I'm still grateful I get to serve Him with whatever time I have left here on earth. I might have a rough eight hours of sleep every night, but I won't let that steal the sixteen other beautiful hours of divine purpose I get to enjoy."

Angel wasn't sure if the tears were pouring down her face more or Tim's face more. Her heart cracked wide open, and the joy of the Lord flowed. "Oh, John." She hugged him. "How beautiful your faith has become! I am touched."

John smiled. "The journey forward might not be smooth, but I hope you and Tim will support me. I'm willing to take it one day at a time."

"Of course, we will." She swiped tears from her cheeks. "And Stephanie too." She glanced at her husband. "Tim, I'd say we spend the night here with John, sleeping on an air bed mattress so, if he has nightmares, we're here to calm him. And then tomorrow, we see a psychologist."

Tim pushed himself off the edge of the bed. "I'll pump air into the one upstairs." He spun to John. "I know shrinks get a bad rap sometimes, but seeking professional help for someone who survived what you did should not embarrass you. It's a sign of courage and not weakness."

John gave a small nod. "I'd hoped I wouldn't need such help, but I'm ready to accept anyone who can help me work through my issues." He shrugged. "I'll likely drag Dr. Ahmed along. He needs a shrink too."

They laughed. "Come to think of it, we all do." Angel went back upstairs and locked up her gun. She took a worship CD downstairs while Tim set up the airbed. She prayed for the peace of God to settle on her brother through the night and calm his disturbances. She slotted the music into the player, turned it low, returned upstairs, and brought them some blankets. Then she and Tim lay on the airbed across from John's bed, and all three soon slept off.

24

"Behold, He Who keeps Israel shall neither slumber nor sleep." Psalm 121:4

Three days later, early in the morning, John rose and went for a walk around the house. He'd been grateful to have company while he slept for two nights in a row as Angel and her husband slept in the basement with him. And he appreciated their support. But, after a session with the psychologist yesterday, he asked Angel and Tim to return to their room upstairs so he could try sleeping alone.

For one, his mind was getting accustomed to being in a free place and the nightmares had subsided considerably. Secondly, he didn't want his recovery to depend on having company as he would have a harder time adjusting later.

So, Angel and Tim agreed. And last night, he slept alone. He was pleasantly surprised he didn't have a single nightmare and had slept throughout. His therapist had encouraged him to go to the gym and exercise so he was tired. That might've helped coax him to a good night's sleep.

Also, he had never been one to stroll before he was kidnapped. But, when he woke up, since his feet had healed considerably, he was itching to go outside and stretch his legs.

He also wished to pray alone. Working twelve hours a day with barely thirty minutes to eat, drink water, and pee, for many years, meant he was not the kind to be idle. He'd thought he was hardworking—until he encountered brutality.

After going past the shopping center and walking around the block, he returned and dialed Angel from the house phone. "Hey, sis." He sank onto the couch, the throw blanket's rough weave scratching his bare arms as he faced the cross on the wall. "I need a phone. A personal phone. But it has to be a random phone I could lose without being traced."

She was silent for a moment. "John, you need a burner phone? For what?"

"I could tell you, but it might put you in danger."

She was silent again. "I'm guessing you didn't tell us everything or you remembered more details you'd like to share with the police. Right?"

"Yes. And I'm a little concerned about sharing them on an open line. There were things I couldn't afford to allow into the official report in case the wrong eyes saw it. Things I need to contact the right federal agencies about."

"Tell me."

"I can't. It could potentially put you in danger, and you are the nucleus of our family. I cannot let anything happen to you, sis. Sorry."

A sigh followed. "Are you sure?"

"Yes. I'm sure. It's too big for you to handle, and such information about traffickers could endanger your life. Like I said, I'd prefer people who are trained to handle such be the ones I involve." He shoved the blanket to the other side of the couch and rested his hand against the smooth cushion. "I'm going to need you most in my personal life. I still need my pastor-sister."

Her soft laughter floated over the house phone. He wished he could gush about how much the memory of her motherly love had inspired him to assist others during his captivity. But he could reserve that for a face-to-face conversation. Right now, he needed to make contact with the right government agency, then head to the one place he'd missed the most.

"All right then. I'll bring a phone home tonight. Make sure you call the SSPD captain to brief him so he can direct you to the relevant agencies and people within them. He'll know people and can help get your information to the relevant parties."

"I'll do that."

"Captain Bailey also mentioned something about you becoming a consultant for the SSPD. With your experience, you can help law enforcement across the nation look at missing persons' cases and identify suspects from those who worked in that compound. That will help bring them to justice. This will be a paid position and won't be announced to the public. Your work and presence there will be classified to protect your privacy. You will also be assigned security around the house during the night in case anyone shows up to seek you out."

John's heart rate picked up, joy warming his chest. "I'm interested in that consultancy, as long as it doesn't jeopardize any of our family's safety."

"Like I said, he assured me of your safety and you will work remotely from my place so only me, you, and those involved will know what you are working on."

He liked the sound of that. "Okay. I'm in. Provided I can also find a job out there to do, so no one wonders what I do for money. I just came home with nothing to my name, so I need a job that has nothing to do with my captivity. I don't need you to search for me. I want God to do it in His own way."

She chuckled. "And who says you're not more of a faith giant than I am? I love you, John. I'll see you later."

"I love you too, sis. And I'm so glad to be home. I'll see you too. Stephanie hounded me to come and see her new place, so I'm off. She's picking me up soon."

"You two enjoy."

"Thanks." He hung up and got ready to leave.

∽

THE FOLLOWING AFTERNOON, AFTER A SECOND MIRACULOUS, restful night, John called Tim to confirm that their church was still at the same location. Then he let him know he was going there.

"I'll be coming for private prayers later too. Maybe we can ride home together then."

"That would be great.'"

"Plus, it's a chance for us to catch up on your spiritual life. I know your faith has held fast through the fire, but it also needs support to build you up now. Sometimes in life, you can swim faster in deep waters than you can walk on land. But, ultimately, you'll need to land and walk, however slow. So, it is with faith in God. You can't sustain in normal environments something refined by the fire of affliction, without adequate, sustained fuel. Some people who stood fast in the storm, fall more easily when their feet are on land. I don't want that to be you."

Just what he wanted to hear. "I was beginning to wonder whether taking me on as a spiritual mentor would be too much to ask. Frankly, I still have questions. You led me to Christ, and I was still a baby Christian when I went into captivity. I survived faith-wise, thank God, but I have not matured. I need your and Angel's wisdom to grow. I appreciate you bringing this matter up, and I'm looking forward to learning from you. So, I'll see you later in church, then?"

"Yes," Tim said.

"Great. Thanks, Tim." John hung up just as another call came in. He wasn't sure if he should answer, but the number seemed familiar, so he picked up the call. "Hello?"

"Can I speak to John, please?"

A smile warmed his face as he recognized the voice. "My favorite doctor, it's me. How are you doing, Ahmed?"

Ahmed laughed. "Well, since you gave me your sister's home number, I wasn't sure I'd get you right away. I'm, um, fine. Mind if I take you up on your offer? Moving to Maryland sounds less scary than committing suicide was."

"I'd love it if you do move. After all, you can't 'doctor' me from afar, and I can't befriend you from miles away. Of course, it's possible, but for two guys who almost died, a face-to-face friendship is better. I don't know if you have a very supportive family, but mine is ready to love you till you drop, figuratively speaking."

Ahmed's warm laughter sent relief through John's mind, so he added, "I'm just as broken as you are, just in a different way. You never know what God can do for us or through us, the broken people," He wasn't sure why he was insisting Ahmed come, but he was sure God placed him across the man's path for a reason. And he wished for their contact to remain regular even if they were not always in the same place. He took him as a brother and wanted to see him succeed. So, he prayed in his heart as he listened. *Lord Jesus, for whatever reason you led me into Ahmed's path, let Your will be done and his soul saved and your divine purpose accomplished, in Jesus' mighty name, amen.*

"I've said goodbye to my folks. Everything else can be handled by email. I'm eager for a fresh start in a new place with new friends. I hope your family won't feel burdened. I will make sure to get a job, maybe at a hospital if my license isn't taken away. The investigation into the medical error is complete, but I'm waiting for their verdict, which might come sooner than expected."

"A good plan. But do you know one thing I've learned in my walk with God, Ahmed?"

"No, what?"

"His plans are greater than our plans and, usually, more efficient. You may plan to get a job here, but He might want you to do something else."

"If you say so. How would I know His plan, then?"

"When you place your trust in Jesus, He makes sure you never stumble blindly through life. He gives you direction. He shows you the way He planned for your life to go. All you have to do is to walk in it one step at a time."

"I heard you, just like you'd shared your faith with me before, but please understand that my family is Muslim. Any conversion to another faith could cost me my life. I can't take the risk, even though what you say sounds true."

"Jesus can protect you too. And if it is not your time to leave this world, no man can take you out of it. I promise you this, if you will give Jesus a chance, He will be a much better friend to you than I could ever hope to be."

"How? When I can't talk to Him?"

"He is here right now. Any time you choose, you can share with Him your frustrations and feelings. He is the only reason I survived captivity for twenty years. I had no other hope, no other reason to continue breathing. I could have given up or taken the supposedly easy way out or cast myself in the path of danger, but I didn't. Because I knew Jesus, and I trusted that, if it was His will for me to live, I would. And even if He had allowed me to die in that circumstance, I would still have thanked Jesus for a life well lived and a chance to have lived here for His pleasure. There is always a purpose for you that God will accomplish through everything you ever face, whether you know it at that time or not. So, please, do trust Him. And He will lead you. In fact, can I pray for you now?"

"I guess it doesn't hurt."

"Father God, I thank You for Ahmed. Thank You for leading me into the path of this wonderful friend of Yours. I am honored. Father God, You know the needs of His heart. You know where the figurative shoe pinches him. I pray You meet him at the point of his need, in Jesus' mighty name. I pray he lets You shine the light of Christ into his heart, life, soul, and spirit. And I also pray he accepts Your offer of friendship. I pray everything that currently frustrates him in his life You will turn around into a divine testimony, in Jesus' mighty name. And finally, Father, whatever reason You have Ahmed moving to Maryland for, may Your purpose be accomplished to perfection in his life. Let him come to Maryland and find hope, love, joy, and peace. Give him a reason to live that no one can take from him. In Jesus' mighty name I pray, amen. Thank You, O God, for answered prayers. I give you praise."

"Amin. That's how we say amen in Islam," Ahmed said. "Thank you for praying for me, my friend. I will see you in Maryland in two days. I have your address so it will be my first stop. Then I will go to a hotel."

"Not a chance. You're not staying at a hotel in a city where I live. You're staying with me here. My sister and her husband are fine with it."

"If you say so, then. Goodbye and thank you. For everything."

"You're welcome, my dear friend. God bless you, and see you soon."

After he hung up, John almost danced. He bowed his head. "Lord Jesus, thank You for Ahmed. Lord, I have no idea why You are leading him to Maryland. I have no plan and no hidden agenda. I simply want to see this man enjoy Your love and fulfill Your purpose for his life, which I don't know. But, as he comes, fill him with joy. Give him Your peace that no man or circumstance can steal from him. Whatever drove him to attempt suicide, the reasons he cannot share, Lord, please handle those permanently and show Him Your lordship in every situation. Guide me to represent You, and when I fall short, please cover me with Your strength and let him see only genuineness and not pretention from me, in Jesus' mighty name, amen."

He rose, dressed, and called a taxi. His sister said he could do that using apps, but he wasn't sure he wouldn't mess up something when there was no one around to help him get it right.

It took another ten minutes to get a call back, letting him know his taxi was on its way. Another twelve minutes and it arrived. When he got in, the man tried to make conversation, but John couldn't speak. The tag on the man's car looked similar to the ones used to transfer the girls and a few boys from one location to another. They used toy names for the car tags. Fun-looking tags avoided suspicion when young girls were spotted inside.

On their way, a thought occurred to him. "Can you please drop me off at any nearby barber's shop? I need a haircut."

"Yes, sir," the muscular driver replied. "Do you prefer a particular one?"

"Anywhere close will do. If you can return in about one hour to pick me up to go to my intended destination, that is appreciated."

"Of course." He searched on his navigator. "I see there's a place about two miles from here."

"Great." John relaxed and exhaled. He'd already shaved all the hair off his face, and feeling his skin was second to none. His shower today had taken much longer thanks to him getting all the hair of captivity off himself.

Now, in order to avoid easy recognition, he intended to shave his head bald. He wasn't sure how his family would react, but he didn't see them having a problem. After all, his hair would grow back.

The taxi dropped him off at a snazzy upper-class salon.

As soon as he entered, John settled in and waited for his turn.

A specialist approached. Then he realized he had only the fifty-dollar bill Angel had given him yesterday in case he needed to go somewhere. "Please, give me one second." He'd also left his phone at home since he wasn't used to carrying one around.

Calling Tim and asking for money felt tough, but he was stuck. So he asked to borrow a phone to make a quick call. "Hey, man, sorry to bother you. I need some money, and I only realized that after I reached the barber's shop en route to the church."

Tim laughed. "Ah well, who would blame a man who quite literally just returned to civilization, huh? Hand the phone to an attendant, and I'll supply my information so they can charge my card. Don't worry about it."

"Thanks, man. I appreciate your help. I owe you one." John did not plan on leaning on them for support much longer. They were already doing a lot to support him. So, he prayed that God led him to where he could apply for a job before he started consulting with the SSPD—for which preparations were already underway—so he could be economically empowered.

About ten minutes later, when it was all sorted out, he sat down and waited behind two other customers before him who were already waiting to be served.

He saw how classy the barber's shop was, though it looked ordinary from the outside. John wondered how much they'd charged for his haircut. An attendant approached. "Sir, the man you called requested for a hundred-dollar cash back to be given to you, so here it is in an envelope."

Stunned, John accepted it. "Thank you." Tonight, he'd tell Tim he didn't need to keep giving him money, and he planned on getting a job soon.

An hour was all it took to reach his turn. He sank into the plush, black leather swivel chair and faced the mirror. The attendant smiled. "Sir, you get up to our deluxe-cut option, so, which style are you interested in wearing? I can bring you our catalog to choose from."

John shook his head. "That won't be necessary. Just shave everything off. I want to be clean-shaven."

"Yes, sir." The attendant got ready.

John exhaled long. *Lord, I need a job.* He wasn't ready to keep depending upon others' benevolence to get by. The words had barely left his mouth when his gaze landed on a note tucked beside the mirror—Help Wanted. That was fast. "Well, I could apply…" He'd never cut anyone's hair before, let alone worked at a barbershop.

In short, he was unqualified.

John waited until the specialist finished cutting his hair. "May I speak with the manager, please?"

Alarmed the specialist drew close. "Sir, did I cut your hair wrongly? Is there a mistake? I promise, I can try to fix it." He set down his tools. "I'll get you a discount for your next visit if I can't fix it."

"You did nothing wrong." John patted his arm. "I'm asking for the manager because I saw the Help Wanted sign, and I'd like to apply for a job."

The younger man exhaled and clutched his chest. "Oh, you scared me for a minute there. Sure, I'll let the manager know you want to see him." He strode toward a door marked Office. John seized the opportunity to pray since he'd acted on a whim and couldn't be sure it was God leading him.

He was also sure of something else—he needed money and was able and willing to work to get it. So, if it wasn't a barber's shop, it would be elsewhere. Looking around at the inoffensive and clean art on the wall, he was convinced the owner was a decent person, and that gave him some hope.

Soon, a middle-aged African-American man emerged—medium height, with a bald center on his head and some beard,

When he reached John, he smiled. "Hello, you'd like to speak to me?"

John returned the smile. "Yes, please." He gestured toward the sign. "I wished to indicate my interest for a job."

The man nodded. "All right. Have you worked at a barber's shop before?"

John gulped. "Sir, I really have not. I've gotten haircuts but have never been the one to give them. But if you give me a chance, I'm willing to learn."

"Of course, I'm willing to give you a chance, but we need to chat for longer than one minute. Come with me, please."

He led John into a clean, well-organized office. A note hung on the wall—I'm Closed On Sundays. Was he a Christian? A family portrait of him, a lovely lady, and three teen boys and a little girl settled on his oak desk behind a tray marked Mail.

He was liking this man.

He pointed to a chair opposite the swivel chair, much like the ones out in the shop. "Please, sit."

John obliged him. "Thank you."

The man observed him. "Before we go any further, I'd like to warn you that I do not work with lazy people. My customers come first. Anyone who works here must be a person of integrity. Do you have integrity?"

John smiled. "Yes, I do. By God's grace."

The man observed him. "Are you a Christian and God-fearing?"

"Yes, I am. If I may ask, are you a Christian as well?"

The man nodded. "Yes. That's part of the reason I don't open the shop on Sundays. It's a day I reserved for worshiping God and relaxing with my family. That is my personal preference. I don't want my boys to grow up without my presence in their lives. Do you have children?"

"No."

"A wife?"

"No."

"Ever married?" The man curled his arms, growing distant as his smile faded.

"Not yet."

"Where was your last job?"

"I worked at a construction site about twenty years ago. That was my last job. Technically-speaking."

Silence settled between them.

"I can explain."

The man tipped his chin. "It had better be a good one and verifiable."

"I can assure you that it is."

"Go ahead."

"My name is John Martinez Emmanuel, although my official name does not include Emmanuel. I added that a few years ago. About twenty years ago, I was a construction worker at a site when I saw an assassin commit a murder. Since my elder sister was a cop, I went to the SSPD to report the crime." John paused, fighting the coming emotions. "Little did I know that the assassin watched me leave, trailed me, and saw when I parked. So, he attacked me and drugged me."

"My goodness." Wide-eyed, the man slowly unfurled his hands.

"Everything I'm saying is fully verifiable. I woke up at the base of a tree in likely another state. I had no idea where I was. But the assassin was right there. He promised to kill me. But, almost as soon as he got in my face, he suffered a seizure. His gun was in his other hand and too far from where I was strapped. But I found an injection on him when he fell so I knew it had to be his medicine. I injected him with it in his leg closest to me. About a half-hour later, he regained himself."

John closed his eyes to keep the tears from falling. "He was an evil man. He'd meant to kill me like he promised. But, after I saved his life, he couldn't do it. So he took me to a border town and sold me to a ruthless gang of drug dealers and human traffickers. There, my twenty years of captivity began. Maybe in the news, you heard that I returned home a few days ago after escaping, and I'm just starting life over. I'm simply asking for a chance to earn money instead of depending on my family as a grown man. Their hands are full already, and I'd hate to become an additional burden."

"Goodness. Your kidnapping was announced at my church." The man pulled out a drawer. "We had prayed for your return, John. We'd prayed and prayed, and it had seemed impossible." He pulled out some forms, glanced at them, and handed them to John. "I'd like to say welcome home, but a better way to welcome you is to give you a job. So, you are hired. We'll start you out cleaning up after our hairdressers and managing the front counter—reservations, financial transactions, customer support, and the like. If you wish to become a full hairdresser, we can talk about attending an academy. Please take those forms home, complete them, and I'll see that you are added to our staff roster by coming Monday. Take the rest of this week to rest and relax with your family. You need it. They need to spend time with you. You can start working next week."

It was John's turn to be wide-eyed. He'd merely expected the man to show empathy, but he got a job too? "Thank you so much. I'm grateful."

"Please let me know if there is anything you need before then. And here is my business card." John accepted them. "I have one question for you."

"Sure." John settled back into the seat.

"Why did you change your name? Why assume a new surname?"

"Because I was in an impossible situation that seemed like I would never get out. Like Naomi in Scripture, all around me was bitterness and sadness. So, instead of turning my back to God, I changed my name. Because when hard times arise, I would rather change my name than change my God."

"Wow. I would rather change my name than change my God. Thank you. You have been a blessing. My middle son is having learning issues, and it's been frustrating to us. Your testimony has renewed my hope."

"We bless God as He did all of this, not me. I did not know this shop, and stopping here on my way to church was completely random. But I know God led me here, so it's amazing to see how He works in mysterious ways."

The door opened a crack and the man who'd cut John's hair poked his head in. "Sorry, there's a taxi here. The driver said you asked him to come get you?"

John had completely forgotten. "Yes, I did. I'm sorry. Please let him know I will be out shortly. Thank you." He stood and extended his hand.

The owner shook it firmly, and his smile returned. "I'm Mr. Gregory Russo. I was a former Olympian but retired due to a back injury. I own this shop, and I'm glad you'll be working here. See you next week. And congratulations."

"I look forward to working with you, sir."

As John left the shop and headed to the taxi, he could

hardly believe how many blessings were tucked away in one little detour. God worked miracles in detours. In one afternoon, less than a week after returning home, he had a job, in an area where he had no expertise.

He smiled as the taxi sped along the highway, past skyscrapers and toward the church in the suburbs. *Thank you, Lord Jesus. My miracle-working God.*

25

"But now, thus says the Lord, Who created you, O Jacob...'Fear not, for I have redeemed you; I have called you by your name; You are Mine.'" Isaiah 43:1

WHEN JOHN WOKE UP TWO DAYS LATER, THE DAY AHMED WAS expected to arrive, he was sure of one thing—God was leading him. When he reached the hospital where he was scheduled to have a routine physical examination, he supplied all of his information. Angel wasn't eager to fill out the form with his new, but not legally changed, name. But she obliged him, stating that she understood why after he'd explained his reasons.

She and Tim had insisted on following him there to spend more time with him. He had told them he got a job, and it had taken a half hour of convincing them after dinner that it had been a voluntary, unexpected miracle. She was ready to call the man and cancel, but John had insisted he get back into the workforce. "My 401k won't build itself. I have to work, sis. I can't depend on you for life. I already lost two decades. Let me work the best I can since I am able to."

They had relented, insisting he spend time with them for the rest of the week. Now, they waited in the hospital waiting room while he consulted with doctors, and then waited for other tests to be done for his eyes to get him new glasses as his vision wasn't all that great.

Later, they went to a Mexican restaurant for lunch.

As soon as they arrived, John was grateful for the cool air inside. "This is so good. Have you gone to my favorite chocolate cake place since I was gone?"

Angel shook her head. "I loved the cake you got me for my birthday, but I couldn't remember where you got it from."

Stephanie, whom he had missed, but who had said she had somewhere to be, joined them. "Hey, guys." She hugged each of them and set her purse on the table before sliding a chair back and sitting down. "What's up?"

One glance at her, and he knew that she wasn't telling them something. A number of years of living in close quarters with women who were unable to say what they wanted had taught him to read between the lines. But he held his peace. "We were waiting for you so we could eat together."

"Sorry, I had to get my car from the shop. It took a little longer than planned due to traffic." She sat back and exhaled. "This air is so cool."

Then, John realized he hadn't told her that he'd gotten a job. For some reason, every time he wished to talk to his sister, he and Angel and Tim had somewhere to be—to get him clothes, the Motor Vehicles for his driver's license, or out shopping for him. "Steph Bear, I missed you."

She chuckled. "Well, now there are two people calling me my nickname around here. How fun. I missed you too, Johnny. It's really good to have you back. You know you can call on me anytime. Especially since I've got my car back." She swept her long dark hair over her shoulders. "And... I'll really like to know how you survived captivity. Angel told me, but I want to hear the details from you."

"Sure. I'll give you my phone number—we got me a cheap flip phone. Long story, but that's what I asked for. I should also tell you I've got a job and I'll be starting on Monday. I'm pretty excited."

Her eyes rounding, she lowered the glass of water she'd been sipping. "What? A job?" Then she spun to Angel and Tim.

"We had nothing to do with it." Angel spread her napkin over her lap. "He went for a haircut and came out with a job and a start date. Only John can swing that."

"I need that hotline connection he's got with God. Seriously. Congratulations." She grinned widely but darted her gaze away. Something was bothering her. He knew it.

But John smiled instead. "Thank you, Steph. Tell me, what have you been up to?"

She exchanged a glance with Angel. "Nothing much. Well, nothing noteworthy at least."

"So... what was that look about?" He pointed at them. "Are you guys keeping something from me? Did something happen?"

Well, of course, things must've happened while he was gone. But Stephanie seemed fine from where he sat.

"Never mind, John. It's nothing for you to bother yourself

about. We're here, all alive and well and for now, that's all that matters."

"Listen, I planned to take my friend, Ahmed, out to lunch tomorrow. Do you want to come, Steph? It will be good to have a family member keep us company." He turned to Angel and Tim. "I also would like you both there when I pick him up from the airport today. I told him my family accepted him, so I would like him to feel that love with your presence. At least, before he starts earnest job seeking. He doesn't really have anyone. And he's scared to receive Christ due to his family's religion. He's going to need a lot of support, and I'll appreciate your help." John drummed nervous fingers on the table, energy pulsing through him in a rush of words that allowed no answer. "Can we accommodate him regardless of our busy schedule? I know it's a lot to ask, but I really believe he's one of the reasons God brought me through the woods. I know he needs Jesus. And I'm willing to be an arrow that points him to Him."

"I'm more than happy to come," Steph responded.

"We'll be there too. Right, honey?" Tim asked Angel, and she nodded. Having Angel and Tim married still amazed John. He prayed that God gave them an enduring marriage.

"Yes, if it's after four in the afternoon, I can surely make it."

"Good. Thank you so much. You all have no idea how much this means to me. I'm glad we at least get to eat together again tomorrow." Those fingers rapidly drilling the table, he turned to Stephanie. "And maybe, by then, you'll be able to tell me what you're hiding. Remember, I'm your brother, and twenty years of absence does not change that."

"I know," Stephanie quietly replied. Her low tone and downcast eyes piqued John's curiosity more. Whatever happened that his family wasn't telling him, he'd definitely get to the bottom of it.

Soon, his cellphone rang, and having given only his own family and Ahmed his number, he picked the call. "Hello?"

"Hi, John. It's Ahmed. I'm here. I just arrived."

"Okay. We'll pick you up. Wait for us at your flight's terminal."

"Thanks."

When Ahmed hung up, John turned to his family. "He's here."

Angel rose. "Awesome. Come on, hunters. Let's go love him like Jesus does."

John chuckled. "I'm glad you're now a hunter."

Stephanie punched his arm playfully, her first attempt at relaxation since she arrived. "We're all believers, and we're all hunters for Jesus' will, thanks to John."

The family left the restaurant in a lighter mood, far from the stress they'd endured for two decades. Stephanie dropped off her car at her place and joined them in Tim's truck to proceed to the airport.

26

"For whoever gives you a cup of water to drink in My name, because you belong to Christ, assuredly, I say to you, he will by no means lose his reward." Mark 9:41

Stephanie hadn't had a day—without Richard in it—more stressful than this one. First, her health insurance coverage had expired due to nonpayment. Then, her application for what could've been the perfect job fell through. Only for her to hear that her brother had gotten a job without even looking beyond where he was sitting and getting a haircut.

All through lunch, she kept thinking about how she would survive, how she would move forward, whether trusting God while going out on a limb, was above her current faith level. Where would she find the kind of job to pay her living expenses? She had less than thirty days to figure it out, and the clock was ticking.

She'd not ask her sister for money. Angel was already stretched thin supporting John. She wouldn't become an added responsibility.

She dug in her heels. She would trust God. She would pass this test. God would make a way.

In the midst of her making these declarations in her heart over lunch, John asked her what was going on in her life. Caught between the lost opportunities of the past and the uncertainty of her present, she had no words.

So, she'd pushed back, much against her wish. Before she spilled about how she ruined her life with a bad boyfriend, she wanted better economic capacity. Telling someone you messed up your life and then asking for financial help was just too hard.

She hungered for a good testimony. For her life to show the goodness of God. So, while everyone ate and chatted, she cried out to God in her heart. *Lord Jesus, I know You love me. I know You won't withhold anything good from me. I know I messed up, but I also know You've forgiven me. Whatever I need to do to come into the fullness of Your perfect purpose for my life, I yield myself completely to You. I have nothing else to lean on. You are my everlasting sustenance. Please, help me. Make a way out for me and bless me indeed.*

She prayed on, and after she dropped off her car and rejoined her family, she felt peace. She couldn't understand how she could have peace when things around her were still so unpredictable. But she chose to allow God's peace rule in her heart.

Maybe there was more to this than her financial security. Maybe God was giving her something better than she could've hoped for.

All she knew was, at this point, she was past the point of

placing her trust in what she could see. Everything she could see and thought she knew had failed her. Yes, her family loved her, but it was time to allow God to build her a new foundation. "Take the remote control of my life, Jesus, and make of me what You will."

As soon as they reached the airport and pulled to a stop at the identified arrival gate, John's alarm drew her back to the present. "It looks like we might have a situation."

A man under the waiting stand looked about her age and an older gentleman in a Middle-Eastern caftan stood next to him. Father and son?

"Wait here." John exited the car and approached both men.

He extended a hand to the older gentleman out of the respect, but the man refused to shake it. Maybe John was right.

"I'm going out to see what's going on." Stephanie pushed the door open.

"We are too." Angel and Tim followed.

Anger and frustration tightened the older man's face. "So, you are the people who are tryin g to ruin my son's life, huh?"

Stephanie stood rooted in shock, but John seemed unfazed as he stepped closer. "Ahmed, my friend, you are welcome. Stephanie," John beckoned her, "would you be so kind as to help Ahmed get his luggage into our vehicle, please?"

Somehow, her legs began to move again. "Sure." She waved Ahmed over. "Please come with me." Together, they took his two pieces of luggage and rolled them toward the truck.

"Thanks." John returned his attention to the older gentleman. "Sir, you must be Ahmed's dad. It's my family's pleasure to meet you."

The man did not respond, but when she and Ahmed returned, the man was speaking. "I raised my son to go and become a reputable doctor. You people convinced him to leave his career at the Regional Hospital, to pursue after foolish religion. You are a bunch of fools."

"I'm sorry, you are mistaken." How could John's tone sound so calm in the face of such confrontation? "I met your son in the woods almost one week ago. I was fleeing from violence, and I saw your son with a gun to his jaw about to kill himself."

He let that sink in. The father was silent.

"I heard some of what he said to himself before he planned to pull the trigger. Your son was not happy. Did you not know? Did you not hear he had tried to kill himself? Have you tried to help him or get him help?"

The man clenched his fist then shook it in John's face. "Listen to me, you raggedy thing of a man, you know nothing about my son! My son did not try to kill himself. You made that up. Now, I want him to return with me and go back and beg to get his job back, as a good son will do."

Stephanie slanted a glance at Ahmed. She could easily understand now why he wished to kill himself, judging from the bout of interaction with his family. Were they all like this?

"Dad, sorry, but you're wrong. I did try to kill myself. And nothing anyone did could've stopped me. I didn't follow through ultimately because this man needed help. I couldn't let him die. I chose to help him and that's why I walked out alive." Ahmed shoved his hands in his pockets, a pleading in his dark gaze as he peered at his father. "I chose to quit my job. He didn't tell me to. I *chose* to do it. I didn't want to study medicine. I did it to make you happy, and yet, you were not happy. I left Regional Medical because that was your dream and not mine. I don't even know what I'm good at because I've always done what you wished, never what I want." He touched the elder man, and he shrank away from his touch. "This is the first time I'm choosing where to go and the people I want to spend time with. This is the first time I'm anywhere close to happiness. I want to be around these people. They seem to have joy, and their faces are not closed like mine. I want something new and good, and I choose to find it myself."

A slap landed across his cheek, and Stephanie gasped. "How dare you speak to me like that, boy?! You are really your mother's son. A rebel! You are not my son anymore." The elder man pointed to them. "And when these people are finished dealing with you and you run back to me, there won't be a place for you in my house."

Pain rippled across Ahmed's face. A pain that must've hurt more than the slap from his father. "I love you, Father, but please know this. I will not return. I hope you can find a way to love yourself someday. Goodbye."

The elder man spun, returned toward the airport, and for a long minute, no one said a word.

John stepped forward first and hugged Ahmed. Then Angel curved her arms around them. Then Tim hugged them. And lastly, Stephanie. They enclosed around him like a human shield, and he burst into tears. As his shoulders shook, they stayed huddled, covered him, shielded his pain and hurt from the view of the outside world.

When he finished crying, they let him go, and John pointed toward the truck. "We are your family, Ahmed. We can never take the place of your natural family. But as they've rejected you, we accept you, and we will love you with everything in us. We'll take care of you when you cannot take care of yourself. We'll fight for you, and we'll be on your side. Never look elsewhere for support. We are your new family. Welcome home."

Ahmed's lips wobbled and whitened at the center as he struggled to contain his emotions. His eyes glistened, and his Adam's apple bobbed. "Thank you so much, John. Thank you, my brother."

And without another word, they moved into the truck and headed home as one family.

∽

Stephanie glanced at the clock on the side of her bed—2:38 a.m.

She'd tried to sleep, but it eluded her. Conflicting feelings she was struggling to reconcile occupied her mind. First, there was the matter of Ahmed. His family's antagonism and ultimate rejection hit her hard—so hard that she'd spent that night on her knees in prayer. She'd thanked God first for the kind of loving family she had. Her parents were good to them when they were alive, according to Angel. And Angel, who stepped up for them after their unfortunate demise, had continued loving them. She could hardly imagine what life growing up had been for Ahmed. Had anyone ever truly loved him before now? She prayed all that night and slept off at dawn. Thankfully, their lunch meeting with Ahmed was moved forward for three days due to John's meetings at the SSPD.

Then she'd prayed again for Ahmed the following night. Then the day after that, she'd prayed yet again for him. Tonight was the third night.

She slid down from the bed and settled on her knees. The burden wouldn't leave her heart. So she bowed her head and prayed yet again. She prayed for Ahmed to open his heart to the love of Jesus and allow God to lead him to the purpose He had for him. She also prayed for God to lead her into His perfect will for this season. She felt some confusion on her end, leaving her unsure where God wished for her to be. Was she just nervous? Or was it her mind blocking her from receiving guidance?

She returned to her prayer for Ahmed. "Lord Jesus, You said the heart of the king is in Your hands and You turn it wheresoever You will. Ahmed's heart is in Your Holy hands. Please turn his heart to seek Your face and follow Your purpose for his life. Please, Lord, save his soul. Nothing matters more than this." Stephanie remained in the posture of prayer for almost an hour until she felt peace in her heart. Then she rose, finally worn down, and as soon as she lay down, sleep came.

27

"Then you shall dwell in the land that I gave to your fathers; you shall be My people, and I will be your God." Ezekiel 36:28

Monday morning came quickly for John. It was time. To start a new job, a new life, and to reintegrate to human society professionally. Was he ready?

He tugged at the outfit—a blue shirt and khaki pants—he'd purchased at the thrift store with leftover change from the money Tim had given him at the barber's shop. He'd washed the clothes, ironed them, and no one would know they were thrifted except his family. He could've bought new ones, but he'd stuck with something cheap in case this gig didn't become a long-term position. Considering his lack of experience, John feared his time there wouldn't last.

So he knocked on Ahmed's bedroom door and waited for an answer before entering. "Come in."

He opened the door and smiled when he saw the man was up. "Hey, bro. Good morning."

Ahmed stared at him. His cheeks reddened. Then he burst out crying.

John stopped his approach. "Did I say something wrong?"

Ahmed shook his head, covered his mouth, and managed to stay the tears. "I've never had a good morning. Father always made me flee the house before he woke up. It was like living in hell." He gulped as John's throat tightened. "Now, for three days, I avoided you and everyone else in the house in the morning, just like I do in my family. But you people showed me love."

Shifting his feet, John lowered his gaze. How was he supposed to react?

Saying and having a good morning was a norm in his family. He couldn't imagine living where it was a strange occurrence. "I'm sorry for how you were treated, Ahmed. I promise that I and my family will support you in every way we can."

Ahmed nodded. "Thank you so much. Please thank your sister, Angel, too, for allowing a man she doesn't know into her home."

Now, John smiled. "Oh no. Angel is a cop and does not allow anyone she doesn't 'know' in. She definitely did a background check before she welcomed you. I can guarantee it."

His first smile curved Ahmed's lips. "I would do so, too, if I was letting a suicidal man into my family."

"She said she did it only to verify any criminal history, not because you attempted suicide. That doesn't bother us."

Ahmed jolted slightly, blinking as he frowned at John. "Why?"

John held the doorknob and prayed his next words could communicate his heart. "Listen, my friend, someone rarely attempts suicide as a result of external factors. Usually, the reasons are close to home. When you escape the circumstances that led you to such desperation, then you can have the clarity of mind to allow God to heal you and make you a new person. Moreover, we know for a fact that Jesus accepts you, so we have no reason not to. You are precious to Him. You can seek professional counsel and have the right environment for such help to be beneficial, including for your nightmares. I heard you last night. I, too, am getting professional help. It's nothing to be ashamed of. Like my sister's husband said, it's actually a sign of courage. I have trouble sleeping thanks to what I've been through."

"Being a war veteran came with a lot more than battle scars. I find it tough to sleep as well. And I will welcome professional help."

"Good. For me, I was in captivity for twenty years, and I'm sure that ruined my psychology somehow. But one thing I know is that, whether I could afford paid help or not, the Word of God shapes me from the inside, gives me hope anew, and lets my light shine."

A quietness enveloped the room. Then Ahmed smoothed the Aztec pattern on the guest room comforter. For a long time, he focused on the geometric shapes and sandy colors. "I want this assurance too. My family has rejected me for a faith I am yet to accept. I've got nothing to lose now since I've lost everything. I might as well try this Jesus thing, and if it doesn't work for me, at least I gave it a shot. It's better than dying."

John lifted his gaze skyward, gave a silent prayer of thanks, and then returned his attention to Ahmed. "I'm glad you made that choice, but if you wish to learn more first, to study and understand before committing to Christ, that's okay. You are under no obligation to choose Christ. It needs to be a completely voluntary choice."

A slow smile curved Ahmed's full lips. "Yes, it is my choice. And there's no better time than now, my friend."

"If so, I will lead you in a prayer of salvation. Please bow your head and repeat after me. And, please know you can say this prayer again later, if you wish to, although once is enough."

"Sure." Ahmed bowed his head, and dark curls tumbled over his face. John's heart broke over the pain, sadness, and disappointments the man must have endured. He hoped his friend would let the love of Jesus wash over him to grant him genuine freedom that cannot be purchased.

"Heavenly Father, I come to You in the name of Jesus, Your only Begotten Son. I acknowledge that I am a sinner and have fallen short of the glory of God. I repent of my sins, and I confess that Jesus is the Son of God Who died and rose to pay the price for my sins with His precious blood. Today, I accept Jesus as my Lord and Savior. I choose to serve Jesus with the rest of my life. Thank you for saving me."

Slow and attentive, as if thinking over each one and weighing their meaning, Ahmed repeated every word.

"Congratulations, Ahmed. You are now a Christian. I will let you discuss with Stephanie, who is arriving shortly to drive me to my new job. She is heading to church for a program tonight, and it would be great for you to go with her and be introduced to other Christians. I have to run along now. God bless you."

Both men shared a brief hug.

"Thank you, John. I feel as though a heavy weight has lifted off my shoulders. I'm glad to have taken this step. I look forward to my new life in Christ."

"It's not me. It's the Holy Spirit who teaches us all things. I was just as skeptical as you when Angel shared Jesus with me. It took me longer because I wanted to be quite sure, but once I took that step of placing my faith in Jesus, my life turned around. You may wonder, why then, did God allow me to get kidnapped?"

"Exactly." Ahmed bobbed a quick nod.

"My trust in God was built up in that place. A place where only darkness surrounded me, where I didn't understand, there I knew the friendship of God and His protection the most. Many died there, but I survived. And sometimes, survival is a greater testimony than never going through something hard. Let me put it this way, God allowed the hard situation to prove He is tougher. Maybe there will come a situation tomorrow that would ordinarily toss my faith overboard, but as long as I remember what God did in the past, I anchor my faith in His Word, and in His past performance to say I know God will deliver me again."

"Wow. That makes sense. For me, if God cared enough about my life to place you in my path in the woods to save me, then I place my faith in Jesus without looking back. After all, between Jesus and my family, it's He Who valued my life above achievements."

"That's a good mindset. We shall also be praying for your family, especially your dad. So he can come to the knowledge of the truth. If anything prompts him to be the way he is, we will pray God will take charge of the situation and change him. Nothing is too hard for God. That is a Scripture. Which reminds me, please let Stephanie know to get you a Bible from church tonight. I have to leave now so I won't be late."

"Okay." Ahmed pushed himself off his bed. "Have a great first day at work. And when you return, I want to hear about how you got a job within days of reaching home, without any relevant experience."

John smiled. "I asked the Lord Jesus, and He gave it to me."

"This is how He works?" Ahmed blinked. "Can I ask, too, and He will do it for me?"

"Yes, if it is in His perfect will for you at this time. Pray, then trust Jesus to guide you. See you later, bro. For real."

A short burst of laughter jumped from Ahmed's lips and his eyes sparkled. "All right, bro, for real."

John left that room and raced upstairs and out of the house with a heart swelling with gratitude.

Against all odds, Ahmed was saved.

∼

STEPHANIE COVERED HER YAWN AS SHE WAITED FOR JOHN TO emerge. As agreed, she was dropping him off at his new job.

When he came out, a huge grin lit his face. "Looks like someone is already having a good morning." She stifled a second yawn as John opened the door and climbed into the front seat.

"And it looks like someone got no sleep at all. Howdy, Steph Bear."

A sigh escaped. "You could say that again, but I promise, it wasn't due to anything terrible. It was due to prayer."

"I need to do that, too, pray extensively for divine leading. But I have a testimony, and you won't believe it."

Stephanie navigated into traffic. "Wow. Can you share?"

"Ahmed has just received Jesus as his personal Lord and Savior."

She heard the screeching tires before she realized it was her car. "Oh, so sorry!" She pulled to the curb and turned the engine off. "What did you say, John?"

He blinked. "Um, that Ahmed is saved. Was that why you nearly crashed us?"

"Yes!" Her hands flew to grip the steering wheel, and laughter flew from her. "I've prayed for him for consecutive nights for him to receive Christ. I mean, the burden was so strong I couldn't sleep. So I got up each night and prayed. I didn't know God was working while I was praying." She laughed joyfully and raised her hands as high as the car allowed. "Oh, thank You, Jesus. I needed this good news so badly."

"Wow. There I was wondering minutes ago why things happened the way they did. Little did I know God had raised an intercessor. I'm so glad you prayed. And sorry you lost sleep."

"You don't have to apologize. It's great news and has bolstered my faith for everything else I'm waiting on God for."

She started the car and reentered traffic. "Lord Jesus, thank You for answering our prayers of salvation for Ahmed. Thank You for leading him into our path. I pray You uphold him and lead Him into what You have planned for him, in Jesus' mighty name, amen."

"Amen," John echoed. "I told him that, since you'd said you were going to church today, he could go with you for fellowship."

She darted a glance in his direction. "Um, I wasn't going there for fellowship."

A frown curved his forehead. "What are you going there for then? Private prayers?"

"Um, not really." Was this the time to spill the beans? "I'm looking for a job. I left the place I'd worked when a former boyfriend threatened my life. So I fled here."

"My goodness. When did all this happen?"

"A couple of years ago until recently when he came here to attack me and the SSPD stopped him. I was away from the faith, too, so I'd walked into that one with my eyes wide open, and the consequences trailed me here. But I thank God for His mercy and for giving me a second chance."

"Thank God you returned safely to your faith. I pray you stay rooted in Christ."

"Amen. I intend staying this time."

"And where is the boyfriend?"

"He's in custody and I'm safe. But I'm basically starting over. I attend a different church from the one we used to go to, although Angel and Tim still go there. I like this new church. The pastor is on fire for Jesus and has a broken past."

"Sounds like a place I'd want to visit. I could go with you and Ahmed. But what are you going there for?"

"I need to meet with the pastor for a spot on the missionary team they announced on Sunday."

"Oh, that's great. Ahmed is also looking for a job so it's perfect. You both go there together and let me know how it turns out if I can't make it there with you." John hardly gave her enough time for a quick nod before he climbed out once they arrived. "I'm almost running late. I don't want to give a bad first impression so I'll see you later for lunch, right? Angel and Tim said they wouldn't make it. You and Ahmed will swing by to pick me up?"

"Yes, we will. Have a great first day." She waved as he left.

Making a U-turn, she reversed the vehicle and returned home. Butterflies fluttered in her belly at the beautiful thought of how God answered her prayers for Ahmed. She could hardly believe her little prayers, said in the middle of the night, were worth anything. But seeing God answer it so powerfully was witnessing a pure miracle. And she had meant it when she'd said it had boosted her faith. She knew God was with her, and there was no greater feeling.

"Father, I need Your guidance. As Ahmed and I go to the church, please show us favor and please reveal Your will." She wasn't sure why she'd chosen to go there, but she felt this was something different from what she'd consider a place to search for a job.

As she drew close to Angel's house, she had an idea. After parking, she rapped on the door, knowing Tim and Angel were out but Ahmed was around.

Moments later, he opened the door and let her in. "Stephanie, good to see you."

She smiled and shut the door. "You too. I dropped John off and was wondering whether you would like to grab lunch in town before we head to the church."

"Yes, that would be nice. What time would you like to meet up?"

"In a couple of hours, say, one o'clock? I think that's when John gets his lunch break. So we can all eat together, if that works for you."

He shrugged. "Lunchtime at the hospital was usually around twelve, but I'm cool with one o'clock too. If my belly grumbles, I can take a snack."

"Okay. But don't spoil your lunch." She wagged a finger striding back toward her car.

"Yes, ma'am." He laughed. "See you later."

She turned. "See you, Dr. Ahmed." Stephanie hoped what

was heating up her cheeks was nothing but the warmth outside because she'd just met the man and an attraction was nothing close to the seclusion she fled to Maryland for. Richard was barely behind her, and she was only interested in seeking God.

"Ahmed. Call me Ahmed," he coolly offered.

"Fine." But as far as she was concerned, their familiarity ended there.

28

"Dwell in this land and I will be with you and bless you..." Genesis 26:3

Around one o'clock, Stephanie sent John a text message.

Can we pick you up for lunch with me and Ahmed?

He replied. *Yeah. That would be awesome. I'll be outside by the time you arrive. My lunch is for an hour.*

She was almost outside Angel's house so she messaged Ahmed with the number she'd been provided with. *I'm outside. Come when you're ready.* She could've asked him about his car, but she didn't wish to embarrass him.

He emerged wearing a light-blue shirt, casual brown pants, and black sneakers. She found her hand clutching her chest. Was her heart beating faster! "No." It couldn't be. It wasn't. She made up her mind to give herself a good lecture later, but as his tall frame slipped inside her car and filled the space, he was impossible to ignore. "Hey."

He smiled, and that lit up a dimple. Then he swept his short, dark curls back. "Thank you for getting me. It was getting a bit lonely."

A smile curved her lips. "You're welcome, Ahmed. We're glad to have you here."

When they reached John's job, she glimpsed him waiting like he'd said, and she pulled up in front of him. She rolled down the window, and joy filled her heart. Her brother was really here. "Get in, Johnny. People are hungry in here."

He chuckled as he slid in next to Ahmed at the back. "Hey, buddy."

"Hey." They fist bumped. "How was your first day so far?"

"Good. Hope my little sister hasn't been giving you a headache."

Stephanie pulled into traffic. "Hey, guys, no gossiping about me. Remember, I'm in the driver's seat, and I'm choosing our restaurant."

"Ha. What will you do?" John sighed. "Plunge us into oncoming traffic as punishment?"

"Or send us to eat at a buffet?" Ahmed added.

"Oh, really?" She swerved a bit when she saw no vehicle coming, and both guys gripped the head grip.

"Goodness, Steph. Was that for real?"

"Relax, guys." She laughed. "You asked what I can do, so I showed you."

"Oh, she is tough." As Ahmed chuckled, his breath rushed forward, warming the back of her neck. "I was thinking of getting to know her better, but she about scared me off already."

"What did you say?" Stephanie almost screeched the car to

a halt. "For the record, considering what I just came out of, I'm not trying to get to know anyone better." She managed to drive to the Asian restaurant. "It's nothing personal against you, just my choice."

Ahmed stayed silent. So did John as they strode into the restaurant. Paper lanterns lent soft light while a hint of peanut oil lingering in the air mingled with the tangy residue of Thai spices.

When the waiter finished taking their orders, John shifted in his hard-backed wooden chair. "Stephanie, so do you mind explaining what you said earlier? Ahmed is a good guy, a Christian. Why did you say you weren't interested in getting to know anyone? I mean, I'm not setting you up with him or anyone, but, as your brother, I'd like to understand your rationale. What happened?"

She glanced at Ahmed, then her brother. "Long story."

"What about a short version?"

"There isn't one. I wish I could cut it and tell you a piece, but it's really a long story. Let's just say, I was hurt a lot, and I'm still recovering."

"Hurt is different from shackled, Stephanie."

She'd been fiddling with the fork on her plate but stilled at Ahmed's words. "Shackled?"

"When you've been in bondage before, the signs are there. Anyone you meet sees a trail of the shackles and can either pick them up and put them back on or tear what's left off you to enhance your freedom. Allow us to help you. We all need help."

Just then, John's gaze fixed on something past her head, so cho opun. He was smiling widely at a little girl trying to dress up her pink doll, but the doll was trapped in the wedge of a large plant. John rose to his feet, went over, and helped her untangle her doll. He squatted, said something, and handed the doll to the grateful girl's hands, and she happily trotted away.

As he returned to their table and the waiter served their drinks, he looked at his sister, and tears framed his eyes. "Being locked in a small space for so long, makes seeing a kid playing, such a blessing." He managed to hold the tears hugging his lashes. "I wished to have a wife and kids of my own by now. They stole that from me. They stole my time."

She understood. "You were taken against your will, and you lost your most valuable possession—time." She pressed her lips tight and lowered her gaze. "On the other hand, I had time, but I blew it on a pointless relationship."

Ahmed reached out and briefly patted her hand, then John's shoulder. "And I, on another level, didn't want the time I had. I felt I had no need for it. I saw little kids playing, and I never realized what a privilege it was. I'm learning to be more grateful for the things I'd taken for granted, because what you valued, I despised."

"We all have lessons to learn from where we missed out and messed up. I believe it's the Lord who brought us here to teach us gratitude."

Ahmed nodded. "In my heart, I'm already repenting for my ingratitude. Maybe I've taken so many things God blessed me with for granted. I was never able to see past my pain in my family to see the blessings I had."

"Me too."

"I second that. I love seeing Angel, Tim, Stephanie, and you, too, Ahmed. But do you know what I appreciate the most? Going to the church and serving God in His house. I missed church so bad."

Her stilted laugh was met with their stares. "We're all so broken."

John shrugged. "With God, that's not a bad thing. The more broken you are, the more flexible you are."

"Amen." Ahmed looked relieved. "Because I think I'm the most broken of all."

"Then I marvel at what God will do through you, my friend." Little did Stephanie know her heart had taken a small step toward this man who wanted the help of Jesus. She liked him, enjoyed his company, and felt free with him. She especially liked how he was eager to grow in his faith, as she was learning to grow in her trust with God. Having a doting elder sister and her loving husband supporting her was good. But this man was giving her direct support independent of any hidden agenda.

She advised herself not to push him away. She could have him as simply a friend and maintain that boundary. There was never, ever going to be another Richard situation where a friendship turned into something else. She'd allow God to teach her how to keep boundaries in relationships, even with believing men.

"Let's pray. We came here to eat, but maybe God had greater plans in mind," Ahmed said. "Steph, why don't you talk to the Lord on our behalf? I'm barely a few hours old in the faith."

John patted his arm. "Sometimes, I feel like the Lord answers the prayers of His babies faster than others." A smile lit his face and chased away the former sadness. "He expects us to be able to handle the tougher stuff. But we still fall flat on our faces and then realize we need Him just as much as new believers. I'd rather you start learning how to express yourself to Jesus, but we'll let Steph take this go around."

"Sure," Stephanie said, "I'll lead us in prayer." Bowing their heads and joining their hands across the table, she prayed. "Lord Jesus, we thank You for bringing us here. We intended to eat here, but we came to find that You'd prepared a table of encouragement and blessings for us. We are so grateful. We are in various stages of our walk. We yearn for faith that moves mountains in our hearts, love that breaks yokes, and hope that never fades for each of us. Lord, grant us the grace to make You our one desire. Let everything else come after You. Thank You, Lord. In Your mighty name, we pray, amen."

"Amen," Ahmed and John concurred.

As she looked up, smiling, she felt the butterflies in her belly flutter again when she saw Ahmed perusing her, and color warmed her cheeks.

"I wish you would share your story," he softly said. "It can't be worse than mine."

She lifted her water glass without raising her gaze. "All bad stories are considered to be worse for the person involved. At the right time, I will. I have to tell John first."

"I understand."

Their waiter placed platters of cashew chicken before them, and John simply stared at his heaping plate as if still struggling to believe such abundance existed. *Thank You*, whispered in Stephanie's heart. *Thank You for the food, for my brother, for the future.* So many thank yous lifted on the steam before she joined hands with John and Ahmed to give thanks.

"On the other hand," John stabbed a curl of onion and chicken with his fork and lifted it to the light, "I need to know how and where you learned to swerve like that. Whoever taught you that could get a bad lecture from me." He dropped the bite in his mouth and wagged his now-empty fork at her.

She laughed. "And the big brother in there just showed up."

Stephanie relaxed, taking surreptitious glances at John as he savored his food and the conversation rotated between football, soccer, baseball, and lastly, medicine. It seemed John and Ahmed were indeed bonding as brothers like John had promised when Ahmed's father denounced him. With the rejection still fresh, their integration of him into their family likely saved Ahmed's life, yet again.

She scooped the last of the spicy sauce, hoping she'd never take another bite for granted, and John checked his watch. "I think I better head back. I wouldn't want the boss to think I left for home. I'll catch a taxi and see you both at church."

"Tim might be coming too. I'm not sure."

"Great. We'll make it a joint time of individual fellowship then. God knows I need it."

She drove them all to drop John off. Then she returned Ahmed to her sister's place. "I'll pick you up around six for the church."

"Thanks," he unclicked the door, then, still gripping the handle, faced her again, "I enjoyed this lunch. I look forward to doing this again—with you."

Stephanie paused. "As long as we're doing it as friends and nothing more, yes, that will be fine. But I'm putting boundaries in my relationships and being careful not to allow friendships to become something I didn't intend for them to become." An exhale whooshed. This was the first time she was really putting up those boundaries she'd carried in her mind. She'd wished to say this before with others but lacked the courage. With the words out of her lips, she felt freer. "I hope you can respect that."

With his free hand, Ahmed pushed his curls back. "Yes, I

can. Your friendship means more to me than anything else." He opened the door. "But I'm open to anything more God might have planned for the future. I'm not making assumptions or pushing you into anything. I just want to maintain an open mind. But I am definitely keeping whatever distance you deem necessary. Your comfort is of utmost priority. I've been through a lot, too, so I need healing and space just as much. I want to learn more about Jesus, grow in my faith, and be of use to the kingdom of God first."

As her shoulders slackened, a comfortable smile laced her lips. "That is a great goal. I'll be praying for you. Pray for me too."

He chuckled. "I already did."

And he spun into the house before she could find out what he'd prayed for her about.

There'd be next time.

29

"Now therefore, go, and I will be with your mouth and teach you what you shall say." Exodus 4:12

THEY SAID IT TOOK A MAN ALMOST TEN YEARS TO REALLY SETTLE into his marriage. Pete Zendel stared at his wife of many years and could hardly believe what she said. "Honey, are you serious? I mean." He tried to stem his frustration, but it was getting harder by the minute. "Babe, I can hardly imagine you asking for this." He spread out his hands. "Why? Why now? You've never asked to go there before."

She curled her arms, equally defiant, more than he'd ever seen her push for something. "You ask why?" Standing there, she grew silent. "Because we both need closure. From your past. From what you have been trying *not* to do since I met you."

"And what would that be?"

"Violet. You have escaped mentioning her except when you

had a guilty moment. Yes, you have mourned and mourned and mourned her loss and your role in it. But she also lived, she hadn't simply died." Patricia drew closer and encircled her arms around him, a move sure to melt his resistance as she stared at him. Those lovely eyes were doing things to his resolve that he wouldn't admit right now.

So, he toughened up—as little as he could—and swallowed hard. "She lived, Pete. Yes, you killed her. Yes, you regret it. Yes, you've paid for your crimes with prison time." She tightened her hold on him. "But have you ever celebrated her life? The things she loved? As in, gone where you knew she cherished and abided there just to honor the person she was? She was a child of God. Don't forget. She left you a beautiful legacy as part of your family, and you can celebrate that."

"I still don't get what you're asking me to do." But her words had choked his throat up already, and his words were trickling out slower now. "How do you want me to...celebrate Violet? She's gone. I wish she wasn't, but she just is. So, how do I celebrate her when she's not here to receive it anymore?"

"The cabin."

They stared at each other. And he knew. His eyes were getting misty. But Pete couldn't get himself to tear them away from the one person he was sure he could bare his soul to and not feel ashamed.

He couldn't speak any longer. Emotions warred within him. Accept to go or decline? He scratched his jaw and mumbled under his breath. Staying away from the cabin and the sweet memories his sister had built for them there had been a temporary solution. He'd had them move her things there from her apartment a few years ago. But Tim, her best friend had contended with him and taken memorabilia that meant something to him and Violet. Pete had allowed him to take them. "Okay." He swallowed again then tore his eyes away and moved a little farther from her too. But her next words froze his steps.

"We can go there with Tim and his wife and spend a weekend."

"*Who?*" Tim considered him an enemy and could even think of shooting him for killing Violet. He saw it in the man's eyes when he drove up to the cabin years ago to let Tim in so he could put Violet's things in his possession there. They'd managed to do what they went there for, without exchanging more than three words—*thanks, bye*, and a third word Tim called him the moment he'd seen him. A word he couldn't bear to repeat.

Pete was reeling, but Patricia wasn't done talking. "Together. As friends. I'd like us to get to know them better. He was Violet's best friend. You could learn a thing or two, especially since President Towers and his wife are no longer around here. And your pilot friend and his wife moved away too. We need new friends, and good old friends wouldn't hurt, if you can get past your bias."

"Pat," he rarely addressed her by name unless it was something he really, seriously, and irreversibly objected to, "I can't do that." He shook his head. "And I don't want to discuss this any further right now." She'd piled too much on him when he'd simply come to have a quiet morning devotion with the woman he loved. She opened her mouth to speak, but he shook his head again. "Please, love. Not now. Okay?" He kissed her and walked slowly away, the memory of her words trailing him and ensuring the rest of his day would be occupied by her gentle voice, serious plea—and Tim's angry face. "Lord Jesus, please help me. I'm going to need much grace today."

IT HAD TAKEN A WHOLE WEEK FOR PETE TO GATHER THE COURAGE to call Tim, knowing how hard the call would be for both of them. Picking up the phone, he dialed the last number he had saved from Violet for Tim—the number from which they'd communicated when he moved Violet's stuff to the cabin with Tim, who knew what was valuable to her. They'd barely managed to get it done without Tim getting at his throat then. He hoped time would've eased some of Tim's pain. Then he whispered a prayer as the call rang, instead of simply hoping.

To his surprise, the call rang through, and a male voice answered. Pete sent a prayer up to God that it was Tim, and that he would talk to him and agree to help him.

"Hello?" The voice sounded familiar enough.

"Hi, can I speak with Tim Santiago please?" He held his breath.

"Yes, this is Tim speaking."

Pete inhaled long. "Tim, this is Pete Zendel, Violet's brother. Not sure if you remember me."

Silence held the line. Then a huff sounded.

"I do. And not in a fond way."

"Listen, I need your help. I—"

The call hung up, sending Pete back to square one. *Just what I thought.*

He heard God say in his heart, "Call him again."

He redialed and Tim picked up. "Tim, I'm sorry about Violet."

Silence. But Tim didn't hang up. "I know I took someone precious from you, and I've regretted it every day. Saying I'm sorry doesn't take away your pain—*our* pain—but it does show

I deeply regret what happened and my role in it. I'm truly sorry. Please forgive me?" He'd asked Tim to forgive him years ago, but the man didn't utter a word then.

"What do you need?" Tim's voice shook. "Talking to you is hard. I'd rather not do it often. I'm sure you can understand. Even your voice is a sad reminder about Violet. And…I forgive you. Though we're not becoming best buddies anytime soon."

Pete exhaled slowly. Some sins did linger in their consequences for life. But knowing God already forgave him and gave him a fresh start made all this bearable. "Thank you, Tim. I appreciate it." So, how could he frame his response to give the shortest version possible? "Before Violet died, she told me a number called her and harassed her. At the time, I had my men look into it, and they found nothing. Next I heard was that the calls mysteriously stopped. And three weeks ago, while I ministered during a Bible study, our system was hacked. I ran a security scan while preaching, but by the time I reached my office, an alarm had gone off."

Hearing no response, he continued. "The SSPD found a message had been coded in a way that seemed like malware. That caused the disruption."

"What does it say?" Tim asked.

Pete repeated the message on the screen. "So, my question to you is this—you dig up old stuff and you know your way around my family's history through Violet. Did she mention anything to you before she died that I might've missed?"

Tim was silent for a long time—so long Pete assumed he'd hung up. But the man was still there. Obviously, he knew something. Likely, he was debating whether or not to tell Pete. "Please, Tim. Help me. If you know anything that can help, please share."

"I can't say this over the phone. I'll be arriving at your church with my family this evening for Bible study and some prayer time they planned to come for. While they pray and listen, I'll meet with you."

Confused, Pete tightened his grip on the phone. He'd never invited Tim to his church. "Wait, you know where my church is? How?"

"I was there three weeks ago, the night you had your breach, if that was the night you were referring to."

"Um..." Too stunned to speak, Pete had to recollect himself to find the right words. Tim was in his church that day? Incredible! "Well, I pray the Lord ministered to you. You should've said hi. You're family. At least, thanks to Violet, I consider you as my family, estranged only due to circumstances."

"I brought my wife and my sister there to accompany them. I wasn't really a guest." The words came out hard. Their obvious symbol hung in the ensuing silence. "And surprisingly, yes, I did enjoy your message. My sister-in-law, Stephanie, received Christ afresh that night."

Oh, he did remember speaking to a Stephanie today. She must be the one related to Tim. "Small world, huh?"

"Small world. I'll see you tonight." Tim sounded about ready to hang up again, but the bitterness lacing his voice had thankfully melted away.

"See you, Tim. And thanks again." Pete ended the call, updated the SSPD, and went home to prepare for the Bible study that evening. If the last three weeks were any indication, the Bible studies in his church were getting hotter than Sunday services—and most unpredictable.

30

"But as it is written: 'Eye has not seen, nor ear heard, nor have entered into the heart of man the things which God has prepared for those who love Him.'" 1 Corinthians 2:9

John arrived at the Living Faith Bible Church quite curious. Stephanie had raved about the church as she drove them there. Tim had already arrived and had a meeting with the pastor scheduled after the service. He didn't look too eager but displayed less angst than Angel had described him as having when he'd discovered who the pastor of Stephanie's church was.

How could one man elicit such raving acclaim from Stephanie and equally strong antagonism from Tim, whom nothing could annoy?

He stepped from the car, expectant to see what kind of man could spur such contradictory reactions.

When the others alighted, John tipped his head back and forth, taking in the vast building. "Wait, there is a church this large in Silver Stone? When you mentioned your church, I imagined a small church by the corner. This," he swept his arms expansively, "this is like a corporation or a complex. I'd like to know the man who runs all this."

Stephanie beamed. "I'd say he's not what you might think. Let God show you who He wants you to see. And," her eyes lit up with a sparkle, "you could make this your church, too, if God leads you to."

John tugged at her long hair. "Steph Bear, you're always dragging us into one place or the other. Your adventurous spirit is alive and kicking."

"Adventurous, and yet she won't give me a chance." Ahmed released a warm chuckle. "I know, you want some distance. I respect that. But, John, if I have your permission, I'd like to pursue this beautiful sister of yours."

They all paused at the church entrance where a welcome team in white shirts were waving and smiling, but they didn't see them. Then they burst out laughing.

"Thank God, you took it in the spirit with which I said it. I thought John might stone me, or you, Stephanie, would kick me out of your sister's house for showing interest in you. I like you, and I won't pretend not to."

A smile thawed Stephanie's face. "I like that you like me, but right now, I like Jesus the most. So, if you can handle that, you can stick around."

Ahmed swiped imaginary sweat. "Well, thank you. That's better than back off."

They laughed again as John walked through the door first, then paused in front of Ahmed. "I'll say this—I can't give you permission, but I can pray for God's perfect will to be done." He curved two fingers and pointed at him. "But I got my eyes on you, bro. If you dare hurt her, I'll make you regret it. I protect her from any more hurt, got it, man?"

"Sounds tough enough. Yeah, I got it. I got it. And," seriousness tightened the lines around Ahmed's eyes and pressed his lips white as he ground his jaw, "never will I do anything to hurt you. You saved my life, and I owe you the joy I have now."

John shook his head. "Never give glory to the vessel. God," he gestured toward the inside of the church, "saved you. He placed me in your path, and He alone gets all the glory. But I understand your intentions and your heart. And your gratitude is appreciated. Now, let's go feast on the Word."

※

John sat and waited as the worship ended. A man of average height and intense personality climbed up the stage with a slight limp. "Is this the pastor?" John leaned in and asked Stephanie.

"He is." Keeping her voice low, she nodded. "And don't let the slow walk fool you. The guy's got fire in his bones. He used to be a dangerous man hunted by the law. Then Jesus arrested him in prison and saved his soul. When he came out, he started this church. Listen."

John straightened, and his heart loosened toward the man facing them now. Hearing the man had been in captivity created a connection. From his own captive experience, John could relate. The man may have a word or two that he could benefit from.

"Good evening, everyone, and welcome to church." The

pastor greeted as he lifted his eyes to meet theirs—intense eyes indeed. John gulped, wondering how far those debts went and how far Jesus had to go to draw him back.

"What you are going through is not about you." He flipped through his Bible. "Repeat it after me. What you are going through or went through or will go through is not about you."

His interest piqued, he repeated the words.

"I want to share a message titled 'The Great Set-up.'"

Beside him, Stephanie opened her notepad and wrote. She took her cellphone out and opened to the Bible App. Then she handed him her Bible. "I noticed yours was worn out. A little homecoming gift for you. I love you." Her smile took the gift deeper into his heart.

"Thank you so much, Steph Bear." John blinked as his eyes grew wet. His Bible was his most treasured possession, but he did need a new one. And having Stephanie realize that need and provide for it without his asking melted his heart—and proved she had truly become dedicated to the things of God.

"'The Great Set-up,'" the pastor repeated, then walked down from the podium and sat down on the first step. He scanned the church from one side to the other. "You know, I've been through a lot of things in my life. I thought, all that time, it was about me. Why did this happen to *me*? Why did *I* go through the things I went through? Why did *I* go to prison? Why did *I* kill and steal and commit all the wicked things I did? Why have people thrown more stones at me after I received Jesus, got saved, and began serving Jesus than they did when I was in the world?" He turned toward a lady at the front. "Why did Patricia go through the pain of losing her son before we met? Why did you go through the pain, the loss, the suffering, the death in the family, the drug addiction, the physical wounds, the emotional wounds, the painful separation, the ugly divorce, the break-up that broke you down?" He rose and walked back to the podium.

"Last time I shared the Word here, weeks ago, we had a powerful message ordained by the Lord. But what you didn't know was that that same day, my wife and I lost our three-month-old pregnancy. The same day."

Murmurs of compassion waved through the church.

"In spite of our pain, she insisted that I come here and share that message. In fact, while I was preaching, she walked into the church. We were in pain. We were mourning. We should've stayed home. Mourned our loss in privacy. But being the woman of God she was before I met her, she once again stepped past her pain and took me to this pulpit and pushed that given Word out of my mouth into your heart. Why?" He waved toward her. "She'd done it before. She'd stepped past her pain of losing her son to allow herself to love me even when her healing was not complete. She chose God's will to save and rescue a man in need like me, over her own comfort. She understood the Great Set-up."

Applause lit up the church.

"Steph, can I have a piece of paper and a pen? I want to take notes." John scooted forward in his seat, eating like a starved man. Every word coming out of this pastor's mouth was sweet, like honey dripping out of a bee's hive.

She smiled, dug through her purse, and handed him the items, then focused on the message again.

"Open your Bibles to Philippians 4 verse 6. Someone read for us."

Stephanie stood and accepted a microphone. "'Do not be anxious for anything. But in all things, by prayer and supplica tion with thanksgiving, present your requests to God.'" She sat back down.

"The greatest root of unbelief, skipping out on God, is anxiety." Needing no microphone, but still using a hand-free one, Pastor Pete's vibrant voice thrummed from one end of the church to the other. "If I trust God and do the right thing, will my family still be provided for? If I trust God and do not sleep with my boyfriend, will anyone still love me or will I still look cool? If I don't do drugs, will the other kids in school bully me? If I don't have an abortion, what will people think of me? If I steal only a little, will anyone notice? If I go with God and the world hates me, will I still succeed in life even when it doesn't seem apparent? When I refuse to sleep with someone I'm not married to and I lose my friends, who will be there for me if I need help? On, and on, and on. These are the roots of the choices we make. And little by little, we stray from His will to please the world. But from going the wrong way most of my life and being in the path now, it has become clear to me that my entire life, all of it—the good, the bad, the ugly, the despicable can't-tell-anyone-about-it stuff, the rolled-in-the-mud-of-sin-and-can't-get-up stuff—is all a set-up. A set-up for what, you may ask?"

John's pen scratched the notepad.

"Isn't it funny how we never see what God is preparing until it's all done? Scripture tells us God prepares a table before me in the presence of my enemies. But while He's preparing the table—chopping up the onions of your life, frying those onions in hot oil, deep-roasting your pride in what seems like shame, pouring out your hope like wine to be served while you run on empty, serving a platter of your dreams with cheese and cream on it—none of that looks like a feast. It looks like a complete destruction. Your enemies are gathered because when God was chopping, dicing, deep-frying, baking, pouring out your life, they thought you were finished. It seemed like it was over. You were never going to make it. You weren't coming out of that situation. It was the end of you. They planned your funeral already, ordered the casket of your dreams, of your marriage, and of your career. They had gathered to celebrate your destruction."

The church went wild. Whistles, roars, wows, and cheers followed.

"What they didn't understand is this—God is the Almighty. He doesn't like uniformity. He likes diversity. Look at man. He created us and made us of every race imaginable. Look around you in this church. It's likely that the person sitting next to you has a different race, language, ethnicity, and national origin from you. They are different. They look different. They speak different. God likes it way. And so do I."

Another round of applause followed, and this time, John joined in. No doubt about it—he'd found a new church home.

"Never laugh at a child of God who is down. Never. Because, when you think it's over for them, their God, the Lord Jesus Christ, Who spoke the world into being, can speak a Word, to reverse their situation beyond your wildest imagination."

Some jumped to their feet and applauded.

"That is why I'm standing before you today, a saved man and a converted soul." He placed a hand on his chest. "I'm not better than any one of you. I'm a child of God, saved by the love of Jesus, washed by His cleansing blood from my numerous sins which the world loves to remind me of."

He stepped one level down. "Every time they remind me of who *I* was, that reminds me of what *He* did. Every time they throw my old sins in my face, I throw the grace of God to meet it up in the air. Every time they cast doubt on my conversion, I affirm the Word God spoke to me and deepen my faith in Him. So, the accusations, the doubts of man, the names I get called are ugly—just like those ingredients God is using to prepare a table before you in front of your enemies today look nothing like what you would call good—but if you keep holding onto your trust in Jesus, those ugly ingredients will work together to become a table of God's display of His mighty power in your life in ways you can never imagine."

Applause shook the place so hard this time it was tough to know the church was barely a quarter-full to capacity. John was applauding too.

"I stand before you to declare—with utmost confidence—everything that has happened in your life, every single one of them, is a piece of The Great Set-up God is putting together to fulfill His purpose that is yet to come. Don't quit on Jesus while He's dicing the onions or while He's frying it or when He's deep-frying the chicken you'd placed your hopes on or while He's pouring out the wine from your life and you feel empty. Please know this—from a man who has seen the other side of the moon you are yet to see—it is a great set-up for God's glory and will do you good at the end. This won't end in shame. It won't end in dishonor. It will end in praise, like all the Great Set-ups God constructed in the past. David, Daniel, Esther, Jesus—none lost because they made a choice, and this is where you come in, they made a determined choice never to give up their faith in God. Hold on to your faith in Jesus, not in a limping I-got-to-hold-on-till-Friday manner, but with full, total, unshakeable confidence that He is God. I can trust Him. His purpose is greater. I will win because I already won through Christ."

Another round of applause ruptured the sanctuary.

"And most importantly, this is not about you. Your testimony after you see the entire set table turn into a feast will serve to bring glory to God and will draw others into placing their faith in Jesus. See, we end where we started this message. God doesn't prepare a table before you for you alone. You can only eat so much." Laughter echoed through the church. "The feast is too big for you alone. But you will invite others to enjoy the feast with you. That is God's purpose. Shine the light so all will see the goodness of God in your life and thank God today while you still hurt, while you can't understand or see where things in your life are going, thank God for the Great Set-up. Thank Him that His purpose is being birthed through you. And praise Him for the grace to stand when the heat of the oil gets too much for you to bear. Who wants to join me to call on Jesus today? Who wants to go ahead and give Jesus glory for the Great Set-up in their lives? Who wants to worship before the throne of God with me? Are you excited that your pain, loss, and difficulty are part of God's Great Set-up in humanity for His purpose? Think bigger, and thank God. If you are in agreement with me, please join me here at the altar and let us thank God and cry out to Him for more grace to endure, more faith to stand, and for the victorious finish we will experience when the Great Set-up is completed."

Everyone thronged forward—including John, Stephanie, Ahmed, and Tim. John briefly glanced to his left, pleasantly surprised to see Tim go to the altar to pray, but he was busy praying for himself long before his knees hit the red carpet there. He thanked God that his captivity had led him to help save Ahmed's life, who now might become someone important to his sister, Stephanie, if all indications were right. He thanked

God that he was now helping law enforcement rescue hundreds of girls who were victims of human trafficking. He thanked God that he'd grown in his faith to a place where he was fully surrendered to whatever purpose God had for his life. John poured out his heart to God, and as the pastor led them in prayer, he yielded even more of his will to God. He worshiped as the worship team took over from the pastor and led them into worshiping God with all of their hearts. His heart was full as they returned to their seats and said the final prayers to end the Bible study.

Tim approached him. "Hey, John. I'm going for a meeting with the pastor. I think Stephanie and Ahmed are going to the church office to apply for jobs. You can come with me or stick with them or hang back here if you'd like to pray more. I know you haven't been to church in, like, twenty years so you've got to be hungry."

John's face hurt as his smile stretched from ear to ear. "Oh yes. Today's Bible study was such a feast. I'd say the Lord prepared this table for me. I want to go with Steph and Ahmed to the church's office to order some of the pastor's older messages."

Tim patted his shoulder. "I'm glad to hear that. He is most unusual, but he's God's choice for this generation and captured half my family, so I'd stick close to this place to visit."

John winked. "Yes, I'll be attending this church, as you didn't ask."

No strain lingered in Tim's slight responding smile. "I figured as much. And your brother and son-in-the-Lord, Ahmed, looks like he will be returning with you. So I've got you, Ahmed, and Stephanie attending this church now. Goodness, I'm going to have some serious words with Pete about how good his messages should remain since he's feeding people I love."

Laughter jumped free from John's throat. "I'm pretty sure he's heard that a lot. Maybe go easy on the man and don't be one of those throwing stones at him. He'll—"

"Make a feast with it," Tim completed, and his eyes crinkled up at the corners. "See you later."

"You too." John navigated toward where the church office was signaled to be, turned left, and met up with Stephanie and Ahmed seated in two kiosks, completing their online applications. He pulled out a seat and began reading up on the Church Facts flyers stuck in a holder, to see how he could integrate and be a part of his new church home.

31

"And he shall be like the light of the morning when the sun rises, a morning without clouds..." 2 Samuel 23:4

Tim entered Pastor Pete Zendel's expansive office and took the offered seat. "Thanks for inviting me. I know it was to discuss what I know about your family's history, but I enjoyed the message you preached."

Pete's eyebrows curved upward. Then a slow smile spread across his lips. "I'm happy to hear that. It's different from how you sounded the last time we talked."

"A lot has changed between the time you and I talked and now. My sister-in-law, brother-in-law, and adopted brother-in-law just decided to become members of your church. So, I now have a stake here. They're my family."

Still smiling, Pete rounded his desk and put his Bible down

on it. "And you want to make sure I take care of them. I will, by God's grace."

"Good." Tim exhaled. "Now, what questions do you have for me?"

Pete's expression changed so fast that Tim blinked. He became businesslike with a firm jaw and stern eyes, almost like the man he used to be, though a softness in his features remained that wasn't there before. "A security breach violated our systems here a couple of weeks ago. We thought it was system-wide but localized it to my own computer. The SSPD intervened and extracted a message designed to look like malware. The message was two questions to me personally. 'Do you know your last name, Pete? Do you know who you really are?' Since then, we've been trying to decode its meaning. I haven't been able to uncover anything. However, I'd hoped that, due to your closeness with Violet, you may know a thing or two that I don't."

Tim bowed his head and prayed for wisdom. He'd made Violet a promise—a promise he'd be breaking now due to the conviction he'd received while the message was going on. A conviction that Pete had really been saved and was now a child of God. He knew it in his spirit.

"Listen, let's make something clear first. I made Violet a promise before she died never to divulge any of what I'm about to tell you. We thought you'd stay the way you were. But, thank God, you're truly saved. I'm only revealing this now because you could be in danger. The hunter is coming."

A frown crinkled Pete's forehead. "Sorry, I don't understand. What is the hunter? And why would he be coming after me?"

Of course, he wouldn't understand. "When Vi was alive, you, she and I went on vacation in Mexico."

"I remember."

"Good. Now, after that vacation, I accepted to join a program with an institution there. In the process, I helped Vi seek out the symbolism of the poem she recited during your dad's funeral. The same poem which triggered mysterious phone calls. A student in my class recognized the poem, and I learned a bit more about it."

"I didn't hear her recite it. Maybe I missed that part." Pete curled his arms and leaned back. "Interesting. That poem about the king and hunter has been in my family for a long time. Our dad liked it and had us memorize it when we were young, but I never thought anything of it. Seemed it was just something fun he was fond of." He rocked his chair slightly, seemingly pensive with past memories. "Is there more to it than meets the eye? Does it have anything to do with my history?"

When Tim didn't immediately answer, Pete drew in a shuddering breath and scratched his jaw. "Sorry for piling on the questions. I should know this stuff since it's my history."

Tim gave his first smile. "Yes, you should. If you were an archeologist. But the last time I checked, you're not into digging up old stuff. I'm the one who does. That's why you originally called me."

Pete laughed, and the sound came funny to Tim's ears. He'd never heard Pete laugh. He'd seen him angry but never happy until now. This was a different man indeed. Christ Jesus had transformed this man into something new and profound. "Well, you can say that again. But how did the poem come to be? And what did it have to do with our family? Zendel doesn't sound like the name of a king to me. At least, nothing I've read in history books suggests so."

"You're right. But...what if Zendel is an assumed name?

Why would someone ask if you knew your last name if it was evident? It means Zendel isn't truly your last name. And it suggests somebody chose to change your last name in your lineage to protect something they didn't want the wrong people to find."

"Like what?"

Tim shrugged. "I'm not sure. But, if a random poem can trigger a phone chase and even after twenty-something years, if someone is still picking at that bone like a dog, then maybe you need to uncover something and protect it. It's a choice you're going to have to make."

"But I'm happy. I have a loving wife, an amazing church and ministry, and a good circle of close friends. I don't want anything to disrupt that. Anything from the past is the past. I'm a Zendel, and I don't think I'm ever changing my name to anything else, even if somewhere in my lineage something changed. That name is fine, even if it just isn't mine."

"You can change one's name, but you can't wash away the identity it stands for. You need to discover who you really are, your true identity. If you don't, someone somewhere will stumble onto something in the future, maybe after you're gone. And if you don't teach this poem to your children, they might never even know if danger was around the corner." Tim braced his elbows on the desk between them and steepled his fingers before his lips. "I don't like disrupting peace either. But peace without a settled mind or where you know danger is lurking is an illusion. Fight this and let the dust over it settle so your future generations won't have to. Whatever you choose, I'll support it."

Pete bowed his head, and Tim assumed he was praying. He waited until Pete finished. When the man raised his head, Tim didn't need to ask. The zeal for protecting his family burned in his eyes. "I choose to find out what was, in order to protect what is. Tell me everything you know. And I'll chase these rats back to their hole."

Tim leaned forward and spilled everything he'd discovered—both before Violet died and after. When he was done, Pete eyed him steadily and nodded.

"Good. You and me and Patricia and Angel will head to the cabin next weekend. I'll find that clue to the secret location somewhere there. Then we'll set out. Pray with me that God will lead us to the information we need and fast too."

"I will. See you next weekend then."

Tim rose, returned to his waiting family, then climbed into his truck, drove behind them, and prayed for Pete on the ride.

∼

Stephanie was chatting with John when Ahmed answered his phone. "Hello?" They'd just left the church office. Pumped about the message, she was already thinking about how to integrate it into her life.

"Yes?" Ahmed's voice carried a hint of anxiety. "I just completed an application."

She exchanged glances with John, and they stopped talking. Both listened as, apparently, Ahmed was being interviewed for a church position less than thirty minutes after hitting Submit on his application.

"I'd like to join your team as an interpreter. I'm excited to meet the immigrant community in Ohio. I'll love working with them."

She exchanged glances with John again.

"One question," Ahmed asked, "when does the position start and how long does it last?"

She held her breath. She liked Ahmed and, although she'd been pushing him away, she'd started warming up to his advances. If he was going away, she wouldn't be too happy. First of all, she liked him even just as a friend.

"Two years sounds great. I need to inform my family. And we'll get back to you. Thank you for the handsome salary offer. I must say it's comparable to what I was being paid at the hospital, and I wasn't expecting a good pay from a church position."

She waited until he wrapped up the call. "They hired you?"

Ahmed's grin spread as wide as from Texas to Washington DC. "Believe it or not, yes. First, it's an interpreter's job for an immigrant Iraqi Christian community annexed to the church. But there's much more. A hospital there needs an Arabic-speaking doctor to work with them so they can treat those patients who can't speak English. They need someone soon so the children's church pastor whom I just interviewed with, who is also a police officer, says she intends to send my resume to them. So, the pay she offered me was a combination of the work I'll do with Living Faith Bible Church and with the hospital. In addition, the hospital in Arizona has cleared me of wrongdoing. So I can keep working as a doctor in this new position, thank God."

Stephanie was quiet. Then after a while, she said, "Congratulations."

Ahmed's frown darkened the rearview mirror. "You don't seem excited."

Her shoulders sloped as she fiddled with the air vent before her. Too bad, he was so astute. "No, to be honest, I have mixed feelings. I can't pretend to either of you so let me just spill it."

She exhaled and prayed they'd understand. "I am very happy for you, for the job and I prayed for a new job for you."

"Then, what's the matter, Steph?" John crossed his arms in the passenger seat.

"Well, I had hoped it would be something around here. I like having you around."

Ahmed laughed. "You played hard-to-get so I accepted the offer thinking it would make you even relieved. Do you like me enough to take a step of faith of closer friendship that could end in marriage, if it's God's will? I want nothing short of that."

Stephanie gulped. This was a long step of faith whose legs stretched from her fear into a faith she was praying she could handle. "Yes. But I want it to go slow, real slow. As in a couple of years slow."

John's laughter caught them up until Stephanie's and Ahmed's joined his, rippling warmth and promise for the future through the car.

"Thank God. I prayed hard for you both in church, now, for God to give us clarity. It's quite awkward to be flanked by two people who have the hots for each other and are too scared to be hurt to admit it. I'm so free right now." John winked, earning him punches from both Stephanie and Ahmed.

"I want to take things slow too. I want these two years so I can grow in my faith. Maybe the Lord is physically separating me from you because you're too lovely not to be a distraction to me. You live in my heart, but maybe my eyes need to be focused on Jesus now. I have a lot to learn, and I wish to focus and learn as much as I can about this Jesus Who would allow a man to enter captivity just to save my life. I want to discover why He made me. Why I'm here. I want to fulfill divine purpose. So, that is where my focus will be. Until the right time, when He wants you and me to be together. Then," Ahmed scrutinized Stephanie then John, "with our family's support, we can take the step of a long-term union together. Agreed?"

The tension, fear from her painful past relationships, and anxiety about her future ebbed away. God saw what she needed and sent him from afar. She was starting over. She still needed to change a lot in her heart to prevent this from becoming like her past toxic relationships. But while Ahmed was away, she'd allow God to work in her. "Absolutely yes. I agree. We each need to find our roots in Christ Jesus before intertwining it with our own. I need to let God work on me, on my character, and my value system while you are away. I won't be idly waiting. I'll find a job, settle into a career, and make myself useful in the Lord's hands. And, even if when you return things change, I won't harbor any ill will. I'll know God's got my life and future in His hands."

Ahmed growled. "No way. There is no man who is taking this beauty from me. He hasn't been born yet. And by the time he's born, we'll be too old for anyone to care." As John chuckled, Ahmed's eyes peered at her in the rearview mirror, his expression solemn, a promise in his eyes. "But seriously, Steph, my mind was made up the moment I set my eyes on you. I knew you were the one. My only one. And I know where my treasure is, and I'll come back for it—for you."

John cleared his throat. "While all this loving is going on, let me confess I wasn't excited for the job for a different reason."

They glanced at him.

"I wanted you here. I wished for you, my brother and friend, to stick close to me, just like Stephanie did. But I accept God's will because I'm certain this is His plan for your life. So, while I pout at God, but also thank Him for making a way for you, I'll say I'm happy you got the job. But most importantly, I'm glad you got it in a place where you'll be surrounded by people who know Jesus and can help you grow spiritually. Your heart is set in the right place. Keep it there. And when you return, we'll see how you and Steph are doing."

At the frown crinkling Ahmed's face beneath his curly hair, John laughed.

"Fine, Ahmed. You've got my blessing—court my sister. But, bro, I'm watching."

Ahmed punched his arm, wearing a wide grin. "I'd be worried if you weren't. And thank you. Your blessing means a lot."

"Let's go home and break all of this news to the rest of the family. I'm sure they'll be thrilled to know all the miracles that happen at Bible studies these days," Stephanie said.

"Yes, they will," Ahmed concurred.

And, heart soaring, Stephanie could hardly contain her joy. God had restored her soul and added love to her banquet of peace. She was complete in Christ, content in Him, and excited to see what God would do for her and Ahmed in the years to come. She now lived without fear for her future.

32

"I know your works. See, I have set before you an open door, and no one can shut it..." Revelation 3:8

THAT WEEKEND, WHEN PETE AND PATRICIA ARRIVED AT THE cabin, along with Tim and Angel, memories swarmed him. Sweet memories assailed him right from when the large rented truck Tim suggested they come in, eased into the driveway and ceased grinding over the gravel. Except for the overgrown weeds and the worn paint, everything was intact.

"Since we won't be staying, I suggest we get started. There's only so much time before the sun sets, and I'm glad we arrived in the morning so we've got at least nine hours to rummage through the whole house."

"Let's get busy then. Tim stepped out of the driver's seat and shut the door.

"Angel and I will try to get to know each other better while we make lunch in the kitchen. Hopefully, the food we brought will satisfy us. If not, we'll cook."

"I'm sure the dishes and all the other stuff are still in the kitchen. I wouldn't use any of those spices as they are very old."

Patricia laughed. "Of course. Now, go."

Pete unlocked the door, led them inside, and sent up a prayer that whatever clue they needed would be found. Whoever sent him that correspondence didn't simply go through all that trouble out of curiosity. Something else had to be at stake.

"Where should we start?" Tim stood in the center of the dust-covered furniture. "It will take longer than a few days to get through all this stuff. So, I'd suggest we start where you likely suspect protected information would be."

Pete scratched his chin and thought aloud. "If I were my parents, I wouldn't leave something important in the living room."

"Nor in the kitchen or dining area," Tim added.

"Nor in the guest bedroom." Pete stopped to touch the rocking chair before the fireplace, thinking of their last Christmas here as a family and his dad sitting there. "We could start in their bedroom."

"Or in the room of the person they would most trust if something were to happen to them and someone came looking for information they'd rather that no one found."

They stared at each other and said simultaneously, "Violet."

Pete led the way up wooden steps that creaked with age. "She spent most of her time in the reading nook, not in her room. Let's go there first."

When they reached it, he stooped under the pirate lantern, which dangled at his move, and the wooden sword she'd used as her coat hanger and smiled. Something hurt his throat. "She loved it here. It was her favorite place, next to the beach."

"She was a reader." Tim surveyed the nook. "And I see she had good taste."

Pete chuckled and nodded. "She did. And she was smart as a whip. I'm so proud of who she was." He was finally seeing what his wife had said about celebrating her life. He saw imprints of the excellent life she lived. "I miss her—her smile, her love, her heart. She was a great example of who a Christian should be."

"Me too, Pete. I ache for all the conversations I wished to have with her and am unable to." He fixed his gaze on Pete. "I blamed you and hated you for taking her from me for a long time." From inside his shirt, he withdrew the locket she'd given him. The locket he hadn't removed, not one time. "But this reminds me of her every day. I know I'll see her again in heaven, but it feels like so long. In the meantime, I've got to keep missing her here. And I forgive you completely. I have no wish to hold a grudge anymore. It's exhausting."

Pete's eyes burned. He closed them and inhaled a fresh beginning. "That means a lot. Now, let's get searching before the ladies wonder why we're taking so long."

Together, they lifted the bed and searched the corners. They took the pillows, cases, closet, and everything covered apart. After a half hour, Pete scratched at his hair. Debris filtered loose. Dust covered him, and the mask he'd put over his face did little to protect him. He'd sneezed enough times to make him sure he'd come down with a cold after this.

"Why don't I check our parents' bedroom while you check here? It's only the books left to check here."

Tim nodded beyond his own shielded mouth. "Sounds good to me."

Pete walked over to their parents' bedroom. Violet had given their clothes away but kept the precious items. He uncovered the bed, searched beneath the pillows, and touched something firm. "Something is there."

He took out a note:

PETE,

If you ever come searching for answers, check the nook. See the book, Raised To Life. Follow the trail. Find the truth. And hide it for good.

Love,
Vi.

"HEY! I FOUND SOMETHING," HE ANNOUNCED, WHICH HAD TIM running over.

"Here." He handed Tim the note. After reading it, Tim turned it this way and that, examining the corners, edges, and the texture. Then he yanked down his facemask and smelled it.

"What is the problem?" Pete folded his arms, perplexed.

Tim glanced up. "Making sure the note is real. I'm roughly verifying the age of the note to make sure it's not planted here, and I think it's real."

"Nobody knows about this cabin except Vi and me."

"And me. She told me."

Pete sighed. "Right." Pete sighed. "You two were super close."

"We were. Let's check the book she mentioned."

They returned to the reading nook and searched until they found the book sandwiched in between a dictionary and an old Yellow Pages. "Here." Tim tugged it free and handed it to Pete. He leafed through it to a letter inside. Bringing out the envelope, he unsealed it and unfurled the letter. Something fell from it, and Tim picked it up. He read:

CHILDREN,

This is your dad. I'm not sure which of you will need to find this note. In fact, I hope neither of you do. I'd prayed and hoped to be the last person in our family to have to deal with this secret. If you are reading this, then someone from the Hunter's family is coming after you, and they won't stop until you're dead. Every one of you. They have one job—wipe out our lineage from the earth. If they find you, then the hunter will come after your children too. So, please do your best to protect them as well.

Zendel is not our last name. You might know this by now. But the journey begins in a town not far from here. Go to this bank xxxxxxxx, find this box xxxxxxxx. I put the key where you can easily access it, and I know Vi would keep it safe. Pete, you are not the most careful person I know.

Now, go in peace, and may the Lord, whom our fathers sought protection under His mighty hand, shield you from the hunter as He alone has done all these years.

I love you.

DAD. (AND MOM.) SHE SAYS NOT TO INCLUDE HER, BUT I WON'T listen.

And, oh, teach the poem to your children. At this point, you have no other choice.

PETE LET THE LETTER DROP FROM HIS HAND, BUT IT DIDN'T HIT the ground as Tim caught it.

His knees grew weak. "I guess I didn't know my family as well as I thought I did."

He turned to Tim, who was searching for something on his phone. "Tim?"

The man looked up, blinked. "Oh, I'm sorry for how you feel, but I was checking for the bank he mentioned. It's not like I don't care. I want to help you get to the bottom of this thing faster. Sorry if it didn't look that way."

Pete waved away his apology. "It's okay. I can process my feelings later." Patricia was always the best person to process his feelings with. "Where is the bank?"

"About seven miles from here. Not far at all."

"All right. I'll get the ladies so we can leave before they get into cooking up a feast."

Both men went downstairs and met Angel and Patricia at the base of the steps, smiling.

"Um, what's going on?" Pete kissed his wife, something he now did that was hard for him to adjust to when they'd married. She pointed to a large dish with a silver bowl covering it.

"Open it." Angel clasped her hands together and tapped her toes impatiently as she smiled. "Please."

Pete chanced a glance at Tim, who shrugged. "Can't help you, buddy. You better go open the plate."

So, Pete walked over, and inhaling long, he lifted the silver bowl and stared at the handwritten note. WE'RE PREGNANT!

The words took a moment to register. Then he gasped, spun to his wife, and lunged into her arms. He hugged her so tightly, while the other couple cheered and clapped. He managed to extricate himself from her long enough to wipe her teary cheeks. "We are?"

She beamed even as tears shimmered in her eyes. "Yes."

He felt his cheeks grow wet and assumed they were his own tears. Since he wasn't given to crying, he hadn't known when the tears leaked from his eyes. "Oh, thank You, my Lord Jesus. I'm so grateful to You for this second chance."

He felt arms around them, turned, and it was Angel and Tim hugging them. "Congratulations to you. We wish you a very safe pregnancy and delivery."

"Thank you." Patricia swiped at her own eyes.

They let each other go. "And what a time to find this out."

When Pete spun to him, Tim's voice sank low. "Yes, you have more to protect now. So much more."

"I do. And I'm willing to go the extra mile. Let's head to that bank. But, first, ladies, here's what we found." Pete gave them the letter, and they read it and all agreed on their next move.

They gathered up their lunch, piled back into the truck, and headed to the indicated bank.

Thankfully, it was still open. So Pete led them inside. After identifying himself, he was allowed access to the safety deposit box. Then he realized he didn't have the key, so he came back out. "Um, I found the box. But I don't have the key."

Tim looked at him. "I do." He uncorked the locket, removed a key, and passed it to Pete. "When you went inside, I remembered this key. I have strong convictions that this is the key you need. Go ahead and try it."

"Thanks." Pete returned to the safety deposit box room. It clicked and unlocked the box. He put his hands inside and extracted a number of contents. Some were shares his dad owned worth quite a sum of money. But then, he saw something drawn on a piece of paper and knew he'd found something precious. Taking all the contents out, he returned the box and closed it.

He thanked the bank official and rejoined the crew. "I found some things inside. They're quite interesting."

They headed to the truck. When Tim resumed driving into town, Pete explained everything, he'd found. "I saw some things personal to my dad, but they're not what we came here for. What we want is this."

He showed Patricia the document and she frowned. "Is that what I think it is? Geographical coordinates?"

He eased it back into his lap. "I believe it is."

"And that's where we find our answers."

"Angel, please use the Earth-Trot app in my phone, plug in those coordinates, and see where they lead."

Angel complied and showed them. "It's a lonely cabin in the woods up in the mountains in a town near Snowy Peaks. And they say the temperatures there are cold."

"Anyone up for mountain climbing?" Pete grinned. "I'm sure Patricia isn't coming because this will be the safest pregnancy in the history of pregnancies."

"No, I'm not mountain climbing any time soon. But you all can go. I'll support you from here."

"Great. I'll get my whole family to join us, and we should

have a great time. Anyone asks, we're going mountain climbing."

Pete smiled at Tim's wit. He'd always known the man to be smart, tactical, and protective of his loved ones. "Let the fun times begin."

33

"For You have been a shelter for me, a strong tower from the enemy."
Psalm 61:3

IT TOOK TWO WEEKS FOR THE WHOLE TEAM TO ARRIVE AT THE mountain base. They had a team of ten. Pete, Tim, Angel, John, Stephanie, Ahmed, Ladi, and Captain Bailey from the SSPD, Mike Argan, a former pilot, and a young tour guide who, during the course of their interaction, playfully nicknamed himself Ed Zendel when he learned Pete's wife was expecting.

"Usually, people don't hike at this time of the year as the mountains have snow almost all year-round even during summer and fall. So, expect very wintry conditions," the young man warned.

But the team was undeterred. Their resolve led them up even when they'd gotten tired and wished to quit. Only their desire to make it back to the base by nightfall kept them going. So they started their trek before the sun rose.

Right around sunrise, they breached the boundaries of the cabin.

"We should be able to reach the cabin soon. I already see the perch of it," Captain Bailey, who wasn't much of a climber but was hanging on, announced.

"Me too. I see it now. It does look like someone lives there. There's a truck out in front." Mike, former pilot to President Towers and a good friend to Pete, nodded toward it.

"Yes, people hike up here often. But whoever lives here wouldn't expect hikers at this time of year." The young tour guide moved a fallen bough aside. He bounced with unspent energy, being about the age of what Patricia's late son would be, and Pete's throat closed at the thought. However, he was equally grateful they were expecting a child again and couldn't wait to hold one of his own in his arms. He stiffened his spine—he *would* find answers, now that he had someone to protect.

After another half hour of climbing, they emerged in full view of the wintry cabin. Snow blanketed the ground but had melted off the trees, leaving lush mountain greenery surrounding them. It was postcard perfect. But he wouldn't live here. It was too cold for his liking. The young guide strode ahead of them, his legs likely more used to the trek. Pete resisted the urge to rub his knees. Hard not to admire the boy's youth—not that old age had brought his aches and pains.

"I'll go closer to see if anyone's home so we can announce ourselves." The guide grinned. "And maybe I'll introduce myself as your son. That should be fun." He whisked around before Pete could object and tell him the many reasons people close to Snowy Peaks might not like the name Zendel. The front door opened. This was Oakland, but it was near enough to Snowy Peaks that people here may recall his negative history with their neighbors.

Just then, a man emerged. "Who are you?" His tone held warning not welcome, and from the suspicious way he peered around the door, it seemed he disliked guests. Pete had seen the sign forbidding trespassing earlier, but they weren't trespassing. They were headed there.

"Ed," their guide replied.

Pete barely made out the next words as a pack of dogs whisked out, barking and rushing downhill toward them.

He grabbed the young man rooted in shock, swung him around, and used himself as a shield for the boy. His thick wool coat protected him as he curled into a ball. Yanking the bones they'd packed in his backpack, and some meat, he tossed it to the ground, and miraculously, the dogs pounced on the food.

"This way!" Captain Bailey led them to the cabin's rear, and they entered through the back from where the dogs had come.

He removed his gun and pointed it ahead. "Police! Don't move." He trained his weapon on the man who sat rocking in his chair.

The man spun, surprised. "You survived the dogs." His eyes narrowed on Pete and recognition sparked as rage reddened the man's face. "You, pig!"

He lurched at Pete, but Captain Bailey intercepted him. He restrained the angry man and slapped cuffs on him. Soon, another party of police officers arrived and entered through the back door.

"Police! Put your hands up in the air," they announced.

"This is getting interesting," their guide, still shocked by the dogs' attack, said with a quivering voice.

"Life is interesting." Pete faced the new arrivals. "Officers, we come here in peace. We only came for information about my father, nothing more."

A man stepped forward with gray hair, clutching the cuffs dangling from his belt. "Oh, really? Is that what you told them before you bought Snowy Peaks—a whole town—and nearly wiped them out? We're not fools out here in Oakland. We're smarter than they were."

Captain Bailey flashed his badge. "Sir, I am the captain of the Silver Stone police department, and I can vouch for this man. He is not the man he used to be. And he is telling you the truth. He means no harm."

"How do you know? You don't know what he did to the people at Snowy Peaks years ago."

"I know. I was there on the side of the law. I knew this man when he was a criminal, and I know him now. It's like night and day. Like I said, we're only here to verify information, and once we find what we want, we leave and never return. Can we please do so?"

Silence occupied the space.

"Fine. But one wrong move, and I'll toss you all out of here. Hurry up," the police officer warned.

"Sounds good to me," Captain Bailey announced. "Guys, lady, you heard the man. Let's hurry it up. We're not welcome here."

Pete approached the man who was restrained with cuffs. "Sir, if you own this house, I have questions for you. I need to know my father's last name. And all the clues point to this house. That's all the clues my dad left me. People might be in danger in the future if I don't uncover this information. Please, help me, even if you don't like me."

The man huffed. "Well, I don't know your father. I'm younger than you are."

"Is there a way you can find out? Is there a safe or something around here where information can be found?"

Silent, lips pursed, eyes narrowed, the man seemed to think for a while. "No. I've never seen a safe."

Growing frustrated, Pete drew closer to the man and struggled to keep his voice even. "Listen to me. Someone called the Hunter is coming, and I need to know who I am before he gets a hold of this information. So, please, if you have any information that can help me, please share it."

That had the man's eyebrows curving upward. "I have heard of the Hunter. My grandfather has something like a poem on the wall about the Hunter. Loosen my cuffs and come with me."

Pete exhaled and exchanged glances with Tim. They were getting somewhere. Captain Bailey undid the man's cuffs, and he led them to an attic. There, by the wall, was a painting similar to the one in Zendel's family cabin. But this one was much older and looked more original, like it was more than one hundred years old. "What's your name?" Pete asked the man.

"Malcolm."

"Thank you for showing us this, Malcolm. Let's examine it. Tim, do you mind helping us since archeology is your thing?"

Tim moved in close and took some pictures of the image. "Of course. I'm thrilled."

While Tim assessed the image, Captain Bailey called the SSPD.

"Pete, do you mind verifying that this is the same poem you and Violet had? It looks the same to me, but I don't have the words memorized. I want to be sure we're looking at the right thing."

Pete drew closer and began to read:

Long may you live, O King!

Escape the Hunter when he comes

His heart is dark, his dagger is cloaked, and his finger is cut

He comes for Kings

And none see him coming

Escape the Hunter every way you can

For the King is favored by God to live

Shield the crown and protect the royal treasury

Live among the orchards, vineyards, and garden of roses and blossom

Fresh as the air, sweet as the berries, and refreshing as the rain

Long may you live, O King!

"Yes, it reads like…wait a minute." He frowned. "There's a statement here that isn't in the one Dad taught us." He pointed to it. "That line, 'Shield the crown and protect the royal treasury,' isn't in our version."

Tim's shoulder loosened. "Good catch. I noticed, too, but I waited for you to say it so I could be sure. Your dad is a smart man. Only someone willing to come this far needs to know that much."

"Is it then possible that the hunter is after the crown and the royal treasury? If there's such, it could be worth a whole lot of money today," Angel said.

"I agree," Captain Bailey concurred. "This could be as much of a witch-hunt as it is a treasury-hunt. We have to tread carefully from now on."

"True. But I have enough money to last my family several generations."

Captain Bailey slapped him on the back. "Man, you have no idea what wealth is until someone tells you what old money is valued at today. I know you're not crazy about money, but someone out there, the Hunter perhaps, is after it. Remember, they are assigned to wipe out your family's generations. So, you find the crown and the royal treasury, and you protect it. Then, you find the hunter or his descendants, and we'll figure out what you'll do. No exacting revenge." He shot Pete a sharp look.

"I won't kill ever again, Hunter or not. He may be responsible for his death at the hands of the law. But I will follow your advice and find the crown and royal treasury." Pete rubbed his jaw. "Does it bother anyone that this may actually be saying ... I'm the son of a king?"

"Well, Patricia would love for your child to know you are the son of the King of kings. Of that I'm sure." Mike settled a hand on his arm. "I know what you're afraid of. That, if you find out your lineage is a powerful one, you might revert to the man you used to be."

Pete gulped but said nothing for a moment. "Mike, power is my greatest weakness. I know how to handle it too well. I'm not eager to return to a place where I'm not a servant."

"You pastor a church of tens of thousands who troop in to hear you every week." Ladi squeezed his arm. "Yes, Pastor Pete, you are still a powerful man. Powerful for the kingdom of God. Now, whatever power God wants to add to what you already have is for a purpose. Find out the purpose, as you find out the power. And use the power for God's intended purpose. The man I'm looking at has enough prayers going up on his behalf to heaven to never go back to the man he used to be. I can guarantee you that. Now, let's take this art down and see the back."

Pete exhaled long, touched by Ladi's words. Relief pulsed through him. Having someone see in him the potential to stay on the straight and narrow path made him resolve to remain faithful despite whatever he uncovered.

Captain Bailey, Tim, and John joined to take the image down. When they turned the back, a form slid downward in the frame, and Pete took it out. Then he read the sheet. "My goodness."

He swallowed and sank to the ground, still holding the

paper. "Immigration documents from Mexico. From what must be my grandfather. King Peralta III. Grandson of the king of Lanzarote." Then he removed a second form. "A change of name filing by my dad when he was thirty. Changed his last name from Peralta to Zendel." He looked up, and Tim held him from passing out. "My last name is Peralta. Fourth grandson of King Peralta of Lanzarote."

"Peralta V," Tim said quietly. "You are nobility, Pete."

"Like we didn't know," Ladi said, and John beamed.

"Kings are born not made. You've led in authority long before you knew details about your bloodline."

"There is a king in all of us. His name is Jesus. I may have royalty in my bloodline, but today, I'm no different from any of you."

"Wait." Tim extracted a sealed document from the frame. "I believe there's more in here."

Someone cleared his throat loudly. "Since you found what you came here for, I think it's time for you to go. I'm not sure the mayor can explain to the people why you're still within our boundaries. You're considered an enemy here. Even if you've changed."

The message he'd shared, about not allowing the way the world holds your past against you to offend you once you understand the Great Set-up, spoke to Pete now. So instead of being offended, he smiled. "I'm grateful you allowed us in. We'll leave shortly."

Leaving the cabin, they carried everything they'd found with them and locked it inside a protective case they'd brought, then began their descent down the mountain and toward whatever reason the Hunter had for shaking this history loose from the past.

EPILOGUE

A FEW YEARS LATER...

Former First Lady of the United States Ruby Towers leaned over the clothing rail in her expansive yard. "Hey, Emerald Eyes, don't just sit there on that porch and watch me. Come, let's hang these dresses to dry out. And you better quit your current action or your granddaughter is going to be purging by this time tomorrow. You keep handing her all sorts of candies."

His laughter, equaled the joy brimming in her heart as he winced and rose, and expressly told their granddaughter, Faith Bailey, to relax with her plate of assorted candy, as she listened on her mobile device to a live worship concert somewhere in the continental US while he strolled over.

Hand in his pocket and strands of gray hair streaking his forehead, he looked only a little different from the little boy who'd become her best friend, then husband, and then President within a few decades.

His Secret Service detail trailed at a leisurely pace, and she wouldn't blame them. "When you have grown children, your job as grandpa is very simple. It rotates between candy bowls and singing rhymes," Robert defended.

Pretending as though she hadn't heard him, Ruby clipped another dress on the line as the evening sky glowed a deep orange. Swiping a bead of sweat with her elbow, she thanked God that she got a chance to live her dream.

A long time ago, while held in bondage by an evil Pete Zendel, she had wanted—no, strongly wished for—a country home where she could spread clothing outside on a farm with Robert and not have a care in the world. Here she was living a long-held dream that had appeared impossible.

And, soon after their daughter, Ritz, nicknamed Sunshine, married, and Ruby and Robert finished his term in office, they bought this farm and moved down South. Welcomed with open arms by their new neighbors, who brought cookies and confectionaries enough to feed a small town—all of which she'd donated to the closest homeless shelter and orphanage, anonymously—she and Robert had settled in to a quiet countryside life while Ritz and her husband, Jaden, pursued their dreams and traveled for missionary work abroad in their spare time. Their dangerous, first-time missionary trip with Pete Zendel hadn't killed the bug both caught for missionary work. And they had remained volunteers after their wedding.

In fact, both of them had just left for Addis Ababa in Ethiopia and dropped off their five-year-old daughter with her and Robert—with strict instructions for her dad not to feed Faith too much candy. Ruby had caught the mischievous wink between Robert and Faith and chuckled, knowing that as soon as the parents disappeared, the pair would set themselves up with sweet-toothed temptations to leave her chasing Faith around once the sugar-high kicked in.

Even now, a small smile creased her lips at the memories flooding her. Robert had changed after Faith was born. She thought she knew a soft side of him that was only hers to explore.

Apparently, he got even softer where Faith was concerned. Love for his granddaughter burned almost as hot in his heart as his love for her. He had assigned paid security, who watched Faith from a distance as she was taken to and from school daily —without her parents' knowledge. Ritz and Jaden wanted Faith to live like everyone else. But for Ruby, knowing Robert was protecting their grandchild also comforted her.

He was a good man, a loving husband, and a doting grandpa, and one because of whom she was not afraid about how the rest of their lives would go.

"Red, you know I love Faith almost as much as I love you." He leaned close to her, and she caught a whiff of his aftershave —signaling he'd done a few miles on their treadmill and showered afresh—and her smile grew. Living in the country didn't take away their sense of sophistication at all. "Almost, but not quite." A long kiss sealed his promise, and by the end, she was caught breathless.

Ruby shook her head. "We're old, and you can still get my heart beating wildly? Maybe I need to go on some missionary trip abroad too."

He laughed and released her, taking the next little one's dress from the bucket and spreading it out. "Like you could just leave without me? No way. Wherever you're going, we're going together."

"Well, for starters, we've got an invitation to travel with a church group. It's a group of new believers who would like to share their faith in hard-to-reach places."

"Could we go? I mean, when the kids return? It's an option."

She glanced at him and shrugged. "It doesn't hurt. Since you're no longer president, I don't see any reason why not."

"We're going to need to check with the kids to see whether they had any other trips planned before we accept anything."

"We could also join them with Pete's group. They go every year, have available security, and we know when." Their security whenever abroad was always a concern on Robert's mind since Ritz's attack.

Robert scratched the gray stubble on his chin. "Great idea. It will give us a chance to catch up with Pete. I miss my friend."

"And what an irony. One of your best friends was once your worst enemy."

He chuckled. "There's nothing Jesus cannot do, I tell you. No heart He can't change, honey. None."

An ache seized Ruby's chest. "I don't feel so good, Robert. Something..." Warmth spread through her arm, and she dropped the last article of clothing.

"Ruby. What's the matter?"

But a sudden belly churn had her knees sinking toward the grass. Robert caught her before she hit the ground. "Call an ambulance!" he yelled out to the Secret Service agent before she passed out.

"I HAVE AN IDEA." PETE STUDIED PATRICIA'S FACE.

"I'm all ears. These days, I no longer know whether to be excited or alarmed." Patricia offered him a disarming smile.

"Why would you be alarmed at my ideas? They wouldn't get you in trouble." Their eyes met. "For the most part."

Twin laughter lightened their mood. "Fine. I have to hear it first so, please, go ahead." She took her seat beside him, straightening her legs out in front of her as the heater blew warm air, filling the room. This winter had stretched longer than expected, and he wished they could have the same warm weather his friends, the Towers, were having in the South.

"I have begun receiving a message from the Lord that I'm excited about." He was pretty sure his eyes shone with excitement, a rarity. "I've prayed all day, every day, for the past week. And I think He wants me to make it a special, long series for the church."

"Exciting!" She kissed him as her eyes lit up. "Wait, was that why you were dictating something to your recorder when I went to use the gas station restroom on our way home last night? I thought it was odd since you hadn't whipped out that recorder stuff in a while." She curled an arm around his shoulder.

Pete nodded. "Exactly. And I look forward to exploring this message series further."

"What is the title? Can you share who or what it's about?" A slow shrug followed as her eyes dimmed. "If not, that's okay too. I'll pray for you and for the message regardless."

"I can share a little. It's from the series I started years ago about Joseph in the Bible. No, it's not like the typical sermons you've heard about him. This one goes deep. Much deeper. I know it was the Holy Spirit revealing them as I explored those passages. I feel like I got insight into deeply guarded secrets of God's wisdom."

"Sounds like Jesus unlocked a treasure chest for you." A smile warmed her face.

"Exactly. It's really an honor. And I can hardly wait to pray through and receive more so I can share."

Patricia placed a finger over his lip. "In that case, don't tell me any more yet. I want to hear the fully developed message. If it's as special as you say it is, I want the whole thing, not piecemeal." Then she let her hand drop, eyes aglow. "I usually love it when God deposits fresh-baked messages. To you, to me, or to any of the other pastors. It makes me know He hasn't forgotten us, even though I know that for a fact. Sometimes, it's good to feel that assurance in the Word too." She tilted her chin and shooed him. "Go. Explore the Word while I take care of the house. Please make this series a good one."

"Of course. As always." Pete felt his head bob. "My job is to yield, and God gives me the messages. Then I write them as they come." With that, he headed up to his study, bent on adding more to what he'd already received.

His cellphone rang as he walked away. He pulled it out of his pocket and answered on the second ring. "Hello?"

Silence met him at first. Followed by a voice he could recognize in his sleep. "Pete. It's Robert."

"Mr. President, good to hear your voice. It's been a while. How's Texas treating you and Ruby? Oh, and your daughter and her husband are fine. I get updates from the team every six hours." The man had never had cause to worry about his daughter's safety as one of Pete's missionaries, but maybe he felt a need to check on Ritz now? Pete cleared his throat when the man said nothing. "Is everything okay? I had assumed you called about Ritz."

"Sorry about the silence, Pete. I was simply..." His voice cracked as he trailed off. "I'm finding it hard to find the right words..."

In the hushed silence, Pete waited. He knew the man. Finding words had never been tough. As a politician, he could sling words like David slung stones. But something got his voice, and Pete wouldn't rush him.

Finally, he sighed. "Can you come to Texas with Mike and Charlie, please? I need you guys. I know you're busy, but—"

"Yes," Pete cut in. "I'll get the guys, and we should be there tomorrow."

"Thanks." Relief loosened President Towers' voice.

"Can I have a hint of what this is about, sir?"

A beat of silence trailed his question. "Yes." President Towers exhaled a long, heavy breath. "It's about Ruby." Another beat of silence followed. "She's been diagnosed with cancer."

Pete's heart turned to a leaden weight and sank deep against his spine. Of course, that would hit Towers hard. The man loved his wife without reservation. "I'm so sorry to hear that. Please know I will be praying, but the guys and I will be at your ranch tomorrow. In the meantime, trust God. See you soon." As soon as he hung up, Pete called Patricia back into the room. He told her the sad news, and she insisted that she was going with them.

"Ruby will need some feminine support too. If I can only be there to pray, it's worth something."

"Sure." Pete arranged with his administrative assistant to have his schedule cleared for three days to accommodate his travel and stay there. Thankfully, their candidates' graduation from the security institute wasn't until a few days' time, so he could ideally make it back in time. When everything was set, he dialed Charlie, then Mike. Both men were equally shocked and immediately confirmed their trip too. Soon, their wives also indicated they would join. Instead of three, they were a traveling party of seven, Robbie, the President's son, would join them as well. Having confirmed the trip, Pete was getting ready to begin packing.

Then the doorbell rang.

∽

HE STRODE TO THE DOOR, STILL REELING FROM THE NEWS ABOUT Ruby and imagining what a tough time his friends were having. "Yes?" Pete stared at his assistant who stood outside the door, waiting.

Arms crossed and slightly leaned on his thigh, the young man appeared flustered. "Sir...um...I mean." He fell silent as his gaze also lowered to the ground.

Pete opened the door wider and stepped aside. "Come on in." He forgot how intense his glances were when he was occupied or worried. "Sorry, something personal came up. In case I sounded distracted, I am."

"Sure." His assistant walked in with hesitant steps, then stopped at the entry to the living room.

"How can I help you? Is there a problem?" Pete hated how his morning, which had started so glowingly, could slide into a worrisome level quickly. But he trusted that God was in control and able to handle whatever life was lurching his way or his friends' way.

The man had still said nothing. He simply tapped his feet on the ground.

Pete grew impatient and slightly more concerned. This man was a sharp guy and usually got his words out but, just like the president, was now having issues. Maybe he needed a gentle prompt. "Listen, whatever it is, man, God can handle it even if I can't." Still, he said nothing. "Is it a personal matter?" This man wasn't the kind to share his personal issues easily, but it never hurt to ask.

"No. It's nothing personal." His gaze stayed lowered.

Pete then crossed his arms, sure his patience had reached its limit. "What then, Simon? You've been with me since you were a teenager, and nothing you tell me would surprise me, honestly. I knew your bad days, and though I never mentioned this before, I know they were very bad. Also, I did a thorough background check on you when I hired you, at your parents' request."

At that, he raised his head, and his left eyebrow perked up. "You did? I know Dad must've asked you to."

Pete didn't respond.

"Well, I'm not surprised. I just didn't think you'd tell me. And that it'd take you this long to share about it." He glanced away, then darted his gaze back to Pete. "That means you know about the...um..."

Pete paused. Then he nodded. "Yes."

"Oh. I could explain."

Pete touched his arm lightly. "There's no need to, Simon. You're not that person anymore. I know that. Why don't you tell me why you're here?"

"Okay." He smoothed his hair back into place. "But I need you to come with me to the office. That's where the stuff is."

The *stuff*? Pete shrugged. "Okay. As long as it's not an emergency."

"Not in that way."

"In that case, give me half an hour to shower and dress up. I'll meet you there."

With a quick nod and strangely avoiding eye contact, Simon left.

∼

RUBY LAY ON THE BED, COVERED UP TO HER CHEST WITH BLUE hospital sheets as Pete and the others walked in and flanked both sides of her. She smiled at him, and he drew close and hugged her lightly. "Good to see you, Madam First Lady." Pete had reverted to calling her by her official title rather than her first name. When she'd objected, he'd asked her to allow it since he'd treated her badly before.

Beside him, President Towers was seated with his head bent as though he'd been praying. He lifted his eyes. As soon as he saw Pete and the other men, he straightened, and light glowed in his intelligent eyes. "Guys," he hugged Pete and Mike and their wives who were not strangers to him and Ruby, "I'm so glad you're here." His gaze rested on every one of them, and for a moment, Pete was drawn back to the preparation process for his mission to Aqua. The same dogged determination in Sergeant Towers to ensure his safe return was clear in those emeralds right now. Except, right now, worry lined his brow.

Knowing the First Lady was the one directly facing the situation, he focused on her. Every one of them could deal with the news later. For now, keeping her spirits up was his goal.

So he leaned in and touched her arm. "How are you?"

A small smile dispelled some of his internal worry and lit her face. Sometimes, while counseling ill church members, it was hard to say whether someone was truly hopeful or not. "Well, I'm happy to see everyone. This feels like a mini-SSPD reunion." She turned her face toward her husband, offering him a reassuring glance, no doubt in an effort to reduce his concern. "I'm doing better."

Good. She wasn't putting on false attitudes.

His shoulders loosened as he gripped her bedrail, the metal cool beneath his touch, the solid object steadying him even while his mind yet reeled. "I'm glad to hear that. We're shoulders to lean on. To pray with. And to cry on. We're not too big to cry around one another, Madam First Lady."

"Call me Ruby, Pete. We're surrounded by inner-circle friends, and there are no outsiders here. You won't pay a penance for your wrongs forever when Robert and I already forgave you."

It sounded like Patricia talking. How come Ruby was repeating what Patricia urged him about? But how could he make them see it was easier to forgive others than to forgive yourself? He resisted the urge to glance in his wife's direction and catch an I-told-you-so look. Though that was unlikely. She loved him. "Okay, Ruby."

Smiling again, Ruby pointed at a seat. Good thing they arrived in time for visiting hours. The hospital was keeping Ruby until the test results came in so they could determine the extent of help she needed, or so President Towers relayed over the phone as they landed. "Please sit. I need a favor from you, Pastor Pete."

The men allowed their wives to settle into the scanty hospital chairs while they stood and some leaned against the wall. Pete lifted a brow. "Pastor Pete? What happened to just Pete? I thought we were doing away with titles around ... inner-circle friends."

The group burst out laughing before a quirky twist moved Ruby's lips. "We are. But I need this pastor's help in a way no one else can assist."

Pete grew curious. All these years, Ruby rarely, if ever, addressed him as a pastor even though she supported her family visiting his church.

"All right. I'm ready to help in any way you need me to."

She swallowed, sat up a bit, and glanced around the room. Her eyes were heavy, and her shoulders sank. But this vibrant light in her eyes couldn't be denied. "I have a confession to make."

Well, that wasn't what they were expecting.

Everyone fixed their gaze on her.

∽

Ruby clutched a fistful of the hospital sheets, and when her eyes met her husband's, a sigh slipped through. "I guess I couldn't keep this a secret forever." Her eyes moved to Pete, whose gaze had never left hers. "I've heard every message you preached in the past five years. Every single one."

"Wait, you came to our church, every Sunday?"

She shook her head. "No, Pete. I ordered a copy of your sermons from the church bookstore and had it delivered every week. I'm sure Lindsay would have put to bed by now. Last time I called in an order, she told me she was due soon and would be leaving the bookstore on maternity leave."

Pete's ears rang, but he managed to compose a response.

"Um, yes, she has delivered, actually yesterday. She gave birth to a beautiful son. Named him Isaac." But his mind was still reeling. "Wait, I'm still a little shocked you listened to my messages. I mean, once would've been an honor. Twice, and I'll throw a party. But every message for *years*? I don't know what to say." He massaged his chin, heart bubbling with gratitude. "Thank you. Thank you so much." His voice broke. "That means so much to me."

She patted his arm and smiled. "I loved every one of them. I just knew that, when a man has been this broken, much light can shine through."

He could hardly contain himself. "I'll frame that recommendation and put it on a wall."

"Could you please do me a favor? Can you share a summary of the latest message, since you're here in person? I'd wait for the tape, but due to ending up in here, I couldn't place the order for it."

The tightness in Pete's belly would make this one of the hardest times he ever shared a message. Speaking to his church was one thing. Sharing the Word with someone whom he considered a spiritual senior and a wise Christian counselor over the years was something else. "Sure." He gulped. "We revisited the famous passage about David and Goliath. I'll start by asking you the same question I'd asked the church on Sunday. What did David kill Goliath with?"

"A sling and a smooth stone." She glanced at Robert, who concurred.

"Yes, he used a sling and a stone." Consensus formed around the room.

But Pete shook his head. "Not really. Physically, yes, he felled Goliath with a sling and a smooth stone. But before the sling and the smooth stone, he already had victory. In other words, David killed him before he killed him."

A knowing smile formed on her lips. "Oh, I see."

"When David faced Goliath, the first thing he did was not to whip out a sling and a stone, because his confidence was not in them. They were mere tools. He could have flung his shoe, and it would have killed Goliath because he'd gotten the victory already. See, it didn't matter what weapon he chose—even though he chose what did the job quickly—but had David chosen physical combat with Goliath, after a bruise or two, he would still have won. But we would then give him the glory. We wouldn't accept that God did it, had David physically engaged Goliath. David had only one goal in his life, when you read through Scripture—to glorify God. Since he found himself at a great disadvantage, he twisted that into an opportunity for God to glorify himself."

"Interesting take," Mike said with a slow nod.

"So, what did David kill Goliath with?" President Towers asked as he settled to sit on the bed his wife lay on.

"To answer that question, I'll ask you all what the first thing David did when he faced Goliath was. Remember what he'd told King Saul. He said, your servant has killed the lion and the bear. He gave Saul the short version. But," Pete felt an unction of the Holy Spirit on him as he stood up from where he sat, "imagine a young David in the wilderness, alone, surrounded by the sheep of his parents' pasture. He was the first and last defense for those sheep. Remember David was not particularly loved by his father or brothers. Home wasn't convenient at all. So, when they send him into the pasture, he fully expects a verbal whipping should any of the sheep get lost. Then, here came a lion."

Pete spread out his arms. "It came in, scattered the sheep, which meant David would have to work hard to gather them together again, but that's a different issue. The most important thing, at this point, is that he remembers what would happen should he return home one sheep short. His brothers would pounce on him, and their father may deliver the ultimate bitter pill of disappointment. So, with those memories at the back of his young mind, he chooses that attacking a lion to get one sheep back was better than what could happen at home."

"Wow." Mike's wife sat up, her eyes brimming with excitement, the same kind Pete had seen in the eyes of his congregation on Sunday. Knowing how the Holy Spirit can always light up His Word whenever and wherever it was spoken always delighted him.

"Please, continue," Ruby urged as she sat up a little more, and Robert slid a pillow behind her back. "Thanks, honey."

With all eyes back on him, Pete continued, "So, he sees the lion disappear behind an imaginary thick grove. He didn't wait. He pursued the lion, and as he came face to face with the animal clutching his precious sheep between its teeth, he realizes how crazy an idea it was to confront a lion—alone and without a weapon. You know what? No one ever asked David what weapon he'd used to kill the lion and the bear. Most would assume he'd used a sword. But, remember, he could not use King Saul's armor because he'd said he 'wasn't used to these.'"

"Oh, wow." Now, President Towers applauded. "Oh, goodness. You are right." He whipped out his cell phone and scrolled through Scripture to confirm it.

While Robert checked, Pete continued, "He also didn't say how or with what weapon he killed the bear. He simply said he killed it. Now, for a young man who was a shepherd not a warrior, who was uncomfortable handling a sword and spear, who had never been in battle, and what could he do when standing face to face with a hungry lion—a fearless animal, highly tactical, and fierce, and much stronger than he was? What he did was to, first of all, realize the animal was greater than him. It was an enemy. It was stronger. It was more experienced in battle. All three of these things applied to the bear. But guess what?"

"What?" the group of friends chorused. Something about hearing the people he counted dear to him, appreciating what God was pouring forth from him, set his heart on fire for God.

Ruby reached out to take her husband's phone and was taking notes on it. So was Mike on his phone, and when Pete spun for a glance behind him, so was Charlie.

In that moment, he felt small in his own eyes and elevated by God in the eyes of these, all at the same time. He could never have planned his teachers would be taught by him. But he knew God could choose to use any vessel at any time. It was left for him to stay humble and remain just that—a vessel for His purpose. *Thank You, Jesus.*

"Those three things also applied to Goliath. Goliath was an enemy. He was stronger. He was more experienced in battle. And he had to be defeated. So what did David do?"

All eyes were pinned on him—as their note-taking fingers paused too.

"He used the same strategy he'd used to defeat the lion and the bear. First, desperation to save the sheep pushed him to confront a lion. He could not retreat. Either he defeated the lion, or it defeated him. One of them would die. So was his situation with Goliath. For both their nations, one of them had to die. But God had taught David a winning formula, which he readily applied beyond the back of the wilderness where he kept sheep. God needed a man whose confidence would never be in his tools or weapons. God needed a heart after him. So, David faced that lion, which was physically stronger than him, and he did what his father, Abraham did. What Isaac did. What Jacob did when faced with impossible circumstances."

He paused, allowing the importance of the moment to seep into their hearts.

"He called on the name of the Lord. He called on the name of the Lord, because it has power and he knew he couldn't kill the lion, but God could. He couldn't kill the bear, but the Lord could. He couldn't kill Goliath, but the Lord could. The name of the Lord was what David used to defeat Goliath before he ever lifted a sling and a stone. The name of the Lord. He said to Goliath, 'I come against you in the name of the Lord...' The same way, we can correctly assume, that was how he defeated the lion and the bear. The weapon wasn't important. Anything could become a physical weapon used for our victory. But we have to get the spiritual victory first, and then the physical will follow. Keep this in mind when facing a challenge—the weapon of victory does not matter as long as your first weapon utilized is the name of the Lord Jesus Christ. Therein lies your and my ultimate victory at all times. Our physical weapons are mere tools, just like I'm simply a vessel being used to share this Word. The real source of power for victory is the name of Jesus, for He is our Lord and Savior. Victory was and is certain in the name of the Lord. Always.

"When you face challenges? Seize the name of the Lord to overcome. Facing debt? Use the name of the Lord. Facing foreclosure? Use the name of the Lord. Facing disease? Use the name of the Lord. He made Himself a blank check for us. Everything else we do after that will be Him utilizing physical weapons to manifest our victory already secured in Christ."

Applause broke out again, and Pete wished they'd keep it less loud for the sake of others in case there were patients admitted into close-by rooms.

"Wow." Ruby's smile now was wider than before. "I needed that message. Lying here, fighting a cancerous enemy that I can't see and which is stronger than me, I needed to hear this, Pete. Thank you so much."

Compassion swirled Pete's heart, and he urged everyone to their feet, sensing the Presence of God in the room. They all gathered around the bed in a circle before he glanced at Ruby and her husband. "You have both been strong emotionally to handle this sad and difficult news. But from now, I want you to know that you are not alone. Each and every one of us will be with you in this fight. This enemy of cancer might be stronger than you. This may be a do-or-die circumstance. And cancer might have more experience with taking lives."

Faith climbed over fear in his heart and took root. "But one thing I'm sure of is that I know a power stronger than cancer. I know someone—Jesus—who carried away all of your diseases and bought your healing with His precious blood on the cross of Calvary. So, I call upon the name of the Lord Jesus Christ, God and Maker of the Universe to activate your healing in Jesus' mighty name!"

"Amen!" chorused around the room.

"We stand as children of the Most-High God and declare with the authority of Christ that you have won the fight. That you will not go down. That you will not only survive this, but your healing will inspire others to believe God for their own healing. I command this in the most powerful name of my Lord Jesus Christ, and it is done."

"Amen," they chorused again.

Still holding hands with Ruby's and her husband's joined to theirs, Patricia tugged at his hand. "Can we give God praise now for her healing? I believe God has answered."

Her smile sealed higher faith to his soul. "I believe it too. No matter how tough the journey to your healing, you simply keep confessing the Word of God's healing, and it shall come to pass."

"Amen," Ruby said as a tear dropped down her cheek.

Patricia led them in singing two songs of thanksgiving, and then they all placed their hands on Ruby and blessed her.

"We are here for you. If you need anything, our contact information will be on a sheet and will also be emailed so you have it in soft copy, in addition to the ones you already have."

Ruby was clearly struggling to keep her tears at bay as she struggled to get her words out. "Thank you all so much. This means a lot to me." She spun to Pete. "Especially the message. It's seared into my soul for good. God gave you that Word for me. I'm sure of it."

Pete choked out, "Me too. And there I was thinking it had been for those who had listened to it first."

As they readied to leave minutes later when the doctors came to attend to Ruby, he leaned close to her ear. "I want you to remember this, Ruby. In the same way the name of the Lord was with David and won for him, cancer does not have you. No, it doesn't. You belong to Jesus Christ—spirit, soul, and body— you hear me? You've already beaten this, both now and in the life to come."

"I know. But thanks for the reminder. I won't forget it."

A handshake with President Towers, and they all left for their hotel rooms to return to their various stations the following day. Pete made up his mind—he was never going to stop praying for Ruby until she won her fight against cancer.

∞

"He shaved."

An audible gasp drew Patricia Zendel away as she parted the curtains to let in daylight. "Is something wrong, dear?" she asked her daughter.

Peering, the girl looked at her dad and grinned. "No, Mom." Their daughter shook her head. "Something is right."

Patricia felt her head dip. "Why?" She had a lot to get done first before getting into a discussion with her girl who worshiped the ground her dad walked on. But she would oblige her for now.

Their daughter pointed at the man, genuinely oblivious to those analyzing him. "Check out the time. It's morning, which means he's happy. If he shaved at night, that's when I leave Dad to you."

Her mom chuckled. "And here was I thinking Pete is smart. Wait till he knows our daughter is smarter." She fully entered the room. "Hi, sweetheart." She kissed him. "How come you're all shaved? Is something going on? You've carried that beard for weeks."

She didn't miss the sparkle when he looked up.

He rubbed the smooth skin on his jaw. "I completed the new message series. The one I've waited on God for. It's finally done." A smile widened his lips. "Three years and four months' journey through three chapters of Scripture." He stood and kissed her back, curling a hand around her waist and drawing her closer. "Let's just say, the Holy Spirit delivered a goldmine of revelation through it, and it will take half a year's sermons for me to deliver all He's placed in my soul." He winked, and she laughed. "Thank you for your support. I love you, Pat."

She touched his face and agreed, yes, his jaw was smooth for a change. "I'm sure the church is ready to listen and absorb it." A slight pause followed. "And I like the clean shave. Please don't carry a beard for three years again, or I'll have to shave it off myself. Or I could call John. Tim said the man is now an expert with barbing."

Pete chuckled and swung her around in a circle playfully, an opposite of the kind of man he was when they met—tough and unsmiling, except to her. His countenance and moods had thawed considerably, which she appreciated about twenty-four years after the fact.

"Oh, my darling. How then am I supposed to focus when I'm digging for divine revelation if I'm wondering how I look? I had no time for that. Fine." He set her down gently on her feet. "I'll keep a clean shave—for now."

She growled, and he tossed a pillow at her. So, she ducked. Oh yeah, Pete Zendel was the best husband and pastor she could ever have prayed to have.

But the phone call earlier today rang in her mind, and she gulped, then shoved it down. No way she would tell Pete she had a stalker. A dangerous stalker who'd discovered their home phone number. No, Pete was happy, and considering the hard life he'd lived before, this was all that mattered now.

While they spoke, the phone rang and before she could say anything, Pete picked up and put it on speaker. "Hey, lady, do you know where your husband is originally from?"

Her husband's frown had her biting her lower lip. "That number called me a few times, and I figured they would go away."

Pete released her and grabbed the phone. "Who are you, and what do you want?"

"I want what you have. And I am the Hunter." The call dropped.

"Pat, you should've told me you were being harassed. Why didn't you tell me?"

Suddenly, the lights went out.

Pete grabbed the phone and dialed 911, but the dial tone was dead. Their line was cut. He grabbed his wife and daughter and shut them in. "Stay here and don't open the door no matter who knocks."

She clutched their daughter, Shalom, who was already crying, to her chest. "Where are you going?"

Pete tossed a phone into her hand, and a Taser she didn't know they had. "You take this and protect our girl at all costs. Call the SSPD and make sure you keep calling and stay on the line until they arrive."

"Pete, I don't want you to go. Please."

He kissed her thoroughly in a way that left her breathless.

∼

"HE SHOULD NEVER HAVE BREACHED MY HOME. I'M GOING OUT there to give the Hunter the hell he asked for." He locked the door, hid the key, and stormed down the steps toward the front door.

Then a loud boom sounded through the front door. It

knocked Pete off his feet, but he scrambled upright and shot at the entryway.

This war might've started hundreds of years ago, but it ended here—today. Then, he ducked for cover behind falling debris and continued firing until he ran out of bullets.

"You are a hard man to find. First, you relocate. Then you change mailing addresses, bank accounts, and everything about you. But you can't change your name, King Peralta V, can you?" A man emerged from the dust. "A man's bloodline always rats him out. Especially that of kings. Your great-grandfather eluded mine. You won't elude me." A wicked grin trailed his words. "You and I have a lot of history. Why don't we fight like our fathers would've the old-fashioned way? Hand to hand combat, fight-to-the-death?" His voice ground like twisted metal, and Pete wasn't sure he'd ever seen eyes that evil.

Pete said not a word.

Simon, his assistant, had given him delivery of secure, registered mail from Malcolm in Oakland—documents detailing more facts about his royal heritage that blurred whatever riches he thought he'd had. His wealth as king was massive—enough to have stunned Simon on the day he got the package detailing this information. And unknown to the Hunter, he hadn't been idle these past years. He had prayed, fasted, waited on God, knowing this day would come. He had also made up his mind not to strike the first blow.

He didn't have to. The man swung an ax, which missed him and fell against his TV, crashing it and shattering its screen. "Does arm-to-arm combat include axes?"

"Argh!" The man lunged at him, and the battle evaded for over one hundred years, clashed two genealogies, from Lanzarote to Silver Stone, and threw both men—one a king and the other a hunter bound by oath not to lose—onto the ground.

"Like King David, I come against you in the name of the Lord Jesus." Pete gripped the man's thigh, unwilling to harm another human being, but also unwilling to die.

He knew.

This was not an ordinary fight. It was a fight to the death—where only one of them would live. And he was determined not to die.

THE END

SERMONS COPYRIGHT

The sermons, messages, and exhortations in this book and series by the character of Pastor Pete Zendel, are original from the author, given to her by the Lord, and have never been preached before. Occasional quotations should be cited. Full delivery or share of any of these sermons requires a written permission from the author.

Thank you.

NOTE TO THE READER

~

Thank you very much for reading **HUNTER**, the next book in this exciting Christian romantic suspense series, and one of my most personal books to date! Writing the book was an emotional roller coaster, so I hope you enjoyed it.

Hunter is a book I will cherish for all my days. It's a book I'll go back to read and get blessed by. I'm in awe of what God wrote through me, and I need those lessons for my own life. I love you guys, but most importantly, I love Jesus for all He has seen me through.

He helped me through many storms and got me to where I wrote this series. I celebrate His love which is greater deeper, stronger, and higher than I could ever have imagined! Right now, if you buy the whole series, I will give to support orphans in need. If you don't buy them, I'll still give whatever I can, but we're better and stronger together. Our efforts are multiplied when we work as a team. So...

Will you support me? If you would, then...

GET THE OTHER BOOKS, AND I THANK YOU IMMENSELY, FOR reading my stories, and for your support!

***

*PRE-ORDER UNSHAKEN LOVE (PLEASANT HEARTS Series Book 4) HERE & ENTER MULTIPLE GIVEAWAYS!

Have you read THE NEW RULEBOOK SERIES? If not, click HERE and enjoy this gripping 9-book acclaimed series today and find out how two orphans grew to become the most powerful couple in the world. **CLICK HERE** and enjoy it now. Read these before HUNTER to avoid some serious spoilers.

Then join my VIP Readers Club here- http://www.joyohagwu.com/announcements.html -to know as soon as the next book releases.

***

DESCRIPTION

How do you escape an enemy you can't see?

When the pursuit begins…no one is safe. A missing brother. A lost sister. A desperate police officer. And a determined husband.

All facing one challenge—escaping danger—while staying alive.

Veteran police officer Angel Martinez has been searching for her missing brother for almost twenty years. Year after year, each trail ran cold and the clues dried up. With only a few dangerous, unwilling witnesses left, will John's kidnapping ever be solved, or is her hope of finding her brother lost for good?

Dr. Ahmed Diaz had no more reason to live—or so he thought. He'd lost everything, and everyone he cared about turned against him. Strolling into the woods to end his life led to a stunning turn of events that would change him for good—and lead him into a path he didn't know existed.

Stephanie Martinez was angry with God for letting her brother, John, get kidnapped. So, she lived life the crazy way she wanted —until the man she loved changed into a person she didn't recognize. Now, faced with danger and more challenges than she can handle, will she turn to the God she abandoned, or give up any chance of a normal life and plunge headlong into hopelessness?

HUNTER, Book One of the Pete Zendel Christian Suspense Series, is the third book in this series. Read WHISPER, the prequel, and THE SECRET HERITAGE, the novella, to better understand this series.

NEWS & NOTE TO THE READER

Thank you so much for getting **HUNTER** the third book of The Pete Zendel Christian Suspense Series! Hunter is Book 1, however, don't miss out on Whisper which is the full-length prequel of this series, and The Secret Heritage, the novella with exciting information about the Zendel family, so please make sure to read those first before. Please expect **HUNTED**, the next book in this series soon by God's grace. It promises to be as exciting! God bless you!

A REALLY COOL OPPORTUNITY

Join my VIP readers club to be the first to know as soon as my books are available for purchase here: http://www.joyohagwu.com/announcements.html

> Want to know when my next book releases?
> And to grab:
> * a free ebook (limited time offer)
> * Release day giveaways
> *Discounted prices
> * And so much more!
> Hit YES below and you're in!
> See you on the inside!

THEN JOIN MY VIP READERS CLUB

DISCLAIMER

This novel is entirely a work of fiction. As a fiction author, I have taken artistic liberty to create plausible experiences for my characters void of confirmed scenarios. Any resemblance to actual innovative developments in any scientific area is purely coincidental. My writing was thorough, and editing accurate; hence active depictions of any kind in this book are attributed to creativity for a great story. It was my pleasure sharing these stories with you! ALL glory to God.

Copyright First Edition © 2018
Joy Ohagwu

LifeFountainMedia

CHRISTIAN FICTION TWINED IN FAITH, HOPE, AND LOVE.
Life Fountain Books and Life Fountain Media logo are trademarks of Joy Ohagwu. Absence of ™ in connection with marks of Life Fountain Media or other parties does not indicate an absence of trademark protection of those marks.

All rights reserved. No part of this publication may be reproduced, stored in a retrieval system, or transmitted in any form or by any means—electronic, mechanical, photocopy, recording, or otherwise—without prior permission of the author, except as brief quotations in printed reviews.

This novel is a work of fiction. Names, characters, incidents, and dialogues are products of the author's imagination or are used fictitiously. Any resemblance or similarity to actual events or persons, living or dead, scenarios, or locales is entirely coincidental. This ebook is licensed for your enjoyment. Unauthorized sharing is prohibited. Please purchase your copy to read this story. Thank you. Christian Suspense 2. Christian Fiction 3. Contemporary Christian Romantic Suspense 4. Christian Romance 5 Faith 5. Fiction

Except where otherwise stated, "Scripture taken from the New King James Version Bible®,

Copyright © 1982 by Thomas Nelson, Inc. Used by permission. All rights reserved.

All glory to God
Printed in the United States of America

✽ Created with Vellum

Made in the USA
Lexington, KY
06 August 2019